Gimu

A Novel of the Pacific War

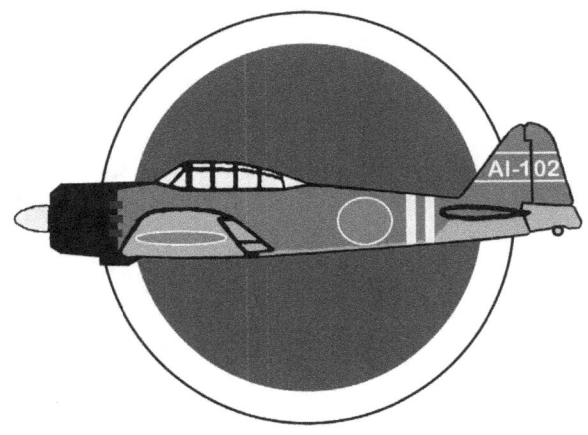

Lenny Flank

Red and Black Publishers, Florida

Gimu: the lifelong duty to loyally fulfill one's obligations and responsibilities to comrades, family, and all of society.

"Death is lighter than a feather,
but Duty is heavier than a mountain."

Contents

Chapter 1
A Childhood in Japan (1920s)

The small coastal hamlet of Sakurada sat at the foot of a jagged cliffside in eastern Japan near the city of Tsu, where the cold green waters of the Pacific Ocean washed against the rocky shore of Ise Bay. The village was a quiet place, its numbers small enough so that everyone knew each other by name. The narrow streets were made of packed earth, worn smooth by the steady passage over the centuries of thousands of bare feet and wooden *geta* clogs.

At the center of the village stood the Shinto temple, with its bright red *torii* gate standing out sharply against the sky. Each year, the local *matsuri* festivals — events marked by processions, prayers, and the offering of food — were held in honor of the *kami*, the divine spirits who protected the land and its people. Villagers would gather to ask for a bountiful catch, for good health, and for protection against disasters. It was here that rituals were conducted to mark important events like marriages, births, and funerals, with the Shinto priest offering prayers for the well-being of the community and for the health of the Emperor, the divine descendant of the Sun Goddess Amaterasu Omikami.

Life in Sakurada was simple, governed by the cycles of the sea and the seasons. As the sun began to rise in the morning, the fishing boats waited, bobbing gently in the shallow water. The larger ones had sails of cotton canvas, but many still used traditional sails laced together from mats of woven rice straw. Each day, the men worked in the boats, hauling in the day's catch and mending their nets on shore, while the women, dressed in simple cotton *kimono*, would stand by the drying racks, carefully arranging split fish for preservation. The process was a time-consuming one, but it was essential for survival, especially in the winter months when the *tai fu* "big wind" became treacherous and the fishing boats stayed close to shore.

The village was a place with a deep history, where every building and every pine tree carried with it the imprint of generations. Here, time moved slowly and the villagers honored their ancestors and kept their practices alive in small everyday rituals: the way the fish were salted and dried, the way the rice was harvested, the way the streets were swept. The people of Sakurada were fiercely proud of their traditional heritage and the simple lives they led, for they knew no other way.

At the edge of the village stood the Sugiyama home, a typical paper-and-wood structure built in the classic Japanese style that reflected the simplicity and adaptability of village life. It had a thatched roof made of straw, wooden beams cut from unpainted cedar planks, and walls made from oiled paper and plastered with a mixture of soil, straw, hemp, sand, and water. The floor was covered with *tatami* mats woven from rice stems. Sliding *shoji* paper doors divided the interior space into rooms, each serving a different purpose: one room for family meals, another for sleeping, and a large *ima* for general living space. The back of the house opened into a modest garden with a well-worn stone path that led to a small shrine dedicated to the spirits of the ancestors. Simple and utilitarian, the family house had been here for centuries, though it had been rebuilt several times after suffering from Japan's frequent earthquakes, storms, and fires.

Like everyone else, their life was tied to the sea. Hideyuki Sugiyama, like his father and grandfather before him, was a fisherman. His deep-set brown eyes always had a stern and serious look, yet they hid an inner kindness that he only rarely expressed outwardly. Though Hideyuki kept mostly to himself, he was known throughout the village as a hard worker and a man of honesty and integrity, as someone who could always be relied upon to help in time of need.

Haruko, his wife, was a woman of gentle and quiet strength. She was well-versed in the traditional arts of weaving, and her small wooden *jikake-ori* loom had been passed down to her through several generations. She used it to make lightweight *kasuri* fabric for summer clothing, heavier cotton for winter garments, and the occasional more expensive "rough silk" *kimono* which she sold to supplement the family income. Her mother had also taught her how to make silk and cotton cord on the small *kumihimo* loom. Haruko's calming presence was the heart of the home.

On the cold morning of February 18, 1915, in the very room where Hideyuki, and his father, had been born, Haruko gave birth to their first child, a son they named Hideyoshi. There was no doctor or hospital in Sakurada, so Haruko was accompanied by the village's *koyo-san* midwife. The boy's first cries had been a loud sharp wail that pierced the air. To Hideyuki, it was a good sign. "He will be strong," he said softly, his eyes glowing with pride as he held the squirming infant in his hands. "The sea will favor him."

The Sugiyama family followed the traditions of their ancestors, and the arrival of a new son meant prayers to the gods seeking blessings for the infant's health and future. Soon after Hideyoshi's birth, Hideyuki carried the newborn to the Shinto shrine where he made offerings for the child's well-being and called upon the *kami* to watch over him and protect him as he grew. The villagers, many of whom were relatives or long-time neighbors, gathered to celebrate the birth. Women cooed over the baby, while the men shared small celebratory cups of *sake*.

From the moment he could walk, young Hideyoshi was an eager participant in village life. In a community as close-knit as Sakurada, every harvest or seasonal change was an opportunity to celebrate together. One of Hideyoshi's earliest memories was of participating in the festival which marked the beginning of the New Year. He would watch curiously as his mother and the other women pounded freshly steamed rice with large wooden mallets before mixing it with sugar and cornstarch and shaping it into sweet sticky *mochi* rice cakes.

Each year, as the weather warmed and the sea grew calmer, the village would also prepare for the spring *matsuri* festival. The children, Hideyoshi always among them, would help gather offerings of rice and *sake* for the gods, working together to make wreaths of wildflowers that would adorn the Shinto temple. The women of the village would perform traditional *dengaku* dances in brightly-colored *kimono*, while the men would pull heavy wooden floats, lit by lanterns and decorated with figures of the *kami*, through the streets.

Most of the young boy's days, however, were spent in the company of other children from the village. They would gather in an open field and challenge each other with games. In *kemari*, the children kicked a small leather ball stuffed with sawdust to each other, trying to keep it aloft without using their hands and not letting it touch the ground. It was a test of balance, coordination, and teamwork. Another popular pastime was *kagome kagome*, where one child (the "*oni* demon") sat blindfolded in the center while the others circled around, holding hands and singing a short chant—the words of which were so old that nobody knew what they meant anymore. At the end of the song, the "demon" child had to guess who it was who stood behind them. During the warmer months, the boys flew handmade kites that they had built from *washi* mulberry paper and bamboo, while the girls played *ohajiki*, a game similar to marbles that used seashells, pebbles or small glass or ceramic pieces.

But not every day was filled with celebration. The life of a fisherman's family was one of constant hard work. Hideyoshi's father was often out at sea all day with the other boats, pulling in nets filled with fish, hauling them to shore, and preparing them for sale or for drying and preserving. Though he was too young to participate in the fishing itself, Hideyoshi would sometimes follow his father along the shore, catching crabs in the rock pools as the fishermen unloaded their catch.

Being a fisherman out on the water was, however, never without its dangers. While the sea provided the bounty that sustained the entire community, it was also a remorseless force, capable of sudden and violent fury. Storms would often appear without warning, and high winds and crashing waves could overturn the little boats with ease. Many in Sakurada had lost a husband or a son or a brother to the sea.

Hideyoshi, though young, learned that the ocean was both a giver and a taker, a friend and a foe. He would often sit on the rocks, staring out at the endless ocean. "What are you looking for?" Haruko asked him one day, her voice gentle. "The other side," he replied simply, his voice carrying an earnestness that struck her. She knew then that her son was indeed someone who looked beyond the horizon.

These simple rituals of village life were embedded in his childhood, and they would form the foundation for his understanding of the world around him. He learned early that the cycle of life was marked by both joy and pain, and that in the face of an often-hostile world "life" was a communal effort. These lessons would remain with him as he grew older and began to dream of a world beyond the little town. But for now, Hideyoshi was content to be a child, living in the embrace of the village that had raised him.

Hideyoshi's uncle, Katsuro Tanaka, was a towering figure in his young life, both literally and figuratively. Thin and tall for a Japanese, Katsuro had served as a gunner aboard the battleship *Mikasa* during the Russo-Japanese War, and, though he worked as a carpenter now, he still showed all the pride of that service in the way that he spoke and carried himself. He often visited the Sugiyama household, his arrival preceded by the sound of his wooden *geta* clogs clacking on the stone path. And from the moment Hideyoshi was old enough to understand, Katsuro would regale him with tales of the triumph at Tsushima, where the Japanese fleet had decisively defeated the Russian fleet. "We stood on the deck," Katsuro would begin, his voice deep and steady, "watching the shells arc through the sky like fiery comets. The *Mikasa* was the heart of the fleet, the pride of our Emperor, and we knew we held the hopes of the nation on our shoulders."

Hideyoshi sat enthralled, his eyes wide as his uncle described the thunder of the battleship's huge guns and the maneuvers of the fleet. "We were outnumbered, outgunned," Katsuro would say, leaning in closer, "but not outmatched. We fought with the spirit of *bushido*. Courage, discipline, and loyalty carried us through." He spoke of his comrades, men seemingly made of steel, who had faced death without flinching—defiantly singing war songs as Russian shells exploded all around them.

Sometimes, Katsuro would let his nephew look at the medals that he had earned during the war, stored in a small lacquered box that was decorated with the Imperial Japanese Navy emblem. As the boy felt the heavy bronze medallions in his hands, Katsuro would say, "These are not just for me. They are for all of us. For Japan. For our family."

But it wasn't only the stories of victory that shaped the youngster's view. Katsuro also spoke with equal solemnity about the terrible costs of war—the friends he had lost, the horrors he had seen, and the sacrifices that every sailor had made. "Remember this, Hideyoshi," he said one evening, his tone unusually somber. "Bravery is not about being unafraid. It is about facing your fear and doing what must be done." He leaned over to look the young boy in the eyes. "Life and death are like the weight of a feather. But duty ..." He looked up and seemed to stare off into the distance. "Duty is as heavy as a mountain."

With the help of his uncle and his father, Hideyoshi crafted a small wooden model boat, carved with great care and attention to detail and painted with Togo's Rising Sun flag. On sunny afternoons he would take his new toy to the nearby rice paddy, imagining it as a mighty battleship in dangerous ocean waters. He would call it the *Mikasa*, just as Katsuro had, and he would wade in and push it through the rice stems, shouting commands like an admiral leading his fleet.

The Sugiyama household was a place where tradition and values were woven together as seamlessly as Haruko's handmade *kasuri* fabrics. From an early age, Hideyoshi was immersed in a world that emphasized above all respect for one's elders, discipline in daily tasks, and a deep sense of community.

Hideyuki believed that respect was the cornerstone of all relationships. He demonstrated this himself in his interactions with the village elders, bowing deeply and listening attentively to their wisdom, and at home he expected the same deference from his family. "When you bow," he told Hideyoshi one day, "you show that you honor the other person. Never forget that every bow is a sign of your character."

Discipline, too, was a value that Hideyuki imparted with deliberate care. Life as a fisherman required early mornings and constant tireless effort, and he sought to instill the same work ethic into his son. Even as a young boy, Hideyoshi was given small jobs to do, like helping to untangle the fishing nets or sweeping the *tatami* mats. "Do everything with purpose," Hideyuki often reminded him. "Be mindful. Even the smallest task deserves your full effort."

Haruko complemented her husband's teachings with a softer touch. She taught Hideyoshi the importance of patience and attentiveness. Whether showing him how she was able to weave threads evenly on her wooden loom or guiding him in planting vegetables in their small garden, she reminded him that painstaking attention produced lasting results. "Haste and inattention leads to mistakes," she said gently as they worked side by side. "Take your time, consider carefully what you do, and you will be proud of what you create."

On evenings when the day's work was done, mother, father and son would gather in the warm glow of the *hibachi* in the main room, and Haruko, seated on a cushion with her *kumihimo* basket at her side, became the evening's storyteller, her soft voice weaving tales as deftly as her fingers were crafting the silken cords in her little round loom.

Hideyoshi, sitting cross-legged on the *tatami* mat with expectant eyes, would wait eagerly to hear his favorite stories. One he always asked for was the tale of Momotaro, the boy born from a giant peach who embarked on a quest to defeat the evil ogres that were threatening his village. "Momotaro was brave," Haruko would say. "But his strength came not just from his courage, but from the friends he had made and the loyalty that they all shared. He knew how to depend upon others and how to cooperate for everyone's benefit." Momotaro defeated the ogres with the help of a puppy, a monkey, and a pheasant—demonstrating that even the smallest companions can make a big difference when they are united and work together.

Another favorite was the tale of Taro Urashima, a fisherman who saved a sea turtle from a group of tormentors and was rewarded with a journey to an undersea palace, ruled by a princess who thanked him for his selflessness. "Kindness is its own reward," Haruko would remind her son. The story always ended with a solemn note, however, as Urashima's curiosity ultimately brought him sorrow when he returned home and opened a forbidden magical box only to find that many decades had passed and everyone he had known was now gone. "Even good intentions must be tempered with wisdom," she would add, her voice thoughtful in quiet reflection.

The story of Hanasaka Jiisan often elicited laughter from the young boy. It told of an old man whose kindness toward a stray dog led to magical rewards of gold, while a neighbor's cruelty and greed brought only ruin. As Haruko imitated the grasping neighbor's angry gestures, Hideyoshi would clutch his sides in glee. Yet there was also the lesson to be learned—generosity brings prosperity, and selfishness brings destruction.

Each story concluded with Haruko smoothing Hideyoshi's hair and saying, "Remember, these lessons are like seeds. They grow if you nurture them."

Always, the importance of "community" was emphasized. The Sugiyamas were never isolated; they were part of a larger network of neighbors and relatives who all relied on one another. Hideyuki would tell his son, "We are strong because we stand together. Alone, we are like a single rice stem, easily bent and broken. Together, though, we are a mighty forest, unyielding to the wind."

One winter, when a villager's fishing boat was damaged in a *tai fu*, Sugiyama was among the first to lend a helping hand. Hideyoshi watched as his father spent hours helping to repair the vessel, patching a hole in the hull while neglecting his own nets and refusing any compensation. "When the sea is harsh," Hideyuki explained, "we have only each other to rely upon." These lessons deeply stirred the young boy, who saw firsthand how even small acts of kindness strengthened the bonds within their community while helping each other to get through the many challenges they faced in life.

Even during meals, the values of "respect" and "community" were reinforced. Hideyuki led a simple ritual before eating: a bow and the thankful words *"Itadakimasu"* ("I humbly receive"), acknowledging gratitude for the food and for all of the many efforts that brought it to the table. Hideyoshi learned that every meal was a reminder of the social network that lay behind it—the fishermen who caught the fish, the farmers who grew the rice, the potters who crafted the bowls, and the family who prepared it with care.

Through these experiences, Hideyoshi came to understand that "respect" was not limited to people but extended also to nature, traditions, and even to one's own efforts. "Discipline" was not about mere obedience, but about cultivating strength and resilience. And "community" was not just a collection of individuals, but a living breathing network of mutual support.

In the spring of 1921, six-year-old Hideyoshi began his formal education. The small, single-story schoolhouse was a modest building of wooden beams and paper-paneled windows. The walls were adorned with scrolls bearing calligraphy phrases extolling "discipline" and "learning", written in bold, confident brushstrokes.

Hideyoshi was eagerly clutching his cloth satchel containing a slate board, chalk, and a few sheets of *washi* paper. His parents had saved for weeks to purchase his supplies, and Haruko had woven him a small bag to carry his lunch — rice balls and a piece of pickled *daikon* radish wrapped in *nori* seaweed.

The teacher, Hayashi-*sensei*, was a middle-aged man with a strict demeanor. He had served in a school in Nagoya before returning to his native Mie province to teach after the government in Tokyo had mandated compulsory education for every child. On the first day, he had addressed the class of a dozen local children. "You are the future of our village, and of Japan," he said, pointing to a large map pinned to the wall. "Here, we will learn not only writing and numbers, but also how to carry the spirit of our ancestors into the modern world."

Hideyoshi quickly proved himself to be an attentive student. While he sometimes found it difficult to grasp arithmetic, he excelled in lessons about history and geography. Hayashi-*sensei* often brought out his prized possession, a worn book, printed in the trade port of Nagasaki, with illustrations of famous explorers and their journeys. The stories of Marco Polo traveling to distant lands and Captain Cook mapping unknown seas fascinated Hideyoshi, and he would sit in wonder as the teacher told tales of these bold men. During recess, while other children played games or chased each other in the schoolyard, Hideyoshi often stayed behind, flipping through the illustrated book under Hayashi-*sensei's* watchful eye.

"*Sensei*," he asked one day, "do you think there are still places in the world left to discover?"

Hayashi-*sensei* smiled faintly, pleased at the spark of curiosity and ambition that was revealed in the boy's question. "Perhaps not in the way the explorers did," he replied, "but there are always new challenges and frontiers. All around us are mysteries waiting to be understood."

Hideyoshi learned to read and write *kanji* and *hiragana*, opening the doors to countless written stories and books. At home, he often practiced his lessons by reading aloud, much to his parents' delight. "Our son will go far," Hideyuki would tell his wife. His voice, however, carried a hint of sadness. Like Haruko, he now understood that their young son's ambitions extended far beyond their little village, and the simple life of a fisherman was not for him.

The people of Sakurada were bound to the land and the sea. In a way, they had always been insulated from the world outside and at the same time deeply connected to it, dependent upon the tides and the seasons but seemingly untouched by the rapid changes that were sweeping across Japan. Many of the villagers had never left Sakurada, and only a handful had been further than the nearby city of Tsu. The outside world was a distant vision, an almost mythical place where railroads cut through the mountains, where great steel ships sailed across the seas, and where flying machines soared through the skies. To the inhabitants of Sakurada, these stories were like fairy tales.

But that was now changing.

It began with small things. A merchant arrived in the village one day with a strange device—a hand-cranked gramophone. He placed it on the veranda of the local inn, and soon a small crowd had gathered round. When the merchant turned the crank and tinny music began to play, the villagers gasped. It was as though a tiny invisible musician had become trapped inside this mysterious thing. Children clapped their hands and laughed, while the older villagers regarded the machine with a mixture of wonder and suspicion. "It's unnatural," one elder muttered, shaking his head. "Music should come from a person, not from a box."

Not long after that, a pair of surveyors arrived in Sakurada. Dressed in Western-style suits and carrying a collection of unfamiliar instruments, they explained that they were surveying and mapping the route for a planned railroad that would connect the village to Tsu. Their presence caused a sensation. Some villagers welcomed the idea, imagining easy and rapid access to markets for their fresh fish. Others worried that the trains would bring trouble—strangers, change, and the erosion of their way of life.

The most significant sign of change, however, came when one of the wealthier fishermen, eager to increase his catch, had saved his money for months to purchase a gasoline engine for his boat. At first, the motor, with its loud, sputtering noise and choking blue smoke, was just a curious novelty. Children ran along the shoreline to watch it in action, and even the most skeptical fishermen couldn't deny its efficiency. But it also brought tensions. The motorboat could venture farther and return faster, with more fish. It threatened to upset the ancient balance of shared fishing grounds and to unravel the cooperative relationships which had sustained the village for centuries.

"Is this progress?" Hideyuki asked himself. "It seems to make life easier, yes. But what will it cost us?"

Hideyoshi listened curiously to the discussions going on around him, though he did not understand all of their implications. To him, the motorboat was fascinating. He was drawn to its ability to conquer the waves with ease through sheer power. Yet, he could also sense the friction it was causing among the adults and the unease that hung in the air.

All of the traditional *matsuri* continued, but even these began to reflect the changing times. At the annual spring festival, a traveling theater group performed a play using electric lanterns instead of traditional oil lamps. The bright, steady light was dazzling, but some people complained that it was too harsh and that it disturbed the harmony and natural beauty of the village, and they lamented the loss of the soft warm glow of the lamps.

Despite all of the mixed feelings, though, Hideyoshi's curiosity about the outside world continued to grow. When he asked his teacher about it, Hayashi-*sensei* replied with a thoughtful smile, "The world is changing, Hideyoshi. What seems impossible today might be commonplace tomorrow. But remember, progress is a blade with two edges. It can bring both opportunity and loss."

For Sakurada, the tide of modernization was inevitable, and seemed to be as unstoppable as the ocean tides. Some villagers embraced the rapid changes, while others tried to cling to the old ways. But for Hideyoshi, they were a spark—an invitation to dream of a world beyond the village.

In the autumn of 1931, there was a hum of excitement through Sakurada. News had spread that a grand event would be taking place in nearby Tsu—a celebration commemorating the Imperial Navy's advancements. Among the attractions was to be an aerial display by the *Sanba Garasu*, the celebrated "Three Ravens," an elite naval aerobatic team. For sixteen-year-old Hideyoshi, this was a chance to witness something extraordinary, something he had only ever read about in school. Imagine, he thought—machines that flew through the air. He had read stories about the Wright Brothers and Santos-Dumont and the Red Baron and Lindbergh, but he had never actually seen an airplane. Neither had any of the villagers.

As Hideyoshi, accompanied by his father and his uncle, approached the makeshift airfield—an empty patch of ground on the outskirts of town—his heart raced with anticipation. Crowds had already gathered, and the streets were lined with booths of vendors selling sweet *mochi*, *omamori* good-luck charms, and small Japanese flags. Imperial Navy officers in their crisp white Western-style uniforms mingled with the civilians, while *kimono*-clad young women playfully watched them from behind paper fans before excitedly whispering to each other and breaking out into concealed giggles.

The Three Ravens were a renowned aerobatic team from the Japanese Navy's air corps, named for their black-painted aircraft. Formed earlier that year, the team had already performed in most of the major cities and had quickly gained recognition for their daring maneuvers and their flawless tight formations. They flew Type 13 Yokosuka K1Y biplanes, sturdy Navy training aircraft which had been repurposed for aerial shows. To the public, the Three Ravens symbolized Japan's mastery of the skies and the Navy's readiness to defend the nation.

At last, with the low drone of engines, three specks appeared on the horizon. The *Sanba Garasu* were flying in perfect formation, before breaking apart in a synchronized maneuver. The crowd was thrilled as the pilots performed loops, barrel rolls, and other intricate aerobatics. At one point, the lead plane climbed steeply before intentionally stalling and plummeting toward the ground, drawing a collective gasp from the viewers—only to pull up at the last moment in a dramatic recovery.

Hideyoshi's eyes closely followed every movement. "How can they do that?" he whispered to his father, who smiled but offered no answer.

During a brief interlude, a naval officer stood on a bench and gave a recruitment speech to the crowd. He spoke of the Navy's role in defending Japan and the need for a new generation of men to embrace the skies. "Ladies and gentlemen," he began, "you are witnessing the skill and discipline of the Imperial Navy's finest aviators. These men represent the spirit of modern Japan—brave, innovative, and dedicated." He paused, and his gaze fell on some of the young men in the audience. "The Navy is not merely a career; it is a calling. It demands courage, intelligence, and a dedication to something greater than yourself. For those of you who dream of the skies, remember this: Japan's future lies in your hands."

When the Ravens returned for their final act, they flew in a triangular formation. The audience erupted in cheers as the planes executed another daring series of loops, crossing paths at dizzying speeds. The pilots demonstrated precision and skill, performing stalling spins and heart-stopping climbs that seemed to defy the laws of physics. One plane performed an Immelmann turn, reversing its direction in mid-air with astonishing speed. Another showcased a slow, controlled roll as it skimmed just above the airfield, its engine roaring like a long thunderclap.

"So," Katsuro said, nudging Hideyoshi with a knowing grin, "what do you think of the Ravens?"

Hideyoshi replied quietly, "I want to be up there someday."

Hideyuki glanced at his son with pride and a hint of concern in his eyes. "Then you must work hard," he said firmly. "The sky is not an easy place to reach."

For days, the performance was the talk of the village. At the Shinto shrine and in the marketplace, neighbors exchanged their excited recollections. Katsura recounted the naval officer's speech to anyone who would listen, emphasizing the message of duty and progress. Navy fliers, he pointed out, were the elite, and only a tiny proportion of all the students who applied for flight training were accepted.

For Hideyoshi, though, the impact went far beyond admiration; the experience had awakened a sense of wonder inside him. He began to spend his free time lying on the grass near the cliffs, looking to the sky and watching the seabirds glide effortlessly over the waves. He would trace their movements with his eyes, imagining himself piloting an aircraft with the same grace and precision. His mind buzzed with questions: How did the planes stay in the air? What powered them? How could one control such a seemingly magical machine? At night, as he lay on his *futon*, he would close his eyes and imagine himself at the controls of a biplane, soaring above the clouds, the village of Sakurada a mere dot below. The dream of flight became a burning flame within him.

Working from memory, he constructed small models of biplanes from gathered scraps of wood and bamboo, painted them with charcoal to mimic the markings of the aircraft he had seen, and proudly displayed them on a shelf in his room. He tied threads to the wings and balanced them on his fingers, testing how they tilted in the wind. He found an old Army manual which included detailed diagrams of military aircraft and studied it intently, though much of it was beyond his understanding.

His uncle encouraged his interest. "During the war," he said during one of their conversations, "we relied on ships to scout the enemy. But imagine the advantage of seeing from above! A pilot holds the power of foresight. It's a noble pursuit, Hideyoshi." His father was less enthusiastic. "The skies are dangerous," he decided one evening as they sat together repairing fishing nets. "A fisherman knows the waves, the currents, the signs of a coming storm. But up there, in the air, you're at the mercy of forces we can't even understand."

During one of his visits, Katsuro watched as Hideyoshi demonstrated how his latest paper model could glide across the room with remarkable stability. "The boy has the hands of an engineer," he remarked to Hideyuki, "and the spirit of a pilot. Let him dream. Dreams have a way of finding their path if you nurture them."

Hideyuki, meanwhile, observed his son's growing obsession with a blend of quiet admiration and caution. The boy's dedication was undeniable—he had a spirit of determination and a clarity of purpose that reminded Hideyuki of his own early years. Yet, as a father, he also saw the challenges that lay ahead. The skies were far removed from the life of a humble fisherman's family. It was not that he doubted his son's abilities—if anything, he believed in them more than he let on. But he knew of the fearsome odds against being accepted by the military flight schools, and he feared the toll that unfulfilled ambition might take on his boy's spirit. The dream of becoming a pilot required not only extraordinary skill but also connections, resources, and the backing of institutions far beyond his reach in Sakurada. Hideyuki knew that the world was not always kind to ambition, and he dreaded the heartbreak that might come if Hideyoshi's dreams were dashed against the harsh realities of life.

Haruko, as usual, struck a more encouraging tone. While she harbored her own fears for her son's safety, she saw the passion in his eyes and the diligence with which he pursued his dreams. "Every path has its dangers," she said gently to Hideyuki. "But if this is the path Hideyoshi is meant to walk, shouldn't we guide him rather than hold him back?"

That night, father and son talked again, over a game of *shogi*. "It is a noble vision you have, Hideyoshi," he pointed out. "But the path to the skies is steep, and not everyone who begins the climb reaches the top." He paused, searching for the right words. "This village has given us a simple but honest life. I worry that your dreams may lead you to a world where the risks are even greater."

Hideyoshi met his father's gaze. "I understand, Father. But I also believe that if I work hard enough, I can make it. The sea is also dangerous, but we still go out because it's what we know, what we're meant to do. I feel the same way about flying."

Hideyuki studied his son for a long moment before giving a slight nod. "Then be prepared to work harder than you ever have. Dreams like yours are not handed out freely. They must be earned."

As Hideyoshi entered his final year of schooling, thoughts of the future began to weigh more and more on his mind. His classmates, he knew, would be fishermen, like their fathers and grandfathers. A few might be taking over family businesses, working the rice paddies, or becoming craftsmen. But his own aspirations were different, and set him apart from them: he wanted to be a pilot. He wanted to fly. Yet, the practicalities of achieving that dream loomed large, there were many obstacles, and he knew he would need a clear plan to make it a reality.

The military seemed like the most viable path. The Imperial Army was a respected institution, stories of its growing air arm were a frequent topic in the newspapers, and it promised not only the opportunity to fly but also a way to serve the nation, a cause deeply respected by his family and the community. Still, the way was difficult. For a poor boy from a small fishing village, the path to becoming a pilot was littered with roadblocks. The military could afford to be choosy, and it only took a small number of applicants each year. Even if he were accepted, the cost of preparing for and traveling to the academy for the entrance exams was a significant burden for a family already living modestly. Entrance into pilot training required not only physical and mental fitness but also a solid foundation in mathematics, physics, and mechanics, and access to resources such as proper textbooks or tutoring was limited in his little rural school. Connections to influential individuals who could provide guidance or support were also virtually nonexistent here. The prospect of leaving Sakurada to train in faraway cities added another layer of uncertainty, requiring not just financial sacrifice but also the emotional toll of leaving his family and stepping out into an unfamiliar and ruthless world.

But nevertheless, despite all the difficulties, Hideyoshi had made up his mind: he would join the military. It seemed to be the only way he would ever be able to touch the clouds.

Chapter 2

The Rise of Militarism (1930s)

The 1930s brought profound changes to Japan, a nation which had become caught between age-old traditions and the relentless push of modernization.

For centuries, Japan had been at war with itself. During the "Warring States Period", local warlords had fought each other relentlessly for dominance. It wasn't until 1600 that the Tokugawa family defeated all of its rivals, established itself as the supreme power, and united the country—only to give itself the ancient title of *shogun* and seize control. Under Tokugawa rule, all of the Europeans and their technology were expelled from the country, Japanese citizens were forbidden to leave Japan or to carry out any foreign travel, and a strict feudal system was imposed in which the Emperor served as a mere symbolic figurehead and all of the real power lay with the *shogun*. Japanese society now became rigidly stratified, with *samurai* at the top and peasants, craftsmen and merchants at the bottom. Foreign cultural, economic and ideological influence was tightly controlled, and only a limited and heavily regulated foreign trade was allowed, conducted through the port city of Nagasaki. This period of deliberate and intentional isolation, known as *sakoku* ("the country in chains"), preserved Japan's unique culture and customs—but it left the islands frozen in time, an endless relic of 16th century feudalism.

By the mid-19th century, however, Japan could no longer avoid the outside world. China had already been carved up by the

European powers, and now Japan was on their plate too. The American Commodore Matthew Perry's arrival in 1853 with a fleet of US Navy warships forced the shogunate to open its ports, and England and France quickly followed with a series of lopsided treaties that the Japanese were forced to sign. The humiliation of these treaties, combined with domestic unrest and economic stagnation, undermined the Tokugawa *shogun's* authority, and *samurai*, merchants, and reform-minded government officials alike began calling for a return to imperial rule, seeing it as a means to restore Japan's strength. In 1868, after a brief but violent civil war, Emperor Meiji was restored to the throne, and the shogunate was abolished.

But the Meiji Restoration was not just a simple return to old traditions. Instead, it became a revolutionary movement to modernize all of Japan, spurred on by the realization that the country needed to match the West in technological, military, and industrial strength in order to protect itself from European domination and to avoid China's fate of foreign occupation. The leaders of this new era embarked on sweeping reforms that transformed Japan's political, social, and economic landscape almost overnight.

The entire old feudal system was dismantled, and the patchwork domains of the *daimyo* regional warlords were replaced by an elected central government under a Cabinet which reported directly to the Emperor. The *samurai*, stripped of their hereditary privileges, were integrated into the new society as bureaucrats, military officers, and businessmen. Land reform policies granted peasants ownership of the feudal plots of land which they worked, though the heavy taxation system often kept them in the same position of poverty which they had always been.

Economically, moreover, Japan was desperate to catch up to the Europeans in terms of production and military power, and the government in Tokyo pursued a single-minded policy of rapid industrialization. They invested heavily in modern infrastructure and frantically built new railroads, telegraph lines, and Western-style factories using all of the latest technology that could be imported from the West.

Education reform was equally thorough. A compulsory education system was introduced for all children, emphasizing literacy and moral training that was based upon Confucian ideas. Older students were sent abroad to universities in Europe and America, where they would receive the best educations that were available in topics that ranged from science to economics, and would then bring their new knowledge along with them when they came back to Japan.

Socially, the Meiji Restoration ushered in a period of rapid change as old Japanese customs were deliberately replaced by Western ideas. Men cut their *samurai* topknots in favor of modern hairstyles, while women gave up their *kimono* for skirts and dresses. Rural agrarian culture rapidly disappeared as more and more people moved to the cities and adapted to an urban society and industrial factory work. The concept of "individualism", introduced from the West, became pervasive in Japan, even as it clashed with ancient and deeply rooted communal Japanese values.

The effect was transformative. By 1914, Japan had been reborn, from a backwards feudal agricultural society into a modern industrial and military power that was now the equal of any Western nation—as was shown by the country's participation in the World War as a full ally of the Entente.

The Great Depression, though, which began in the United States in 1929, quickly rippled across the globe, leaving no nation untouched. Japan was no exception. During the feverish industrial expansion of the Meiji Restoration, Japan's economy had become deeply intertwined with global export markets in Europe and the US. As demand abroad for Japanese goods now plummeted, though, the nation found itself mired in a deep and persistent economic downturn that upended people's lives and widened existing social divides.

For the average Japanese family, the impact was immediate and devastating. Exports of silk, one of Japan's primary commodities, collapsed as Western nations and the domestic market cut back on luxury purchases. Farmers in rural areas, who depended on silk and textile production to supplement their meager incomes, saw their livelihoods vanish almost overnight as silk prices fell to just a fraction of their previous value.

In urban areas, meanwhile, unemployment surged as factories were shuttered and businesses declared bankruptcy. Workers who had migrated to the cities during the boom years of the 1920s now found themselves without jobs or money. Bread lines and soup kitchens became increasingly common in industrial hubs like Osaka and Yokohama, harsh reminders of the human toll of the economic collapse. Meanwhile, the *zaibatsu* – Japan's powerful conglomerate companies owned by wealthy families – tightened their grip on the economy, consolidating their wealth even as small businesses struggled to survive.

All of this was then exacerbated by Japan's growing population, which was crowding more and more people onto the tiny islands. Most of Japan was mountainous and unsuitable for farming, and this lack of arable land led to a food crunch as there simply was not enough rice being produced to feed everybody.

In Sakurada, the effects of the Depression were felt in subtler but equally painful ways. The fishing industry, already a precarious trade, became even more difficult as market prices dropped. Hideyuki, like so many fishermen, found himself forced to sell his catch at a loss or to barter his fish for basic necessities like rice and vegetables to make ends meet. Still, many people were going to bed hungry.

The promise of democracy which had been given during the Restoration period now unraveled, and the economic hardships of the Great Depression fueled widespread dissatisfaction with the government. Many rural families viewed the Cabinet in Tokyo as a distant and uncaring authority, corrupt, ineffective, and more concerned with protecting the wealthy urban *zaibatsu* elites than with alleviating the suffering of ordinary people. Protests became more and more common.

This disillusionment, in turn, created fertile ground for radical ideas. Nationalist groups like the *Kokuhonsha* ("Society for the Preservation of the National Essence") and the *Ketsumeidan* ("Blood Brotherhood League") now capitalized on the public's frustrations, advocating for a return to "traditional Japanese values". Supported by high-ranking military officers, the nationalists began to advocate for the expansion of an overseas empire to "make Japan great again" and to solve the nation's economic woes by providing more living space for a growing population, new markets for Japanese industry, and cheap sources of raw materials like oil, iron and rubber.

These extremist factions were not content with mere rhetoric. Assassinations and coup attempts were directed at anyone who criticized or opposed the militarist agenda. In 1932, the May 15 Incident shocked the nation when a group of young naval officers assassinated Prime Minister Inukai Tsuyoshi, believing his policies were too conciliatory towards the Western powers. The assassins, who received widespread public sympathy during their trial, underscored the growing disillusionment with "democracy" and the acceptance of intimidation and violence as a legitimate means to achieve political ends.

Meanwhile, the military continued to gain unprecedented influence over Japan's government, claiming to be the true stewards of the nation. Senior generals frequently bypassed civilian authority, pressuring the government to increase military spending and enable an aggressive and expansionist foreign policy. In February 1936, over a thousand young naval officers temporarily seized control of parts of Tokyo and attempted to assassinate several government officials before being arrested by government troops. The incident demonstrated the deep divisions within the armed forces, but it also further weakened the civilian government.

As the militarists gained more and more power, they began to tighten their grip by imposing severe restrictions on free speech and political dissent. The Peace Preservation Law, initially enacted in 1925 to suppress Communist activities, was broadened to target any form of opposition to the authoritarian state. Intellectuals, journalists, and activists who advocated for democracy or who criticized the military government now faced arrest and imprisonment. By the late 1930s, political discourse had become narrowly throttled, with the militarist narrative dominating the public discourse and all other viewpoints being censored and suppressed.

Amid this political upheaval, the lines between the military and the government became increasingly blurred. The cabinet positions of War Minister and Navy Minister were now reserved solely for high-ranking active-duty officers, giving the military direct control over national policy. Politicians who resisted the militarist agenda faced open threats of assassination. The authority of the Diet and the Prime Minister's office eroded and faded, allowing the militarists to declare that the civilian politicians were weak and incapable of addressing the challenges facing Japan. This rhetoric found a place with a population that had been battered by the economic depression and was now yearning for strong leadership.

Internationally, Japan's actions reflected its internal instability.

On the evening of September 18, 1931, a small explosion occurred near the tracks of the South Manchuria Railway outside the city of Mukden in northeastern China. The railway, owned and operated by the Japanese-controlled South Manchuria Railway Company, was a vital military and economic asset. The damage was minimal, insufficient even to disrupt train operations, yet it served as a convenient excuse for the Japanese militarists.

The Japanese Kwantung Army, stationed in Manchuria to protect Japanese interests, quickly blamed Chinese guerrillas for the alleged sabotage. Without awaiting instructions from Tokyo, the local generals launched a full-scale military operation, swiftly capturing Mukden and advancing across Manchuria. Within days, the Kwantung Army had seized several major cities and strategic points, effectively taking control of the entire region.

The truth behind the explosion would not emerge until much later: the bomb had been the work of the Japanese Army itself, and the Mukden Incident had been intentionally orchestrated by local officers of the 29th Infantry Regiment, acting without orders from Tokyo, as a pretext for invasion. Discontented with the civilian government and eager to expand Japan's territorial influence, these officers had sought to provoke a conflict that would justify a large-scale military intervention.

At home, the Mukden Incident and the invasion of Manchuria were celebrated as a triumph of Japanese military prowess. Newspapers and propaganda outlets lauded the Kwantung Army's actions, presenting the occupation of Manchuria as a necessary step to protect Japanese citizens and their interests in the region. The public, still grappling with the economic hardships of the Great Depression, saw Manchuria as a land of opportunity and a solution to many of Japan's problems.

However, the Mukden incident also demonstrated that the Army could act independently on its own, even against the will of the civilian government, without facing any consequences, and could impose its will onto the entire nation with impunity. The democratic government in Tokyo had ceased to effectively function, and from now on, the Army was in *de facto* control of Japan. The consequences would be dire.

Following the Mukden Incident, Japan wasted no time before consolidating its hold over Manchuria. The Kwantung Army, once again acting independently of the civilian government but with tacit approval from the militarist factions in Tokyo, continued its swift campaign of occupation. Military strikes seized more and more Chinese territory.

In 1932, Japan proclaimed the creation of the puppet state of Manchukuo, ostensibly an independent nation, but in reality a virtual colony governed by Japan. To lend the new state an air of legitimacy, Japan installed Pu Yi, the last emperor of China's Qing Dynasty who had been overthrown in 1911, as its figurehead ruler. His authority in Manchukuo, however, was purely ceremonial, and the real power lay with the Japanese military and civilian officials who controlled the administration, economy, and infrastructure of the puppet state.

The militarists displayed Manchukuo to Japan and to the world as a model of pan-Asian unity in a "Greater East Asian Co-Prosperity Sphere". This was, however, solely a propaganda effort aimed at portraying Japan as the liberator of Asia from Western imperialism. In truth, the region was being systematically exploited for Japan's own benefit, and Manchuria's vast natural resources were extracted to fuel Japan's industrial and military needs. Japanese companies were given special privileges and incentives, while Japanese settlers were encouraged to migrate to Manchukuo, where they were given land and opportunities unavailable in Japan's overcrowded cities and struggling rural areas. The local Chinese population lived under discriminatory policies and harsh conditions, and those who opposed the harsh Japanese rule faced severe repression.

The League of Nations, under pressure from China, conducted an investigation into the Mukden Incident and Japan's actions in Manchuria. The resulting Lytton Report, published in 1932, concluded that Manchukuo was "not a legitimate state", and called for Japan to withdraw its forces from Manchuria. However, the League's recommendations were non-binding, and its lack of enforcement mechanisms rendered the report ineffectual and powerless. In response, Japan refused to recognize the jurisdiction of the League of Nations and withdrew from it in 1933, signaling its willingness to defy international opinion and to pursue its expansionist agenda unchecked.

The sweeping political and economic changes of the 1930s did not spare the Sugiyama family. For centuries, they had weathered the natural cycles of scarcity and abundance with the quiet stoicism born of a fishing village life. But the upheavals in Japan's broader society now began to intrude forcefully into their small isolated world.

Hideyoshi noticed it first in the way his father grew quieter during their family meals. Once a man of steady words and measured humor, Hideyuki now spent long hours staring into the distance, his face clouded with concern. The discussions he shared with Haruko in the evenings were often hushed but tense, their voices rising occasionally before falling into silence. Hideyoshi, listening from his *futon*, couldn't always make out the words, but he sensed the division and worry that seemed to hang over the household.

Katsuro was the most vocal. Over cups of tea, he spoke of Japan's need to build foreign colonies as a way of promoting economic growth just as the European powers themselves had already done all over the world, and defended the imperative to expand the Japanese military as protection against European or American domination. "We are just following the example set for us by the Anglos," Katsuro declared. "And without the strength of an Army and Navy, we could lose everything to foreign powers."

Hideyuki, who rarely indulged in politics, fidgeted uncomfortably. "The military says they're protecting Japan," he softly replied. "But look at Manchuria—they say it's for our prosperity, but I don't see any prosperity here. Just more taxes and more men leaving for the Army." He slowly sipped his tea. "The

Army gets rice, the Navy gets steel, and what's left for us? Empty nets and promises."

Haruko tried to be the peacemaker and steer her brother's conversation toward calmer waters. "The times are changing. But war won't fill the fishing nets. We must focus on what we can control."

Still, the rising tide of militarism could now be seen everywhere.

The atmosphere in Japanese schools had shifted dramatically. Education was no longer merely a means to impart knowledge and basic skills; it had become a vital tool for shaping young minds to align with the nation's growing ambitions. Across the country, classrooms were transformed into a forum where loyalty to the Emperor, reverence for the nation, and readiness for sacrifice were instilled into the young and impressionable.

Morning ceremonies became required. Across cities, towns, and rural villages, students would gather in orderly ranks in their schoolyards and, at the sound of a whistle or bell, turn toward the flagpole and bow deeply to the rising sun emblem which symbolized Japan's divine destiny. The national anthem, *Kimigayo*, was sung with enthusiasm, and teachers delivered words of encouragement meant to foster national pride and personal devotion.

Hayashi-*sensei's* classroom was no exception. Every day began with a solemn reminder of each student's role in the nation's future. "You are the heart of Japan's strength," Hayashi-*sensei* would declare. "Through your efforts, the Empire will grow ever greater."

The school textbooks had changed as well. Once devoted to practical subjects and to moral lessons rooted in classical Confucianist writings, the new materials from the Ministry of Education were steeped in the ideology of patriotism, loyalty and sacrifice. Stories of explorers and inventors were replaced by tales of ancient *samurai* and their unswerving devotion to their *daimyo* lords. Lessons on Japanese history emphasized military victories and the nation's divine mission to lead Asia.

In Hayashi-*sensei's* classroom, a newly introduced lesson on *bushido*, the *samurai* code of honor, captured the attention of the students. As the teacher placed a *bokken* wooden sword on his desk, his voice took on a reverent tone. "*Bushido* is the soul of Japan," he said. "It teaches us to be courageous, loyal, and selfless. These values will make you strong—not just as individuals, but as sons and daughters of our great Empire."

Physical education also reflected the changing times. Military drills became a standard part of the curriculum, with students learning to march in formation and to instantly respond to commands with precision. Boys often trained with wooden sticks as a simulation of rifles and bayonets, while girls were prepared for home-front duties.

For many teachers, this shift was a matter of duty, though some wrestled privately with its implications. For the young students, who knew nothing of war, most naively embraced these military ideals wholeheartedly, finding a sense of belonging in the pageantry and patriotism. The marching, the flags, the uniforms, the chanting and singing—it all became a sort of glorious game to them.

Soon government-issued posters began appearing in towns and villages across the nation, emblazoned with bold slogans urging vigilance against external and internal enemies. In newspapers, editorials emphasized the heroism of Japanese soldiers, describing their sacrifices in vivid detail while trumpeting Japan's military victories in Manchuria as a benevolent act to bring order and prosperity to a troubled region. Foreign powers, particularly Britain, France, and the United States, were depicted as oppressors and occupiers intent on controlling all of Asia and on undermining Japan's rightful place as the continent's natural leader.

Radio broadcasts featured patriotic songs, speeches by military leaders, and dramatized accounts of Japan's historical triumphs. One recurring program, *Voices of the Rising Sun*, concluded each episode with the message: "Through unity, strength, and loyalty, our Empire will shine eternal."

Religious institutions were also co-opted into the effort. Shinto shrines, already central to Japanese spiritual life, now became sites for ceremonies promoting reverence for the Emperor. Priests conducted rituals to bless soldiers and their families, while including messages about the moral duty of citizens to support Japan's divine mission.

Entertainment and culture did not escape the influence of propaganda, either. New theater performances and films frequently included nationalist themes, glorifying Japan's *samurai* heritage or portraying foreign powers as deceitful antagonists.

At the same time, the government promoted the idea of "*Hakkō ichiu*" (the "eight corners of the world under one roof")—a vision of global harmony achieved through Japanese leadership. This concept was presented as both an idealistic mission and as a justification for Japan's military actions.

For Japanese citizens, the pervasive propaganda was difficult to escape. While most people voluntarily embraced its messages wholeheartedly, finding pride in the vision of a strong and unified Japan, some others viewed it with quiet skepticism and feared that it would lead the country to destruction. However, dissent was dangerous, and even those who harbored private doubts about the government's policies found it increasingly difficult to voice any disagreement in the face of overwhelming public enthusiasm.

And always there were the *Kempeitai* (Military Police Corps) and the *Tokko* (Special Higher Police). They were the primary instruments of state control which were used to suppress dissent and enforce loyalty. The *Kempeitai*, originally a military police force within the Imperial Japanese Army, soon extended its reach into civilian life — conducting surveillance, rooting out "anti-government activity", and enforcing ideological conformity. The *Tokko*, meanwhile, specialized in monitoring and suppressing subversive elements, particularly communists, socialists, labor organizers, and critics of the Emperor or the militarist government. Together, these organizations worked to stifle dissent through widespread spying, arrests, and brutal interrogations, often employing torture. Citizens were encouraged to report any suspicious or disloyal people they knew, thus fostering a climate of fear and suspicion in which nobody trusted their neighbor and no one dared to speak out.

Even in the little fishing village, though, there were contrasting reactions. Katsuro strongly supported the nationalist movement. He often spoke of Japan's duty to expand and secure its place as a world power. "The victory over Russia," he would say, "proved that we are capable of defeating even the strongest Western nations. Japan must seize this moment to fulfill its destiny."

Hideyuki, in turn, would shake his head and murmur, "Wars are easy to start, but hard to end," but he rarely pressed the issue further. He understood the strength of Katsuro's convictions and the influence that his war service carried in the eyes of others. Instead, he focused on teaching Hideyoshi the value of hard work and caution, quietly trusting that his son would temper his ambitions with wisdom.

For Hideyoshi, the whole issue was confusing and unsettling. The tales of Japanese soldiers building an empire stirred a pride within him, and he admired the bravery of those who fought for their country, but the strain it was placing on his family and community made him question the cost.

Meanwhile, Hideyoshi's guarded criticisms of the government grew sharper over time. He began to express concern about conscription, which was becoming more common as the military expanded the war in China. "It won't be long before they start coming to villages like ours, taking the boys and leaving the rest of us to fend for ourselves," he warned one evening. His words sent a chill through Hideyoshi, who couldn't help but wonder if he, too, might one day be called upon.

On one particular evening, as the family gathered around the small *hibachi* hearth, Katsuro leaned back against the wooden frame of the house, his eyes fixed on the ceiling as if reliving a distant memory. "The Navy," he began, his voice steady, "is the path for those who want to serve with honor and skill. The Army, they'll take anyone—farmers, laborers, men who've never seen a map. But the Navy ... the Navy is different."

Hideyoshi listened intently, his interest piqued. His father, Hideyuki, sat quietly, his expression neutral but attentive.

Katsuro continued, glancing at his nephew. "Whenever I saw the Army men, they were treated like machinery, nothing more. The officers had no regard for them, and the conditions were brutal. But the Navy? It's a place for men with ambition, for those who want to rise above their station. They value skill, intelligence, and discipline. And let me tell you, Hideyoshi, the Navy is the future of Japan's strength."

Katsuro's stories now often returned to a particular battle, the siege of Port Arthur. His descriptions of the Army's struggles against the Russians were vivid, recounting the arduous marches, the bitter cold, and the poorly coordinated assaults that cost thousands of lives. Yet he always contrasted this with the decisive naval engagements, where strategy and precision had turned the tide in Japan's favor.

"Do you know why we won that war?" Katsuro asked, his voice rising slightly. "It wasn't the Army slogging through mud and blood. It was Admiral Togo and the Navy at Tsushima. The Navy broke the Russians, not the foot soldiers. Remember that."

Hideyoshi's father finally spoke, his voice cautious but calm. "You speak highly of the Navy, brother-in-law, but let's not forget that war itself is a heavy burden. Whether it's the Navy or the Army, it demands sacrifice. It demands blood."

Katsuro nodded, acknowledging the truth of his words. "That's true, Hideyuki. But if a man must serve—and mark my words, Hideyoshi, with the way things are going, you may not have a choice —then he should serve where his life or death will mean something. The Navy will give you skills, discipline, and maybe even a future after the war. The Army? You'll just be another body."

The next morning, as Hideyoshi helped his father repair the fishing nets, he cautiously broached the subject. "Father, what do you think of what Uncle Katsuro said? About the Navy?"

Hideyuki looked up, his hands steady as he worked the net. "Your uncle speaks from his own experience. He sees the Navy as a better path because he's seen the worst of the Army. But you must understand, Hideyoshi, that every choice comes with its risks. The Navy isn't an easy life, either. It has its own dangers, and it demands discipline and hard work."

Hideyoshi nodded, taking his father's measured words to heart. But the seed had been planted. His uncle's words still echoed in his mind. If circumstances were to force him to serve in one way or another, then the idea of being drafted into the Army, with its tales of hardship and brutal conditions, was far less appealing than the structured and merit-based environment that Katsuro described in the Navy.

The pressure to make a decision had already been building for months. Soon he would be eighteen, and soon after that he would graduate school. Japan's military recruiters were relentless, and with the escalating war in China, every young man of his age was a target for conscription. In school, Hayashi-*sensei's* lessons frequently touched on the glory of serving the Empire, reinforcing the inevitability of military service for most of the students.

For Hideyoshi, the decision was also fueled by more than just practical concerns. Ever since he had watched the *Sanba Garasu* perform their aerobatic display, he had been captivated by the idea of flight and aviation, and the thought of being conscripted into the Army, marching endlessly through muddy fields and forests only to be bayoneted or blown apart, filled him with dread. The Navy represented freedom, adventure, and a chance to see the world beyond the shores of Japan. By enlisting voluntarily, he concluded, he would at least be able to choose his branch of service—and possibly even steer his career toward aviation.

The Navy, he knew, had one of the best flight programs in the world. But he also knew that the most direct way to be accepted into the Navy's flying corps was to either obtain a private pilot's license and enlist, or to attend pilot training in a university and graduate as a pilot in the reserves. Neither of those were possible in Sakurada.

That left two other options, in the form of two new programs that were specifically designed to recruit large numbers of new pilots for the war in China. He could apply directly to the Naval Academy as part of the *Yoka Renshusei (Yokaren)* aviation course, and, if accepted, become a flight student. But only a tiny fraction of the thousands of young men who applied each year were accepted. The odds were slightly better in the Navy's *Soju Renshusei (Soren)* program, which required potential pilots to enlist as an ordinary sailor, serve a period of time on duty aboard ship, and then apply for flight training.

In the end, there was really only one decision that he could make.

On a chilly morning in February 1933, having just turned eighteen, Hideyoshi made his way to the recruitment office in Tsu, accompanied by Katsura. The office was a bustling hub of activity, filled with young men like himself, eager to serve. The walls were adorned with patriotic banners and with photographs of naval ships cutting through the waves and planes soaring above the clouds.

The recruitment officer, a gruff man in his mid-forties, spoke with practiced authority. "The Navy is the heart of the Empire's strength," he declared to the assembled group. "We need men of courage, discipline, and intelligence to defend our nation and secure its place in the world. Join us, and you will not only serve the Emperor with honor as a *samurai* — you will carve your name into the history of Japan."

When it was his turn, Hideyoshi stepped forward, his heart pounding. The officer asked a series of questions about his background, education, and physical health. Katsura stood nearby, offering silent support. When the moment came to sign his name, Hideyoshi hesitated for a brief second, feeling the significance of the commitment he was about to make.

Then, with a deep breath, he signed.

Chapter 3
Joining the Japanese Navy (1933)

The day of Hideyoshi's departure was heavy with unspoken emotions. The village bustled with the usual early morning activity, but for Hideyoshi and his family, this was no ordinary day. It was a day of endings and of beginnings.

His mother had been up before dawn, preparing a special breakfast of rice topped with *umeboshi* pickled fruits, and *miso* soup. The table was set carefully, as if the artful arrangement might somehow ward off the inevitability of their parting. Hideyuki sat at the head of the table, in contemplative silence.

Hideyoshi ate quickly, barely tasting the food, though his excitement to leave and begin his naval career was tempered by the bittersweet sorrowfulness of the occasion. Haruko fussed over him, arranging his hair and making last-minute adjustments to his clothing. "Remember to write to us," she said softly, her hands lingering on his shoulders. "And take care of yourself. The world outside isn't like Sakurada."

The family walked together to the village's edge, where a narrow dirt road led toward the newly-finished railway station. Along the way, neighbors and friends stopped to bid Hideyoshi farewell. One of them presented him with a folded *yosegaki* flag: it had been signed by most of the village men, and each of them had added a brief message wishing good luck and success. Other people shouted messages of encouragement as they went by. "Make us proud!" "Glorious victory!" "*Banzai!*" Children, too young to fully grasp the meaning of the moment, waved excitedly as he passed.

At the station, the mood grew more somber. The train platform was deserted except for Hideyoshi's family and a few travelers who were passing through to Tsu. Katsura handed him a neatly wrapped *bento* box containing some rice balls, his rough hands lingering as he passed it over. "Remember your duty to the Emperor," he said, his voice gruff. "But don't forget where you came from."

Haruko then pressed a folded piece of cloth into his hand. It was a *senninbari*, a "thousand stitch belt", calling upon the *kami* to confer good luck, good health, and protection from harm. In addition to asking the village women, Haruko had stood all afternoon at the train platform in nearby Tsu, imploring each woman who had passed by to add a single red stitch until there were one thousand of them.

As the train whistle sounded in the distance, Haruko's composure broke. She pulled Hideyoshi into a close embrace, tears streaming down her cheeks. "Be brave," she whispered. "And come back to us." Hideyoshi held her tightly.

The train arrived with a hiss of steam, and he climbed aboard, carrying his small satchel of belongings. He turned to look at his family one last time, their faces a mixture of pride and sadness. As the train began to pull away, he leaned out the window, called, "I love you!", and continued to wave until they were no longer in sight.

The rhythmic clatter of the train wheels matched the pounding of his heart. Already, Hideyoshi felt an ache he hadn't anticipated — a longing for the familiar warmth of home and family. For the first time, the enormity of what lay ahead truly hit him. He was leaving behind everything he had ever known, and stepping into the unknown.

The winter air was crisp as the train pulled into Yokosuka. Hideyoshi stepped down onto the platform, clutching his satchel bag with one hand and adjusting his cap with the other.

Yokosuka Naval Base, in Tokyo Bay, had been established by the Tokugawa *shogun* in 1866. During the Meiji Restoration, however, it had been greatly expanded as Japan sought to build up a modern Navy that could stand up to any foreign opponent. The country's first home-built battleship, the *Satsuma*, had been constructed here in 1905. At over 250 acres, the base now contained a shipyard, several airfields, drydocks, and a naval gun factory, as well as the primary training facilities for new recruits. Japan's newest carrier-based aircraft, the Type 92 Kugisho biplane torpedo bomber, was being designed in the Naval Air Technical Center, and the shipyard was just finishing their work on the Imperial Navy's latest aircraft carrier, the *Ryujo*. More were already being planned.

After being issued his trainee cadet uniform, Hideyoshi joined a group of young men gathered near an officer who was yelling out orders. The officer immediately turned to him and shouted, "Line up! You are no longer boys of your villages! You are now trainees of the Imperial Japanese Navy. Act accordingly!" The recruits scrambled into formation, and Hideyoshi found himself standing shoulder to shoulder with others who, like him, were just now beginning to realize what they had really gotten into.

The recruits marched in silence. As they approached the gates, the sheer scale of the base came into view. Fences surrounded the entire sprawling compound, and inside were rows of barracks, training grounds, and administrative buildings stretching out in perfect order. Uniformed men were everywhere, marching around in ordered groups or dashing alone from place to place to carry out somebody's orders. It reminded Hideyoshi of an ant hill.

Inside the gate, a senior petty officer met them. His uniform was immaculate, his face stony, and his eyes sharp as he scanned the new arrivals with a look of barely-concealed contempt. "You will address me as Petty Officer Motashi," he barked out, in a voice that dripped with authority. "From this moment on, you belong to the Navy. Your old lives are over. Forget your comforts, forget your families. Here, you will learn discipline, loyalty, and strength." Then his face softened for just a moment. "Welcome to Yokosuka Naval Base."

They were led to their barracks, simple wooden buildings that smelled faintly of fresh sawdust. The cots were arranged in neat rows, and each was accompanied by a small locker and a stool. "Settle in quickly," Motashi commanded. "Your training begins tomorrow at dawn. You'll need every ounce of rest you can get."

That evening, Hideyoshi found himself in the mess hall, surrounded by dozens of recruits and trainees. The clatter of bowls and chopsticks filled the air as the men ate their simple meal of rice, *miso* soup, and *udon* noodles. The recruits were too nervous or tired to say much, and Hideyoshi exchanged polite nods with those near him but remained mostly silent. Everyone seemed lost in thought, and most, like Hideyoshi, were quietly contemplating the choice they had made.

The next morning, reveille came early with the blare of a bugle. The new cadets stumbled out of their cots, still groggy, and hurried to assemble outside. The chill of the pre-dawn air bit at their skin, but no one dared to complain. Motashi strode among them, inspecting their uniforms and posture. "You are here to serve the Emperor and the nation," he declared. "Keep that in mind, every second of every day."

After inspections, the cadets were marched off to begin their classroom courses. The building, a utilitarian structure of gray stone, seemed as imposing as the instructors who awaited them. The walls were adorned with maps of the Pacific, photographs of naval ships, and portraits of Japan's naval heroes, a silent illustration of the legacy that the cadets were expected to uphold.

The first lecture was on naval history, delivered by Commander Saito. He began by recounting the triumphs of the Imperial Japanese Navy, from the victory at Tsushima in the Russo-Japanese War to its expanding presence in the Pacific. Hideyoshi listened intently, captivated by tales of daring naval maneuvers and the courage of sailors who had come before him. Yet, there was little room for romanticism in Saito's delivery; every victory, he emphasized, was the result of discipline, training, obedience to orders, and unwavering loyalty to the Emperor.

Hideyoshi was also introduced to the *Gunjin Chokuyu*, the "Imperial Rescript". Presented by the Emperor Meiji and 1882 and memorized by every military member since then, the Rescript listed and described the Five Requirements of every serviceman: "The military man is loyal. The military man is polite. The military man is brave. The military man is trustworthy. The military man is thrifty."

The day ended with a long lesson in naval discipline and protocol. They were drilled on the proper way to salute, how to address superior officers, and above all to always respect the rigid hierarchy that defined every aspect of life in the Navy. And, as cadet trainees, they were at the very bottom of that hierarchy.

By the time the day concluded, Hideyoshi's arm ached from repeated salutes, but he quickly learned that this would not be the worst part of his training regimen.

From the very first day, the tone was set: this was not merely an academic school, but an anvil that was meant to forge obedience, resolve, and unhesitating loyalty to the chain of command. Even minor missteps—the tiniest delay, a sloppy uniform, or a missed salute—could invite a sharp reprimand. Or worse.

Discipline was enforced with an iron hand, and punishments for mistakes were swift and brutal. Cadets were fortunate if they escaped with a humiliating tongue-lashing. Instructors would get into their face and scream "I can't hear you, little mouse! Speak up like a Navy man!"

Just as often, even for the most minor of offenses, they would be the victims of corporal punishment, the favored form of which was being beaten with the *Gunjin Seishin Chunyubo* or "club to instill military spirit," a heavy wooden stick that was carried by every officer. The Navy's philosophy was clear: you will learn obedience and respect even if we have to beat it into you. Cadets were subjected to a constant barrage of orders, drills, and inspections, all carefully designed to strip them of any individuality, to dehumanize them, and to produce an instinctive and absolute willingness to do whatever they were told.

This harshness was deliberate. The Navy's leaders believed that such rigorous conditioning prepared recruits for the extreme stresses of combat, where any hesitation or disobedience could mean death for the entire crew. It was also rooted in the deeper cultural values of social conformity. The Japanese have always had a saying, "The nail that sticks up must be nailed down", and the military applied that maxim with ruthless effect.

The cadets were, therefore, mercilessly punished for everything or for nothing, and every day carried with it the risk of painful and humiliating brutality. The naval cadets at Yokosuka had already learned that they counted for nothing and that any flaw or mistake, however minor, would lead to swift and severe repercussions. "Uncle Katsuro was wrong," Hideyoshi ruefully thought to himself. "In the Navy, too, we are just another body."

One afternoon, Hideyoshi was sitting cross-legged on his cot, hastily polishing his boots before the morning inspection. Around him, the barracks hummed with subdued murmurs and the sharp scrape of brushes against leather.

The first signs of trouble came when a senior petty officer swept into the room like a storm cloud, his "military spirit" stick resting ominously on his shoulder and his eyes scanning the room with hawk-like intensity. Stopping abruptly near one locker, he crouched down and plucked a thin strand of lint from the otherwise pristine interior. "Who does this locker belong to?" he demanded, his voice sharp enough to cut steel.

The unfortunate cadet stepped forward and saluted, trembling. "Sir, it's mine!"

The petty officer's lip curled in disdain. "Your locker is filthy. Unacceptable!" Turning to the other cadets, he bellowed, "The beekeeper is coming to check on his hive!"

Instantly, all of the cadets scrambled toward their wooden lockers, each no larger than a small cupboard. Hideyoshi barely managed to wedge himself backward into the cramped space with his shoulders pressed uncomfortably against the edges of the frame and his knees jammed against the sides. Together, as one in unison, the cadets began flapping their hands in tight, frantic motions and buzzing like bees.

"Buzz louder!" the petty officer roared, stalking the row of recruits. "Do you call that a hive? Pathetic!"

Hideyoshi flapped harder, his wrists aching as he mimicked the drone of a bee. A cadet near the end of the line stumbled, his buzzing faltering into a gasp. Without missing a beat, the petty officer dashed over and slapped him hard across the face.

After what felt like an eternity, he finally ordered them to stop. The cadets spilled out of their lockers, gasping for breath and hoping that their punishment had ended. But their reprieve was short-lived. "Fall in!" came the command, and they hurriedly formed ranks on the wooden floor.

The next penalty came almost immediately. The officer strode rapidly toward one of the cadets and stood almost nose to nose. "You are out of position!" he shouted. "How dare you disrespect the formation!"

Without further warning, he swung the stick, cracking it across the cadet's thigh with a thud. The boy staggered but managed to remain upright. When the officer struck again, this time across his shoulders, the cadet involuntarily cried out in pain.

"Do you understand now?" the petty officer snapped, his tone cold and merciless.

"Yes, sir!" the cadet choked out, trembling as he fought to hold back tears.

The petty officer's eyes narrowed. "Weakness is contagious," he sneered. "Your lack of discipline disgraces this entire barracks." He turned sharply to the assembled cadets. "If one of you fails, you all pay the price. Stand at attention!"

The cadets exchanged uneasy glances but hastily obeyed. The officer paced before them, the "spirit injection stick" swinging freely in his hand. "You will learn that there are no individuals in the Imperial Navy," he said. "When one fails, all suffer. Now, bend over."

The cadets hesitated for a fraction of a second, and his voice exploded. "Bend over, I said!"

Reluctantly, the young men complied, their hands resting on their thighs as they braced for the inevitable. The petty officer moved methodically down the line, delivering a blow to each cadet's backside. The sound of the stick striking flesh echoed across the room, mingling with muffled grunts and gasps of pain.

When the stick reached Hideyoshi, he clenched his jaw and resolved not to cry out. The blow landed squarely across his lower back, sending a sharp jolt of pain through his body. He bit down on the inside of his cheek, tasting blood, but he refused to make a sound.

By the time the petty officer reached the last cadet, the group was visibly shaken, their faces pale and their postures rigid. He then stepped back, surveying his work. "Let this be a lesson," he growled. "I am not doing this because I hate you—I am doing this because I like you and I want to turn you into sailors. We are the Imperial Navy, not a band of bumbling farmers!"

The cadets shuffled back to their cots in silence, too sore to move further. Hideyoshi sat cross-legged, rubbing his aching back. He exchanged a brief glance with the cadet whose locker had first incurred the officer's wrath, a boy whose tear-streaked face was now a mask of guilt and shame. No words were exchanged, but the message was clear.

Despite the hardships, there was always a sense of camaraderie among the cadets. They often helped one another through difficult academic topics, and shared moments of triumph when a particularly harsh instructor offered a rare word of praise to one of them.

One evening, as Hideyoshi sat reading a manual, a fellow recruit named Minoru leaned over. "You're from Mie, right?" he asked. Hideyoshi nodded, and the cadet grinned. "My uncle's a fisherman there. Maybe our families know each other."

Teruo, a young man from Osaka with a quick wit, also became a fast friend. "So, Sakurada, eh?" he had remarked one evening, lying on his cot after a day of drills. "Never heard of it. Must be one of those places with more fish than people." His barb earned a laugh from Hideyoshi, a rare moment of levity in their rigid and restricted world.

The trio soon became inseparable. They bonded over shared hardships during training and found small ways to break the monotony of their regimented days. Late at night, when the barracks were finally silent, they whispered jokes or reenacted their instructor's more ridiculous outbursts, muffling their laughter in their pillows to avoid being overheard. Teruo's impressions of Petty Officer Ando—complete with exaggerated scowls and an overly dramatic swing of an imaginary stick—had Hideyoshi stifling his laughter so hard his sides hurt.

Their camaraderie wasn't limited to the confines of the barracks. Whenever they were granted a rare leave they ventured out beyond the base, where the bustling streets of Yokosuka and Tokyo offered a tantalizing taste of freedom and a stark contrast to their regimented life. One memorable outing led them to the Ginza, where Teruo convinced them to spend their meager pay on bowls of steaming *udo* at a crowded street stall. "This," Teruo declared, gesturing with his chopsticks, "is what we're really fighting for—freedom to eat good food whenever we want."

Later that same evening, they wandered into a small, dimly lit bar. The smoky room buzzed with chatter as a jazz band played in the corner. They were too young and too poor to drink much, but Minoru managed to charm the waitress into giving them an extra round of *sake*. "It's my first time in Tokyo," he told her with an innocent grin. "This is practically a cultural experience, right?"

Despite their strict curfew, the trio often cut their returns perilously close. One night, rushing back to base under the glow of the streetlights, they were nearly caught by an officer on patrol. "Quick, this way!" Minoru hissed, leading them down a dark walkway behind one of the buildings. They pressed themselves against a wall, holding their breaths as the officer's footsteps echoed past. Once the coast was clear, Teruo whispered, "I think my heart just stopped," earning muffled laughter from his companions.

Even during the endless drills, they found ways to inject humor into the stifling routine. During one particularly tedious marching exercise, Mihara stumbled theatrically, earning a sharp rebuke and a slap from the instructor but also a hidden smirk from Hideyoshi.

Yet, despite their playful side, they remained fiercely loyal to each other. When Minoru struggled to memorize a knot-tying technique, Hideyoshi stayed up late to tutor him, patiently demonstrating until his friend finally mastered it. When Teruo's *tabi* socks wore through—an offense that would certainly bring an injection of "military spirit"—Minoru pooled what little money he had with Hideyoshi to buy a secondhand pair for him.

Weekends also brought a welcome reprieve from the regimentation of naval training. As part of the Navy's effort to cultivate humility in its sailors and to forge bonds between them and the civilians, cadets were assigned to spend their Sunday free time with local families. This practice, called *katei homon* ("home visit"), was explained to them during a morning assembly. "You are here to serve Japan, not just the Navy," the officer had told them. "Understanding the lives of ordinary people will teach you the values of service and gratitude."

Hideyoshi found himself assigned to the Kimura family, who lived in a modest home near Yokosuka's bustling harbor. The head of the household, Yasuo, was a steelworker in the shipyard who took pride in his work crafting the vessels that were the backbone of Japan's naval might. His wife, Fumiko, was a warm, industrious woman with a knack for keeping their two young children, Keiko and Haruto, in line. Each Sunday, Hideyoshi would take the autobus from the base to the Kimura home, carrying his Navy-supplied dinner along with him (the Navy did not want its cadets to be a burden on anyone, and also wanted them to learn self-reliance.)

On his first visit, the Kimuras welcomed Hideyoshi with polite curiosity, then Fumiko immediately set him to work peeling *daikon* radishes for pickling. His clumsy attempts drew giggles from Keiko, a precocious six-year-old, and an encouraging smile from her mother.

Over time, the tasks grew more demanding. Hideyoshi helped carry buckets of water from the well, and repaired a sagging fence. One morning, Yasuo handed him a shovel and led him to a patch of rocky soil behind the house. "We're planting a garden," he announced. Hideyoshi, who had never given much thought to agriculture ("I'm a fisherman", he reminded Yasuo) spent hours breaking up the tough clods of earth and digging neat rows. By the time the sun dipped to the horizon, his arms ached and his hands were blistered, but the family's gratitude made it worthwhile.

On another visit, Fumiko asked Hideyoshi to teach Haruto, who idolized sailors, how to properly fold a naval uniform. The boy's enthusiasm was contagious, and Hideyoshi found himself explaining the importance of every crease and fold. Haruto's laughter echoed through the house as he earnestly tried to mimic the technique.

Despite these lighter moments, the visits carried a serious purpose. The Navy thought that it would deepen their commitment to serving the nation, and by living among ordinary families and engaging in chores, recruits were meant to absorb the essence of "Japanese spirit and fortitude".

One evening, as the family sat around the table, Fumiko asked, "Why did you join the Navy, Hideyoshi?" The question caught him off guard, but he answered honestly. "I wanted to fly and see the world," he said, then added, "But I also wanted to serve Japan in the best way I could."

Yasuo nodded solemnly. "A sailor's strength," he said, "is not just in his muscles or his mind—it's in his heart. Never forget the people you serve."

The words stayed with Hideyoshi long after he left the Kimura home.

For the next several months, the cadets attended classes on naval history and seamanship. The daily schedule was exhausting. Physical conditioning drills consumed the early hours, often involving long runs carrying heavy gear or repeated calisthenics that left muscles burning and lungs gasping. They also played sports like baseball, rowing, and volleyball, which were intended to teach them teamwork and cooperation.

After a quick breakfast, the cadets marched to their classrooms, where the instructors, whether officers or senior enlisted men, demanded perfection. Their critiques were often delivered with a shout or, in many cases, by a quick strike with a "military spirit" stick. Barely a day went by without Hideyoshi acquiring another bruise, usually for no discernible reason other than to forcefully demonstrate to the cadets who was in charge.

Navigation classes were among the most technical of the lectures, with instructors drilling into the cadets the importance of accuracy. Hideyoshi learned to read charts, calculate distances, and understand the complexities of currents and tides. Mistakes were not tolerated, and those who struggled were often reprimanded in front of the entire class.

Weapons training was also a vital part of their training. Cadets spent hours learning about the Navy's arsenal, from the operation of torpedo tubes to the maintenance of small arms. On the firing range, Hideyoshi struggled at first with shooting the standard infantry Arisaka rifle, but soon developed enviable accuracy. There were also endless hours of gunnery drills on an old almost-derelict training ship that was docked out in the harbor, with teams taking turns to rapidly reload and dry-fire the 12cm batteries and the 20mm anti-aircraft guns until they could have done it blindfolded in the dark.

One of the most draining but important parts of their preparation involved emergency procedures and damage control. Hideyoshi and his fellow cadets were constantly undergoing surprise fire suppression drills, often racing against the clock to contain and extinguish simulated fires. They also trained for shipboard flooding, learning how to seal compartment leaks and how to operate pumps. The instructors made it clear that these skills would mean the difference between life and death in combat.

There was little time for rest during this phase of their training. After classes and drills, cadets were expected to study and prepare for the next day. As summer turned into autumn, the pace of their studies began to pick up, and they knew that it would not be long now before they were assigned to duty posts at sea.

The news came on a crisp September morning in 1933, delivered at the end of the daily assembly. Petty Officer Kawahara's voice boomed out over the assembled cadets. "Assignments have been posted. You are dismissed to check your orders." The young men scrambled toward the bulletin board, anxious to learn their fates.

Hideyoshi pressed forward through the throng, his heart pounding. His eyes scanned the list until they found his name: "Sugiyama, Hideyoshi – Assigned to Destroyer *Akatsuki*". Relief and pride surged through him. The *Akatsuki*, a sleek and fast vessel, was one of the Navy's newest ships.

Later that afternoon, Hideyoshi met with Minoru and Teruo to share their assignments. Minoru declared, "I'm heading to the *Hayate*. Another destroyer, but she's older than yours," he said, punching Hideyoshi lightly on the arm.

Teruo, however, was less enthused. "Radio communications," he said, his voice flat. "They're sending me to train with the signal corps. After that, I'll be stationed at command headquarters on Saipan."

Hideyoshi frowned. "Saipan? That's far."

Teruo nodded. "Too far. I doubt we'll cross paths again."

The trio spent their last evening together walking along the Yokosuka docks. "We've been through a lot," Minoru said, breaking the silence. "But this is the Navy. Everyone goes their own way eventually."

Teruo's usual wit was subdued as he added, "Just remember us when you're out there, Hideyoshi. Don't let the sea swallow you whole."

The morning of the graduation dawned bright and crisp and the February chill bit at the cadets' exposed hands and faces as they lined up on the Yokosuka Naval Base's expansive parade ground. Hideyoshi and his fellow cadets stood rigidly at attention in their freshly pressed uniforms.

A drumbeat echoed across the ground as the base commander, Rear Admiral Nakatomi, ascended the podium. "Cadets," he began, "today marks a significant moment in your lives. You stand on the threshold of service to the Imperial Japanese Navy, the guardian of our sacred homeland and the embodiment of our nation's strength and honor. It is not merely a career you have chosen—it is a calling, one that demands your utmost dedication, sacrifice, and loyalty."

Admiral Nakatomi's tone deepened. "Make no mistake—your path will not be easy. The sea is an unforgiving master, and our enemies will test you in ways you cannot yet imagine. Some of you will not return." He paused a moment before going on. "But know this—your sacrifice will be honored for eternity. You will embody the spirit of *Yamato-damashii*, the indomitable spirit of Japan. Through your service, you will ensure the prosperity of our nation and the safety of its people."

"I have faith that each of you will rise to the occasion. You have endured the rigors of training, the harsh discipline, and the sacrifices required of you. You are ready."

The next morning, Hideyoshi boarded a train to Sasebo, where the *Akatsuki* awaited her crew. Through the whole journey, he stared out the window at the passing countryside, his thoughts divided between the future ahead of him and the friendships he was leaving behind.

The *Akatsuki* was a marvel of engineering. She was fast, agile, and bristling with weaponry — everything a destroyer should be. Her deck bustled with activity as sailors prepared for her voyage.

Hideyoshi reported to the officer of the deck, and after getting his gear settled he was taken to his station in one of the destroyer's main 12.7cm gun turrets, intended for use against aircraft as well as surface targets. The *Akatsuki* was already preparing to leave port: her next mission was a routine patrol along Japan's southern coast. It was still dark as the *Akatsuki* slipped out of her dock and headed out into the open sea.

Below deck, Hideyoshi reported to the magazine room of the Number One gun turret where Chief Petty Officer Kondo, a gruff veteran with a face weathered like an old oak, was in charge. It quickly became apparent that he did not think much of raw recruits. "Listen up, farm boy," Kondo bellowed. "Your job is simple: carry ammunition, clean the breach, and do whatever you're told. You mess up, and it won't be just the captain you'll answer to."

Hideyoshi's tasks seemed straightforward, but although he had done gun drills in training, the equipment on the *Akatsuki* was newer. Kondo demonstrated the loading process. "Speed and precision," the chief emphasized. "In combat, lives depend on it. The more shots we can get off, the longer we will live."

Hideyoshi's first test came during a surprise drill ordered by the captain. "General Quarters" alarms blared, sending men rushing to their stations. He dashed to the ammunition storage and loaded the brass shells into the transfer rack with trembling hands, sweat dripping into his eyes and his muscles straining under the weight as he hauled the heavy rounds.

"Faster, farm boy!" Kondo shouted, his voice cutting above the noise of the machinery. Hideyoshi bit back a retort, focusing instead on the rhythm of the task. Load. Transfer. Step back. Load. Transfer. Step back. His arms burned, but he forced himself to keep moving.

By the end of the drill, Hideyoshi collapsed against the bulkhead, gasping for air. Kondo glanced at him and gave a grudging nod. "Not bad for a first-timer. Keep it up, farm boy, and you might just make it."

The days blurred together as the *Akatsuki* patrolled the seas. Hideyoshi grew accustomed to the routines: dawn inspections, repeated drills, and long hours at the turret. The gunnery team's easy camaraderie was a welcome relief from the unyielding discipline he had suffered during his basic training. During quiet moments, the gun crew shared stories over bowls of rice and *udon*, laughing at tales of mischief from their youth.

One night, though, the crew was jolted awake by the sound of an alarm calling them to stations. A shadowy vessel had been spotted on the horizon, running dark without lights. The *Akatsuki* altered course to intercept, and Hideyoshi found himself back at his turret, heart hammering in his chest.

"Enemy ship or smuggler, maybe. We don't know," Kondo informed him. "Stay sharp."

As the destroyer approached its target, the tension grew thick, but as they got closer, the shadowy vessel turned out to be a battered fishing trawler, its crew waving frantically in surrender. The *Akatsuki*'s officers boarded the vessel, spoke with the crew, and confirmed it was a local craft blown off course by a recent storm. The destroyer escorted the trawler back toward safer waters.

In the autumn of 1933, the *Akatsuki* received unexpected orders to set course for Germany as part of a goodwill tour to strengthen Japan's diplomatic ties with Europe. For the crew, the prospect of visiting a distant and exotic nation stirred everyone with excitement and curiosity. The ship's captain assembled the senior officers to review the itinerary and protocols for the visit, emphasizing the importance of projecting discipline and professionalism in every interaction. "We are not just representing the Imperial Japanese Navy," he reminded them. "We are representing our entire nation."

As the *Akatsuki* steamed across the Pacific, the crew worked constantly to ensure that the destroyer was in pristine condition. Decks were scrubbed until they gleamed, brass fixtures polished to a mirror shine, and uniforms meticulously inspected. Conversations buzzed with speculation about what they would see in Germany and what the Germans would think of them.

The long voyage across the vast expanse of the Pacific Ocean, though, was a challenge for the crew of the *Akatsuki*. Day after day, the destroyer cut through the endless blue, the horizon stretching unbroken in every direction, the monotony interrupted only by occasional stops at some remote islands. Hideyoshi found a sense of calm in the routine: maintaining the ship's gunnery systems, drills and exercises, scrubbing anything that didn't move, and swapping stories with his crewmates during the rare moments of rest.

As they neared Panama, the faint outline of land on the horizon stirred a ripple of renewed energy among the crew. Soon, the legendary Panama Canal came into view, signaling their arrival at the gateway between oceans.

The *Akatsuki's* sleek hull sliced through the green waters as she approached the entrance to the Canal. For Hideyoshi and much of the crew, this was a marvel they had only read about in geography lessons. Now, as the destroyer prepared to navigate this engineering masterpiece, anticipation buzzed among the sailors.

From the deck, Hideyoshi could see the distant outline of the Miraflores Locks. "It's like something out of a dream," he said to a nearby crewmate, who nodded with equal fascination. The massive gates of the locks loomed ahead, and a canal pilot came aboard, greeting the officers and taking charge of navigating the ship.

As the *Akatsuki* entered the first lock, the crew marveled at the precision of the operation. Massive concrete walls rose on either side of the ship, and powerful machinery began to fill the lock with water. The rising waters lifted the destroyer slowly but steadily, and Hideyoshi leaned over the railing, watching the water churn below.

"It's like the ship is floating on a mountain," another sailor remarked.

Hideyoshi grinned. "A mountain built by men."

The journey through the canal was not without its challenges. There was not a lot of clearance inside the locks, and the crew had to maneuver the ship carefully. The canal pilot calmly issued precise instructions, and the *Akatsuki* responded with the disciplined efficiency that had been honed to a sharp edge by the countless drills.

The crew's excitement peaked when the *Akatsuki* entered Gatun Lake, a sprawling artificial body of water at the heart of the Canal. A lush tropical landscape surrounded them. Monkeys chattered in the distance, and colorful birds flitted among the trees. For a brief time, the deck crew forgot their duties and simply took in the beauty of the scene.

After several additional locks and more hours of careful navigation, the *Akatsuki* emerged into the Caribbean Sea. A few days later, they anchored in the harbor of Kingston, Jamaica. Here, a vivid scene of aquamarine water and palm-covered hills greeted the sailors as they stepped ashore. The Caribbean air was thick with the scent of tropical flowers and coconut trees. It was a stark contrast to the snowy mountains of Japan.

For Hideyoshi, this was his first time setting foot on foreign soil. He looked around, wide-eyed, as a brass band played a welcoming tune on the pier. The local governor and a delegation of British officials welcomed the Japanese officers with formal handshakes and polite speeches. Meanwhile, the crew received a warm reception from the local population, who had gathered to catch a glimpse of these exotic visitors from faraway Asia.

The Captain permitted a day of shore leave for each of the crew, and Hideyoshi and a small group of shipmates seized the opportunity to explore. They wandered through Kingston's bustling streets, marveling at the colorful markets and the colonial-era buildings. The sailors, in turn, dressed smartly in their crisp white uniforms, drew curious stares and friendly smiles from the locals.

At one market stall, Hideyoshi watched as a vendor deftly sliced open a coconut with a machete. "Try it!" the man said, offering the fresh fruit with a grin. Hideyoshi hesitated but then accepted, sipping the sweet coconut water.

As the group wandered further, they encountered a lively calypso band performing on a street corner. The rhythmic music was unlike anything Hideyoshi had ever heard, and he found himself tapping his foot to the beat. Usugi, one of his shipmates, clumsily attempted a dance, drawing laughter from the sailors and applause from the gathered crowd.

Later, a group from the ship visited a plantation on the outskirts of the city, arranged by the local officials as part of a goodwill tour. The sailors learned about Jamaica's history of sugar production and its role in global trade, though the darker aspects of its colonial past were only hinted at by their guides.

That evening, in return, a reception was held aboard the *Akatsuki*, with local dignitaries and a few invited citizens mingling with the officers and crew. The Japanese sailors did their best to represent their nation with formality and respect. Hideyoshi found himself in a halting conversation with a young Jamaican man who spoke only English. They exchanged some basic phrases and shared laughter over their well-meaning but only partially-successful mutual efforts to communicate.

The next morning, the *Akatsuki* departed Kingston, with the crew lining the deck in dress uniform as they waved farewell to the crowd gathered at the harbor.

A week later, the ship steamed into the German port of Kiel. Germany, with its naval tradition and its controversial politics, was an intriguing destination for the Japanese crew, and when the *Akatsuki* sailed into the harbor, the dock was lined with German naval officers, dignitaries, and curious citizens equally eager to see the visiting warship from distant Japan.

As the ship docked, a band struck up both the Japanese and German national anthems, and the German sailors saluted sharply. Their precision and discipline was, Hideyoshi reminded himself, a reflection of the Prussian military tradition that the Japanese Navy had itself studied so closely during the Meiji years.

The formalities were brisk and efficient. The *Akatsuki's* captain exchanged greetings with his German counterpart, and an official delegation welcomed the Japanese officers ashore. For the enlisted men, however, the real excitement began later when shore leave was granted.

Kiel, with its neat and orderly streets where everything was in its proper place, presented a stark contrast to the vibrant chaos of Kingston or the bustling docks of Japan. The sailors were taken on a tour of the Kiel Naval Academy, where they marveled at the state-of-the-art facilities and the impressive training regimens.

Over a lunch in a mess hall which they shared with German sailors, Hideyoshi found himself seated across from a young *Unteroffizier* named Gerlach who spoke some rudimentary Japanese and Chinese (his father, he explained, had been in Tsingtao during the Great War). After finding someone to translate for them, the two men exchanged pleasantries and compared life in their respective navies. The German sailor, blond and square-jawed, proudly described his ship, the battle-cruiser *Hessen*, and whispered conspiratorially that he soon might get his real wish, which was to serve on the new "pocket battleship" *Graf Spee*. Germany's land, naval, and air forces, Hideyoshi knew, had been severely limited by the Treaty of Versailles which had ended the World War.

In the afternoon, the sailors were given time to explore the city on their own. Hideyoshi and his friends admired the gothic spires of St. Nicholas Church and the imposing Kaiser Wilhelm Canal. They also stopped at a small *kaffeehaus*, where they sampled black bread and sausages; the rich flavors were foreign to their palates, but surprisingly good.

As the day wore on, the group visited a local beer hall, an outing organized by their German hosts. The atmosphere was jovial, with the sound of clinking steins and hearty laughter filling the air. Hideyoshi sipped cautiously at his dark hearty beer, its bitterness contrasting with the milder *sake* that he was accustomed to. His shipmate Kinami, less reserved, raised his glass high and shouted, "*Prost!*" to the amusement of their German counterparts.

Despite the lighthearted moments, however, the undercurrent of militarism was visible everywhere. Adolf Hitler had just been appointed Chancellor a few months earlier, putting the National Socialist Party into power. The Japanese sailors couldn't help but notice the Nazi Party posters extolling German strength and unity that seemed to be posted on every wall, along with the red and black swastika flags that fluttered from every home. A number of shops on the street had a Star of David roughly painted on their door, a few accompanied by the slogan "Don't buy from Jews".

The German officers all greeted each other with *"Heil Hitler!"* salutes. Some of their hosts spoke with pride about their hopes for the nation's resurgence under the new government, and their wish for Germany to emerge from economic ruin and once again take her place among the great nations of the world. It was, Hideyoshi noted, similar to the speeches that were coming from the Army Generals who ruled in Tokyo.

Hideyoshi's experience on the goodwill tour had transformed him from a wide-eyed recruit into a capable and disciplined sailor. Life on the *Akatsuki* was demanding but rewarding. His role as a gunnery assistant kept him busy, and he gained proficiency in everything from ammunition handling to the precise calibration of the ship's guns. Within a few months, he had earned a promotion to Seaman, Second Class.

In the spring of 1935, Hideyoshi received new orders transferring him to the heavy cruiser *Chokai*, a new ship with an advanced design. He was elated and proud, but also nervous. The *Chokai* was a different beast altogether—larger and far more complex than the little destroyer, and equipped with all the latest cutting-edge technology. It would be a challenge.

During his first week aboard the *Chokai*, Hideyoshi was assigned to the team responsible for maintaining the ship's two Mitsubishi F1M scout seaplanes (known to the Americans as "Pete") and their catapults. He spent countless hours studying the plane's systems, from the intricate details of its engines to the precise mechanisms of the catapults that launched it into the sky.

The *Chokai's* missions provided ample opportunities to put his new skills to the test. During reconnaissance exercises off the China coast and in the Philippine Sea, Hideyoshi's meticulous work ensured that the seaplanes were always mission-ready.

His dedication did not go unnoticed. By the end of his first year on the *Chokai*, he was promoted again, this time to Seaman, First Class. With the new rank came greater authority and responsibility: he was placed in charge of the seaplane maintenance crew, a role that required him to oversee not only the technical upkeep of the aircraft and catapults but also the training and discipline of his subordinates.

But now Hideyoshi wanted more. For months, he had watched the seaplanes launch and return, their pilots embodying a freedom that he could only dream of. Unlike the ship's crew, who were viewed as (and treated as) mere interchangeable swabbies, the seaplane pilots were treated with deference and respect—not only because they were officers, but because their job on the ship was exotic to most and seemed almost magical.

Fixing these planes, Hideyoshi decided, was rewarding in its own way, but it wasn't enough. He wanted to be the one in the cockpit, feeling the wind rush past as he soared above the waves. He wanted to fly.

One evening, as the ship sat anchored in port, Hideyoshi found himself standing on the deck, staring at the horizon where the sky melted into the sea. The *Chokai's* captain approached quietly.

"You've done good work here, Sugiyama," the captain said, his voice steady. "The seaplanes wouldn't fly without men like you keeping them in top shape."

"Thank you, sir," Hideyoshi replied, hesitating for a moment before voicing what had been on his mind for months. "But if I may speak freely, sir ... I've always dreamed of flying them myself."

The captain raised an eyebrow, his expression unreadable. "Flying, eh? That's a different path altogether. Have you considered applying for the *Sōjū Renshusei* program?"

"I have, sir," Hideyoshi admitted. "But I wasn't sure if I was qualified yet to apply."

The captain placed a hand on Hideyoshi's shoulder. "You've shown dedication and discipline here. Those qualities will serve you well as a pilot. If this is truly what you want, I'll support you."

By February 1936, Hideyoshi had submitted his application, with the captain's formal recommendation attached. A few weeks later, he was assigned to take the entrance exams, and found himself standing outside a nondescript naval building back in Yokosuka Naval Base. He was pleased at being back in his old school, this time as an Imperial Navy sailor, but at the same time he had a worried feeling gnawing at him. The "*Soren*" pilot training program had a reputation for being one of the most challenging paths in the Imperial Japanese Navy, accepting only a select few and with a high rate of wash-outs.

The morning began with the written exam, held in a stark, utilitarian classroom filled with rows of metal desks. Hideyoshi sat among dozens of other candidates, all clad in the crisp white uniforms of the Navy. An officer distributed the exam papers, and he took a deep breath before picking up his pencil. The room was silent except for the faint shuffling of papers and the occasional cough.

The questions covered a wide range of topics: advanced mathematics, physics, meteorology, navigation, aerodynamics, and mechanical engineering. Hideyoshi's hands moved swiftly, his mind racing through calculations and recalling diagrams that he had studied late into the nights aboard the *Chokai*. He double-checked his answers again, and then yet again, not wanting to make even the smallest mistake.

By midday, the candidates were led to a field for the physical fitness tests. The air was chilly as they were put through a tiring series of exercises. Hideyoshi sprinted, climbed ropes, and performed calisthenics, his muscles aching. A Navy officer shouted out orders, his tenacious gaze evaluating their every movement. It reminded Hideyoshi of his old cadet days, but this time, at least, nobody was "instilling a military spirit" into him with a stick.

"Push yourself, Sugiyama," he muttered to himself, gritting his teeth as he completed the final lap of a timed run. Around him, some candidates faltered, collapsing onto the grass.

The most nerve-wracking part came in the afternoon: the interview. Hideyoshi sat stiffly in front of a panel of senior officers, who asked probing questions about his motivations, his knowledge of aviation, and his experiences aboard the *Chokai*.

"Why do you want to become a pilot?" one officer asked.

Hideyoshi met his gaze steadily. "Sir, I've always admired the courage and skill of the Navy's pilots. I want to serve my country to the best of my ability, and I believe I can do so in the air."

The officers exchanged glances, jotting down notes. Another officer leaned forward. "You've worked on seaplanes as a mechanic. Do you think that gives you an advantage as a pilot?"

Hideyoshi nodded. "Yes, sir. I understand the machines, their strengths and weaknesses. I believe that knowledge will make me a better pilot."

The interview concluded with polite nods, but Hideyoshi could not decipher their expressions.

The weeks of waiting that followed were agonizing.

Then, one afternoon as he was examining one of the *Chokai's* seaplanes, a voice called out to him from behind. He turned to see Petty Officer Kashiwahara walking toward him, a folded piece of paper in his hand.

"A message for you," he said, handing it over. "It came through the communications center this morning."

Hideyoshi accepted the paper with steady hands, though his heart raced. Unfolding it, he quickly scanned the lines of text. His eyes widened.

"To: Hideyoshi Sugiyama, IJN Cruiser *Chokai*

"Subject: Orders for Assignment

"You are hereby notified of your acceptance into the *Sōjū Renshusei* aviation program as a pilot trainee. You are to proceed to the Kasumigaura *Kokutai* training base by the first week of June 1936. Report to the commanding officer upon arrival for further instructions."

He read the message again to ensure he wasn't dreaming. It was real. He had been accepted.

"Well?" Kashiwahara prompted, raising an eyebrow. "What's the news?"

Hideyoshi looked up, a smile breaking across his face. "I've been accepted into the aviation program. I'm going to Kasumigaura."

Kashiwahara let out a low whistle. "That's no small feat, Hideyoshi. Congratulations."

The news spread quickly among the crew. Some offered congratulations, while others gave him friendly words of advice.

The following morning, as Hideyoshi boarded the train bound for Kasumigaura, he was no longer just a sailor. He was on his way to becoming a pilot.

Chapter 4
Training as a Pilot (June 1936 to September 1937)

Hideyoshi's travel orders were neatly folded in his jacket pocket, and his duffel bag rested at his feet, containing everything he owned: a few changes of clothes, a carefully pressed spare uniform, and the boundless hope of a man on the verge of realizing a lifelong dream.

The base loomed in the distance, a sprawling complex of hangars, barracks, and airstrips, bordered by the sparkling waters of Lake Kasumigaura. He could already see aircraft—Type 95 trainers—soaring overhead.

A petty officer met him at the station, clipboard in hand. "Sugiyama?" he asked.

"Yes, sir!" Hideyoshi replied, standing stiffly at attention.

The officer nodded curtly. "Follow me. We've got a long day ahead of us."

Hideyoshi hefted his bag and fell into step as they approached the guard booth at the gate. Once inside, he was struck by the scale of activity. Aircraft taxied along the runways, ground crews scrambled to refuel and repair machines, and cadets marched in tight formations.

The petty officer led him to the administration building, where Hideyoshi completed a series of check-ins: paperwork, medical evaluations, and equipment. By midday, he had been assigned to a barracks.

After stowing his belongings, Hideyoshi stepped outside and took a deep breath, savoring the moment. "This," he said to himself, "is the only place I want to be." His thoughts were interrupted by the sound of an officer's whistle, summoning the new arrivals to the parade ground.

As he joined the others, a senior instructor, Lieutenant Commander Matsuda, addressed the assembly. "Welcome to Kasumigaura *Kokutai*," he said, pacing before the cadets. "You are here because you have shown promise, but let me make this clear from the start — promise alone means nothing. Over the coming months, you will endure the most rigorous training of your lives. Many of you will fail. Those who succeed will earn the right to call themselves aviators of the Imperial Japanese Navy. The sky does not forgive weakness, nor do we."

The cadets were then divided into groups and led on a tour of the base. Hideyoshi's group was assigned to Lieutenant Mitori, a lean, sharp-eyed instructor. "This way," he said, gesturing for the group to follow.

Their first stop was the hangar, where a pair of two-seater Yokosuka K5Y biplanes sat on the tarmac. Their bright orange paint scheme allowed student pilots to easily see each other in the sky, but it also led to the plane's nickname — the "Red Dragonfly".

"These will be your first aircraft," Mitori explained, patting the wing of one plane affectionately. "They are reliable and forgiving, but don't mistake that for 'easy'. They will expose every flaw in your technique."

The tour continued to the classrooms, where blackboards were covered with complex diagrams of math equations and navigation charts. "You'll spend as much time here as in the air," Mitori noted. "Understanding the science of flight is just as important as mastering its mechanics."

At midday, the groups gathered in the mess hall for lunch. Hideyoshi found himself sitting with a few other cadets he had met during the tour. Among them was Masaaki Oba, a soft-spoken young man from Fukuoka, and Kenji Sugai, whose boisterous laugh quickly filled the room.

"So, where are you from?" Sugai asked, breaking the ice.

"Mie Prefecture," Hideyoshi replied.

Oba grinned. "Bet you don't see skies like this back home, do you?"

After lunch, the cadets were gathered in an auditorium for a detailed overview of the training program. Senior instructor Hasegawa outlined the curriculum: academic studies in aerodynamics, meteorology, and navigation; physical training to build stamina and resilience; and, of course, flight training, beginning with basic maneuvers and culminating in solo flights.

"Your days will begin at sunrise and end long after sunset," Hasegawa said. "Every moment here is designed to prepare you for the challenges of the sky and the battlefield. Those who cannot keep up will be sent home."

The orientation day ended with another lecture. Commander Harashi stood before the trainees to explain the organization of the Imperial Japanese Navy's air groups. It was a system that Hideyoshi and his classmates would need to understand intimately, as it formed the backbone of their operational structure.

"In the Imperial Navy," Harashi began, "air power is not just an extension of the fleet—it is an essential component. To achieve this, we organize our aviators and their aircraft with care, from the largest air groups down to the smallest formations."

He gestured to a chalkboard, where he had sketched a hierarchy. At the top was the *Kokutai*, or air group, the largest operational unit in the naval air service. Named after its home base, each *Kokutai* served a distinct purpose: training, reconnaissance, or combat. "For instance," Harashi said, tapping the chalkboard, "Kasumigaura *Kokutai* focuses on training, while operational *kokutai* like Yokosuka or Sasebo may be tasked with defense, patrols, or offensive missions. A *kokutai* is a self-contained unit with its own command structure, maintenance crews, and personnel. The commander of a *kokutai* carries immense responsibility, overseeing both its aircraft and its men."

Below the *kokutai* were smaller units called *hikotai*, or flight units. These groups specialized in specific missions, such as fighter interception, torpedo bombing, or reconnaissance. "The *hikotai* is the practical division of aircraft," Harashi explained, "designed to focus on a particular mission while still integrating with the larger *kokutai's* goals."

Harashi's chalk slid down to a smaller circle on the diagram. "Within each *hikotai*, you will find the *chutai*—what other countries might call a 'squadron'. Typically, a *chutai* consists of nine to twelve aircraft. This is a combat-ready formation, commanded by a senior officer, and it is often the primary unit deployed in the field."

Finally, Harashi drew three small circles connected by lines beneath the *chutai*. "At the most fundamental level is the *shotai*, or flight. This is the unit you will likely become most familiar with as pilots. Each *shotai* consists of three aircraft. The leader—the most experienced pilot—flies in the center, with two wingmen to support him. The *shotai* is the building block of our air strategy. Formation flying, mutual support, and coordinated attacks all stem from the *shotai*."

The trainees listened intently as Harashi continued. "The lead pilot has the task of attacking enemy aircraft. The job of the two wingmen is to keep the enemy off of the leader and to protect his tail. It is no place for hot-dogs or for glory-seekers." He emphasized the importance of discipline and hierarchy within the system. "The *shotai* must function as a single entity, with each pilot anticipating the other's movements. Disobeying formation or deviating from your position to run off on your own will lead to disaster — not only for you but for your comrades."

Harashi's voice took on a more reflective air. "This structure reflects the broader doctrine of the Navy. We emphasize coordination and cohesion because we believe in the power of the group over the individual. When you fly in a *shotai*, you are not three separate planes; you are a single weapon. When your *kokutai* takes to the skies, it is not just a group of aircraft — it is the focused might of the Empire."

The next day marked the beginning of actual flight instruction in Ground School.

Hideyoshi joined the other trainees as they gathered on the parade grounds. Their day would always begin with physical training — rain or shine. All of the students were already in superb physical condition, but that was not the purpose of these exercises. They were intended, as one instructor informed them, to "strengthen your warrior spirit". To this end, the "games" they played were brutal.

Martial arts instruction had been a core component of their training ever since Kasumigaura, but here, the intensity reached new heights. Their instructor, a short but imposing man named Lieutenant Kato, strode into the center of the circle. His sharp eyes scanned the assembled cadets like a tiger searching for the slightest weakness. "You are warriors of the Imperial Japanese Navy," he shouted. "Discipline and spirit are as essential to you as your skill in the air. Without them, you will falter at the critical moment." He paused for a moment before continuing. "A fighter pilot must be always on the attack and must always take the fight to the enemy. Here, we are going to fill you with the spirit of the *samurai*."

He then motioned for the cadets to divide into pairs. "Begin with *kendo*. One hundred strikes each. Then switch roles. Do not hold back, and do not relent."

Hideyoshi paired with Hashida, their *bokken* wooden swords raised in formal salutes before the first strikes began. The rhythmic crack of wood echoed across the yard as they alternated blows.

After the *kendo* drills, Lieutenant Kato shifted the focus to *naginata-do*. Used like bayonets, the long shafts and curved blades were an homage to the traditional weapons of *samurai* women. The fluid, sweeping movements required balance and control, in contrast to the explosive energy of *kendo*.

Once the martial arts drills were concluded, the instructor ordered the cadets to form a large circle. This exercise called for a seemingly endless wrestling match where two cadets would face each other until one was defeated. The winner then left the circle, while the loser would remain in the center to face a new opponent. If necessary, the losers would stay in the circle the entire time, then begin again the next day — until they had either defeated somebody or were washed out of the program for "lack of warrior spirit". Since nobody wanted to be expelled from the program, these matches often turned vicious, and the instructors did not interfere. Bloody noses were commonplace, and broken bones were not unknown. It was a Darwinian game akin to "kill or be killed", and it was fully intended to weed out those who were not sufficiently aggressive or bellicose.

Lieutenant Kato pointed to the center. "Matsuda, you begin with Sugiyama."

Matsuda lunged, attempting to grapple Hideyoshi's torso, but he twisted away, using his opponent's momentum to throw him off balance. The match ended quickly, with Matsuda pinned beneath Hideyoshi in a well-executed hold.

"Next!" Kato shouted.

Hideyoshi returned to the circle as Matsuda stayed to face the next challenger. After seven matches, he eventually managed a victory, and his vanquished opponent, Tanaka, now took his place in the center. It continued until every student had stepped into the circle.

As the exercise ended, Kato called them to attention. "Well done," he said. "In battle, there will be no rest, no respite. You must find the strength to continue, no matter how tired, no matter how outnumbered. That is the warrior spirit."

After a couple hours of this, the students moved inside to their classroom. This was austere yet functional. Wooden desks were arranged in perfect rows, and a large chalkboard dominated the front of the room. The walls were adorned with motivational slogans in bold *kanji*: "Discipline and Dedication Bring Victory." "One Hundred Million With One Spirit". "Asia for Asians."

Commander Harashi stood at the front, his gaze sweeping over the assembled cadets. "Today," he began, "you embark on the intellectual foundation of your aviation careers. Flight is not merely a matter of skill — it is a science, a discipline. If you cannot master these lessons, you will not fly."

The first lecture delved into the principles of aerodynamics. Hideyoshi listened intently as Harashi sketched the outline of a wing on the chalkboard, explaining how air pressure and lift worked in tandem to keep an aircraft aloft. "This," Harashi emphasized, underlining the diagram with a swift stroke of chalk, "is what separates us from the birds. Understand it, or you will never leave the ground."

As the day progressed, the cadets were introduced to an array of different subjects: meteorology, engine mechanics, and navigation. The meteorology instructor, a thin lieutenant with a penchant for dramatic storytelling, described how a sudden downdraft had once nearly sent his aircraft into the side of a mountain. "Nature does not forgive ignorance," he warned, pacing across the front of the room.

In the navigation class, an instructor named Ozawa—a grizzled warrant officer who seemed to have flown over every ocean on the planet—stressed the importance of accuracy. "A mistake of one degree on your compass," he said, tapping a map with his knuckle, "can mean the difference between landing safely on a carrier and being lost at sea."

By mid-afternoon, the cadets were released for a brief lunch. Hideyoshi sat with a few classmates under the shade of a tree, the group poring over their notes while sharing bits of rice balls. Sugai, who had been accepted to the aviation school from high school through the *Yokaren* program, nudged Hideyoshi with a grin. "So, what's harder—plotting a course in the air or on the *Chokai*?" Hideyoshi chuckled, and Oba, who had like Hideyoshi been accepted through the *Soren* exam, piped in with, "Be glad you didn't have to serve on a boat, Kenji. I was seasick the entire time."

The final lecture of the day focused on aircraft engines. The instructor displayed a disassembled radial engine at the front of the classroom, pointing out each component and its function. "You must understand this machine as if it were part of your body," he said. "When you are in the air, it is your lifeline."

As the sun dipped below the horizon, the cadets were finally dismissed and the day was over.

There would be many more days like it.

After 14 weeks of ground school, Hideyoshi was getting restless and was beginning to wonder if he would ever get to fly, but he had earned high marks in every subject, proving himself to be a serious and capable student.

Then, finally, one morning the classroom instructor ordered his students out to the airfield hangar, telling them, "Today you get your first taste of flying." Lined up neatly in front of the hangar were three bright orange K5Y biplanes. Like all trainer aircraft, there were two cockpits, one behind the other, and each had their own complete set of controls, allowing the plane to be flown from either one. Normally the student would sit in the front and the instructor would watch him from behind and take immediate control if it became necessary. Most of the students were unaware of the rate at which new pilots crashed their planes, but the flight instructors understood it all too well. For this orientation flight, though, the student was in the back so he could see what the pilot was doing.

Lined up in front of the hangar, Hideyoshi and the other trainees stood at attention as the flight instructor, Lieutenant Yamazaki, a seasoned veteran who had flown missions over China, explained that they would be taken up in the trainers, one at a time. "You are an observer and are there to watch," he declared. "So don't touch anything on my airplanes. And if you need to throw up, please try to do it over the side. The ground crew gets very upset if they have to clean your breakfast out of the cockpit."

For the next three hours, the instructors escorted each trainee to one of the planes, helped them strap in, then started up the engine, taxied for a bit, revved the propeller and took off. The flights were short: just a climb up to a few thousand feet, a lap around the airfield with a few turns, then in for a landing. Several of the students, Hideyoshi noticed, looked distinctly pale after they had clambered out of the plane and back to the ground. They were not seen on the base again.

When Hideyoshi's name was finally called, he eagerly stepped forward, and Yamazaki gestured briskly for him to climb into the front seat. As soon as he was strapped in, Hideyoshi had an irresistible urge to wrap his hand around the control stick in front of him, but a glaring look from the instructor, who seemed to have read his mind, told him that would not be a good idea.

Yamazaki climbed into the front cockpit, then turned around and held up the speaking tube where his student could see it. Once Hideyoshi had it in place, the pilot, yelling to be heard over the noise of the big radial engine, told him, "Pay attention. Watch everything I do. Soon enough, you'll be the one up here flying." Hideyoshi nodded in response.

The engine roared more loudly, and the vibration of the fuselage rattled through Hideyoshi's body. The aircraft taxied to the end of the runway and, with a quick glance back, Yamazaki pushed the throttle forward. The K5Y began its takeoff roll. Hideyoshi felt the wind rushing past his face even through the goggles.

The moment the wheels left the ground, Hideyoshi was struck by an overwhelming sense of awe. The earth fell away beneath him as the K5Y climbed steadily into the sky, and the world turned into a patchwork of green and brown fields with the silvery glint of a river snaking through the landscape to the sea and the mountains on the horizon. It was breathtaking.

Yamazaki performed a series of gentle maneuvers—banking left, then right, climbing, and descending—explaining each movement over the speaking tube. "Feel the rhythm of the plane, Sugiyama. It's alive in its own way. You must learn to listen to it." The K5Y was graceful yet sturdy, a perfect match for its role as a trainer. Hideyoshi focused intently, his eyes darting between the instruments in the front cockpit and the horizon ahead.

Enthralled, Hideyoshi did not want it to end, but after what felt like too short a time, Yamazaki turned into a bank and brought the plane back toward the airfield. The descent was smooth, and Hideyoshi braced himself as the wheels touched down with a soft bump. The plane rolled to a stop, and the roar of the engine faded into silence as Yamazaki cut the power.

When Hideyoshi climbed out of the cockpit, his legs felt a bit unsteady, but it was from excitement, not fear. Yamazaki gave him an appraising look. "You handled that well, Sugiyama. Pay attention, work hard, and you'll be flying solo before you know it."

Hideyoshi bowed deeply, unable to suppress a grin. "Thank you, sir."

Over the weeks that followed his initial flight, Hideyoshi's training on the K5Y progressed methodically, beginning with basic flight maneuvers and steadily advancing to more and more complex exercises.

Initially, he spent hours in the rear cockpit with Lieutenant Yamazaki or another instructor demonstrating how to execute essential maneuvers like takeoffs, straight-and-level flight, turns, and controlled descents. The focus was on developing a feel for the aircraft—its responsiveness to control inputs, the steady hum of its engine, and the slight vibrations that telegraphed its movements. Hideyoshi made mistakes which the instructors never hesitated to criticize harshly, but he took their words as a challenge to improve.

A few weeks later, after mastering the basics, Hideyoshi moved on to the front cockpit and to more advanced lessons, including coordinated climbs and descents, steep turns, and stall recovery. One of the most challenging steps was learning to land. Yamazaki drilled him relentlessly, forcing him to practice proper alignment with the runway and the delicate control required to flare up just before touchdown. Any error—a bounce, a skid, or coming in too steeply—

was met with sharp rebukes. "You are a Navy flier," he pointed out, "and you will need to land on an aircraft carrier someday. You have no room to make the slightest mistake." But Hideyoshi persisted, refining his technique until the movements became second nature.

As the days turned into weeks, Hideyoshi's confidence grew. He began to understand the intricate interplay between the aircraft, the environment, and his own actions. His hands and feet began to move instinctively on the controls, and he found that he was able to anticipate the plane's reactions. His instructors started giving him more responsibilities during flights, allowing him to take control himself for extended stretches before they took over again.

By the 10th week of training, Hideyoshi was introduced to emergency procedures, practicing simulated engine failures, forced landings, and other contingencies. These exercises were nerve-wracking but vital, and they taught him the crucial lesson to keep calm and focused, even when placed under overwhelming pressure.

Finally, after 14 weeks of rigorous preparation and nearly 40 hours of dual instruction, Yamazaki informed him that he was ready for his first solo flight. "Sugiyama," the instructor said one evening after a particularly smooth landing, "tomorrow, you'll fly alone. Don't let me regret it."

The next morning, with the sun barely up, Hideyoshi stood at the edge of the tarmac, staring at the Yokosuka biplane in front of him as if he were seeing it for the first time. The previous months had been a whirlwind of classrooms and training flights. Now, the culmination of all that effort loomed before him: his first solo flight. As Hideyoshi adjusted his flight helmet, his mind raced with thoughts of procedures and possible contingencies. He had flown many times under the watchful eyes of instructors, but this would be the first time he would be truly alone in the cockpit. There would be no one to guide him, no one to correct any mistakes. And he had been here long enough now to see far too many cadet pilots who had made mistakes. Usually they were fatal.

His instructor, Lieutenant Yamada, approached with a clipboard in hand and gave an encouraging nod. "You're ready, Sugiyama," he said. "You've shown precision and control in every maneuver. Today is about proving to yourself what I already know—you can handle this."

Hideyoshi nodded, and Yamada handed him the clipboard. "You know the drill. Pre-flight inspection, start-up, and follow the pattern we've practiced. Remember, keep your climb steady, and don't rush the landing. Trust your training."

"Yes, sir," Hideyoshi replied, trying to keep his voice steady.

Yamada clapped him on the shoulder. "One more thing," he said, lowering his voice slightly. "The first solo flight isn't just a test of skill—it's a test of composure. Stay calm, no matter what."

Hideyoshi saluted, then turned toward the biplane assigned to him for the flight. At the plane, a mechanic stood waiting, wiping his hands on a rag. "Sir," the man greeted with a smile. "She's in perfect shape. I checked her myself."

"Thank you," Hideyoshi said, bowing slightly before beginning his walk-around inspection. He ran his hands over the fabric-covered wings, checked the tension of the control cables, and examined the landing gear. The familiarity of the routine steadied his nerves. By the time he climbed into the cockpit, he felt his mind beginning to shift from "anxiety" to "focus".

Seated in the cockpit, Hideyoshi reached for the throttle lever, his fingers steady as he eased it into the "idle" position. Next, his hand moved to the fuel mixture lever, adjusting it carefully to the "rich" setting. There was a distinct click as it locked into place.

Reaching for the primer pump, Hideyoshi grasped the handle and gave it three deliberate strokes, feeling the resistance with each pull. He remembered his instructor's words: "Not too little, not too much. Three to five strokes—just enough to get the engine breathing." He counted them in his head, ensuring that he didn't rush.

Now his hand moved to the control for the cowl flaps, which he opened with a quick motion. The metallic clicks as the flaps adjusted were faint but audible. The open flaps would allow vital cooling air to flow around the radial engine once it roared to life, preventing it from overheating.

He sat back for a moment, scanning the controls and gauges to confirm that everything was set. The throttle at "idle", the mixture "rich", the primer pump engaged, and the cowl flaps open—it was all as it should be.

With the engine controls set, Hideyoshi turned his attention to the airfield crew standing nearby. He raised his right hand and gave the signal—a sharp deliberate motion that instructed them to "pull through" the propeller.

The ground crewman, a burly man with grease-stained overalls, nodded briskly. He approached the propeller and, with a practiced grip, began spinning the blades slowly by hand. Each turn circulated oil through the cylinders, reducing the risk of a hydraulic lock. Hideyoshi could see the man's muscles tense with each pull, the effort evident even in the methodical pace. He repeated the motion several times, and when he finished, the waiting crew chief stepped back, giving the pilot a thumbs-up. Hideyoshi leaned out of the cockpit and called out, "Clear prop!"

He scanned the immediate area, insuring that no one was standing near the arc of the spinning blades. An accident here would be lethal. The ground crew stepped away, standing at a safe distance as they awaited the next stage.

Satisfied that everything was safe, Hideyoshi turned to the controls and double-checked the magneto switches, confirming they were set to "on."

The Yokosuka was not as sophisticated as the more modern mono-wing fighters, so it relied on a manual ground-starting procedure rather than an onboard electric starter. Hideyoshi leaned out of the cockpit once again and signaled to the crew chief, who approached the propeller with a starter crank in his hand. He positioned himself carefully, making sure that he was clear of the prop and that his footing was solid, then gave a sharp nod.

With a strong heave, the ground crewman cranked the propeller, spinning it into motion. The engine coughed once, a deep guttural vibration, and then caught. Hideyoshi quickly adjusted the throttle, nudging it just enough to maintain a steady idle as the engine hummed with power, produced a vibration through the entire airframe and shaking Hideyoshi in his seat.

Once again, he looked over the instrument panel, especially at the all-important tachometer, oil pressure gauge, and temperature gauge readings. Everything was within the normal range. Satisfied that all was well, Hideyoshi gave a thumbs-up signal to the crew chief, who grinned and stepped away, his task complete. The plane was alive now, ready to take flight.

Leaning forward slightly, Hideyoshi noted that the oil pressure needle was climbing steadily into the green zone, and the temperature gauge had already begun its slow ascent. He let the engine continue to idle at low RPM, resisting the urge to push it up too quickly. The instructors had drilled this into all of them—not allowing enough time for the engine to warm up properly would lead to poor oil lubrication and overheating and cause a disastrous engine seizure in flight.

After two minutes, the now warmed-up engine was running smoothly and the vibrations had dampened a bit. It was time to check the magnetos. Hideyoshi flipped the first magneto switch, cutting off one side momentarily. The engine sputtered but continued running, albeit slightly rougher. He nodded in satisfaction —this magneto was working. He switched it back on, then repeated the process with the other magneto. Again, the engine sputtered but stayed alive. Both were functioning as expected.

His hand returned to the throttle, giving it a gentle nudge forward to bring the RPM up slightly, and felt the plane begin to roll forward. The wheels rumbled on the uneven ground. He loosened his grip on the control stick and placed his feet lightly on the rudder pedals, ready to make adjustments if necessary. On the ground, with no powered wheels, the plane could only be steered by using the rudder. It demanded a light touch: too much rudder could result in a ground loop and a crash.

He kept up a close watch on the tachometer, ensuring that the engine RPM stayed in the safe range. Too much throttle during taxiing could also lead to overheating, a mistake he had seen others pay for during training. Hideyoshi carefully taxied the plane toward the designated takeoff point.

Reaching the end of the runway with the plane's nose pointed into the wind, Hideyoshi eased the throttle back to "idle", letting the biplane coast to a stop.

He began his final checks. Gripping the control stick, he moved it through its full range of motion, looking from side to side to confirm that the ailerons and elevators were responding properly. His feet worked the rudder pedals from side to side, confirming the rudder's operation.

The K5Y trainer had an open cockpit, so he made sure his goggles were snug and secured the thin strap beneath his flight helmet, then took a moment to adjust the elevator trim wheel beside his seat. He rotated it carefully.

Ready now for takeoff, Hideyoshi looked towards the control tower, where a traffic controller was observing the field. A sharp nod came in reply to Hideyoshi's raised hand.

"Permission to proceed."

Hideyoshi took a deep breath as his hand moved to the throttle lever. "Here we go ... " he said to himself. He began to push it smoothly forward, and the engine responded with a rising howl. The biplane was now straining at the brakes, eager to break free and leap into the air.

As the throttle reached full power, the propeller wash began rushing past him, tugging at his flight suit. He gently let up on the brakes, and the biplane rolled forward, slowly at first, then gaining speed.

Hideyoshi now felt the force of the engine's torque, trying to pull the aircraft to the left, and his right foot pressed down on the rudder pedal with just enough force to counteract the drift. If he made a mistake now both he and the airplane would end up as a mangled heap on the runway.

As the K5Y continued to accelerate down the runway, he felt the tailwheel lift off the ground. The biplane was now balancing on its main undercarriage. Hideyoshi glanced down at the airspeed indicator: the needle was hovering just above 55 knots.

The moment of truth.

He eased the control stick back, and the nose of the aircraft rose gracefully. For a moment, the tires continued to kiss the earth, and then they lifted off the ground and the K5Y was airborne. The rough rumble of the wheels over the runway was replaced by the smooth hum of the engine and the rush of wind past the open cockpit.

Hideyoshi's heart pounded in his chest with an overwhelming sense of exhilaration. He was flying—truly *flying*—on his own for the first time.

As the biplane continued its ascent, Hideyoshi maneuvered the control stick to maintain a steady climb angle and keep the airspeed indicator near 65 knots, the Yokosuka's designated climb speed. Below him, the airfield fell away, its neat rows of hangars becoming steadily smaller. He glanced at the instrument panel, confirming the climb rate and engine temperature. Everything was in the green.

At two thousand feet altitude, he eased the control stick forward and leveled out. His left hand moved to the throttle, gently pulling it back to reduce power, and the K5Y responded obediently as the engine transitioned to cruising mode at around 60% of its maximum output. Hideyoshi adjusted the fuel mixture lever, enriching it slightly to compensate for the altitude and give the best engine performance.

With his hand steady on the control stick, he initiated a gentle bank to the left, simultaneously applying coordinated rudder pressure with his feet. He could hear his instructor's voice in his head: "Smooth inputs". The plane arced into a turn. Hideyoshi kept his eyes on the horizon, glancing occasionally at the turn-and-bank indicator on his instrument panel.

After leveling out, he took a moment to soak in the scene around him. Above, the boundless sky seemed to embrace him. It felt both exciting and humbling.

After a few minutes, as the airfield came into view on his left, he began his descent into the landing pattern. The nose dipped gently downward as he eased back on the throttle.

Carefully, Hideyoshi aligned the biplane with the center of the runway and adjusted the throttle to hold a steady descent speed, keeping it just under 60 knots. The ground now rose slowly to meet him, and he smoothly eased the throttle back even further, letting the plane's descent gradually increase.

When the biplane was just a few feet above the ground, Hideyoshi again pulled back lightly on the stick, lifting the nose in a controlled flare. As the K5Y lost lift, it settled gently down onto the runway. The main wheels touched the ground, and the airframe shuddered. The rumble of the ground beneath the wheels once again replaced the whistle of the wind, and Hideyoshi eased the throttle down to "idle", letting the engine slow to a low hum.

He carefully taxied the biplane toward the edge of the runway, keeping his movements steady and monitoring his engine RPM to prevent overheating. The ground crew members waved him toward an open space, and he gave a small nod of acknowledgment. As he brought the biplane to a gentle stop, he pulled the throttle all the way back, then cut off the fuel mixture control to end the flow of fuel to the engine. The powerful radial coughed once, then sputtered into silence. The propeller stopped. Finally, Hideyoshi flipped the switches for the magnetos and the master electrical system to the "off" position, ensuring that all of the power was safely disconnected.

He leaned back in his seat for a moment, taking a deep breath, then gently patted the side of the cockpit. He had done it.

As Hideyoshi was climbing out of the cockpit, Yamada and some of the ground crew were already running over. One of them handed him a damp cloth to wipe his face. "Smooth landing for a first solo," he said, nodding appreciatively. Another ground crewman gave a playful salute. "Looks like you'll be flying circles around everyone soon enough!"

That afternoon, Hideyoshi strolled toward the mess hall, his body still electric with the lingering adrenaline of his solo flight.

"Hideyoshi!" Oba waved him over. Beside him, Sugai sat with his sleeves rolled up, gesturing animatedly as he recounted some tale.

Hideyoshi joined them, pulling up a bench. "Still reliving the glory, Kenji?" he teased, though the sparkle in his eyes, he knew, probably betrayed his own excitement.

"Reliving? I'll be telling this story until my dying day," Sugai shot back with mock indignation. "There I was, climbing into the heavens, free from instructors screaming in my ear. It was like ... liberation! Like soaring out of a cage for the first time."

Oba laughed, shaking his head. "Free? Maybe until you came down for landing. I heard Ogata muttering something about your approach being as graceful as a sack of rice falling off a truck."

Sugai clutched his chest dramatically. "Harsh words for a man who brought his plane down in one piece!"

"And all in one piece it was," Hideyoshi added with a chuckle. "I'll admit, though, I was nervous during the takeoff. It felt strange without someone sitting behind me, ready to step in if I made a mistake. But once I was up there ..." His voice trailed off as he searched for the right words. "It felt like I was finally alive. Everything just clicked."

Oba nodded, his expression softening. "Same here. Once I got over the nerves, it felt natural, like I was meant to be there. But I'll tell you this: turning back toward the airfield felt harder than any maneuver. I didn't want it to end."

Sugai leaned forward, smirking. "Well, not all of us had perfect takeoffs or landings, but at least none of *us* ran off the runway. Poor Yamashita's name will go down in history for that one."

The three of them burst into laughter, but then Hideyoshi added wistfully. "He's a *Soren*, from the *Mogami*. Poor guy—now he'll get sent back to his ship in disgrace and have to bear all the shame of everyone knowing about his failure."

The thought made everyone go quiet.

After completing their solo flights, the focus of student training shifted to more advanced skills. Their days now often began with navigation exercises, tracing pre-planned routes over Lake Kasumigaura and the patchwork of fields beyond, or over the Pacific out of sight of land. With only a compass and visual cues to guide them, the trainees had to calculate their positions and adjust their headings, all while maintaining what they called "situational awareness", an unerring grasp of where everything and everyone was in relation to them, in all three dimensions. It was a vital skill for a pilot.

The real challenge, however, was flying in formation. Hideyoshi was assigned to a three-plane *shotai* led by Lt. Kibana, who flew in the lead position. It was the assigned task of the two wingmen to stick to the leader and to keep enemy fighters off his tail. It demanded precise flying, at very short distances. The possibility of a fatal collision was always there, and in every class there were a number of trainees who made fatal mistakes. But it was a vital skill both for fighters, who had to protect each other in combat, and for bombers, who needed to drop their payloads together into a concentrated area.

"Stay close, but not too close," Kibana had warned during the briefing. "And stay with me no matter what happens."

Once they were in the air, Hideyoshi found himself hyper-focused. The Lieutenant banked sharply to the left, and Hideyoshi followed, keeping his eyes on the leader's wingtips while at the same time watching out for the other wingman. The close proximity was unnerving, and he could feel his stomach tighten as he fought to match Kibana's movements and stay in position.

Once the students were proficient in their formation, there came a series of lessons in hand signals. The Navy's frontline fighters had no radios, and the pilots had to master an entire repertoire of signals for in-flight communication. Instructors on the ground demonstrated gestures that conveyed commands—climbing, diving, turning, and regrouping—until the students knew them all by heart and they became second nature. Kibana then tested them in the air.

But not all the news was good.

One afternoon, Hideyoshi was seated under the shade of a tree near the barracks with his flight manual spread out on his lap, reviewing some procedures.

"Hideyoshi," a familiar voice called, breaking his focus.

Looking up, he saw Sugai approaching, his usual springy stride noticeably subdued. There was a pained look in his eyes. Hideyoshi sat up, closing the manual. "Kenji, what's wrong?"

Sugai stopped a few feet away, hesitating as if he were searching for the right words. "It's Oba," he said finally, his voice low.

Immediately a tight knot formed in the pit of Hideyoshi's stomach. Dreading the answer he might get, he asked, "What about him? Is he hurt?"

Sugai shook his head and sat down heavily beside him. "No, he's not hurt. He's ... gone. They told him this morning that he's been reassigned. He's washed out."

Hideyoshi's heart sank. "Washed out? But he was doing fine— better than fine, even. His solo flight was solid. He said he felt like he belonged up there."

Sugai sighed, rubbing the back of his neck. "That's what I thought too, but the instructors didn't agree. They said his formation flying was shaky. He tried to plead his case, but it was no use. They've already reassigned him to logistics work at a depot near Nagoya."

For a moment, neither of them spoke. Hideyoshi stared at the ground, grappling with the news. Masaaki had been one of the first friends he'd made at Kasumigaura.

"Did you see him before he left?" Hideyoshi asked finally.

Sugai nodded. "Yeah, I caught him just before he boarded the truck. He seemed . . . I dunno . . . resigned, I guess. He said it's not the end of the world, that he'll find a way to serve even if it's not in the cockpit. But I could see it in his eyes—he was crushed." He clenched his fists. "It's not fair. He worked just as hard as any of us."

"I know," Hideyoshi said quietly. "But not everyone makes it through. That's the reality of this training. They demand perfection because anything less out there"—he gestured toward the sky —"could mean disaster."

The two sat in silence for a while.

"Do you think it could happen to us?" Sugai asked finally, his voice barely above a whisper.

Hideyoshi didn't answer.

As weeks turned into months, Hideyoshi's skills sharpened. Formation flying became second nature, and his navigation skills improved to the point where he could plot a course with confidence.

After a time, Hideyoshi began his instrument-flying lessons, using an odd-looking contraption called the Link Trainer. Tucked away in one corner of a hangar, its blue-painted body resembled some sort of miniature-airplane child's toy. Yet the Link instrument-flying trainer, or "Blue Box," as it was often called, represented a technological leap in training for instruments-only flight at night or in bad weather.

Developed in the United States by Edwin Link in the late 1920s, the trainer was a clever product of mechanical ingenuity. Link, a civilian aviation enthusiast who had been frustrated by the high cost of learning to fly, had used his knowledge of organ bellows and pneumatic systems to design and build a "flight simulator" capable of mimicking the movements of an aircraft and allowing pilots to practice flying without ever leaving the ground. It caught the attention of military air forces worldwide—including the Imperial Japanese Navy, which promptly purchased several of them.

As Hideyoshi waited his turn in the device, he studied it closely. It was a compact miniature airplane with a full-size cockpit (sporting comically small stubby wings and a tail) mounted on a mechanical base that allowed it to pitch, roll and yaw just like an actual aircraft. Inside, the pilot had an instrument panel with gauges duplicating those in a real airplane. The closed hatch-like cover blocked off all view to the outside, forcing the student to depend entirely upon his instrument panel. The controls—a joystick, rudder pedals, and throttle lever—responded realistically to the pilot's inputs through a complex system of pneumatic bellows and mechanical linkages, which translated his control movements into corresponding tilts and turns.

Nearby, the instructor's control station contained a "course plotter," a mechanical table with a moving pen that traced the pilot's theoretical flight path onto a paper map. This setup allowed instructors to monitor the pilot's performance in real time and provide instant feedback. Together, the trainer and control station created a realistic and immersive simulation for instruments-only flight—a vital necessity for a pilot who would be flying at night or in bad weather.

Sliding into the snug cockpit, Hideyoshi found a familiar set of instruments—altimeter, artificial horizon, airspeed indicator, and compass. The instructor closed the canopy, sealing him in, and Hideyoshi's world instantly shrank to the dimly lit panel in front of him.

A voice crackled through the intercom, instructing him to "fly the instruments." Outside the trainer, a small group of cadets watched the instructor manipulate the controls at his station. As the Link hummed to life, the Blue Box tilted slightly, and the pen on the course plotter began tracing Hideyoshi's progress on a paper map.

"Maintain altitude and heading," came the command. "After 50 kilometers, change your bearing to zero three five."

The artificial horizon dipped slightly, and Hideyoshi corrected with the control stick, watching the needle stabilize. For the next half-hour, the trainer tilted and turned. At first he was disoriented—his time in the Yokosuka biplane had accustomed him to the "feel" of the plane as it maneuvered, and now he did not have that source of sensory input. It took several sessions for him to learn to fully trust the instruments and the information that they gave him.

Over several months, he became more and more comfortable with blind flight, and it wasn't long before he was "flying" the little Link as smoothly and confidently as if he were up in the sky in a Red Dragonfly.

The Imperial Navy had a meticulous system for assigning trainees to specialized roles, insuring that each individual was matched to the position that was best suited to their abilities and also matched the Navy's own needs.

From the moment they entered the program, trainees were constantly assessed for their potential. Whether they arrived through the elite Naval Academy or as enlistees in the *Yokaren* or *Soren* programs, the process was the same. Basic training provided a foundation in flight skills and navigation, but it also allowed instructors to evaluate every student's strengths and weaknesses, taking note of their flight performance, technical understanding, reflexes, and decision-making under pressure.

At the end of their basic training, once they were proficient in their basic skills, the new pilots were directed into one of several specialized tracks, which were dependent upon their own individual aptitudes and also upon those replacements that the Navy currently had a specific need for. Those destined for fighter cockpits would go on to learn advanced aerial combat techniques. Bomber pilots would be further trained in formation flying and mission planning. Navigators would go on to learn celestial navigation and mapping, while radiomen would be taught the intricacies of signal transmission and coded cryptography.

For every student, as they reached the end of their basic flight training, this process was the subject of much anticipation. They knew that every flight, every maneuver, and every exam they had done was contributing to this decision that would shape their future. Everyone, of course, wanted to be a heroic fighter pilot and fly the hottest new planes. But most of them would not be—they would be assigned instead to less glamorous roles like rear gunners or cargo pilots or bombardiers.

In February 1937, Hideyoshi and the remaining pilot trainees graduated from basic flight school. They were now "Airmen". Of the 37 students who had originally started in the group, only 12 remained. Three of them had died in accidents: 22 of them had been discharged from the program for "failure to meet standards".

The remaining students, now a tightly bonded group, gathered in their immaculate dress uniforms (with freshly-supplied "winged Rising Sun" Naval Pilot insignia over their left breast pocket) on the parade ground at Kasumigaura. Admiral Fujimoto, the school's commanding officer, delivered a brief but stirring address.

"Today, you are no longer students," he declared. "You are naval aviators, entrusted with the honor of defending our Empire in the skies."

Later that day, orders for assignments were distributed, each envelope containing a name and a destination. As the graduates gathered together to open them, the air was charged with anxiety and anticipation.

Hideyoshi unfolded his envelope carefully. Written in the crisp strokes of an officer's hand were the words: *Saeki Air Group – Advanced Fighter Training, Oita Prefecture.*

He looked up to see Takumi scanning his own orders. "Well, what did you get?" Hideyoshi asked.

"Yokosuka Air Group," he replied, disappointment evident in his voice. "I'll be training as a radioman. Not what I hoped for. But it's critical work. They say it's like being the eyes and ears of the whole flight team."

"True enough," said Sugai, who had joined them with his own orders. "I'm heading to Kisarazu. Torpedo planes." He grinned wryly. "Seems I'll be flying low and slow over the waves. Guess someone has to do it."

Shigeru, another classmate, opened his envelope. "Advanced navigation training for me," he said. "They're sending me to Sasebo. Bomber squadrons. It'll be my job to keep the crews on course and the bombs on target."

"Sounds like pressure," Sugai remarked, shaking his head. "And you, Hideyoshi? What's your fate?"

"Saeki," Hideyoshi replied, his voice tinged with excitement. "Advanced fighter training."

The group exchanged envious looks. "The hotshot," Sugai teased. "Well, try not to get too cocky up there. Not all of us can dance in the clouds like you fighter types."

Hideyoshi smiled. "And not all of us have the nerve to fly straight at enemy ships like you torpedo pilots."

The steady roar of the Yokosuka's engine filled Hideyoshi's ears as he scanned the coastline below looking for the runway. The flight to Saeki Air Group had taken him over towns, rice fields, and forested hills to the Seto Inland Sea. Adjusting his course, Hideyoshi examined the windsock at the edge of the airfield and began his descent. The biplane glided over the threshold of the runway before its wheels settled on the ground with a satisfying thump. The K5Y rolled to a gradual stop, and Hideyoshi guided it toward the cluster of waiting ground crew.

As he pulled his duffel bag from the cramped storage space behind his seat, a petty officer approached briskly, clipboard in hand. "Sugiyama, correct?" the petty officer asked, glancing at the aircraft's tail number.

"Yes, sir," Hideyoshi replied.

"Good. Your orders included delivering this aircraft, so you're done with that part. Now, welcome to Saeki Air Group. Follow me."

As they walked, the petty officer pointed out key locations. "Mess hall is over there. You'll eat three times a day, no exceptions. Maintenance hangars are to the east—don't wander in unless you want to get chewed out. That's the flight line ahead, but you'll only be there with your instructors. And there," he said, stopping abruptly and pointing to a long, single-story wooden building, "is Barracks B-3. Welcome to your new home."

The petty officer led Hideyoshi to an empty space near the back. "This is yours. Unpack, stow your gear in the locker, and report back outside in twenty minutes for a base orientation."

As soon as the petty officer left, a student on a nearby *futon* approached, grinning broadly. "You're new here, huh? I'm Toyoda," he said, extending a hand. "Welcome to Saeki. You flew in, didn't you? Airplane transfer? Lucky. Most of us had to take the train."

The next day, Hideyoshi sat in the classroom, his cap resting neatly on the desk in front of him. The cadets snapped to attention as the door opened and their instructor entered. Without a word, Lieutenant Mitsubari walked to the front of the room, his boots scraping on the wooden floor.

After surveying the room, he set his cap on the desk and faced the cadets. "At Kasumigaura, you learned how to fly an airplane," he said, his gaze moving deliberately across the room. "Here at Saeki, you will learn how to use it."

The room remained silent.

"This is not a pleasure craft," he continued. "We are not flying for fun. The fighter plane is a weapon of war, and in war, you must be able to kill your enemy before he kills you. And here is where you will learn how to do that." The impact of Mitsubari's words, striking at the heart of why they were there, settled heavily over the room.

He took a step closer to the students, his eyes narrowing. "Some of you will excel here," he said. "You will prove that you have the skill, the discipline, and the courage to master this weapon. Others will falter. Not everyone here will graduate. We do not tolerate mistakes here. But if you commit yourself fully, you will leave this place ready to face whatever any enemy can throw at you."

Mitsubari turned to the blackboard and began sketching the outline of an aircraft with practiced efficiency. "We will start with a review of the Type 95 fighter, its strengths and weaknesses. Then we will move into formations, aerial tactics, and gunnery. This is not just about flying; this is about survival and victory. Pay attention, take notes, and prepare yourselves. You are no longer students of flight. You are students of war."

The instructor paused for a moment, then turned back to the blackboard, where he had drawn the silhouette of a Type 95 fighter. With the chalk in hand, he circled the aircraft's sleek wings and distinctive fixed landing gear.

"This," he began, "is the Type 95 Mitsubishi A5M. Our enemy calls it the Claude. It is the mainstay of the Imperial Japanese Navy Air Service and the fighter you will be mastering during your advanced training here at Saeki."

Mitsubari set the chalk down and faced the room. "The Type 95 was introduced in 1936, and it represents a significant leap forward for naval aviation. Until its arrival, most naval fighters were biplanes like the trainers you have already flown, slow and less maneuverable. The Claude changed all that. It is the world's first carrier-capable monoplane fighter to enter service, and it has set a new standard for speed, agility, and combat effectiveness."

He began pacing slowly, his hands clasped behind his back. "Powered by a Nakajima Kotobuki radial engine, the Type 95 has a maximum speed of 440 kilometers per hour and a service ceiling of 9,800 meters," Mitsubari intoned. "It is armed with two 7.7mm machine guns mounted in the cowling, synchronized to fire through the propeller arc."

He stopped and gestured to the blackboard. "This aircraft has been tested and proven in combat over China, where it has been deployed extensively since the outbreak of hostilities. Its primary adversaries in that theater are the Soviet-built Polikarpov I-15 biplane and the Polikarpov I-16 monoplane, both of which have their strengths and weaknesses."

Mitsubari picked up the chalk again and quickly sketched rough profiles of the Polikarpov fighters next to the Type 95. "The I-15, with its biplane design, is slower than the Claude but highly maneuverable, especially at lower altitudes. The I-16, on the other hand, is faster and more heavily armed, with a pair of 20mm cannons in some variants, but it lacks the Type 95's agility."

He turned back to the class, his expression serious. "In engagements over China, the Claude has consistently outfought both of these aircraft, provided the pilot uses proper tactics. Its light airframe and responsive controls allow for tight turns and quick recovery, qualities that are indispensable in a dogfight. However, its lack of armor means that you cannot afford to make mistakes. One well-placed burst from an I-16's guns can end your career — and your life."

"This aircraft rewards skill and punishes carelessness. It is not forgiving, but in the hands of a capable pilot, it is a deadly weapon. You will learn to exploit its strengths and compensate for its weaknesses. Remember, in combat, your survival depends as much on your ability to read the situation as it does on your technical skill. Know your enemy, know your machine, and know yourself."

The room was silent, the cadets absorbing the instructor's words. After a moment, Mitsubari nodded. "Tomorrow, we will begin with in-depth technical drills on the Type 95's systems and maintenance. Today, I expect you to study its performance characteristics and familiarize yourselves with its operational history. This knowledge is not optional; it is essential. Dismissed."

After several more days of classroom instruction, Hideyoshi and the other cadets found themselves standing in one of Saeki Air Group's sprawling hangars. Inside, several Type 95 fighters were parked. They were low-wing monoplanes, sleek and modern — a work of art compared to the dumpy-looking Yokosuka biplanes they had been flying.

When Hideyoshi's turn came, the mechanic supervising the group motioned for him to climb up. "Get in and get comfortable. Familiarize yourself with the layout, and don't touch anything," the man instructed.

Hideyoshi hauled himself onto the wing and eased into the cockpit. The Yokosuka's cockpit had been relatively spacious, but the Claude, designed strictly as a single-seat fighter, offered no such room. Every lever, switch, and dial was positioned for efficiency in the heat of combat, leaving little space to spare. The inclusion of a gun sight mounted above the dashboard was a grim reminder of the aircraft's sole purpose.

The first difference Hideyoshi noticed was the enclosed cowling surrounding the radial engine directly in front of him. The control stick and rudder pedals felt different as well. The Yokosuka's controls had been forgiving and intuitive, designed for ease of training. The Claude's controls required a firmer hand and more controlled inputs. Hideyoshi could already tell that flying this machine would demand a higher level of concentration.

Reaching down, he felt the sturdy throttle lever and noticed the placement of the trim controls, which were more accessible than on the Yokosuka. The Claude's designers had clearly prioritized the pilot's ability to make rapid adjustments in combat situations.

What struck him most, though, was the visibility—or rather lack of it. The Yokosuka's open cockpit and biplane configuration had offered excellent downward and lateral views. In the Claude, the monoplane wings and the more enclosed cockpit significantly reduced his field of vision. The rearward visibility, in particular, was almost nonexistent due to the high fuselage behind the cockpit. Hideyoshi made a mental note to compensate for this blind spot during flight.

The ground crew member's voice interrupted his thoughts. "Time's up. Next!"

A few days later, after everyone was familiar with the cockpit layout, the students were allowed their first flight in the Claude.

The lead instructor, Lieutenant Takumi, gathered the students around. "It's time to take these machines into the air. This is a step up in every way from what you've flown before. Respect the aircraft and its capabilities, and it will reward you. Underestimate it, and it will punish you."

Hideyoshi performed his pre-flight checks methodically, reviewing each step as he had rehearsed. Fuel—adequate. Control surfaces—responsive. He climbed onto the wing and into the cockpit, and the mechanic gave him a thumbs-up and signaled to start the engine.

Hideyoshi pulled the starter lever, and the engine roared to life, the propeller spinning in a blur. The vibration of the big Nakajima radial engine was more pronounced than in the Yokosuka.

Following the ground crew's signals, he taxied to the runway. The Claude responded crisply to his inputs, much more sensitive than the Yokosuka. Hideyoshi eased the throttle forward. The engine surged and the Claude accelerated rapidly, the tail lifting off the ground within moments. He used gentle rudder inputs to counter the torque, keeping the nose aligned with the runway. At 90 kilometers per hour, he pulled back slightly on the stick, and the plane lifted gracefully into the air.

The Claude climbed with a nimble responsiveness that surprised him. The speed was intoxicating. He quickly adjusted the trim and stabilized the aircraft at 1,000 meters. Leveling off, he glanced at the instruments. Oil pressure and engine temperature remained stable.

There, under the watchful eye of an instructor in another Claude, he performed basic maneuvers: steep turns, climbing spirals, and shallow dives. Half an hour later, he was back on the ground.

It was, Hideyoshi decided, a beautiful airplane.

The weeks following Hideyoshi's first flight in the Type 96 were filled with training flights, three each day.

The mornings usually began with a briefing in the squadron ready room with Takumi. "Today, you will begin dogfighting drills," he had announced. "This is where you learn to fight, to use your aircraft as a weapon. Speed and maneuverability are your strengths. Exploit them. Keep your wits about you, and never lose sight of your opponent."

Once airborne, the group formed into loose formations, each *shotai* of three planes led by an instructor. The drills began with basic tactical maneuvers. Takumi demonstrated how to execute a high-speed climbing turn to evade an enemy or how to drop into a steep dive to close distance. Hideyoshi followed each move.

Once the students had learned the advanced aerobatic maneuvers that were a part of air combat, the lessons moved on to actual dogfighting drills. Takumi would break off, signaling his students to engage him one at a time. The instructor's Claude danced through the sky, nimbly rolling and diving to escape their pursuit. Hideyoshi pushed his plane to the limits as he tried to stay on his tail, but Takumi's experience in the nimble fighter was undeniable, and just as Hideyoshi thought he had the advantage, Takumi looped upward and slipped behind him, signaling his simulated "kill" with a sharp wing waggle.

"Good effort, Sugiyama," Takumi told him after they had landed. "But you were too eager. Patience is as important as speed. Anticipate, don't react." The critique stung, but Hideyoshi nodded, determined to improve. Over the next few rounds, he learned to vary his approach, feinting to try to draw Takumi into a vulnerable position. Though he didn't score a "kill", he managed to evade Takumi longer with each attempt.

After a while, the drills shifted to formation tactics. Flying in tight *shotai* formations demanded a high level of skill. Each pilot had to maintain their position relative to their wingmen while executing gut-wrenching maneuvers to both defend and attack. They practiced formations of three against three, three against two, and two against three. By the end of each day, the cadets were physically and mentally exhausted.

Back on the ground, they gathered around Takumi, who offered feedback on their performance. "You're improving, all of you," he said. "But you still have much to learn. Combat is unforgiving. Every mistake is a potential death sentence. Don't ever forget that."

As the cadets walked back to the barracks, some of them reflected on the day's lessons. Hideyoshi asked his barracks-mate Kanawa, "So, what did you think?"

"It's harder than I thought," Kanawa admitted, wearily rubbing his shoulder. "Takumi makes it look effortless."

"Because he's been doing it for years," Hideyoshi replied. "We'll get there, too. We have to."

After several weeks of these mock dogfights, the trainees were surprised one morning to see six dull-green stumpy-looking aircraft parked on the tarmac, each with foreign markings that had been hastily painted over with Rising Sun insignia. They were Polikarpov I-15 biplanes and I-16 monoplanes, the standard fighters used by the Chinese.

Their instructor, Lieutenant Osaki, gestured towards the unfamiliar planes.

"These are the Polikarpov I-15 and I-16 fighters," Osaki began. "Captured in China. Many of your opponents will be flying these. Today, you'll be dogfighting with some of our experienced Japanese veterans from those campaigns. They've flown against the Chinese and their Soviet advisors and they know the tactics you're likely to encounter. Pay attention. They are here to teach you how to survive."

The veterans were introduced—Lieutenant Commander Namba and Warrant Officer Ishizami, both decorated combat pilots. Their demeanor was professional, and their eyes were like cold steel. They knew what "war" was like.

Namba, a tall man with sharp features, spoke to the trainees. "We are not here to coddle you. If you make a mistake, we will exploit it. Learn quickly, or you won't last long in combat."

A short time later, Hideyoshi found himself climbing into his Claude, the cockpit now feeling like a familiar second skin. The Mitsubishi, unlike the Yokosuka, came equipped with a radio, but it was new technology and it was unreliable, often conking out. Many of the combat units in China, he had learned, were removing them altogether, considering them useless dead weight and hoping to gain a few more precious kph in speed. Without their radios, they were still dependent upon hand signals and wing-waggling to communicate.

The trainees flew in a three-ship *shotai* while the veterans flew as a pair. Hideyoshi stuck close to Kanawa, maintaining formation as they climbed for altitude.

The exercise began with simple maneuvers. Namba and Ishizami, flying the Polikarpovs, demonstrated the tight turning abilities of the I-15 and the surprising climb rate of the I-16.

Then, Namba's I-15 suddenly waggled his wings and broke hard to the right, rolling into a tight spiral. It was an invitation to catch him. Hideyoshi banked sharply after him, his Claude groaning under the aerodynamic strain. Despite his best efforts, though, the maneuverability of the I-15 allowed Namba to escape easily.

The next set of drills focused on coordinated tactics. Namba and Ishizami demonstrated the "drag and bag" tactic. In this maneuver, one plane would lure the trainees into a chase while the other swooped in for an attack from behind. Namba flew along a straight and steady path for a few seconds—a fatal error in a dogfight. Seeing his opportunity, Hideyoshi closed in for what he assumed would be an easy victory. Instead, Ishizami, flying the faster I-16, exploited his distraction and took advantage of his target fixation. Looping around and diving from above, the combat veteran came within fifty meters of the Claude, simulating a burst of fire with a waggle of his wings.

Back on the ground, the veterans offered critiques. "You had speed and altitude advantages in the Claude," Namba told the group. "Use them. Do not get into a turning fight with an I-15. Strike from above and disengage before it can counter."

Ishizami added, "The I-16 has a faster roll rate than your Claude, but it's unstable at low speeds. Force it into a slow-speed engagement, and you'll have the upper hand. Always think two moves ahead of your opponent."

For the next few days, the cadets engaged the two veterans, who easily evaded them time after time. During one mock engagement, though, Hideyoshi climbed to gain an altitude advantage, then executed a diving attack on Ishizami's I-16. The Polikarpov broke away to evade, but this time Hideyoshi stayed disciplined, resisting the urge to follow into a fatal high-speed turn. Instead, he climbed again, forcing Ishizami to abort his counterattack and evade him. He was learning.

By the end of the week, the exercises had opened their eyes to the realities of air combat. The veterans departed with a final piece of advice. "Your Claude is a weapon," Namba said, "but it's the skill and training of the pilot that will win or lose the fight. The plane is just an extension of your own brain and hands. Use it wisely."

The final phase of Hideyoshi's training was the most daunting yet—the art of carrier landings. Even the most skilled of pilots regarded this as aviation's greatest challenge. Landing on a long stationary airstrip was one thing; touching down on the tiny pitching and rolling deck of an aircraft carrier at sea required skill, nerve, and lots of practice.

The Americans had a specially-trained "Landing Signal Officer" or LSO who stood at the back of the flight deck and used a pair of brightly-colored paddles to guide airplanes in for a landing. The Japanese, however, had no LSO. Each pilot was responsible for his own safe landing.

To help guide them, though, especially in bad weather, Japanese carriers were equipped with a system of colored lights. If the two rows of colored lights were even, it meant the plane was on the proper glide angle for landing. If one row was above the other, it meant you were too high or too low.

Carrier takeoffs were less dangerous, but could still be hazardous. The flight deck was much shorter than any runway, and there was not enough room to run up to full takeoff speed. This required that the carrier turn to face into the wind whenever it was launching planes, allowing the moving air to give enough boost in lift to get airborne. An engine failure on takeoff, though, meant that the plane would roll off the front of the flight deck. A pilot could then drown before he could get out of the wreck, or he could be run down by the still-moving 35,000-ton ship.

The training began with a runway that had been painted with a slew of white lines that mimicked the deck of an aircraft carrier. They spent an entire day studying diagrams of carrier landing patterns and learning the techniques. Their timing and angle had to be precise so that the arrestor wires that were strung across the carrier deck would be snagged by the Claude's tailhook, which would bring it to a stop.

Osaki drilled them on the importance of managing airspeed precisely. Too fast, and they'd overshoot the wire. Too slow, and they would stall and crash into the deck.

For several weeks, they practiced taking off and landing. Anyone who strayed outside of the lines was "dead". On landing, they had to hit the exact spot on the deck which put them over the arrestor wires. They also learned to push the throttle ahead to "full" at the moment of touchdown. If they missed the arrestor wires or if the tailhook failed to engage, they had to immediately speed down the flight deck and take off again, going around the landing pattern for another attempt. It was the most embarrassing thing a carrier pilot could do.

At first, the cadets made many mistakes. In Hideyoshi's first practice attempt, he hit the simulated carrier deck with a jarring thud and bounced over the painted "wires". Osaki's critique was merciless. "You came in too hot and too steep. Do it again." But with constant practice, they were soon hitting the mark every time.

After a few weeks, they were ready for the real thing. To become "carrier-qualified", they had to make six successful landings on an actual carrier. The *Ryujo* was assigned to cruise in the Pacific just offshore, and the cadets were to take off from Saeki, navigate to the carrier and land, then take off and fly back to Saeki. Six times. "Today, the stakes are real," Osaki reminded them. "If you mess up out there, the ocean will be your landing strip."

When his turn came, Hideyoshi flew his Claude out to sea and navigated towards the pre-arranged rendezvous spot. From the air, as he descended, the *Ryujo* looked impossibly small, bobbing on the waves. The landing signal lights held steady as he approached, then crept up, nudging him to ease off the throttle. The deck loomed closer and closer. Hideyoshi felt the wheels touch down with a jolt, then the sudden deceleration as the wire caught his plane and pulled it to a shuddering halt. His first carrier landing was a success.

With his carrier qualification, Hideyoshi's training was complete, and he was promoted to the rank of Naval Airman First Class. Soon, he knew, he and the other cadets would receive their orders for new assignments, and they would be placed on active duty.

In the meantime, they were put to work flying patrols out into the Pacific and along the coastline. "Today's mission," he had been told, "is a coastal patrol. You will fly a pre-arranged route, maintaining a tight formation while scanning for any unusual activity. This is not a drill. You are to treat this as you would any operational mission. Stay alert, and follow your lead's instructions."

Finally, after a few weeks of routine patrols over mostly empty ocean, Hideyoshi received his orders: he was to report to the 1st Kokutai at "an operational airfield in Shantung Province, China" for combat deployment. The instructions outlined his departure schedule, the chain of command at his new station, and the protocols he was to follow during the transfer.

His time at Saeki had come to an end, and he would not be flying peacetime patrols anymore. He was going to war.

Hideyoshi met Kanawa near the hangar, where they had shared countless hours of camaraderie and friendly rivalry. He was also leaving Saeki. His orders were sending him to the carrier *Hiryu*, a coveted assignment.

"So, you're going off to the front," Kanawa said, clapping Hideyoshi on the back. "I guess you'll have to tell me what it's like when we meet again."

"And you'll have to tell me about life aboard the *Hiryu*," Hideyoshi replied with a grin. "I've heard stories about the food on carriers. Better than what we've had here."

The two laughed, but the levity couldn't mask the reality of the moment, and Kanawa's expression turned serious. "Stay sharp out there, Hideyoshi. From what I've heard, those Chinese pilots are no slouches."

"I will," Hideyoshi said. "And you—don't let the carrier landings get to you."

Kanawa smirked. "I've got that down already. Just don't let me hear you've been shot down. I'll never let you live it down."

The next morning, Hideyoshi stood on the tarmac, a small duffel bag slung over his shoulder. Parked nearby was a chubby Nakajima L2D transport plane, a license-built copy of the American DC-3. The plane's crew had been ordered to ferry supplies to a forward base on the Chinese mainland, and Hideyoshi had been assigned a spot in the cargo bay for the journey. It wasn't unusual for fighter pilots to hitch rides, and operational logistics often called for flexibility.

The plane's pilot greeted him with a polite nod. "Welcome aboard. It won't be the most comfortable ride, but it'll get you where you need to go."

"Thank you, sir," Hideyoshi replied, bowing before stepping inside. The walls were lined with crates strapped down for the journey, and he secured himself into a jump seat as the crew completed their pre-flight checks.

The flight to the mainland was long, even with the L2D cruising steadily at altitude. Hideyoshi exchanged a few words with the co-pilot, learning more about the airfield they were heading to. It was a major hub for operations in China, bustling with activity as squadrons rotated in and out of the conflict zone. "From there," the pilot told him, "you'll likely be ferried out to your assigned squadron."

Two days later, after bouncing along crater-pocked dirt roads on a long and tiring trip by Army truck, Hideyoshi arrived at Koto Airfield, near the port city of Tsingtao. It would be his new home for the foreseeable future.

Chapter 5
China (October 1937)

The day after his arrival at Koto, after checking out his A5M Claude fighter with a brief flight around the airfield to learn the local landmarks, Hideyoshi and the rest of his squadron was ordered to a briefing, which was held in a canvas tent hastily erected near the edge of the dusty runway. Wooden crates served as makeshift tables, and the pilots sat on rough benches that had been cobbled together from planks. A single kerosene lamp flickered in the corner.

One of the senior officers, Lieutenant Commander Horiuchi, stepped to the front, and the chatter stopped.

"To our new replacement pilots," he began, "I have only one message. You have been brought here for one reason: to fight. This is not a training exercise. You are now on the front lines of a conflict that will define the future of our nation."

He moved to a large map of China which had been pinned to the side of a wooden crate. Red and blue lines marked the contested areas. "This will be a routine patrol. Our mission is to ensure air superiority over these key regions," he said, tapping a finger on locations near Shanghai and Nanking. "The Army doesn't have any fighters in this region, so it is relying on us to dominate the skies and protect their advances. We must also neutralize the enemy airfields and provide cover for our supply convoys."

The briefing then shifted to the political context of the war, delivered by an officer from the Ministry of Naval Affairs. "This war," the Major began, "is about securing resources vital to our

Empire's survival. The actions you take will contribute to Japan's rightful place as the dominant power in Asia. The League of Nations and Western powers may denounce our efforts, but remember: we are fighting for the future of our nation. We expect every man to perform his duties to the utmost."

The Second Sino-Japanese War, which would grow to engulf the entire Pacific, had its origins in a single explosive confrontation at a small bridge just outside Peking (now known as Beijing).

After the Meiji Restoration in the late 19th century, Japan had transformed itself into an industrial power. This rapid modernization, however, had created a voracious appetite for resources — coal, iron, oil, and arable land — that Japan's own islands did not have, and had to obtain from outside sources. The puppet state of Manchukuo and the invasion of Manchuria had provided a temporary solution, but the militarists who controlled the government in Tokyo now looked towards further expansion into China itself and the complete domination of Asia, declaring this as essential for Japan's survival. And the incident in Peking gave them the perfect excuse.

Since the time of the 12th-century, the Marco Polo Bridge had crossed the Yongding River and provided a connection between the tiny Chinese town of Wanping and the countryside just outside of Peking. On the night of July 7, 1937, Japanese troops from the Army's North China Garrison, stationed nearby, were conducting a nighttime military exercise. The training drills involved gunfire with blank ammunition to simulate combat. While such exercises had happened before, they always provoked tension with the local Chinese population, who feared that the Japanese had expansionist designs on their territory, and who believed there was a good possibility that the Japanese would invade.

Shortly after the July 7 exercises began, a Japanese private went missing. A Japanese Army officer (fearing, he said, that the soldier had been captured by Chinese guerrillas) sent a request to the nearby Chinese garrison at Wanping, demanding that his men be allowed to enter the town and search for the missing trooper.

The Chinese commander at Wanping, however, was immediately suspicious, and concluded that if he allowed Japanese troops to enter Wanping's gates, they would never leave. He refused the request. The Japanese made threats and moved more men to the area around the bridge. The Chinese, now anticipating a Japanese attack, in turn reinforced their positions around Wanping.

Just before midnight, shots were fired. (Both sides would later blame the other.) The firefight lasted only a few minutes, but it put both sides on edge.

Later that morning, with the Japanese soldier still unaccounted for, fighting once again broke out. Japanese artillery batteries began shelling the town of Wanping, and Chinese forces replied with machine guns. Then Japanese troops tried to cross the bridge, but were repelled by Chinese fire. In the middle of all this, the missing Japanese soldier finally turned up—he had become lost during the training exercise. But now events had already spun out of control. The Japanese commander sent his forces swarming into Chinese territory and marched them towards Peking and Tientsin (modern Tainjin). They were met by a Chinese counteroffensive, and what had begun as a minor clash now erupted into full-scale war.

Japan's Kwantung Army, stationed in Manchuria, moved swiftly in a series of coordinated campaigns to consolidate control over northern China, escalating from skirmishes to coordinated military campaigns. The initial focus was Peking and the nearby port city of Tientsin, critical strategic points.

The Japanese objective was clear: to seize the cities and establish a foothold in northern China. The campaign began with a two-pronged assault led by elite divisions of the Kwantung Army. Superior in training, weaponry, and coordination, the Japanese forces overwhelmed the Chinese 29th Army, commanded by General Song Zheyuan. Though the Chinese defenders fought fiercely, they were outgunned and lacked the heavy artillery and air support that the Japanese could bring to bear on them.

By late July, Japanese forces had encircled Peking, launching relentless artillery barrages and air raids to weaken its defenses. The city's ancient walls, built to defend against spears and arrows, crumbled under the Imperial Army's assault. On July 28, the city fell to the invaders.

Tientsin, situated along the Hai River and a key port city, was next. Japanese forces unleashed a lethal series of flanking maneuvers to capture the city, despite stiff resistance. By the end of July, Tientsin too was under Japanese control.

After capturing Peking and Tientsin, the Japanese turned their attention to the provinces of Hebei and Shanxi. These regions were vital for their agricultural output and their strategic proximity to key industrial targets deeper in the Chinese interior.

The Chinese government, led by Chiang Kai-shek, attempted to organize a defense, and even worked out a temporary alliance with his old enemy Mao Tse-Tung and the Communist Red Army, but China was crippled by petty jealousies among regional warlords and a lack of coordinated actions.

Japanese forces captured Baoding, an important city in Hebei, and then moved westward into Shanxi Province, where the industrial city of Taiyuan became the next target. At Niangzi Pass, Chinese forces were able to use the rugged terrain to their advantage and temporarily slow the Japanese advance, but the superior Japanese artillery and air power forced a breakthrough, and Taiyuan was quickly surrounded.

Despite these advances in the north, however, Japan's generals recognized that controlling northern China would not be enough to force Chiang to surrender. The Chinese had already moved their capital from Nanking to Chunking. So the Japanese turned towards Shanghai, a vital economic resource as well as a symbolic stronghold of Chinese resistance.

Japanese forces launched their attack on Shanghai in August. While Japanese bombers carried out near-daily air raids on the city, Imperial Navy gunships in the Yangtze River pounded the city with shells. Japanese troops moved into the streets of Shanghai, confidently expecting a quick victory. Instead they ran into China's best troops, the elite 87th and 88th Divisions, who had been ordered to defend the city at all costs. The result was a grinding stalemate.

The League of Nations once again condemned Japan's actions, even though Japan had withdrawn after its earlier invasion of Manchuria and was no longer a member. The League issued a resolution condemning Japan's invasion as an illegal act of aggression and urged its member nations to provide support to China. But the League was toothless and did not have any way to enforce its decisions, and Tokyo simply ignored them.

Some nations did act on their own, however. The United States, which was already beginning to view Japan as a potential military rival in the Pacific, imposed an embargo on the export of arms and war materials to Japan and supplied US-made weapons to China, including aircraft.

Britain and France, which both had economic interests in China, voiced their concerns about Japan's expansionism and urged Japan to respect China's sovereignty and avoid further escalation. But their governments, preoccupied with the rising threat of Nazi Germany and facing their own economic troubles, were unable to take any stronger actions.

The Soviet Union, which shared a border with Japanese-occupied Manchuria, took a more pragmatic approach. While publicly condemning Japan's actions, Stalin secretly supplied weapons to Chinese forces, including Russian-built fighter planes and advisors to train Chinese pilots to fly them.

But in the end, Japan's leaders viewed the League of Nations as ineffectual and dismissed Western criticism as hypocritical, arguing that they were not doing anything in China that the Europeans and Americans had not already done themselves.

The day after arriving in China, Hideyoshi made his way to the makeshift bar that was tucked unobtrusively in a faraway corner of the base. Although it was strictly against Navy regulations, the base commander recognized its value in allowing the pilots to let off a little steam and unwind, and turned a blind eye to it provided that the pilots never broke his one firm rule—no one was ever to drink anything the night before they were to fly a mission.

Inside, men sat in small groups, and the sound of conversation filled the air.

"Ah, you must be Sugiyama!" a booming voice called out as Hideyoshi entered. "I'm Lieutenant Takayuki Osaki, your *shotai* leader."

Hideyoshi snapped to attention and saluted. "It's an honor to serve under you, Osaki-*Taicho*."

Osaki smiled and shook his head. "No need to be so formal around here. In the air, in combat, we're all equals and we all watch out for each other." He gestured toward the rest. "Come on, I'll introduce you to the rest of the men."

The first was Kunio Iwashita, a tall man with sharp eyes and an easy smile. "Welcome to the squadron, Sugiyama. Hope you can keep up with us."

"I'll do my best," Hideyoshi replied with a grin.

Next was Jun Nakagawa, the youngest in the group but with a confident air that belied his age. "Don't let my baby face fool you," Nakagawa said, smirking. "I've downed my share of targets."

"Just don't let it go to your head," Iwashita quipped, eliciting laughter from the group.

Over the course of the morning, Hideyoshi got to know the rest of the squadron members. Each had their own quirks and personalities, but there was an unmistakable bond among them, held together by the dangers they all faced. Several of them took Hideyoshi to a wooden table where they sat sipping *sake* and trading stories.

Iwashita leaned back in his chair, gesturing animatedly as he recounted a particularly close call during a training mission. "I swear, the ground was so close I could see individual blades of grass," he said, his voice full of mock drama.

"You probably mistook them for rice paddies," Nakagawa retorted, earning a round of laughter.

Hideyoshi shared a story from his own training, recounting the wrestling match drill that had left him bruised.

"I remember those days. It seemed like the instructors were trying to turn us into *sumo* wrestlers, not pilots," Osaki joked.

As the day went on, the group moved to the airstrip for a routine inspection of their aircraft. Osaki took the opportunity to quiz Hideyoshi on the Claude, testing his knowledge of the plane's capabilities and limitations.

"Good," Osaki said after Hideyoshi correctly answered a series of technical questions. "But knowing your plane is only half the battle. The rest is instinct and teamwork. We all have to know that we can count on you."

That evening, the squadron gathered in the mess tent for dinner. The atmosphere was lively, the air filled with the clatter of utensils and the hum of conversation. Hideyoshi sat between Iwashita and Nakagawa, feeling more at ease now with his new comrades.

His gaze eventually fell on the pilots from another of the airfield squadrons clustered together in a corner of the room. They were older, their uniforms bore the marks of long service—faded insignia, frayed cuffs—and their faces carried an easy confidence that younger aviators like Hideyoshi couldn't help but admire.

Iwashita, seated beside Hideyoshi, nudged him and nodded toward the veterans. "Fourth *Kokutai*. They're telling combat stories again," he whispered with a grin. "Come on, let's go listen."

The two of them rose, followed by Nakagawa and Osaki, and approached the group. One of the older pilots, Lieutenant Hino, noticed Hideyoshi and waved them over. "New meat for the grinder, eh?" he said with a grin. "Take a seat, boys. You might learn something."

The younger men settled in as Hino continued his tale. "It was just a week ago, near Nanking. We were escorting bombers, and sure enough, the Chinese showed up to meet us. Russian-made I-16s, tough little planes. Fast, too, in a dive."

Hino leaned forward, his voice dropping slightly. "They don't fight like us, though. They hit and run, trying to wear us down. They know they can't match us in a dogfight, not with our training and the A5M's maneuverability. But they're aggressive—brave, I'll give them that."

Another veteran, Lieutenant Yamashiro, chimed in. "Bravery doesn't always mean good tactics, though. One of them came straight at me, guns blazing. I sidestepped with a sharp roll, got on his tail, and gave him a burst. Watched him spiral down." Then he paused, his expression darkening.

"But not all of us came back," Hino finished for him. He turned to the younger men, his eyes hard. "Remember this, rookie: no matter how skilled you are, there's always someone better. My wingman, Samimito, was hit that day. Engine fire. He bailed out, but … " Hino's voice trailed off, and the group fell silent.

Osaki broke the tension. "What happened?" he asked quietly.

Hino glanced at him, his jaw tight. "The locals found him before our ground team did. Let's just say, it wasn't a quick end. They're angry, and they have every reason to be. This war has devastated their homes."

Hino sighed and softened his tone. "But it's not always grim. I've seen our men pull off feats that would make the gods jealous. Osamu Taki — now there's a flyer. He once shot down three in a single sortie. The last one tried to out-turn him, but Taki was too good. Got the kill with barely any ammo left."

The younger pilots exchanged awed glances.

Hideyoshi finally spoke. "Is it true that the I-16s can outclimb us?"

Yamashiro turned to him. "It depends on what altitude you're at. But speed and climb aren't everything. What you do, that's what counts. It's the pilot that wins air fights, not the airplane."

Hino added, "And don't forget your training. Know your plane, know your enemy, and always watch your six. Flying is the easy part. Fighting — that's where your wits will save you."

The pilot barracks were a modest arrangement, just simple wooden structures. Despite the bare accommodations, though, life was unexpectedly eased by the presence of a local man named Zhou, who had been hired to perform chores for the pilots. He was middle-aged, but looked older — the product of a life of hard labor. He spoke little Japanese beyond basic phrases but was good at understanding what was needed.

His service had been arranged through a local intermediary, likely coerced into cooperation with the occupying forces. There were even occasional rumors that he was a spy for Mao's Communists and was reporting on Japanese troop movements in the area.

Each morning, however, Zhou arrived at the barracks before sunrise, carrying a woven basket on his back. He would collect the soiled uniforms piled in a corner and haul them to the nearest stream, where he would scrub the fabric against smooth stones until they were clean again. By the time the pilots returned from their morning briefing, their clothes would be hanging neatly on bamboo poles to dry.

Zhou also cooked for the men, using the rice and rations they provided. His simple meals — a pot of steaming rice with Chinese vegetables from the local market, and occasionally some chicken or pork — were a welcome change from the military's field rations. Though some of the flavors were unfamiliar to the Japanese, the pilots found themselves warming to the meals, teasing Zhou by declaring him a better cook than their Navy mess. Zhou would bow modestly in response, a faint smile on his lips.

In the afternoons, while the pilots were in the air, Zhou swept the barracks clean of dust and tidied the cots. He kept the kettles full of hot water for tea and even patched worn uniforms with scraps of fabric that he had scrounged up from somewhere. He also took care of the squadron mascot — a macaque monkey named Hanzo that someone had found in a Chinese market and had brought back to the barracks, thereby rescuing the little fellow from the cooking pot.

Despite the language barrier, Zhou's relationship with the pilots seemed to be cordial, marked by an unspoken arrangement of mutual benefit: Zhou providing comfort and service, and the pilots in return giving him whatever they could spare. Rice, dried fish, a bottle of *sake* on occasion, and, most valuable of all, cigarettes. These items, while ordinary to the Japanese servicemen, were precious luxuries in the impoverished countryside that Zhou called home. Hideyoshi had always assumed that he was selling his gifts on the black market and was living off the money. Nobody knew if he had a family.

Sometimes, when the *sake* had flowed more freely, one of the pilots would try to engage Zhou in conversation, gesturing wildly and using the few broken Chinese phrases which they had picked up. Zhou would laugh softly, shaking his head, and mutter a response that no one understood, but which always seemed to lighten the mood.

One day, Zhou brought a small bowl of *yu mian* noodles as a gift for the men. It was his way of expressing gratitude for their generosity. The pilots, in turn, pooled their cigarettes to send Zhou home with more than usual.

Though Zhou's presence was taken for granted by some, Hideyoshi was disturbed by the idea of a Chinese man serving as a household worker for them, and found himself watching the man closely at times, struck by his quiet dignity and the resilient strength that was evident in his eyes. His presence was a blunt reminder of all the local people whose lives had been upended and disrupted by the war. For Zhou, this arrangement was likely not a choice, but a harsh necessity. The man may even, deep down inside, have hated these people who had invaded and occupied his country. And yet, he always carried himself with a stoic patience that was humbling to see.

By the time Zhou left each evening, the barracks felt cleaner, warmer, and somehow more bearable. It was a small thing, but for the men who were far from home in the midst of war, such small things often meant the most.

For several days since Hideyoshi had arrived, the weather was bad and things had been quiet. Other than occasional patrols when the clouds broke, nobody was flying. He decided to take advantage of the lull to venture out beyond the perimeter of the air base, accompanied by two other pilots, Iwashita and Kageyama. Walking along the pockmarked dirt road that led into town, they were struck by the extent of the devastation. The Chinese bombs had been intended for their airfield, but many of them had missed their target and hit the village instead. Most of the houses had been reduced to charred skeletons, their roofs shattered and their walls blackened by fire. A Taoist temple at the village's center bore gaping holes in its structure, its once-ornate carvings now splintered and broken. All the civilians were gone, either dead or evacuated, and the only signs of life were a few stray dogs scavenging through the rubble.

"War leaves nothing untouched," Iwashita said, his voice low. "This was someone's home once. A place of peace, laughter, and life."

Takashi nodded, kicking a piece of debris out of his path. "And now it's nothing more than ashes. This is what we're a part of, whether we like it or not."

Hideyoshi didn't reply.

That evening, as he sat in the mess tent with his fellow pilots, Hideyoshi remained quiet. He had received orders to fly another combat mission tomorrow morning, but oddly, he wasn't thinking about that. Instead, his mind was continually replaying the images of the village and its haunting empty silence. The training and discipline that he had gone through had prepared him to be a pilot, a soldier, and a warrior. But nothing had prepared him for the brutal reality of war, the human cost that lay beneath all the strategic objectives and military maneuvers. Training for war was one thing: seeing it up close was another.

"You're unusually quiet tonight, Sugiyama," Iwashita said, nudging him with an elbow. "Nervous about tomorrow?"

Hideyoshi managed a faint smile. "Just thinking. About everything we've seen today."

Iwashita sighed, leaning back in his chair. "It doesn't get easier. But you'll learn to compartmentalize it. Focus on the mission, on what needs to be done. You'll need all of your wits tomorrow."

Chapter 6
Combat (Oct-Dec 1937)

In a little wooden shack at the Koto airfield, Hideyoshi and his squadron-mates gathered around a low wooden table. A map of the operational area was spread out with its corners weighted down with spent anti-aircraft cartridge casings.

Lieutenant Osaki, their *shotai* leader, tapped the map with a pointer, its tip hovering over a cluster of red circles drawn in grease pencil. "This," he began, "is where we expect the Chinese fighters to be operating. Intelligence reports indicate increased activity along this sector, near a railway junction critical to enemy supply lines."

Hideyoshi leaned forward, studying the marked positions. The red circles were clustered around a town that had seen heavy ground fighting in recent weeks.

"We'll be flying a sweep today, aiming to intercept and engage any enemy aircraft. Priority targets are their fighters."

Iwashita, always quick with a quip, raised an eyebrow. "And if they decide to run?"

"Then we chase them," Osaki replied without hesitation, bringing a ripple of chuckles from the squadron. "But keep your eyes open. The Chinese have been known to lure our planes into ambushes. If it looks suspicious, it probably is."

Tomachi fidgeted with his gloves. "Sir," he asked, "what about ground fire?"

"It'll be heavy," the lieutenant replied. "But we'll stay above 3,000 meters whenever possible. Keep an eye out for tracer fire and avoid diving too low unless absolutely necessary."

A maintenance officer entered the tent, saluted briskly, and handed Osaki a clipboard. "All planes are fueled and armed, sir. Engines are ready."

Osaki nodded in approval and addressed the group again. "Once we're airborne, stay in tight formation. I'll lead, with Sugiyama and Iwashita on my wing." Hideyoshi knew why he had been assigned to fly with the most experienced pilots—they wanted to keep an eye on the new guy in case they needed to bail him out of trouble. "Nakagawa, you'll fly with Saito and Tanabe. Follow the plan, and watch each other's backs."

Hideyoshi glanced at his wingman, who gave him an encouraging grin. "Looks like we'll be keeping each other out of trouble," Iwashita said.

"Just don't get too far ahead," Hideyoshi replied with a smile. "I'd hate to have to save you."

As the pilots filed out of the tent, Osaki called after them, "Final word of caution: remember why we're here. This mission is about clearing the skies. Focus on the objective, and we'll make it back in one piece."

Outside, the base was already alive with the sounds of activity. Ground crews swarmed around the silver Claudes, performing final checks amid the rumble of engines being warmed up and the occasional shout of a mechanic.

Hideyoshi walked to his aircraft, running a hand along its fuselage as he approached. Fighter sweeps, he knew, were unpredictable. Often they didn't find anything. But sometimes they did.

One by one, the squadron's planes taxied to the runway and climbed into the air. Hideyoshi glanced to his right, where Iwashita flew in perfect formation. Ahead of them, Lieutenant Osaki led the squadron in a tight V-shaped group.

The steady chatter of the engine was the only sound in the cockpit. The radios, deemed too unreliable and weighing the planes down, had been removed. Every kilogram saved added a few precious kilometers per hour to their speed, a crucial edge in combat. Communication now relied solely on the language of hand signals and on instinctive teamwork.

Below, the outskirts of Tsingtao rolled by, giving way to the Chinese countryside. There were occasional villages, some of them reduced to smoldering piles of wreckage by the relentless advance of the Imperial Army.

Then, a rapid series of wing-waggles and hand signals from Iwashita flashed the message to them—"enemy planes ahead". Hideyoshi scanned the horizon and spotted a group of small black dots in the western sky. Osaki raised his arm sharply, signaling everyone to spread out while holding altitude.

Hideyoshi's eyes narrowed as the silhouettes of Chinese fighters became clearer—stubby little I-16s. They were in a loose formation, and flying straight and level.

Again Osaki's hand rose over his head, forming a fist to signal "patience". Hideyoshi watched the enemy planes grow larger. His pulse raced.

The Chinese pilots still had not spotted them, as the approaching Claudes had the sun at their backs. Now the Japanese squadron began to maneuver into position, splitting into two groups as prearranged. Osaki led Hideyoshi and Iwashita to maintain their altitude advantage, while the second group, led by Nakagawa, veered off to set up a turning attack.

With a sharp downward thrust of his arm, Osaki gave the signal to dive. The three Claudes dropped like falcons, hurtling through the air toward their unsuspecting prey. The wind buffeted Hideyoshi's plane as he pushed the throttle forward, the enemy fighters growing rapidly in his gunsight. Their Chinese "blue sun" insignia were now visible on the wings.

Suddenly, chaos erupted. The I-16s scattered, their surprised pilots reacting with sharp maneuvers as the Japanese planes streaked toward them. Machine guns rattled and tracers sliced a web of fiery threads through the sky. Hideyoshi's hand trembled on the control stick, his eyes darting from one target to another. He couldn't seem to focus; the scene unfolded too quickly, a confusing clamor of motion and sound.

A sudden twinkle of light—an I-16 firing at him—snapped him to attention, and he instinctively yanked the stick to the left. The Claude rolled hard, pulling him away from the incoming fire, but the sudden motion left him disoriented. His pulse pounded wildly in his ears as he scanned the sky, trying to make sense of all the chaos. He spotted Iwashita's plane banking sharply to avoid an enemy fighter.

For a moment, Hideyoshi felt panic creeping in. The sky was alive with twisting blurry shapes, all moving too fast for him to track. He was overwhelmed by the adrenaline coursing through his veins.

Then, as if a voice in the back of his mind had spoken, he remembered Osaki's words: "Trust your training."

Hideyoshi forced himself to take a deep breath, and his eyes focused on the horizon, steadying himself as he loosened his too-tight grip on the control stick and scanned around for a target. He spotted an I-16 off to his side, weaving erratically to avoid the fire from a diving Japanese plane.

Now calmer, Hideyoshi rolled his Claude, aligning himself with the enemy fighter's path. He pushed the throttle forward and his plane surged ahead. The training that had been drilled into him now came back like a muscle memory—the steady approach, the calculated lead.

The I-16 pilot leveled out for a moment and seemed to be unaware of his approach. As Hideyoshi came closer and slipped behind it, he carefully lined up the Polikarpov in his gunsight, with his thumb hovering over the trigger. The enemy plane grew larger as it made a slow rolling turn to the right, then suddenly made a snap roll to the left and nosed down into the start of a dive. Hideyoshi had been spotted. At almost the same instant, he squeezed the trigger, and the Claude's twin 7.7mm machine guns opened up.

Tracers streaked toward the Chinese plane, stitching a deadly path along the left wing and fuselage. The enemy plane shuddered, thick black smoke pouring from its engine as Hideyoshi's rounds found their mark. The I-16 began to dive more steeply, trailing black smoke as it lost altitude.

For a moment, Hideyoshi could hardly believe it. The enemy fighter continued its death spiral, the pilot unable to regain control. Finally, the plane hit the ground far below, exploding in a burst of flame and debris.

Hideyoshi clenched his fist in triumph and let out an involuntary shout as he pulled up and climbed away. He had done it —his first victory. He leveled out and quickly scanned the sky, searching for another target.

But the brief period of chaos that had consumed the air only moments before seemed to have disappeared, and the skies around him were suddenly, eerily, empty. The twisting dogfights, the streaks of tracers, and the smoke trails had vanished as quickly as they had appeared. A quick glance over his shoulder confirmed that the surviving I-16s were retreating, streaking away toward the horizon.

Another movement caught his eye—a pair of planes banking together in the distance, their silhouettes unmistakable. They weren't the stubby shapes of the I-16s; they were Claudes, their wings displaying the familiar Rising Sun emblems.

Hideyoshi nudged the control stick to the side, bringing his plane into a shallow turn to close the distance. As he approached, he saw the familiar tail markings of Iwashita and Nakagawa in tight formation. Iwashita raised a hand, giving a brief, sharp wave, and Nakagawa waggled his wings, a gesture that meant "form up on me". Hideyoshi acknowledged with a nod, pulling into position on their left and settling into formation. The three planes flew together in a loose triangle.

Faint streaks of blue smoke trailed from the exhaust pipes of Iwashita's engine, while Nakagawa's Claude displayed a row of new bullet holes along the upper wing. The sight reminded Hideyoshi of his own plane, and he glanced at his instrument panel, noting that everything was still within normal limits.

Iwashita then signaled with a hand gesture, pointing toward the southeast—the direction of their base. They turned for home and, after an uneventful hour, touched down at Koto, their wheels kicking up clouds of dust as they rolled onto the runway. Ground crew rushed forward.

As he climbed out of his cockpit, Hideyoshi held up one triumphant finger, and was met with enthusiasm. The mechanics clapped him on the back, beaming with admiration and congratulating him on his first victory.

"Not bad, Sugiyama!" Nakagawa called, grinning as he approached.

Hideyoshi returned the smile, but before he could respond, a figure strode toward them at a purposeful pace. Lieutenant Osaki's broad-shouldered frame seemed even more imposing as he approached, his expression unreadable.

He stopped a few paces away, his sharp eyes locking onto Hideyoshi. For a moment, he said nothing.

"Well done, Sugiyama," he said slowly. "Your first air victory is an achievement worth celebrating."

Hideyoshi's chest swelled with pride, and he bowed deeply. "Thank you, Osaki-*taicho*," he said, the words brimming with gratitude.

But before Hideyoshi could savor the moment, Osaki's smile vanished, replaced by a hard glare. "However," he began, his tone turning cold, "what you did today was reckless."

Hideyoshi froze, his satisfaction evaporating in an instant.

"You broke formation," Osaki continued, his voice rising. "You abandoned your *shotai* in the heat of battle, leaving them vulnerable. Do you understand what could have happened? To them, and to you?"

"I—" Hideyoshi stammered, the weight of Osaki's words crashing down on him. "I'm sorry, *Taicho*. I didn't mean to—"

"Intentions mean nothing in combat!" Osaki snapped, cutting him off. "We are not here for individual glory, Sugiyama. We are here to protect each other, to insure that the mission is accomplished, and that as many of us as possible return home alive."

The other pilots stood in silence, their expressions somber. Hideyoshi felt his face burn with shame as he absorbed the rebuke.

Osaki stepped closer, his eyes boring into Hideyoshi's. "You got your victory today," he said, his voice softer but still firm. "But if you keep flying like that, it will be your last. And worse, it could cost the lives of your comrades. Do you understand me?"

"Yes, *Taicho*," Hideyoshi murmured, respectfully bowing his head. "I understand."

Osaki held his gaze for a moment longer, then nodded curtly. "Good. Learn from this, Sugiyama. Next time, I expect you to do better."

As Osaki turned and walked away, Hideyoshi remained rooted to the spot. The thrill of his victory had been replaced by the harsh reality of his mistake. He glanced at Iwashita and Nakagawa, who gave him small nods of encouragement but said nothing.

It was a hard lesson.

The days following his first combat victory blurred into a series of briefings, sorties, and tense moments in the skies.

Early one morning, he and the other pilots were summoned to the operations room. The ground war had intensified, and Japanese troops were pushing deeper into contested territories. Their task today was to conduct a series of ground-attack and close air support missions to disrupt enemy positions and to assist the infantrymen who were advancing through a strategically vital valley.

"The enemy has established fortified positions here," Osaki said, tapping a cluster of red markers. "We have received reports of heavy resistance in these areas. Our task is to clear the way for our advancing units."

He looked around at each of the pilots around him. "These missions are critical to maintaining our momentum in the campaign. Understand this: we fighters are part of a larger machine. A single cog, yes, but a vital one. Without us, the bombers can't strike. Without the bombers, the Army stalls. Without the Army, the war is lost."

The squadron took off in staggered formations. Although the A5M was primarily an air-superiority fighter, it was also equipped to carry small anti-personnel bombs and was capable of performing ground-attack missions, though all the heavy work was always left to the twin-engined bombers. So all of the Claudes carried a 30kg bomb under each wing.

As they gained altitude, Hideyoshi's thoughts briefly drifted to Sakurada, wondering how his mother and father were doing amid the chaos of the times. He had been writing to his family almost daily, but the mail delivery to his airfield was sporadic. He had told them of his air victory over the I-16, and his father's response was filled with pride and encouragement. He had not told them about the tongue-lashing he had received afterwards.

Reaching the target area, the squadron split into smaller elements. Hideyoshi joined up with Osaki and Nakagawa, and they descended sharply.

The ground erupted into a blanket of fire as they dove. Plumes of smoke rose from foxholes and bunkers as Japanese artillery pounded the area. Hideyoshi spotted the faint sparkle of enemy machine guns below, their muzzle flashes visible even from the air.

Ahead of him, he saw Osaki drop his bombs and instantly tripped his own "release" switch, feeling the sudden weight shift as they dropped away. Immediately, he pulled up sharply, and the strain of the maneuver pressed him back into his seat and made the Claude's wings rattle. Below, the explosions rippled through the enemy line, sending debris and flame skyward.

The three planes regrouped and, once again diving low to almost treetop level, began a series of strafing runs, their machine guns spitting out bullets at the enemy troops. The Chinese fought back fiercely. Their own machine gun tracers arced through the air at them, some passing dangerously close to Hideyoshi's plane and some making loud tinny noises as they impacted. He maneuvered sharply, zigzagging to avoid the fire.

After several strafing runs and with everyone's bombs gone and ammunition running low (everyone was careful not to expend all their ammo, since they knew they could always encounter Chinese fighters on the way home), the squadron regrouped at the prearranged rendezvous point and returned to base.

Later, as he sat near his plane, watching the ground crew patching up the bullet holes, Hideyoshi reflected on the day. He was now more confident in his abilities and more comfortable in the air. The Claude had become his sword in this war, and as he gained experience with each sortie, he was becoming a sharper blade.

A few days later the squadron was flying another patrol when Osaki, at the head of the formation, waggled his wings—a signal to get the squadron's attention—and pointed. Below them, a formation of enemy aircraft came into view.

Osaki adjusted his position slightly, pulling closer to Hideyoshi and Iwashita. He again pointed downward toward the bombers, clearly indicating his intent. This was their target, and he wanted Hideyoshi and Iwashita to engage.

Osaki's plane peeled away, climbing slightly to take a covering position. From this vantage point, he maintained a protective watch, scanning the skies for enemy fighters. Hideyoshi and Iwashita were now on their own.

Together, the two Claudes tipped forward, plunging into a steep dive. Hideyoshi's focus narrowed to the enemy planes that were growing larger in his sights. He adjusted his angle, moving towards a position slightly below and behind the bombers—a tactic that would minimize the gunners' ability to fire directly at him. He was now close enough to see the flash of gun muzzles as they opened fire.

Beside him, Iwashita was already lining up for his first pass, and he struck first. His Claude unleashed a burst of gunfire at the leftmost bomber and the tracers found their target, tearing into the enemy's fuselage. Smoke and flames erupted from one of the engines, and the plane began to drop away from the formation. The gunners, however, quickly retaliated, sending a hail of bullets in Iwashita's direction. He broke away sharply, climbing back toward the safety of Osaki's protective orbit.

Hideyoshi seized the opening and pushed his Claude forward, zeroing in on the rearmost plane. He could see the gunner at the tail, frantically swiveling his weapon toward him. Adjusting his angle of attack, Hideyoshi pressed the trigger.

The first burst missed, with the tracers falling harmlessly below the bomber's tail. Adjusting quickly, Hideyoshi fired again, this time striking the right-hand engine. A plume of flame billowed out, and the propeller stopped spinning. The bomber shuddered in midair, losing altitude as its pilot fought to stabilize it.

The tail gunner returned fire, and bullets zipped past Hideyoshi's cockpit. He gritted his teeth and pressed forward, firing another burst. The bullets shredded its rudder. The enemy plane lurched to one side, flames now engulfing its wing as the damaged engine burned. Hideyoshi pulled up sharply, climbing away from the falling wreckage as it disappeared into the haze below and hit the ground with a bright orange flash.

He glanced around the sky, searching for Iwashita or any signs of enemy reinforcements, and saw Osaki and the other Claudes in a steep dive. They downed two more of the bombers, and within moments the battle was over. The lead bomber, now smoking from its left engine, banked hard to the west, signaling retreat. The remaining aircraft followed.

With a sharp waggle of his wings, Osaki signaled for the squadron to regroup. One by one, the Claudes joined him as they took stock of their numbers. Hideyoshi was relieved to see that every member of the squadron had returned.

A few days later, the group was flying another fighter sweep. They had not encountered any enemy planes for some time now, and this time they were penetrating deeper into enemy territory, hoping to draw the Chinese into battle.

Suddenly, Osaki waggled his wings, and the entire formation followed his lead as they turned toward a cluster of specks in the distance. Their stubby angular profiles were unmistakable—it was a flight of American-made Curtiss Hawk 75M fighters, patrolling at a lower altitude and unaware of the Japanese formation sweeping in from above them.

"Engage!"

Osaki's quick hand signal sent the Claudes fanning out, each taking up a position to exploit the higher altitude and superior maneuverability of their planes. The Hawks were a serious opponent.

The fight unfolded quickly. Claudes twisted and turned in the skies, but the enemy pilots were experienced, and were diving and banking themselves to evade the faster Claudes. Amid the chaos, Hideyoshi spotted Osaki in a tight turn with an enemy Hawk glued to his tail, firing bursts of machine-gun fire that were coming dangerously close.

Instinct took over. Hideyoshi pushed hard on his stick, diving into a steep pursuit. The Hawk pilot, fixated on Osaki, didn't notice the Claude bearing down on him. It was a fatal mistake. Hideyoshi closed the gap, centered the Hawk in his sights, and pressed the trigger.

The enemy plane shuddered, black smoke pouring from its engine as it pitched downward, trailing fire. Osaki rolled away to safety, giving a quick, emphatic waggle of his wings in acknowledgment before rejoining the fray, targeting one of the Hawks still lurking at the edge of the battle. He fired in short, precise bursts, his tracers striking true. The enemy's wing buckled, and the plane spiraled downward.

Hideyoshi scanned the area, searching for more threats. It was then that he noticed something chilling—a Claude trailing black smoke, its movements sluggish.

It was Iwashita. Riddled with bullets, his plane was struggling to maintain altitude. Hideyoshi could only watch in horror as the damaged aircraft began a slow descent. The pilot was clearly attempting an emergency landing, but the harsh mountainous terrain below offered no clear space, and as the Claude disappeared into the hills, Hideyoshi felt a heavy knot in his stomach.

The order arrived unexpectedly one chilly morning: nine pilots, including Hideyoshi, were to transfer temporarily to the forward airfield at Danyang, near Nanking. "Pack light," Osaki instructed. "We leave at dawn tomorrow."

As they descended toward Danyang, the airfield was a sharp contrast to the well-maintained Koto. The grass airstrip here was uneven and lined with hastily constructed revetments made from tree trunks. A few tents dotted the perimeter. Trucks and men moved around between the aircraft that were already stationed there, a mix of reconnaissance planes and light bombers.

"Not exactly comfortable, is it?" Nakagawa quipped, jumping down from his plane and slinging his flight bag over his shoulder.

"Comfort isn't the priority here," Osaki replied curtly as he approached. "Stay focused. We're not here for rest and relaxation."

They were greeted by the airfield's commanding officer, a harried-looking Major named Suzuki who seemed perpetually caught between exhaustion and urgency. He gave a brief rundown of their assignment. The pilots from Koto would provide additional cover for bombing runs into Nanking and would fly sweeps to keep enemy fighters at bay. The pace, he warned, would be grueling.

Their quarters consisted of a few shared tents with thin mats laid on the dirt floors. Supplies were limited, and meals consisted mostly of rice and dried fish.

Despite the conditions, the men settled in quickly. By the second day, they were running orientation patrols over the surrounding area, familiarizing themselves with the terrain. Hideyoshi noted how close they were to the frontlines — artillery fire could be heard faintly in the distance, and troop trucks regularly rolled through the camp, coated in mud, either taking fresh troops to the fighting or bringing wounded troops back from it.

That evening, the pilots gathered around a makeshift heater, sharing cigarettes and stories to lighten the mood. Osaki maintained a watchful distance, occasionally chiming in with a dry comment but mostly observing.

Hideyoshi crouched close to the heater, rubbing his hands together to coax more warmth into his fingers. Beside him, Nakagawa sat cross-legged, chewing on a piece of dried fish with exaggerated effort.

"This place makes Koto look like a palace," he said through a mouthful of fish. "I didn't think it was possible to miss those flimsy cots back home."

Igarashi leaned back against a crate, smirking as he exhaled a plume of cigarette smoke. "You complain too much, Nakagawa. Be glad we have tents. I've heard some of the Army boys are sleeping in trenches not far from here."

"Trenches don't bother me," Nakagawa shot back. "But this—whatever this is they're feeding us—it tastes like they scooped it out of a muddy field."

"You're too soft," Igarashi said, chuckling. "A real pilot can eat anything and keep flying."

Osaki glanced over with a raised eyebrow. "A real pilot doesn't complain at all," he said evenly.

As the conversation lulled, Hideyoshi broke the silence. "Do you think this assignment will be different from Koto?"

Igarashi stubbed out his cigarette against the side of the heater. "Different? Definitely. We're right in the thick of it now. Every mission will feel like a coin toss—heads, you're fine; tails ..." He trailed off, letting the sentence hang ominously.

Nakagawa frowned. "You don't have to make it sound so grim."

"It's the truth," Igarashi replied with a shrug. "But don't worry, baby face. Osaki will keep us alive."

"Enough," Osaki said. He leaned forward. "We're here to do a job. Stay in formation, watch your wingmen, and listen to my orders. Do that, and you'll make it back."

By November 1937, after months of brutal and costly fighting, the Japanese Imperial Army had secured the port city of Shanghai. That gave them a strategic foothold for further operations along the Yangtze River, the vital artery that connected Shanghai to Nanking and the vast interior of China. With Shanghai under their control, Japanese forces could begin an advance up the Yangtze with the goal of capturing Nanking, the wartime capital of China.

Nanking (modern-day Nanjing) held immense symbolic and strategic importance. It was not only the seat of Chiang Kai-shek's Chinese government but also a significant cultural and economic hub. For the Japanese, its capture was seen as a critical step toward breaking Chinese resistance and forcing a swift conclusion to the war.

The United States, Britain, France, and other European nations were still officially neutral in the conflict, bound by treaties and reluctant to intervene in what they perceived as a regional war. However, their interests in China were far from minor. Nanking was home to large European and American expatriate communities, businesses, and missionary organizations, all of which now found themselves in the path of the advancing Japanese Army. Western diplomats watched the situation with growing alarm, particularly as stories of Japanese atrocities against civilians began to filter out.

As Japanese troops approached Nanking in early December 1937, the foreign community in the city scrambled to evacuate, and Western diplomats enacted plans to ensure the safe withdrawal of their citizens. Several gunboats from England and the United States were stationed on the Yangtze River near Nanking to protect these evacuation efforts. But the situation grew increasingly uncertain as the Japanese Army surrounded Nanking and began its final assault into the city.

Hideyoshi's patrol that morning had started as uneventfully as any other. The skies over Nanking were clear, but he could see that the Japanese grip on the city was tightening, with columns of smoke marking the path of their advance. He scanned the horizon continuously, alert for any sign of enemy activity.

As he approached the Yangtze River, a convoy of small ships could be seen in the waterway. They were refugee ships, taking civilians across the river and away from the city. One of them, he he had been told at the mission briefing, was the *Panay*, an American gunship. Her captain had already notified the Japanese government of her position.

Hideyoshi's attention was drawn not by the ship itself, however, but by the unmistakable silhouettes of the Japanese Yokosuka B4Y Type 96 bomber planes and Nakajima A4N Type 95 fighters that he could see moving down the river towards it. They were in an attack formation.

At first, Hideyoshi thought he must be mistaken. The *Panay* was a neutral ship, and its American flag was clearly displayed for all to see. Yet, as he watched in stunned amazement, the Japanese planes unleashed a wave of bombs and strafing runs on the tiny vessel. Explosions rocked the water, and clouds of smoke and fire began to engulf the ship.

"Fools," Hideyoshi muttered angrily to himself. "What are they doing?"

Without a radio in his Claude, he had no way to communicate with the attacking planes or warn them of their catastrophic mistake. But, desperate to act, he banked sharply and descended toward the melee. He approached one of the bomber planes, waggling his wings frantically as a signal to cease the attack. The pilot either didn't notice or deliberately ignored him, continuing its bombing run. Hideyoshi made another pass, this time directly in front of one of the Nakajima fighters, forcing it to break off its strafing run. He waggled his wings again, gesturing upward in a desperate plea for them to pull up and stop the assault.

But then one of the fighters, apparently taking him for an enemy plane, turned toward him and fired a burst from its machine guns, the rounds slicing the air dangerously close to his Claude. Hideyoshi instinctively pulled into a sharp climb and maneuvered away from the attack. Rolling out, he then banked to expose the bright red insignia markings on his own wings, signaling his identity as a fellow Japanese pilot. The Nakajima turned away.

The attacking planes, their mission seemingly complete, began to pull away, leaving behind a scene of devastation. Hideyoshi circled back, helplessly watching as the *Panay* burned, its crew scrambling into lifeboats to escape the inferno. His frustration and fury boiled over as he turned his plane back toward Danyang.

Upon landing, Hideyoshi wasted no time. He stormed into Major Suzuki's office, his flight suit still streaked with sweat. Suzuki looked up from his desk, surprised by Hideyoshi's abrupt entrance.

"Lieutenant Sugiyama, what is the meaning of this?"

Hideyoshi snapped to attention but couldn't suppress the urgency in his voice. "Sir, I must report that, during my patrol, I witnessed Japanese planes attacking an American ship on the Yangtze. It was the *Panay*. I could see her flag, clear as day. I tried to stop them, but they ignored me. One of them even fired at me!"

The commander's eyes narrowed. "Are you certain of what you saw?"

"Absolutely, sir," Hideyoshi replied firmly. "There is no mistake. Those were Yokosuka torpedo planes and Nakajima fighters, and they carried the Rising Sun insignia. And the American flag was unmistakable."

The room fell into a heavy silence as the commander absorbed the report. Finally, he leaned back in his chair. "This will be forwarded to higher command," he said gravely. "For now, you are dismissed."

That night, Hideyoshi sought out Osaki. The *Taicho* was seated by the stove, its weak flame flickering against the cold air. He glanced up as Hideyoshi approached, and gestured for him to sit.

"You're troubled," Osaki said, breaking the silence.

Hideyoshi hesitated, then nodded. "I can't stop thinking about it, Osaki-*taicho*. The *Panay*. Those were our planes. They attacked an American ship flying their flag. It doesn't make sense. Why would we provoke them?"

Osaki leaned back, his expression thoughtful. "War is full of things that don't make sense, Sugiyama. Sometimes, orders are given that we don't understand. And sometimes, mistakes are made."

"But this wasn't a mistake," Hideyoshi argued. "They could see the flag. I saw it! We all know what the consequences could be if we anger the Americans."

"You're not wrong." Osaki let out a sigh. "But it is not our place to question why. We're *samurai*, Hideyoshi. We carry out orders, whether we agree with them or not. It's the way of things."

Hideyoshi looked down, a puzzled expression on his face. "Does that mean we just accept it? That we look the other way when something like this happens?"

Osaki's gaze softened, but there was a weariness in his voice. "You're young. You still think war is about 'honor' and 'reason'. But war ... war devours everything. It is chaos dressed as order. If you dwell on the things that don't make sense, it will devour you too."

That night, Hideyoshi lay awake in his cot, staring at the wooden beams above him. For the first time since joining the *Soju Renshusei* program, he questioned the path that he had chosen.

Over the following days, news filtered in about Japan's official response to the incident. An apology had been issued to the Americans claiming the attack was an error, a regrettable accident of war. There was talk of reparations, promises to avoid such an incident in the future. The Americans accepted the apology, at least on the surface, but Hideyoshi could sense the deeper damage. Trust, between nations and between people, was not easily mended, and this breach would linger like a crack in a stone foundation.

As the fighting increased near Nanking, the entire 1st *Kokutai*, including the Danyang detachment, was transferred to the Daijahang airfield on the outskirts of the city. The new base had been hastily fortified to serve as a forward operations center for air operations over Nanking. It was rough, but it was a significant improvement over the spartan conditions at Danyang.

As Osaki's detachment landed at Daijahang, their gaze fell on a row of Claudes already parked at the airfield, bearing the familiar tail markings of their *kokutai*. "Looks like the rest of the unit beat us here," Osaki remarked, nodding toward a group of pilots gathered near a makeshift command tent.

Hideyoshi nodded. "It feels strange to be back with everyone. Danyang was quieter."

"Don't get used to being quiet. If anything, things will only get more intense here."

As they walked toward the command tent, the familiar faces of their comrades came into view. Nakagawa, with his perpetually boyish grin, was chatting animatedly with a pair of mechanics. Shigemitsu, their squadron's stoic veteran, stood nearby. A few faces were missing.

Osaki went off to report to the *kokutai's* commanding officer, Captain Igarishi. The captain broke into a brief smile and declared, "Ah, Osaki. Good to see you've made it in one piece. How was the transfer from Danyang?"

"Uneventful, sir," Osaki replied. "The planes performed well, and the crews are settling in."

"Good," Igarishi said, nodding. "You'll find things more organized here. The entire *kokutai* is together again, which means we'll be rotating missions more efficiently. But don't get too comfortable—enemy activity in the region is increasing. We'll need every man and machine at their best."

Over the next few hours, Hideyoshi and his comrades were assigned tents near the edge of the airfield, where they unpacked their gear and staked out sleeping spaces. The mess tent offered a hot meal—a rarity during their time at Danyang—and the mechanics quickly got to work ensuring that the Claudes were combat-ready. Daijahang was closer to the front lines, and the low rumble of artillery and the occasional glow of fires on the horizon served as constant reminders of the war's relentless advance.

That evening, the pilots gathered around a small campfire, sharing stories and catching up on all the events that had unfolded during their separation. Nakagawa was in fine form, regaling the group with exaggerated tales of his exploits. "I tell you, those Chinese gunners couldn't hit the broad side of a battleship," he declared, prompting a mix of laughter and skeptical groans.

As the fire burned low, Osaki addressed the group. "This airfield isn't just a base; it's a symbol of how far we've come and how much farther we have to go. We're here to support the army as they move deeper into enemy territory. Our missions will be critical in ensuring their success. So I expect everyone to do their duty to the best of their ability."

The rumors had begun to circulate almost immediately after the fall of Nanking. Pilots returning from reconnaissance missions whispered about columns of smoke rising from the city, about bodies seen floating in the Yangtze River. Ground crews spoke of soldiers bragging about "clearing operations" in the captured city. At first, Hideyoshi dismissed the stories as exaggerated or out-of-context fragments of Chinese propaganda. But as the days passed, the rumors became harder to ignore.

It was in the mess tent one evening, over bowls of rice and soup, that Hideyoshi overheard Shigemitsu confiding to another pilot. "I heard from an army liaison. They're rounding up anyone they suspect of being a guerrilla."

Osaki, seated across from them, shot a sharp glance at Shigemitsu. "Enough. We don't deal in hearsay. Focus on the missions."

But Hideyoshi couldn't shake the unease that settled in his gut. Days later, when he and Nakagawa were granted a rare day of leave, he suggested that they head into the city. "I want to see for myself," he said as they climbed into the back of an Army truck that was heading into Nanking. Nakagawa, usually cheerful and talkative, was uncharacteristically quiet.

The city they entered bore no resemblance to the bustling, vibrant capital it had been just weeks earlier. Nanking was now a landscape of ruin. Entire neighborhoods were reduced to rubble, the streets choked with dust, debris and the smell of smoke. Hideyoshi's stomach churned as the truck jolted over a pothole, the movement revealing a pile of bodies stacked haphazardly against a crumbled wall. Some were civilians, their hands bound, others were soldiers in ragged Chinese uniforms. Flies buzzed thick in the air.

The truck stopped near a makeshift Army checkpoint, and the two pilots got out, walking cautiously through the ruined streets. Japanese soldiers moved about in small groups, some looting shops, others corralling frightened civilians. Hideyoshi and Nakagawa kept to themselves, their Navy-issue flying uniforms drawing a few curious glances but no interference from the Army men.

They rounded a corner and froze. In an open square, a Japanese Army sergeant stood over a kneeling middle-aged Chinese man, a long *katana* in his hands. A small crowd of soldiers jeered and laughed as the sergeant screamed accusations of guerrilla activity, while the gaunt man pleaded in rapid, desperate Mandarin, words that Hideyoshi didn't understand but whose meaning was horribly clear.

"Stop him," Hideyoshi whispered, his voice barely audible. "We have to—"

"No," Nakagawa hissed, grabbing Hideyoshi's arm. "We can't do anything about it."

The sergeant raised his sword, and with a single fluid motion, brought it down. The Chinese man collapsed, lifeless. Hideyoshi felt his breath catch, his chest tightening. The soldiers cheered, one of them patting the sergeant on the back as though he had just scored a run in a baseball game.

Nakagawa turned away, his face pale, and Hideyoshi followed. They walked aimlessly through the streets, the impact of what they had seen pressing down on them like a physical force. They passed more evidence of the atrocities: a burnt-out schoolyard littered with corpses, a woman sobbing uncontrollably and clutching the body of a child as soldiers rummaged through the ruins of her home nearby.

The ride back to Daijahang was silent. Nakagawa stared blankly out the side of the truck, his jaw clenched, while Hideyoshi's hands were trembling. That night, as Hideyoshi lay in his cot, the images replayed endlessly in his mind. The laughter of the soldiers, the pleading of the man, the decapitated body collapsing to the ground.

The days following Hideyoshi's visit to Nanking passed in a blur of routine. He found escape in the structured rhythm of military life. Every morning began with the same drill: dawn briefings, equipment checks, engine startups, and the roar of the Claudes taking to the sky. It was a reprieve from the grim reality on the ground, but it also served as a reminder of his duty.

The concept of *gimu*, or "obligation", had been instilled in him since his youth. It was the cornerstone of Japanese identity, encompassing duty to one's family, one's community, and ultimately, to the Emperor. It was not a choice, but a fundamental part of existence—a moral imperative that demanded self-sacrifice and unwavering commitment. And, Hideyoshi knew, it included an unwavering commitment to his comrades in the squadron. No matter what he thought about the war, he had an obligation to his fellow pilots. He could not let them down. He had to perform his duty. It was a matter of *gimu*.

Over the next weeks, the missions came in rapid succession. Escorting bombers, strafing troop convoys, attacking supply depots, fighter sweeps—it all blurred together into a relentless cycle of violence. Each sortie added to Hideyoshi's experience and deepened his standing within the squadron. He was no longer "the new guy". Yet, with each mission, he felt the widening gap between the man he had been and the man he was becoming.

One evening, after a particularly tiring mission, Hideyoshi found himself alone by the airfield, gazing out at the dim silhouette of Nanking.

Nakagawa approached. He too had changed: his youthful exuberance was now dimmed by the constant grind of the war. "Hideyoshi," he said quietly, "do you ever wonder what all this is for?"

Hideyoshi hesitated, searching for an answer. "I wonder," he admitted. "But I also know we can't stop. We have to do what's asked of us. It's our place."

Nakagawa nodded, though his expression remained thoughtful. "I suppose so."

As they stood in silence, the distant hum of engines signaled another flight returning from a mission. There was one plane missing.

The relentless combat operations left the pilots hollow-eyed and weary, their laughter forced and their camaraderie tempered with the knowledge that any one of them could be gone in the next sortie. The constant strain of flying, fighting, and losing friends weighed heavily on everyone.

Hideyoshi sat in the briefing room, his gloves resting on his lap. Their latest orders were straightforward: a ground-attack on retreating Chinese troops who had set up defensive positions near a key supply route. It was another routine mission.

Osaki stood at the head of the group, his authoritative presence a rare island of calm. "Remember," he said, pointing at the map, "we strike hard and we get out quickly. Don't linger. Watch each other's six."

Over the target area, Hideyoshi followed Osaki's signal, diving low and unleashing his guns on a cluster of trucks. Tracers lit up the ground and explosions bloomed, sending men scattering. The Chinese soldiers fired futilely at the sky as Hideyoshi climbed to rejoin the *shotai*.

In the chaos, Hideyoshi almost missed the warning—a frantic waggle of Osaki's wings. Enemy planes. A flight of Chinese I-16s emerged from the haze, their guns blazing as they charged the Claudes. Hideyoshi twisted his plane into a tight turn, narrowly avoiding an enemy fighter on his tail. He dived sharply, pulling up just in time to see Nakagawa in trouble.

Nakagawa's Claude was trailing smoke, an I-16 glued doggedly to his tail. "Break! Break!" Hideyoshi shouted instinctively, though the uselessness of the words struck him immediately. Nakagawa couldn't hear him. Hideyoshi tried to maneuver closer, his guns spitting bursts of fire, but the I-16's pilot was skilled, evading his shots while continuing to hammer Nakagawa's plane. Then, with a shuddering explosion, Nakagawa's Claude disintegrated in midair. Pieces of the plane and its young pilot tumbled earthward.

The dogfight raged on for what felt like hours, though it was only minutes. By the time the Chinese planes broke off and retreated, another pilot, Mimura, was also gone—his Claude seen spiraling out of control into a hillside.

The surviving squadron members regrouped and limped back to Daijahang. Silence greeted them on the ground as they climbed out of their planes, their faces ashen. Shigemitsu slammed his cap onto a bench, his frustration and grief erupting in a sharp curse. Hideyoshi sat heavily on a crate, staring at the dirt beneath his boots.

That evening, Osaki gathered the remaining pilots around the makeshift heater in their barracks. "We have all seen what this war can do. It takes and takes, and it will not stop taking. But we are here, and we owe it to each other to keep fighting and staying alive. Nakagawa and Mimura, they did their duty. Let's honor them by ensuring we don't join them unnecessarily."

The war was grinding all of them down, piece by piece.

The end of December 1937 brought a biting chill to the airfield at Daijahang. The frost that coated the wings of their Claudes in the morning mirrored the somber mood of the squadron. Weeks of relentless missions, dwindling supplies, and the constant threat of death had taken their toll on them all.

Hideyoshi sat in the barracks, his fingers numb as he laced his boots, when an orderly stepped in.

"Sugiyama," the man said, "orders from headquarters."

Hideyoshi set his boots aside, opened the envelope, and unfolded the paper inside. His eyes scanned the *kanji*, and he froze when he reached the words: "Return to Japan ... Assigned as an Instructor ... "

The unexpected announcement stirred conflicting emotions in him. Relief was immediate—he would leave the chaos, the carnage, and the relentless war behind. He had had enough. But his relief was also spiked with guilt. His squadron mates would remain here, still flying, still fighting, still dying. It felt like abandonment, even if the orders weren't his choice.

The word spread quickly among the other pilots. By the time Hideyoshi emerged from the barracks, Shigemitsu and Osaki were waiting. Shigemitsu offered a grin. "So, you're heading back? Lucky bastard."

Osaki crossed his arms, his expression unreadable. "It's not luck. Everyone has their time." He glanced at Hideyoshi. "When do you leave?"

"Two days," Hideyoshi replied. The words felt heavy in his mouth.

Osaki nodded. "Make sure you pack everything. And don't leave any mess for us to clean up." His tone was dry, but the faint twitch of a smile softened the jab.

That evening, the pilots gathered around the fire, a ritual that had grown to define their long nights at Daijahang. Someone produced a small bottle of *sake*, a rare treat that had somehow survived all the supply shortages. Shigemitsu poured a modest cup for Hideyoshi and raised it.

"To Hideyoshi," Shigemitsu said. "May he enjoy the comforts of home while we're still here freezing our asses off."

The group laughed, though the humor was thin, stretched over the cracks of their shared exhaustion. Hideyoshi accepted the cup and raised it. "To all of you. May you stay warm and drink more *sake*."

The warmth of the *sake* did little to banish the cold.

The following morning, Hideyoshi packed his few belongings and climbed into the back of an Army truck, his bag slung over one shoulder. Shigemitsu and a few others stood by the barracks, watching him leave.

The truck jolted forward, taking him away from the cold, the war, and the memories.

As the ship carrying him back to Japan cut through the grey waters of the East China Sea, Hideyoshi stood on the deck, staring out at the horizon. The steady hum of the engines beneath his feet was the only sound, save for the occasional cry of a seabird circling overhead. His mind was far away, replaying the past three months in haunting detail.

He thought of the faces first—Nakagawa's boyish grin, Mimura's quiet resolve, Iwashita's sharp wit. And all the others. They had been with him at the beginning, their presence a comfort in the chaos. Now, their absence was a hollow ache.

His thoughts shifted to the missions. The exhilaration of his first sorties, the pride of earning a respected place in the squadron—all of it was now overshadowed by a lingering unease. Each victory, each bullet fired, had a cost. He had seen the wreckage left behind—the shattered planes, the burning villages, the lifeless bodies of soldiers and civilians alike. He clenched his fists around the railing, the cold metal biting into his palms.

Most of all, the horrors of Nanking would not leave him. He had seen it, the undeniable evidence of brutality and savagery. For the first time, he had questioned not just the wisdom of the war but the very nature of the men waging it. He had looked away then, unable to stop it. Now he wondered if that made him complicit.

He thought of his parents, of the life that eventually awaited him again back in Sakurada. Would they recognize him now, this hardened combat pilot with so many doubts burned into his soul?

As the Japanese coastline grew closer, Hideyoshi made a silent vow. He would continue to serve to the best of his ability—his *gimu* demanded that—but he would do so with his eyes open, questioning what he fought for and why. The war was far from over, and he knew he would return to the skies. But he also knew that the man he had become would never again see the world in the same way.

Chapter 7
Return to Japan (January 1938)

Hideyoshi reached the harbor at Yokosuka a few days later. He stepped off the deck and gazed at the familiar coastline. Japan. Home. Yet the sight of it seemed bittersweet. The landscape was the same as when he had left, but he was not.

After a short debriefing at Yokosuka, Hideyoshi received orders to report to Ise Airfield in Mie Prefecture. Located near his home village of Sakurada, the assignment seemed almost too fitting, as if fate had granted him a reprieve to reconnect with the world he had left behind. Throughout his deployment in China, Hideyoshi had written letters to his family with unwavering regularity, pouring his thoughts onto paper in the dim light of barracks in between missions. Yet, each letter had to be carefully crafted, stripped of anything that might invite the attention of the military censors. The brutalities of combat, the close calls he had been through, and his growing disillusionment with the war were topics he could not put into words. His correspondence instead became a series of assurances: his health was good, his spirits high, he was fulfilling his duty, and on every mission he was wearing the "thousand-stitch belt" that his mother had given him. Now, stationed just a short journey away from his family's village, Hideyoshi looked forward to seeing them in person.

Ise Airfield was a relatively new installation, its construction driven by the growing demands of Japan's escalating war in China. The base had been hastily built in the shadow of Mount Asama, chosen for its proximity to the port city of Tsu and its position along the eastern coastline of Ise Bay. Its creation was part of the Navy's broader effort to expand its pilot training programs in order to meet the rising need for trained aviators in the ongoing conflict.

The train ride to Ise carried him through familiar landscapes. Fields lay dormant under a thin frost, and the occasional red-tiled temple roof gleamed in the winter sunlight. It was the Japan he remembered, yet he felt like an outsider passing through it. Fellow passengers gave polite nods to the young man in uniform, but he sensed their curiosity, their unspoken questions about where he had been and what he had seen.

When the train finally pulled into the small station near Ise, Hideyoshi shouldered his bag and stepped into the crisp air. A Navy truck awaited him, with a young sailor in the driver's seat. "Sugiyama?" the sailor asked.

"That's right," Hideyoshi replied.

The ride to the airfield was brief. At the gate, he was met by an Ensign with a clipped mustache. "Sugiyama, reporting as ordered," Hideyoshi said, saluting and handing over his orders.

The officer returned the salute. "Welcome to Ise Airfield. Follow me."

The officer led him to a small administrative building where the airfield's commander, a stocky man in his forties, awaited him. He gestured for Hideyoshi to sit and opened a folder on his desk.

"You're being assigned here as an instructor for advanced fighter training. It's a critical role, and I expect you to apply the same discipline here that you have demonstrated in combat."

"Yes, sir," Hideyoshi replied.

"There's one more matter," the commander continued, sliding a sheet of paper across the desk. "As of today, you are promoted to Petty Officer. Congratulations."

Hideyoshi blinked, momentarily caught off guard. "Thank you, sir," he said, taking the document. The promotion was an unexpected honor.

The commander stood, signaling the end of the meeting. "You'll be shown to your quarters. Take the day to familiarize yourself with the base. Your duties begin tomorrow."

Life at Ise Airfield settled into a steady routine of training flights, classroom lectures, and evaluations. Hideyoshi found himself both teacher and role model, guiding a new generation of student pilots who were eager to prove their worth. For many cadets, he was an example of the combat experience they hoped to achieve. Yet, Hideyoshi quickly realized that molding these young men into capable pilots required more than technical instruction; it demanded patience, understanding, and the ability to lead by example.

One morning, a student misjudged a turn during a simulated dogfight and nearly collided with another Claude. Hideyoshi, flying as the instructor observer, intervened with a sharp roll and a warning signal. After the planes landed, Hideyoshi approached the shaken student.

"You were too fixated on your target," he explained. "In combat, you'll face enemies, friends, and the ground—all at the same time. Learn to see everything, not just the prey in front of you."

The cadet nodded, visibly chastised, and Hideyoshi took a moment to soften his tone. "We learn from our mistakes here where the stakes are lower, so we don't make them in combat. Take this as a lesson, not as a failure."

Hideyoshi's combat stories inevitably became the center of interest, and during downtime in the mess hall they peppered him with questions. Many were technical—how to outmaneuver an opponent, how to judge the enemy's intent—but others revealed the cadet's youthful curiosity about the realities of war.

One evening, a student approached him.

"Petty Officer Sugiyama," the young man began, his voice tentative, "did you ever feel afraid in combat?"

Hideyoshi regarded the cadet thoughtfully, his mind flashing back to dogfights over Nanking and the chaos of battle. "Every time," he admitted. "But fear is not the enemy. Let it sharpen your focus, not control you. The moment you think you're invincible, you'll make a mistake, and mistakes will kill."

On another occasion, during a training flight, Hideyoshi demonstrated some complex maneuvers with a level of precision that left the cadets in awe. He explained that such drills were not just about mastering the aircraft but about developing instincts that would take over in the heat of combat.

"If you hesitate up there," he said, pointing skyward, "you might not get a second chance. Practice until these moves become second nature."

Another cadet, a boisterous and overconfident young man, reminded him of Nakagawa, his energetic comrade from China. The student's bravado often masked his insecurities, and Hideyoshi worked to temper the boy's overconfidence without dampening his enthusiasm.

"You have talent," Hideyoshi told him after a particularly reckless maneuver during a training flight. "But talent without discipline is dangerous. You're part of a team here. Your actions affect everyone."

Once, a soft-spoken yet fiercely determined student asked Hideyoshi about his personal philosophy on flying.

"To know the aircraft is to know yourself," Hideyoshi replied, after some reflection. "Trust your machine, but also respect its limits. And never forget that you are its master, not its passenger."

Through these interactions, Hideyoshi found a renewed sense of purpose. Training cadets was vastly different from the adrenaline-fueled missions he had faced in China, but it was no less important. He took pride in shaping the future of Japan's naval air force.

After a few weeks, Hideyoshi was granted a leave, and he immediately jumped at the chance to visit his family in Sakurada. As the truck from the airbase rumbled down the dirt road lined with rice paddies and bamboo groves, the air smelled of the faint salt of Ise Bay and of freshly tilled earth, an aroma he had not realized he missed.

The truck stopped near Sakurada's Shinto temple, and Hideyoshi climbed down, his dress white naval uniform crisp and adorned with his new rank insignia. A cluster of villagers had already gathered, drawn by news of his arrival. Children scampered around, pointing excitedly, while older men and women stood with wide smiles.

"Hideyoshi!" his mother's voice rang out, and he turned to see her hurrying toward him. His father followed, his gait slower but his expression brimming with pride.

"Mother, Father," Hideyoshi greeted, bowing deeply.

Haruko embraced him before pulling back to examine his face. "You've grown thinner," she said, her brow creased with concern.

"It's the training," Hideyoshi replied with a smile. "They keep us busy."

Hideyuki clapped a hand on his shoulder. "It's good to see you, son. You've done us proud."

Hideyoshi looked around for a moment, then asked, "Where is Uncle Katsuro?"

Haruko hesitated. "Your uncle ... he left over a month ago," she said softly. "He joined the Patriotic Volunteer Corps." There was a hint of resignation in her voice. "You know how fervently he believes in the Empire's destiny. He said he wanted to devote himself fully to supporting our soldiers and their mission." She sighed, and the pain of her brother's departure was still evident on her face. "He's traveling to different towns, speaking at rallies and participating in patriotic events. They say veterans like him inspire the people with their stories, reminding them of Japan's strength and unity." She forced a smile and added, pensively, "I suppose he's finally found the cause he's been seeking."

Hideyoshi nodded slowly, picturing his uncle in his old Navy uniform, standing before a crowd with his commanding presence and his booming voice extolling the virtues of duty and sacrifice. Katsuro's deep-seated nationalism, like that of Japan itself, seemed to have taken on a life of its own.

As the family walked together toward their modest home, more villagers approached, each eager to greet him. Some bowed deeply, others offered small gifts—rice, dried fish, and even a bottle of *sake*. One of the village elders, a stooped man with a long beard, addressed him solemnly.

"You honor us with your bravery, Hideyoshi," he said. "Our village is proud to have one of its own serving the Emperor."

That evening, the village held a small celebration in his honor. Tables were set up in the central square, laden with simple but plentiful food. Lanterns hung from the eaves of nearby houses, casting a warm glow over the gathering. Children giggled as they chased one another, while the adults raised endless cups of *sake* in toasts to Hideyoshi's health and success.

As the evening wore on, Hideyoshi found himself seated among a group of people with his father beside him. They asked him about his time in China.

"I'm afraid I can't say much," Hideyoshi replied, aware of the military's strict censorship rules. "But our mission was successful."

One of the men nodded gravely. "We hear stories," he said. "The newspapers say Japan is bringing peace and order to China. Is that true?"

Hideyoshi hesitated. "It is what we are ordered to do," he said finally, in a careful tone.

Hideyuki, sensing the tension in his son's voice, changed the subject. "Hideyoshi, you'll stay the night, won't you?"

"I will," he said, his smile returning.

Later, as the celebration wound down and the villagers drifted back to their homes, Hideyoshi sat with his parents in the warmth of their *hibachi*. Haruko placed a tray of tea before him and sat down, her hands folded in her lap.

"You've seen much, haven't you?" she asked softly.

Hideyoshi looked into the flickering coals, his expression unreadable. "Yes," he admitted. "More than I ever expected."

Hideyuki leaned forward. "War changes a man, Hideyoshi. But never forget where you come from. This village, this family, we are always here for you."

The next morning, as he prepared to return to the airbase, the villagers gathered once more to bid him farewell. Haruko handed him a bundle wrapped in cloth—homemade rice balls and bean cakes for the journey.

"Take care, Hideyoshi," she said, her voice thick with emotion.

"I will," he promised, bowing deeply. "Thank you for everything."

When Hideyoshi returned to the village for his next visit, it was late spring and the air seemed lighter, but the welcome was just as warm. The villagers had arranged another small gathering at the shrine, not as elaborate as the first but still lively. Hideyoshi arrived to find familiar faces and a few unfamiliar ones, among them a striking young woman who was speaking to Haruko, her posture graceful and her *kimono* a soft lavender hue that complemented her delicate features.

His mother noticed his gaze and waved him over. "Hideyoshi, come meet Aiko Yoshino. She is visiting from Tsu."

Aiko turned as he approached, her dark eyes meeting his with a quiet confidence. She bowed politely, and he returned the gesture, noting the subtle curve of a smile on her lips.

"It's a pleasure to meet you," Hideyoshi said, keeping his voice steady.

"And you as well, Petty Officer Sugiyama," she replied. Her tone was politely formal but carried an inviting warmth that intrigued him.

They soon found themselves walking together along the sea cliffs at the edge of the village. The villagers milled about, allowing Hideyoshi and Aiko to converse without interruption.

"Your mother mentioned you've recently returned from China," Aiko said, glancing at him. "It must have been difficult."

Hideyoshi hesitated, as he always did whenever the topic came up. "It was challenging," he admitted. "But I'm grateful to be home, even if only for a short time."

Aiko nodded, her expression thoughtful. "My brother serves in the Army in Korea," she said. "He writes to us, but the letters sound guarded. I wonder what he's truly experiencing."

Hideyoshi looked at her, sensing a depth of understanding that few others shared. "The letters are often that way," he said. "It's hard to put certain things into words, even if we were allowed to."

They walked in silence for a moment, the conversation hanging between them. Then Aiko changed the subject, her face brightening as she turned to him. "Your village is beautiful. It must be a comfort to return here."

"It is," Hideyoshi said with a smile. "The people, the land—it reminds me of what we fight for, though sometimes the reasons seem far away."

They stopped near a small bridge that crossed a narrow stream. The water flowed quietly down to the sea, and the trees overhead cast dappled shadows on the path. Aiko leaned on the railing, her hands clasped loosely.

"You're different from what I expected," she said suddenly, her gaze fixed on the stream.

Hideyoshi raised an eyebrow and looked at her. "Oh? And what did you expect?"

She laughed softly. "I'm not sure. Perhaps someone more ... boastful. More consumed by the stories of war."

"I've seen enough of war," Hideyoshi replied, his voice quieter now. "It's not something to boast about."

Aiko turned to face him. "I think that's why I find you interesting, Hideyoshi-*san*."

The use of his first name surprised him, but he didn't object. Instead, he felt a warmth in her words that reached past the armor that he had built around himself.

Before long, the sun dipped lower in the sky, and the sounds of the village began to call them back. As they walked, Hideyoshi found himself constantly glancing at Aiko, noting the way she carried herself with an air of elegance and strength.

At the gathering that evening, they sat together, talking more about their families, their lives, and their hopes. The villagers noticed and gave them space, their quiet smiles speaking volumes.

When it was time for Aiko to leave for Tsu the next morning, she bowed to Hideyoshi once more. "It was a pleasure meeting you," she said. "Perhaps we'll meet again."

"I hope so," Hideyoshi replied.

As she walked away, he found himself watching her go, and a feeling he hadn't expected was stirring within him.

Over the next few months, Hideyoshi and Aiko's paths continued to cross. Whenever his duties allowed, Hideyoshi made the journey from Ise Airfield back to his village, and on most visits, Aiko was there. Sometimes she stayed with her aunt in the village; other times, they would meet in Tsu, the bustling city where she lived with her father.

Their time together was never hurried. They walked along the village paths, sat by the stream where they had first spoken, and shared quiet moments under the ancient trees that dotted the countryside. In Tsu, Aiko introduced Hideyoshi to her favorite places: a quaint teahouse tucked away in a side street, a bustling market where the aroma of fresh seafood mingled with the scent of spices, and a small park where cherry blossoms would soon be blooming.

One late afternoon in the village, Aiko brought a small picnic basket to their meeting spot by the stream. "I thought you might like something homemade," she said with a smile as she set out the carefully wrapped sweet *mochi* bean paste treats.

Hideyoshi sat cross-legged on the grass, watching her unpack. "This looks wonderful," he said. "You didn't have to go to so much trouble."

"It's no trouble at all," she replied. "Besides, I wanted to repay you for all the stories you've shared."

As they ate, the conversation drifted from the mundane to the profound. Aiko had a way of asking questions that made Hideyoshi think—about his time in China, about his hopes for the future, and about the life he envisioned beyond the war.

"What do you want to do when all this is over?" she had asked one day, her voice gentle but insistent.

Hideyoshi hesitated, his gaze fixed on the horizon. "I've never thought much about it," he admitted. "It feels so distant. Unreal. And I'm a military man. We all know what could happen."

Aiko studied him, her dark eyes searching. "You should think about your future," she said softly. "The war won't last forever."

Her words stayed with him, lingering even after he had returned to the air base.

Their bond deepened with each meeting. Hideyoshi found himself looking forward to their conversations, to the sound of her laughter and the way she seemed to see right through the walls he still put up around himself.

One evening, as they walked along the beach near Tsu, the setting sun painted the sky red, and they stopped to watch the waves lap at the shore.

"Aiko," Hideyoshi began, his voice uncharacteristically hesitant, "I wanted to thank you."

She looked up at him, puzzled. "For what?"

"For being here," he said. "For reminding me that there's more to life than duty and war."

Aiko smiled, a soft, knowing smile. "You're welcome, Hideyoshi. But I think you already knew that. You just needed someone to remind you."

As the weeks turned into months, their budding relationship became the worst-kept secret in the village. The women whispered approvingly, and Haruko couldn't hide her delight. "She's a good match for you," she said one evening as Hideyoshi sat in the tiny garden. "Strong, thoughtful, and kind."

He didn't reply. He had always been pragmatic, focused on the demands of the present. Yet with Aiko, he found himself thinking about a future—a future where the war was over, and the life he had fought to protect could finally be lived.

The next time he visited Tsu, he carried with him a small token: a simple silver hairpin shaped like a *sakura* blossom. When he gave it to Aiko, she blushed as her fingers traced the delicate design.

"It's beautiful," she said, her voice barely above a whisper.

"Not as beautiful as you," Hideyoshi replied, his usual reserve softened by the moment.

They stood there for a long time, the noise of the city fading into the background. In that moment, neither thought of the war, of duty, or of the uncertainties that lay ahead. For now, there was only the promise of what might be.

As he approached his family's home, Hideyoshi nervously fingered the gift-wrapped parcel in his hands—a selection of fine tea leaves he'd picked up in Ise. His heart raced with anticipation.

Haruko knelt outside, gently brushing debris from the veranda. She looked up at the sound of her son's approach and smiled warmly. "Hideyoshi, you're early today. It's good to see you."

"I thought I'd make the most of my leave," he replied, bowing and handing her the parcel. She unwrapped it with care.

"Such a thoughtful son," she said, beckoning him inside. "Your father's been fixing his nets. He'll be happy to see you."

Inside, Hideyuki sat near the *hibachi*, a weaving shuttle in hand as he mended a torn fishing net. He looked up as Hideyoshi entered and gave a slight nod. "You're here earlier than expected. Good. Sit."

Hideyoshi knelt formally on the *tatami* mat, his hands resting stiffly on his knees. He glanced at Haruko, who had settled beside him, and then turned his attention to his father.

"Father, Mother," he said, his voice steady, "I have something important to discuss."

Hideyuki paused his work, setting the net aside. Haruko tilted her head, her expression bearing a knowing smile.

"I've been spending time with Aiko Yoshino," Hideyoshi continued. "We've grown close, and I have come to care for her deeply." He took a deep breath. "I wish to marry her, with your blessing."

Haruko's eyes sparkled with emotion, though she remained composed. "Aiko is a lovely girl," she said softly. "I could see the way you two looked at each other when you first met. I had a feeling this day might come."

Hideyuki leaned back as he studied his son. "You've thought this through?"

"I have," Hideyoshi said firmly. "Aiko understands the demands of my career, and I am confident that we can build a life together despite them. She is kind, intelligent, and supportive. I believe she will be a strong partner."

Hideyuki nodded slowly, his expression thoughtful. "Marriage is a union of families as much as individuals. Have you spoken to her parents?"

"Not yet," Hideyoshi admitted. "I wanted to seek your approval first. If you consent, I plan to visit her family to formally ask for their blessing."

Haruko reached out, placing a hand on Hideyoshi's arm. "You have our support, my son. Aiko will make a fine wife, and I'm sure her family will welcome you."

There was a hint of pride in Hideyuki's eyes. "You've grown into a responsible man," he said. "You have our blessing."

Relief and gratitude swept through Hideyoshi, and he bowed deeply. "Thank you, Father. Thank you, Mother."

As Haruko rose to prepare tea, Hideyuki resumed repairing his net, his movements deliberate. "When the time comes to meet her family, we'll stand by you," he said. "But remember, this is only the beginning. Marriage is not just a commitment to Aiko, but to the path we all walk together."

"I understand," Hideyoshi replied.

A few days later, Hideyoshi was even more nervous as he approached the Yoshino family home in Tsu. His naval uniform was impeccably pressed, every button gleaming.

When Aiko opened the sliding door, her smile eased some of his nerves. "Come in," she said, stepping aside to let him enter. The interior of the house was modest but tidy, with the fragrance of green tea wafting from the kitchen. Aiko's mother, Emiko, appeared in the doorway to greet him. She was a petite woman with a kind but penetrating gaze, dressed in an elegant *kimono*.

"Welcome, Sugiyama-*san*," she said, bowing deeply.

"Thank you for having me, Yoshino-*san*," Hideyoshi replied, bowing in return.

Emiko led them to the small garden, where a low table was set with tea and a plate of neatly arranged sweets. As they sat, Aiko's younger sister Michiko, a girl of about twelve, peeked shyly around the corner. When their eyes met, she giggled and darted out of sight, leaving Aiko shaking her head with an affectionate smile.

"Please excuse my younger daughter, Sugiyama-*san*," Emiko said, pouring tea with practiced grace. "She's curious, but a bit timid."

Hideyoshi smiled. "It's quite all right. I was much the same at her age."

Just then, Aiko's father, Hiroshi, entered the room. He was a tall, broad-shouldered man with strict eyes that softened only slightly when he acknowledged Hideyoshi with a short nod. Hideyoshi bowed deeply.

"Father," Aiko said, rising to greet him, "this is Hideyoshi Sugiyama, whom I've told you about."

Hiroshi studied Hideyoshi for a long moment before sitting across from him. "You are a pilot, I hear."

"Yes, Yoshino-*san*," Hideyoshi replied. "I've served with the Imperial Navy for several years now. I recently returned from operations in China."

Hiroshi nodded, his expression unreadable. "Military service is an honorable path. My own father served in the last war."

Emiko interjected to lighten the mood. "Aiko tells me you grew up near Sakurada village. It is beautiful there."

"Yes," Hideyoshi said, seizing the opportunity. "It's a quiet place. My parents still live there."

As they continued to talk, Hideyoshi answered Hiroshi's probing questions about his career, his family, and his intentions in life. He was keenly aware that he was being auditioned and evaluated as a suitable marriage partner for Aiko.

After what felt like an eternity, Hiroshi leaned back slightly and sipped his tea. Though his expression remained reserved, there was a hint of approval in his eyes. "You speak well, Sugiyama-*san*," he said finally. "And it seems you've been raised with proper values."

Hideyoshi bowed politely. "Thank you, Yoshino-*san*. My parents have taught me the importance of honor and respect."

The visit ended on a cordial note, with Emiko presenting Hideyoshi with a small package of sweets for his journey back.

As he and Aiko stepped out into the fading light of the evening, he released a breath he hadn't realized he'd been holding.

"That went smoothly," Aiko said, glancing at him with a teasing smile.

Hideyoshi laughed softly. "I think your father was sizing me up for a *katana* duel."

"He's just protective," she replied. "But I think he liked you."

The formal meeting between the Sugiyama and Yoshino families was set for an early spring afternoon, held at a neutral location—a tea house in Tsu that offered privacy and an air of formality. The arrangements had been carefully made, with both families agreeing on a time and place that would allow them to evaluate each other without the pressures of being hosts or guests.

Hideyoshi arrived with his parents well ahead of time. His father, dressed in a subdued traditional *haori* and *hakama*, carried himself with the quiet dignity of a man who had worked hard all his life. Haruko, in a *kimono* patterned with subtle cherry blossoms, exuded her usual warmth and composure.

The Yoshino family arrived shortly after. Hiroshi was also in traditional attire. Emiko, with her characteristic grace, carried a small gift wrapped in *furoshiki* cloth—a gesture of goodwill. Aiko walked behind them with her younger sister Michiko, who clung shyly to her older sister's side.

After formal bows and greetings, the two families were seated around a low table. Tea was served by the attendants, and pleasantries were exchanged. Haruko spoke first, offering gratitude for the Yoshino house's hospitality toward her son during his visits to Tsu.

"It's been our pleasure," Emiko replied with a smile. "Aiko has spoken highly of him. We are grateful for the kindness he has shown her."

Hiroshi, ever direct, turned his attention to Hideyuki. "Sugiyama-*san*, your son's service to the nation is commendable. My family respects his sacrifices and the honor he has brought to your name."

Hideyuki bowed his head. "Thank you, Yoshino-*san*. It has not been an easy road, but Hideyoshi has proven himself capable and dutiful."

The conversation shifted to family histories, shared values, and expectations. Haruko spoke fondly of their life in Sakurada, of tending the fishing boat and upholding traditions. Emiko, in turn, described the Yoshino family's roots in Tsu and Hiroshi's work as a merchant, emphasizing their commitment to discipline and hard work.

Throughout the discussion, Aiko and Hideyoshi sat quietly, occasionally exchanging glances but leaving the talking to their elders. They knew this was a delicate dance. While both families knew of their affection for each other, marriage was much more than a love match—it was a social contract. Many Japanese marriages were still arranged, set up by a neutral go-between who negotiated things much like a business merger. Though Hideyoshi and Aiko clearly loved each other, there were many other considerations which had to be accounted for.

Hiroshi eventually addressed Hideyoshi directly. "Sugiyama-*san*, you've made a name for yourself as a pilot. The war in China must have demanded much of you."

"It has, Yoshino-*san*," Hideyoshi replied. "But I have been fortunate to return home and to find someone who has brought me peace amid the chaos." His gaze briefly flicked to Aiko, whose cheeks flushed at the compliment.

Hiroshi's expression softened, though his voice remained measured. "It is clear that my daughter respects you. That speaks to your character."

After what felt like days but was only a single afternoon, the meeting concluded. Haruko presented the Yoshino family with a small lacquered box containing tea leaves, a gesture of mutual respect. Hiroshi accepted it with a nod, signaling his approval.

As the families departed, Aiko and Hideyoshi lingered behind for a moment, watching their parents exchange parting words.

"I think that went well," Aiko said, her voice tinged with relief.

Hideyoshi smiled. "Let's hope it's the beginning of something good."

The engagement ceremony, known as *yuinou*, was a deeply significant moment for both the Sugiyama and Yoshino families. It symbolized not only the union of Hideyoshi and Aiko but also the merging of their family futures. The ceremony was held in the Yoshino family home in Tsu.

In preparation for the event, Haruko carefully oversaw the selection of the gifts from the Sugiyama family. Each item was chosen with great care, as the symbolism behind these offerings carried profound meaning. She enlisted the help of neighbors in Sakurada to prepare everything to perfection. The gifts included a bundle of dried kelp for longevity, a pair of dried cuttlefish to symbolize fertility, and a bolt of pristine white linen, representing purity and a fresh start for the couple.

On the day of the ceremony, Hideyuki carried the gift tray, wrapped in an elegant silk cloth, as they entered the Yoshino home. The Yoshino family had prepared a low table decorated with seasonal flowers. Aiko's father Hiroshi sat at the head of the table, with Emiko and Michiko beside him. Aiko knelt respectfully on the *tatami* mat, her hands folded gracefully in her lap.

Hideyoshi and his parents knelt opposite them, bowing deeply as they presented the gifts. "Please accept these tokens of our respect and commitment," Hideyuki said solemnly.

Hiroshi leaned forward, carefully unwrapping the silk cloth to reveal the gifts. Each item was examined with a slow, deliberate nod, finally concluding with, "These are thoughtful and generous. We are honored to accept them and welcome your son into our family."

Hideyoshi glanced at Aiko, who lowered her eyes demurely but couldn't hide the small smile that played on her lips. The union was now publicly acknowledged and accepted by both families.

As the formalities concluded, the Yoshino family presented their own reciprocal gifts: a beautiful lacquered box containing fine local tea and a small bag of polished rice. This gesture symbolized their gratitude and blessings for the marriage. Hideyuki accepted it graciously, bowing deeply.

With the formalities complete, the mood lightened. Tea was served, and the conversation turned to plans for the wedding itself.

Michiko, finally relaxing, peppered Hideyoshi with questions about his life as a pilot, while Emiko and Haruko discussed wedding arrangements. Hiroshi, ever formal, inquired about Hideyoshi's schedule and how the upcoming nuptials might fit around his duties at Ise Airfield.

The next step in Hideyoshi and Aiko's journey to marriage took them to the Shinto shrine in Sakurada. Nestled among ancient cedar trees at the edge of the village, it was here that Hideyuki and Haruko had themselves been married decades earlier.

The families gathered at the shrine dressed in traditional attire, and Hideyoshi and Aiko approached the priest, an elfin man in his sixties named Matsukawa. After the customary bows and offerings at the shrine's altar—a small dish of rice, a sprig of *sakaki* leaves, and a few coins— he led them into the adjoining consultation room and knelt behind a low wooden table, a collection of scrolls and texts spread before him.

"The fortunes of the heavens guide us," he began solemnly, "but they also require respect and understanding. Let us seek clarity for this union."

The priest began by asking for the dates and times of Hideyoshi and Aiko's births and recorded the information on a parchment, softly chanting brief prayers to the *kami* as he worked.

He then consulted an *omikuji*, a sacred lot-drawing ritual, to foretell the future fortunes of the couple. From a lacquered box filled with papers, he drew a single slip inscribed with delicate calligraphy. As he read it, his face remained neutral, but he nodded approvingly.

"This is a favorable match," he announced. "The union of Sugiyama and Yoshino is blessed with harmony and mutual respect. There will be challenges, as in all paths, but the *kami* smile upon this marriage."

Relieved looks spread across the faces of both families, and Hideyoshi felt a wave of reassurance. He had faced countless challenges as a pilot, but navigating the traditions and expectations of marriage had been a different sort of test for him. Aiko, kneeling beside him, seemed to be more comfortable with it all.

Next, Matsukawa calculated an auspicious date for the wedding, based upon the couple's birthdates and the lunar calendar. His fingers traced patterns on a chart, and he paused several times to consult his scrolls. After a few moments, he looked up.

"The second day of the sixth month," he said. "It is a *taian* day, the most fortunate of all. The blessings will be strong, and the ceremony will proceed smoothly."

The families exchanged nods of agreement. It was a good date, far enough away to allow time for preparations but not so distant as to prolong the wait.

Before concluding, Matsukawa offered each family a protective talisman, inscribed with prayers for the couple's health, happiness, and prosperity. These small, ornately decorated amulets would be kept in their respective homes as symbols of the blessings which had been invoked that day.

As they departed the shrine, the families lingered briefly on the steps, taking in the serene surroundings. Michiko, always curious, asked Matsukawa about the significance of the *omikuji*. The priest chuckled softly and explained, "It is not merely a prediction but a reflection of your energy and intentions. When a couple is as committed as these two, the *kami* often respond favorably."

Later, as Hideyoshi and Aiko walked back to her family's home, he glanced at her and said, "I didn't realize how nervous I was until now."

Aiko took his hand and smiled.

In March 1938, under a cloudless sky that promised blessings for the future, Hideyoshi and Aiko were married in a traditional Shinto ceremony at the shrine in Sakurada. The event was steeped in centuries-old customs that bound them not only to each other but also to their families and the divine spirits.

The morning began with a procession from the Sugiyama home to the shrine. Aiko, her white silk *kimono* decorated with intricate embroidery of cranes, symbols of longevity and fidelity, was carried in a *jinrikisha*. Her head was adorned with a traditional *tsunokakushi*, a white hood that symbolized her humility and her readiness to enter her husband's family.

Hideyoshi, in his Navy dress whites, walked at the front of the procession with his parents. Behind him, Aiko's family followed in equally formal attire. Villagers lined the streets, bowing respectfully and offering quiet congratulations as the couple passed.

The shrine had been meticulously prepared for the occasion. The air was filled with the scent of incense and cedar, and the sacred space was adorned with white paper streamers and evergreen branches, symbols of purity and renewal. Matsukawa awaited them, dressed in his ceremonial robes.

The ceremony began with a purification ritual. The priest waved a *haraigushi*, a wand with paper streamers, over the couple, chanting prayers to cleanse them of impurities and prepare them for their new life together.

Next came the prayers to the *kami*, invoking their blessings for the couple's union. Matsukawa led the families in bowing and clapping in unison, a gesture meant to call the attention of the divine spirits.

Then, Hideyoshi and Aiko stepped forward for the *san-san-kudo* ritual, the heart of the Shinto wedding.

Three small cups of *sake* were placed before them, each representing heaven, earth, and humanity. They alternated sips from each cup, three times each, in a precise and deliberate manner. The act symbolized their union, not only with each other but also with the spiritual world.

Once the ritual was complete, Aiko's white kimono was exchanged for a richly colored *uchikake*, a formal robe embroidered with vibrant red and gold motifs. This change marked her transition from a maiden of her family to a wife of the Sugiyama household. As she stood beside Hideyoshi, the transformation was both literal and symbolic, capturing the essence of their new life together.

The priest offered final prayers and presented them with an *omamori* talisman to protect their marriage. The new couple accepted it with a deep bow.

The post-ceremony banquet, or *kekkon hiroen*, took place in the largest hall of Sakurada's inn. The room was transformed for the occasion, its *tatami* mats freshly replaced, walls decorated with banners of good fortune, and long, low tables laden with a feast.

As the newlyweds entered the hall, everyone rose to their feet, bowing deeply in respect. Aiko walked gracefully beside Hideyoshi, her colorful *uchikake* robe flowing behind her. They knelt at the head of the room, bowing deeply to the assembled guests in a gesture of humility and gratitude.

Hideyuki rose to give the opening toast. His voice, usually quiet and measured, now carried a tone of pride. "Today, we celebrate not only the union of two wonderful young people but also the joining of two families. Hideyoshi, we are proud of the man you have become, and Aiko, we are grateful to welcome you into our family. May your journey together be filled with harmony and happiness."

The guests clapped enthusiastically as *sake* was poured into tiny porcelain cups and passed around. Everyone raised their glasses in unison, shouting "*Kampai!*" before taking the first sip.

The meal began in earnest. There was grilled sea bream, a traditional symbol of good fortune; bowls of steaming rice topped with sesame seeds and pickled plums; and an assortment of vegetables arranged artfully on lacquered trays. Sweet *mochi* rice cakes, shaped into cranes and turtles to represent longevity and fidelity, were served as dessert.

Midway through the feast, Hideyoshi's commanding officer from Ise Airfield stood to deliver a speech. "Petty Officer Sugiyama," he declared with a mix of formality and warmth, "is a man of great courage and even greater honor. His service to our nation has brought pride to his family, and now he embarks on a new mission —one of partnership and family. Aiko, I have no doubt you will be the perfect partner for him."

The applause that followed was boisterous, punctuated by laughter and cheers from Hideyoshi's fellow instructors, who had traveled from Ise to attend. One of them, a bold and mischievous pilot named Ishido, couldn't resist adding his own quip. "Here's to the only man I know who can land a combat fighter and a bride in the same year!" The room erupted in laughter, even as Hideyoshi shook his head with a sheepish smile.

Traditional entertainment followed the speeches. Michiko performed a *mai ogi* dance, her movements graceful and deliberate, and the room fell silent in admiration. A musician from Tsu played the *shamisen*, her fingers plucking out melodies that spoke of history and home.

Toward the end of the evening, the couple performed a traditional gesture of gratitude. They knelt together, first facing Aiko's parents and then Hideyoshi's, bowing deeply to thank them for their love and guidance.

Married life for Hideyoshi and Aiko began in a modest home near the heart of Tsu. The house, a small wooden structure with a tiled roof, had been arranged by Hideyoshi's father as a wedding gift. It stood on a quiet street lined with cherry trees. Though humble in size, the house was filled with warmth, and it soon reflected Aiko's meticulous touch and Hideyoshi's appreciation for simplicity.

Their days quickly settled into a routine. In the mornings, Hideyoshi would don his uniform and bicycle to Ise Airfield, a brisk ride that cleared his mind before the day's duties began. Aiko, meanwhile, busied herself with setting up their home. She arranged *tatami* mats in the living area, embroidered cushions for their low wooden table, and filled the kitchen with the scent of freshly brewed tea and simmering *miso*.

Evenings were their time. Hideyoshi would return from the airfield tired but eager to recount his day. Aiko listened attentively, her questions thoughtful, though she worried about the toll his work took on him. She understood the weight of his responsibilities and admired his dedication, even as she wished for more peaceful times. After dinner, they often walked through the streets of Tsu, enjoying the cool night air and the soft glow of lanterns from nearby homes. Their conversations were easy and full of laughter.

Their neighbors quickly took notice of the young couple. Hideyoshi's reputation as a combat pilot preceded him, and his presence in Tsu was a source of pride for many. Aiko, with her graceful demeanor and genuine kindness, was equally well-liked. Women from the neighborhood often stopped by with small gifts, from freshly caught fish to handmade sweets, a gesture of goodwill that Aiko always accepted with heartfelt gratitude.

One afternoon, as they walked through the bustling market, Aiko paused at a stall selling potted plants. She picked up a tiny *bonsai* tree, its delicate branches expertly pruned. "For our home," she said with a smile, cradling it carefully. Hideyoshi nodded, amused by how much thought she gave to even the smallest details. Later, the *bonsai* found a place in their tiny garden, becoming a quiet symbol of their growing life together.

Despite their happiness, there were moments of adjustment. Hideyoshi's military discipline sometimes clashed with Aiko's more spontaneous nature. Early on, he had voiced frustration when she spent hours chatting with a neighbor instead of completing her errands. Aiko, in turn, gently reminded him that not every aspect of life needed to be planned with military precision. These differences, though minor, taught them the importance of patience and understanding.

One evening, as they shared a cup of tea, Aiko mentioned her wish to start a family. "I'd like to hear the sound of children's laughter in our home," she said quietly. Hideyoshi smiled, setting his cup down. "Someday," he said. The thought of raising a family while Japan's future seemed so precarious weighed heavily on him, but he didn't voice his concerns. For now, he chose to focus on the present.

Their life in Tsu was not without challenges. The growing tensions in the world were impossible to ignore. Newspapers spoke of Japan's continued campaigns in China, and Hideyoshi deduced that things were not going well there. Whispers of strained relations with the Western powers reached even their quiet corner of the country. Hideyoshi, a military man, knew what this could lead to. He carried these worries silently, though, and was always outwardly calm—though inside he was unsure of what the future might demand of him. And, anyway, there was nothing he could do about it. The Japanese had a saying, *Shigata ga nai*. "It cannot be helped."

Yet, even in the face of these uncertainties, Hideyoshi and Aiko found solace in each other. On Sundays, when Hideyoshi had leave, they often visited his parents in Sakurada or walked to the nearby shores of Ise Bay to watch the waves lap gently on the sand. It was during these moments, away from duty and the world's troubles, that Hideyoshi felt most at peace.

The years 1939 and 1940 marked a turning point in the international political landscape, with growing tensions that increasingly shaped Japan's military ambitions.

Japan's war in China, which had begun with overwhelming public support, was proving far more protracted and costly than anyone had expected. Despite the Imperial Army's successes in seizing major cities and ports, the Chinese forces continued to resist fiercely. The United States, though not directly involved in the conflict, provided military equipment to the Chinese and became a harsh vocal opponent of Japan's expansionist actions.

At the same time, Japan sought to bolster its international position through diplomacy. In 1940, the signing of the Tripartite Pact solidified an alliance with Germany and Italy, creating the "Axis Powers". Official statements in Tokyo celebrated the pact as a triumph of shared values and mutual defense, but privately, many officers, including Hideyoshi, questioned its practicality. Germany's military successes in Europe, while impressive, did nothing to help Japan's immediate issues in Asia, and Italy's performance in Africa was far less effective.

Meanwhile, tensions with the United States continued to grow. The Lend-Lease Act, passed in March 1941, allowed America to provide massive military aid to China. Shipments of frontline American fighter planes including the Curtiss P-40 Warhawk, and the recruitment of American volunteer pilots to train and fight alongside the Chinese—known as the American Volunteer Group (AVG) or "Flying Tigers"—added new difficulties to Japan's challenges in the air war. Hideyoshi had seen firsthand how difficult the air campaigns in China were even against the now-obsolete I-16s. And the possibility of provoking a confrontation with the United States—the most powerful economy in the world—troubled him greatly.

The military briefings at Ise Airfield grew more and more strident. Officers were instructed to prepare for the possibility of an expanded conflict beyond China. Hideyoshi recognized that Japan's aggressive policies were forcing it into a corner. The need for resources, particularly oil, was driving increasingly reckless talk from Tokyo, and the possibility of war with the Western powers felt less like an abstract threat and more like an inevitability.

The development of the Mitsubishi A6M Zero, an aircraft that would come to dominate the skies in the early years of the Pacific War, was a product of this growing military necessity. By the late 1930s, the Navy had recognized the need for a new generation of fighters to replace the Claude, which had proven itself in China but was now already beginning to show its age.

In 1937, the Navy issued specifications for the new fighter, known as the 12-*Shi* program. The requirements were ambitious, even audacious—designed not only for short-range land combat in China, but also for long-range island warfare over the vast expanse of the Pacific Ocean. The new aircraft had to have a top speed of at least 310 knots, have a range of over 1,000 nautical miles, and possess exceptional maneuverability. No other fighter aircraft in the world could come even close to that level of performance. For the engineers at Mitsubishi, led by the brilliant Jiro Horikoshi, the challenge was seemingly impossible.

To meet those sweeping requirements, Horikoshi and his team had to make a number of bold decisions. The requirements could be met, they decided, but only if the resulting aircraft were incredibly lightweight. The new design, christened the A6M, would, therefore, be an all-metal low-wing monoplane like the Claude, but unlike the A5M it would have retractable landing gear and a closed cockpit. The monocoque design would be made from the latest alloys, including the lightweight but strong duralumin, and would be assembled using a new flush riveting system to reduce drag and increase speed.

To save weight, the engineers stripped away all of the cockpit armor as well as the self-sealing fuel tanks—features that were standard on Western fighters. While this lightened the Zero, made it faster and gave it longer range, the lack of protection also made the plane and pilot vulnerable to enemy fire.

By 1939, the prototype was ready for its maiden flight. It performed beyond all expectations. The Zero demonstrated impressive agility, being capable of tight turns and high climb rates that left other fighters scrambling to keep up. It was armed with a pair of 7.7mm machine guns and two 20mm cannons, giving it enough firepower to bring down a heavy bomber. It was without a doubt the best naval carrier fighter in the world at the time.

In the spring of 1939, as the Zero was just beginning production, Hideyoshi was selected to test-fly and evaluate the revolutionary fighter. From the moment he first laid eyes on the Zero at the Ise airfield, he knew this aircraft was different from the Claudes that he was accustomed to. Its long, tapered wings and lightweight frame screamed out "speed and agility".

His first flight in the Zero was exhilarating. As he climbed into the cockpit, he noticed the snug fit, designed to make the pilot feel like an extension of the machine. The controls were smooth and responsive, and as he taxied down the runway and took off, the aircraft's power was immediately apparent. The Zero's climb rate left him momentarily breathless, and once at altitude, the plane responded to his slightest touch, banking sharply, rolling effortlessly, and executing tight turns.

Over the weeks, Hideyoshi pushed the Zero to its limits, testing its capabilities in simulated dogfights and mock ground attacks. The aircraft's agility was unmatched, allowing him to outmaneuver even the best of his fellow instructor pilots in training exercises. Hideyoshi declared that it "climbed like a hawk and flew like a sparrow". Yet, it demanded careful handling. A reckless pilot could quickly find himself in trouble with it.

One particular flight tested both his skills and his nerve. During a high-altitude maneuver, a sudden crosswind caused the Zero to stall. Hideyoshi's heart raced as the aircraft plummeted. Drawing on his years of experience, he corrected the spin with a combination of rudder and elevator adjustments, leveling out just in time to avoid a disastrous crash. Back on the ground, his instructors praised his composure. For Hideyoshi, the incident was an indication of the Zero's unforgiving nature. "The Zero isn't just a machine," he told his fellow pilots. "It's a living thing."

By the end of the evaluation program, Hideyoshi was enthusiastic about the Zero. It was a fighter that mirrored his own style as a pilot: elegant yet lethal, disciplined yet daring.

It was late in the spring of 1938 when Aiko shared the news with Hideyoshi. Her cheeks flushed as she placed his hand over her belly and whispered, "We're going to have a baby." The words filled their home with quiet anticipation that grew as the months passed. Together, they prepared for the new arrival, with Aiko sewing tiny garments and Hideyoshi spending his evening spare time carving wooden toys.

When Aiko and Hideyoshi shared the news of her pregnancy, their families responded with unrestrained joy. Haruko clasped her hands together, her eyes glistening as she murmured blessings for a healthy child, while Hideyuki nodded approvingly, his reserved demeanor softening as he patted Hideyoshi's shoulder. "You've made us proud," he said simply. Aiko's parents were equally thrilled, with Emiko immediately offering motherly advice on everything from remedies for morning sickness to nutritional meals to ensure a strong baby. Hiroshi, though less vocal, broke into a rare smile, visibly pleased at the prospect of becoming a grandfather.

Both families began making plans for the arrival of the baby, exchanging suggestions on names and promising to visit often.

In the quiet of a February morning in 1939, then, the first cries of a newborn echoed through the small home. The midwife handed the swaddled infant to Aiko, who cradled him against her chest. Exhaustion softened her features, but her smile radiated pure happiness. Hideyoshi knelt beside her, his heart swelling as he studied the tiny face of their son. The baby's small hand curled instinctively around his finger.

"He's strong," the midwife remarked. "A healthy boy, as all firstborns should be."

Hideyoshi nodded. He reached out a hand to brush his son's cheek. "Ichiro," he said quietly, the name already decided between him and Aiko. It was a name that symbolized both tradition and promise—"first son," a nod to his role as the start of a new generation.

Aiko smiled. "Ichiro," she repeated, her voice soft. "He'll grow up to be strong, like his father."

The days following Ichiro's birth were a blur of new routines and adjustments. Hideyoshi, who had spent years navigating the challenges of combat and aerial maneuvers, now found himself in unfamiliar territory. He learned how to hold Ichiro properly and how to soothe him when he cried, and marveled at every tiny expression or movement. Aiko took naturally to motherhood, and her calm demeanor was a steady anchor in their new world.

Word of Ichiro's birth spread quickly, and soon the house was filled with well-wishers. Neighbors, friends, and even some of Hideyoshi's fellow aviators came bearing gifts—small toys, bundles of clothing, and words of congratulations. Hideyoshi's parents arrived from Sakurada, with their pride apparent in every smile and gesture. Haruko held Ichiro for hours, softly singing gentle lullabies to him.

"This boy will carry on the Sugiyama name," Hideyuki declared. "You've done well, Hideyoshi."

Aiko's parents visited as well, bringing their own blessings and hopes for Ichiro's future. Emiko fussed endlessly over the baby, and Hiroshi showed a quiet respect. Over a shared cup of tea, he expressed his gratitude. "You've given Aiko a good life," he said. "And now you've given us Ichiro."

One evening, as Hideyoshi returned from the airfield after a long day of training, Aiko greeted him at the door with Ichiro in her arms. Aiko's face lit up. "Look, Hideyoshi," she said. "He recognizes you."

Hideyoshi leaned in, and Ichiro's tiny eyes seemed to focus on him, a toothless smile spreading across his face. It was a small moment but one that filled Hideyoshi's heart.

Ichiro's birth brought Hideyoshi a deep joy, yet it had also opened the door to an inner conflict that he now found increasingly difficult to ignore. In the quiet hours at night, he would sit by the crib, watching his son sleep, and wondered, "What kind of future would Ichiro inherit if the storm clouds of war continued to gather?"

Even among his peers at the airfield, there were signs of unease. "A wider war feels inevitable," one senior officer confided to him during a break in training. "It's only a matter of time before we clash with the Americans. And when that happens ..." He trailed off, but the meaning was clear.

Hideyoshi listened without comment, his face impassive. He knew better than to voice his own thoughts, especially in an atmosphere where any disagreement could be construed as disloyalty. Yet privately, his mind wrestled with the implications. He had flown missions over China, seen the destruction and suffering of war firsthand, and had even justified it as part of his duty. But now, as he held his son's tiny hand or listened to Aiko hum lullabies in the next room, the moral calculations felt less clear.

One evening, as they sat together after dinner with Ichiro asleep in his cradle, Aiko sensed that something was wrong and reached for his hand. "You've been distant lately," she said softly.

Hideyoshi hesitated before replying, unsure how much to reveal. "I'm just thinking about the future," he said finally. "What's to come, for all of us."

Aiko tilted her head, studying him. "You're a father now. It's natural to feel torn."

Her words struck a chord. "Torn" was exactly how he felt — torn between his obligation to his country and the growing realization that the world was teetering on the edge of something catastrophic.

He was a soldier, bound by duty, but he was also a father and a husband, and the balance between them was precarious, especially as the clouds of war grew darker.

A little over a year later, Hideyoshi stood at attention before Commander Matsuo, the base's commanding officer.

"Petty Officer Sugiyama," Matsuo began, handing him a sealed envelope marked with the Imperial Navy's insignia. "These are your orders. You are to report to the Kure Naval Base for reassignment to the air group of the *Akagi*."

Hideyoshi accepted the envelope with a nod, his heart steady but his mind racing. He knew the *Akagi* by reputation — one of the Imperial Navy's foremost carriers, a cornerstone of Japan's growing fleet. To serve aboard her was an honor, but the suddenness of the reassignment caught him off guard.

"Commander," Hideyoshi said after a brief pause, "if I may speak freely?"

Matsuo gestured for him to continue.

"With respect, sir, I must ask—would I not serve Japan better by continuing my work here at Ise? The need for pilots is only increasing, and my experience in training cadets could help prepare more men for the demands of combat."

Matsuo regarded him with a look of understanding. "Your concern is valid, Sugiyama, and your work here has been exemplary. But Japan's needs are evolving. Our carriers are the cutting edge of naval warfare, and their air groups must have the most capable and experienced pilots. Combat veterans like you bring knowledge that cannot be taught in a classroom or even in training flights."

He continued, leaning forward slightly to emphasize his point.

"The *Akagi* is transitioning to the A6M Zero, an aircraft that will redefine air combat. The men assigned to her must master it quickly and under the guidance of those who have faced the realities of war. You are one of those men, Sugiyama. That's why you've been chosen."

"I understand, sir," Hideyoshi said after a moment. "I will do my duty."

Matsuo nodded. "I know you will. Report to Kure in two weeks. Until then, make your preparations. Dismissed."

That evening, Hideyoshi sat with Aiko in their small home. Ichiro lay cradled in Aiko's arms. Hideyoshi studied them both.

"You've been quiet," Aiko said gently, her gaze meeting his.

Hideyoshi nodded, reaching out to touch Ichiro's tiny hand. "I received new orders today," he began, trying to keep his voice calm. "I am to report to Kure in two weeks. They've assigned me to the air group of the *Akagi*."

Aiko's face betrayed no shock, though her eyes softened with understanding. She was a military wife, and she had always known this day would come. "The *Akagi*," she said. "It's an honor, isn't it?"

"Yes," Hideyoshi replied. "It is. But it means I'll be away for a long time. And this time ..." He hesitated, searching for the right words. "This time, I leave more behind."

"We knew this life would not be easy, Hideyoshi. But you are doing this for us—for Ichiro. For Japan." Aiko reached for his hand. "I will be here, waiting for you, just as I always have."

Her words were steady, but he could hear the effort it took to keep them that way. "She is strong and brave," he thought to himself. He pulled her close, pressing his forehead to hers. "I'm grateful for you, Aiko. I don't know if I've said that enough."

"You say it every day," she replied, smiling. "Even if not with words."

The following days were filled with quiet preparations. Hideyoshi ensured that everything was in order for Aiko and Ichiro. He made arrangements with friends in Tsu to check in on them, and spent every spare moment he could with his wife and son. He did not know when he would see them again.

On the morning of his departure, the three of them stood at the edge of the road, waiting for the Navy truck. Hideyoshi knelt to Ichiro's level, though the toddler was still too young to understand. "Be good to your mother," he said softly, his finger brushing the baby's hair.

As he rose, Aiko adjusted the collar of his uniform, her hands lingering for a moment longer than necessary. "Write to us," she said. Her voice was steady but her eyes were glistening.

"I will," he promised. "Every chance I get."

As Hideyoshi walked away, he forced himself not to look back. Duty called, and he would answer, but his heart remained in Tsu.

At Kure Naval Base, the towering masts of warships rose against the horizon, the clang of hammers echoed from the drydocks, and sailors rushed around from place to place.

The *Akagi* loomed ahead, a giant among the ships at port. Her long, flat flight deck was seemingly endless, and her distinctive three-tiered bridge rose proudly above it. The ship carried a crew of 1600—larger than the entire population of Sakurada. Even among Japan's impressive naval vessels, she was a marvel—a proud symbol of the Empire's growing power.

Hideyoshi reported directly to the air group's office, where a senior officer, Commander Chidoshi, greeted him with a curt nod. Impatiently, he motioned for Hideyoshi to sit.

"Petty Officer Sugiyama," Chidoshi he said, glancing over Hideyoshi's service record. "You come to us with an impressive background. Combat missions in China, instructor experience, and most importantly, qualification as a Zero pilot. That makes you uniquely valuable to the *Akagi* at this time."

"Thank you, Commander," Hideyoshi replied. "It's an honor to serve aboard the *Akagi*."

Chidoshi nodded but didn't look up. "The *Akagi* is undergoing a critical transition," he continued. "We are phasing out the Claude and integrating the A6M Zero into the air group. The Zero is a superior machine, but it requires adjustments for our pilots in techniques, tactics, and mindset. We need pilots who know how to handle this new airplane and can guide others. That's why you're here."

Hideyoshi hesitated for a moment before speaking. "Commander," he said carefully, "I'll do everything I can. If I may ask, will I be flying combat missions, or is my role strictly transitional?"

Chidoshi leaned back in his chair. "Primarily transitional, at least for now. Your combat experience and Zero training will be key in getting the rest of our fighter wing up to speed. However, this is the *Akagi*. You should always be ready to fly into battle. Once we complete the transition, we'll assess the situation."

Hideyoshi nodded. "Understood, sir. I'll ensure the men are prepared."

Chidoshi closed the file and stood, signaling that the meeting was over. "You'll be quartered with the senior pilots. Your first task is to check out the Zeroes we've already received and begin assisting with training flights. Report to Lieutenant Yamaguchi tomorrow morning for a full briefing."

The *Akagi* moved steadily through the vast expanse of ocean, her flight deck alive with the hum of activity as aircraft were prepped, checked, and launched in a carefully orchestrated series of actions. For Hideyoshi, sitting on deck in the cockpit of his Zero fighter, this was familiar territory. His time at Ise Airfield, training naval air cadets and maintaining his own carrier qualifications, had ensured that he remained sharp in the skills demanded of a naval aviator.

The deck crew signaled, and the Zero roared to life, its engine responding with a satisfying growl. With practiced ease, Hideyoshi guided the aircraft down the flight deck and into the open sky.

Circling back, he aligned with the *Akagi* for his first landing of the day. Hideyoshi adjusted his descent, mindful of the carrier's uneven rise and fall. Touchdown came smoothly, the aircraft jolted to a halt, and Hideyoshi taxied forward as the deck crew rushed to secure the plane.

"Not bad," one of the deck crew remarked as Hideyoshi climbed out of the cockpit.

Hideyoshi grinned. "It's good to be back on a real deck."

Beyond his own work, Hideyoshi also took time to observe the *Akagi*'s routines. He studied the coordination of the deck crews, the flow of aircraft from hangar deck to flight deck and back, and the interplay between the pilots and the ground crews. The *Akagi* was a finely tuned machine, with every element working together with just one goal—to put warplanes into the air.

As a combat-experienced pilot, Hideyoshi also found himself taking on the mantle of mentor among the younger aviators. Many of them were fresh from training, their confidence still developing as they adapted to both the Zero and to the realities of carrier life. Life on the *Akagi* was better than on most ships, but it was still no summer picnic.

"Carrier operations aren't just about skill," he would tell them. "They're about trust—trust in your training, trust in your aircraft, and trust in the crew that supports you. The key is to stay focused and to learn from every landing, every maneuver."

The pilots nodded, their faces showing both confidence and nerves. Hideyoshi recognized that look—it was one he had worn himself, years ago.

As the *Akagi* continued her voyage, Hideyoshi began his job of familiarizing the pilots with the new Zero. He had each of them sit in the cockpit and memorize every switch and dial. Once they were thoroughly familiar with the plane, they began doing takeoffs and landings. It wasn't until they were all comfortable with everything that he began taking them up for operational combat air patrols around the carrier group.

Standing near his aircraft on the flight deck, Hideyoshi reviewed the mission plan with his two wingmen, Yoshikawa and Igarashi.

"We'll focus on formation discipline and maneuvering," Hideyoshi explained. "The Zero's agility is unmatched, but it's only an advantage if we work together. Watch your spacing and anticipate each other's movements."

"*Hai*, Instructor Sugiyama!" the two replied in unison.

Moments later, the three Zeros roared down the deck and lifted into the morning sky.

Hideyoshi led the patrol over open waters, his eyes scanning the horizon. Although the mission was a routine exercise, he approached it with the same focus he had learned during combat in China. Looking back over his shoulder, Hideyoshi raised his left hand and extended two fingers, signaling Yoshikawa to tighten his position. Like the Claude, the Zero came equipped with an air-to-air radio, but like the Claude, the device was so unreliable that most combat units stripped it out to save weight. The trailing aircraft responded to the signal by easing closer.

As they flew, Hideyoshi introduced maneuvers designed to showcase the Zero's strengths. A series of coordinated turns and climbs highlighted the fighter's exceptional agility, while mock interceptions allowed the pilots to practice their timing and coordination.

During one maneuver, Hideyoshi signaled the start of a steep climb. His wingmen followed seamlessly, their formation holding steady as the Zeros ascended.

Hideyoshi had told them, "The Zero excels in turning maneuvers. Use that to your advantage. But be cautious — our lack of armor means you can't afford to take any hits."

Over the following days, Hideyoshi conducted several more patrols, each one building on the previous, and the younger pilots began improving as they grew more comfortable with the Zero.

When all of the *Akagi's* fighter pilots had been fully checked out in the Zero, Hideyoshi expected that he would be returned to instructing trainees at Ise, where he could be with Aiko and Ichiro again. Instead, he found himself permanently re-assigned to the *Akagi*. It was a crushing disappointment, but, after a two-week leave back home, Hideyoshi settled into his place on the *Akagi*. His life became a routine of patrols and drills.

In November 1940, Hideyoshi stood at attention before some of the ship's senior officers, and Captain Kasumo stepped forward with a document in hand.

"Petty Officer Sugiyama," Kasumo began. "In recognition of your leadership, combat experience, and exemplary service to the Imperial Japanese Navy, you are hereby promoted to the rank of Ensign. This promotion comes with the responsibilities of command within the carrier air group. Congratulations."

Hideyoshi bowed deeply. "Thank you, Captain. I am honored by the trust placed in me, and I will strive to meet the expectations of this new role."

The other officers nodded in approval, and Kasumo bowed. "You have earned this, Sugiyama. Your excellent performance both in combat and in training has not gone unnoticed. You will now command a *shotai* of three Zeros. Lead them well."

The following day, Hideyoshi joined his wingmen in the hangar, where the fuselage of his Zero now bore the freshly-painted two red vertical stripes of a *shotai* leader. Petty Officers Igarashi and Yoshikawa, greeted him with salutes and a sense of anticipation. Both had already flown with him many times on patrols.

"We're a team now," he told them. "A *shotai* must move as one, think as one. My role is to guide you, but it's also to ensure that we support each other in every mission. Trust in your skills, and trust in each other."

"Yes, sir!" they replied.

Igarashi and Yoshikawa were already confident in their abilities and in their leader.

Chapter 8

Planning Pearl Harbor (1941)

Even as the war in China continued to drag on, Japan was already looking elsewhere. The signing of the Tripartite Pact in September 1940 cemented an alliance with Nazi Germany and Fascist Italy, as Japan sought to deter interference from the United States and Britain while expanding its sphere of influence in Asia. Meanwhile, the militarists in Tokyo exploited France's defeat to intimidate the Vichy government into allowing Japanese troops to occupy northern Indochina in 1940, securing a foothold near the trade routes and natural resources in Southeast Asia. So, by the spring of 1941, the stage had been set for another confrontation.

In July 1941, the United States, in direct response to Japan's occupation of Indochina, imposed a complete embargo on oil exports to Japan and froze all Japanese assets in the US. This was a devastating blow. Japan, an island nation with few natural resources of its own, had been importing nearly 90 percent of all its oil from America. Without that supply, estimates suggested that the current oil reserves could sustain Japanese military operations for only about two years, even with severe rationing. After that, with no fuel for ships, vehicles or aircraft, Japan's entire military machine would grind to a stop. It would literally run out of gas.

For Japan's civilian population, the American sanctions also produced economic hardship. Supplies of everyday goods dwindled, prices rose, and rationing became serious. The asset freeze worsened the situation further, cutting off Japan from foreign currency reserves and making it impossible to purchase critically necessary materials on the international market.

These economic pressures created a profound sense of urgency in the military and the government. The choice was harsh: they had to either negotiate a withdrawal from China and Indochina to appease the United States and restore renewed trade relations, or they had to seize all of those resources which Japan needed, by force. For the militarists, withdrawal from their occupied territories was simply unthinkable—it would, as they saw it, be a humiliating retreat that would undermine Japan's standing as a world power and would waste all of the sacrifices they had already made during the long war in China.

The only acceptable option, as they saw it, was war.

That conclusion in turn intensified the division and rivalry between Japan's Army and Navy. For years, an internal argument had raged within Japan's military hierarchy over strategic priorities. This clash centered on two competing visions for expansion: the northern strategy (*hokushin-ron*) and the southern strategy (*nanshin-ron*).

The northern strategy focused on expanding up into the Soviet Union. Proponents of this view, mostly from the Army, considered the vast resource-rich territory of Siberia as the answer to Japan's growing need for raw materials. Also, not coincidentally, this thrust would put the Army at the center of operations, entitling it to the lion's share of military resources. The Army's plans for a war against Russia hinged on exploiting what they perceived as Soviet weakness, especially after Stalin's purges in the late 1930s. After all, the Army argued, Japan had already beaten Russia before, in the 1905 war.

On the other hand, the southern strategy, favored by the Navy, proposed expanding down into Southeast Asia instead, particularly towards the Dutch East Indies and British Malaya. Not surprisingly, this would put the Navy in charge of the operation. The southern strategy, however, meant direct confrontation with the United States and Britain, and while London was already fighting for its life against Hitler's Germany, the United States would be the most formidable opponent that Japan had ever faced. But, the Navy argued, America, which had sat out most of the Great War, was weary and was suffering from economic troubles, and would want to negotiate a quick settlement to avoid another long and brutal war.

In the summer of 1939, the debate over strategy came to a head with the Nomonhon Incident, also known as the Battle of Khalkhin Gol, a border conflict that unexpectedly broke out between Japanese Manchukuo and Soviet forces in Mongolia. It proved disastrous for the Japanese, who suffered over 17,000 casualties and were decisively defeated by the Soviets.

The crushing loss at Nomonhon settled the strategic question once and for all: Japan was simply not strong enough to take on both the USSR and China at the same time. The Army reluctantly agreed, and Japan now focused its attention on Southeast Asia.

That left the United States as the primary obstacle to Japan's ambitions. With its Pacific Fleet stationed at Hawaii, the US Navy posed a formidable threat to any Japanese move southward. Japanese leaders knew that once they began their offensive into Southeast Asia, the United States would inevitably respond in force, and they knew that Japan could not afford to engage in a lengthy conflict with a nation that vastly outmatched them in industrial capacity and resources.

Thus, the decision was made to strike first, decisively and devastatingly. The strategic imperative was clear: Japan had to neutralize the US Pacific Fleet quickly before it could interfere with the planned operations in Southeast Asia and before the Imperial Army and Navy ran out of fuel reserves and could no longer fight.

That in turn sparked another debate, this time within the Navy itself, over how best to accomplish this. At the heart of this argument was the conflict between two differing viewpoints: on the one side were the traditionalist admirals, who viewed battleships as the backbone of naval power, and on the other side were the air power advocates, who recognized that the punch of modern naval power now lay with carrier-based aviation.

The traditionalists within the Navy viewed battleships as the ultimate instruments of power and believed that a war with the United States would hinge on a single decisive engagement—a modern version of the Battle of Tsushima that had brought victory in the Russo-Japanese War. They believed that Japan's existing fleet, including the new *Yamato*-class of super-battleships already nearing completion, would give the Imperial Navy an edge in a direct toe-to-toe slugfest with the US Navy.

On the other side of the debate were the carrier proponents, led by the Navy's Admiral Isoroku Yamamoto. He had spent time in the United States and had seen firsthand America's immense industrial strength and economic power, and he had always been opposed to the idea of war with the Americans. Now, as Commander-in-Chief of the Navy, it became his duty to plan for just such a war.

Yamamoto saw aircraft carriers as key to any realistic military strategy. He argued that carrier-based aviation had revolutionized naval warfare, giving Japan the ability to project power far beyond the range of even the biggest battleship guns. Under his leadership, the Navy had already begun developing a powerful carrier force and training an elite corps of naval aviators. Now, if there was to be war with the US, this force provided Japan's best hope for victory.

Yamamoto pointed out that the US Navy's Pacific Fleet, stationed at Pearl Harbor, was the linchpin of American power in the region. Destroying it in a sudden attack would not only give Japan free rein to seize the resources of Malaya and the East Indies but also demoralize the United States and force it to negotiate peace on terms favorable to Japan.

Ultimately, Yamamoto's view won out. His reputation and authority as Commander-in-Chief carried significant influence, and his argument that Japan's only chance for victory lay in a sudden and devastating initial strike was difficult to counter. By mid-1941, Yamamoto had convinced the Navy's leadership and the Tokyo government to adopt his plan. The *Kido Butai* "Mobile Force", consisting of six aircraft carriers and over 400 aircraft (the largest carrier strike force ever assembled), would attack the United States fleet at Pearl Harbor.

The success of the plan rested on intelligence gathering. As a matter of routine, the Japanese intelligence services already had a number of operatives in Hawaii, including spies who were posing as local residents and embassy staff and who were carefully observing the patterns of naval activity at Pearl Harbor. Now these efforts became more focused, sending back regular reports on the American fleet's movements and the status of Oahu's airfields, and obtaining specific requested information such as the depth of the harbor waters. (A matter of crucial importance to the planners, since special modifications would need to be made to the aerial torpedoes to insure that they could operate effectively in the shallow waters of Pearl Harbor.)

Working out the logistic and supply issues were equally vital. The fleet would have to put to sea from the remote Kuril Islands in northern Japan and cross the stormy northern Pacific, avoiding the regular shipping lanes and maintaining a strict radio silence so they could not be tracked by American listening posts. Supplies, including fuel and provisions for the long voyage, had to be calculated. Refueling at sea was a critical element as the fleet had to avoid port calls, and this hazardous operation had to be practiced and perfected.

While Yamamoto and the Navy were optimistic about the operation, elements within the Japanese Army and even some naval officers remained skeptical, and Yamamoto himself knew that he could not achieve a total success. At best, the attack would buy Japan some crucial time — perhaps six months or a year — to consolidate its gains in the Philippines, Malaya, and the Dutch East Indies, and to form a hardened defensive perimeter to force the Americans to negotiate a settlement that would allow Japan to keep its conquests.

The final plan was a masterpiece of naval air tactics. The opening moves of the attack would focus on Hawaii's airfields, with the goal of demolishing the American fighter planes on the ground and preventing them from mounting any effective air defense. Next, the torpedo planes and dive bombers would strike the US carriers and battleships that would be berthed in the harbor, destroying them. A short time later, a second attack wave would target any remaining undamaged vessels and also the military base's infrastructure. The attack would be scheduled for early on a Sunday morning, when the American forces would be least prepared.

On the *Akagi*, Hideyoshi and the other Zero pilots were suddenly ordered into a seemingly unending string of training flights, and now carried out near-daily exercises designed to simulate the stressful conditions of an actual combat mission. Early morning briefings outlined specific complex maneuvers and flight formations, with the focus often on coordinating with the carrier's Nakajima B5N "Kate" torpedo bombers and Aichi D3A "Val" dive bombers.

In several such drills, the Zeros flew mock escort missions with groups of Kates, charged with protecting the vulnerable bombers from hypothetical interceptors. Hideyoshi and his fellow pilots practiced weaving protectively around the bombers in tight formations, ready at any moment to break off and engage in simulated dogfights. At times, veteran pilots in older "Claude" fighters played the role of "enemy aircraft", attacking aggressively to test the readiness of the Zero pilots and their ability to protect the bombers.

The dive bombers added another layer of complexity to the drills. Val formations dove steeply toward mock targets on the ground, with Zero escorts shadowing them from above to ward off any simulated attacks.

While they weren't told what was going on, the pace and intensity of their preparation had made it obvious to everyone that they were being prepared for something unusual. Hideyoshi began to wonder if they were about to be sent back to China.

There would be six fleet carriers in the strike force.

Kaga had been originally laid down in 1921 as a fast battle-cruiser, but she had been hastily converted into an aircraft carrier in the middle of her construction. A number of modifications in the

1930s had enlarged her flight deck and hangar and increased her aircraft capacity to 75 combat-ready planes and 18 crated spares. *Kaga* had already seen action in China, launching air support missions during the fighting around Shanghai.

The *Soryu* and *Hiryu*, were purpose-built aircraft carriers, smaller than *Kaga* but faster and more maneuverable. They had entered service in 1937 and 1939. Each carried 57 combat aircraft. A combat detachment of *Soryu's* planes had been temporarily sent to land bases at Nanking, and *Hiryu* had been in Indochina but saw no action.

Shokaku and *Zuikaku*, both commissioned in early 1941, were the newest carriers in the Navy and incorporated all of the lessons that had been learned earlier, with reinforced flight decks, better armor protection, and state-of-the-art hangar facilities. Each could carry 72 combat aircraft, their pilots new and mostly untested.

A powerful covering force would also be dispatched to accompany and protect and support the carriers, including the battleships *Hiei* and *Kirishima* and a number of cruisers, destroyers, and supply ships. There were also oil tankers for mid-voyage refueling.

Hideyoshi's own ship, *Akagi*, would serve as the flagship of the operation. A sister ship of *Kaga*, she too had been originally designed as a battle-cruiser and later converted into an aircraft carrier, and had undergone extensive modifications in the 1930s. She carried a combat mix of 75 Zero fighters, Val dive bombers, and Kate torpedo bombers.

The atmosphere aboard the *Akagi* grew increasingly tense as the days stretched into late October 1941. Hideyoshi first noticed the change during a routine drill when a small group of ferry boats brought a group of senior officers to the carrier. The number of high-ranking officers visiting the ship seemed to multiply overnight, and soon the ship was, as one mystified ground crewman noted, "crawling with admirals".

At first, Hideyoshi dismissed the visits as routine inspections or strategic consultations, but as the days passed, it became apparent that something else was going on. One afternoon, Vice Admiral Nagumo himself came aboard, accompanied by his staff. His arrival was quiet but was noticed immediately; it was the kind of news that quickly made its way through the entire crew. Within hours, the corridors leading to the ship's command spaces had been cordoned off, and the senior officers disappeared into closed-door meetings.

Conversations between crew members rapidly turned to whispered speculation, though no one dared voice their guesses too loudly. Some suggested that the fleet was preparing for a massive operation in China. Some were convinced that they were about to sail for Siberia, reigniting the conflict with Russia. Others whispered about a plan to enter the Mediterranean Sea and assist their German allies in North Africa. One wild rumor claimed that their upcoming mission was to escort a secret convoy transporting Emperor Hirohito to oversee operations himself in China—a theory so absurd that it left the more seasoned sailors rolling their eyes.

Hideyoshi kept his thoughts to himself, concluding that the chain of command would tell them whatever they needed to know in due time—and wouldn't tell them any more than that. For now, then, his focus remained on his duties.

Something big was up, though—that much was obvious to everyone. And it was not difficult to piece together at least some of the fragments of information. All the unusual drills, the increased security, and now the presence of Nagumo, pointed to a mission of extraordinary importance.

Hideyoshi sat on his cot in the cramped quarters that he shared with three other pilots on the *Akagi.* He paused, a blank sheet of paper in front of him, absently tapping the end of his brush against the inkstone as he gathered his thoughts.

Although all Japanese servicemen were encouraged to write home often to their families as a way of keeping up morale and of demonstrating to the public that Japan's soldiers and sailors were being well-treated and well-provided for, he had also been instructed that all outgoing letters would be inspected by the *Kempeitai*, the military security police, to ensure that no sensitive information about their procedures or operations leaked out, so he could say nothing about where he was or about the endless drills for war that consumed most of his day. But he wanted to write something that would make his wife smile and feel connected to him despite the distance.

"My dearest Aiko", he began.

The words came slowly at first, but soon the ink flowed as he described as much as he could about life aboard the carrier. He wrote about the early morning wake-ups, the joy he felt at being in the air, and the camaraderie of his fellow pilots as they traded stories and laughter over bowls of rice in the mess hall.

"It feels like living inside a giant, floating city," he wrote. "But it's a city that never stops moving, though the horizon is always the same. Sometimes, I stand on the deck and I imagine the waves are carrying me back to you."

"I think of you every day," he added. "When I hear the wind or feel the sun on my face, I imagine you walking beside me, your voice in my ear. I miss you more than words can say."

After rereading everything to ensure that he hadn't included anything the censors might strike out, he folded the letter carefully. Tomorrow morning he would deposit it in one of the special boxes on board the ship, where outgoing mail was held until it could pass censorship. It would then be delivered onshore when the ship reached port and would be sent on its way.

Weeks passed, and the routines of carrier life continued with the days blending into one another. Then Hideyoshi's name was called during mail call. A small package, neatly wrapped in soft paper, bore Aiko's handwriting.

Inside, along with her letter, was a small *omamori*, a charm for good fortune and protection—something often purchased at Shinto shrines to safeguard travelers, students, or sailors (who always tended to be a superstitious lot). The amulet's silk covering was embroidered with protective *kanji* in golden thread, and the faint scent of incense still clung to it.

"My dear Hideyoshi", her letter read. "Life must be so different out there, so far from home. I hope this small token will bring you protection and remind you that my thoughts are always with you. Please keep it close to your heart."

Hideyoshi held the *omamori* between his fingers, feeling its smooth fabric. He slipped it over his head and tucked it under his uniform, where it rested against his chest.

That night, as he lay in his bunk listening to the soft hum of the propellers and the occasional creak of the hull, Hideyoshi reached up to touch the *omamori* again. He closed his eyes, picturing Aiko's face, the quiet streets of Tsu, and the sound of the waves in Ise Bay.

Chapter 9
Pearl Harbor (December 1941)

On the morning of November 26, 1941, the *Kido Butai* fleet prepared to depart from Hitokappu Bay in the frigid northern waters of the Kuril Islands.

Hideyoshi stood near the edge of the *Akagi's* flight deck, watching the endless expanse of ocean roll beneath the carrier's hull. Around him, the fleet loomed like steel giants against the slate-gray sky. His breath formed clouds in the icy air and the frigid cold seeped through his gloves, but he hardly noticed.

Akagi's engines roared to life, and the massive carrier began to move. Across the water, the other ships of the *Kido Butai* followed suit. The fleet was a formidable sight: six carriers—*Akagi, Kaga, Soryu, Hiryu, Shokaku,* and *Zuikaku*—flanked by battleships, cruisers, and destroyers. Together, they formed the most powerful naval strike force Japan had ever assembled.

In the mess hall, the conversations were subdued. "Where do you think we're heading?" Yoshikawa asked one evening, his youthful curiosity getting the better of him. Igarashi shrugged. "There are heaters all over the hangar deck, so it looks like we're going somewhere cold," he said, his voice low. "Russia, maybe."

And indeed the weather grew colder as the fleet advanced northward, skirting the edge of the stormy Pacific. The crew on the icy deck bundled themselves against the freezing temperatures, their movements cautious and deliberate as they performed their duties.

Below deck, the crew worked constantly to maintain the ship and their aircraft, making sure that every system remained fully operational even in the harsh arctic conditions.

The fleet was accompanied by several oil tankers, which indicated to alert crew members that their destination, whatever it was, was far enough away to require at-sea refueling. This was a particularly delicate and potentially dangerous operation, requiring delicate maneuvering in the rough seas. The oilers assigned to the *Kido Butai* would pull alongside each warship in turn, their decks bristling with hoses and crew. Men worked in coordinated teams to secure the lines, a difficult job made all the more dangerous by the icy decks, the steep waves, and the risk of collision.

Hideyoshi watched with curiosity as the *Akagi* slowed to match the oiler's speed and the massive flat-top carefully moved into position alongside the much-smaller ship. The rough waves tossed them both around, but the crews managed to secure the hoses and begin the long process of pumping fuel into the immense carrier. "It's like threading a needle," another pilot declared. Hideyoshi added, "While inside a washing machine."

Secrecy and stealth were paramount. Navigators pored over their charts, ensuring that the *Kido Butai* remained on course while avoiding all of the commercial shipping lanes. Lookouts continuously scanned the horizon looking for any sign of other vessels or aircraft. The entire fleet was under a strictly-enforced radio silence: the ships could receive radio signals, but were under firm orders not to send any.

After several days at sea, the fleet turned southward, and the weather began to shift as the bitter cold gave way to milder temperatures. Hideyoshi stood on the deck alongside Igarashi and Yoshikawa, feeling the welcome warmth of the sun on their faces. The three men gazed out at the endless ocean, their thoughts unspoken but shared. "Whatever this is, it's going to be big," Yoshikawa said finally, breaking the silence.

Several days later, the *Akagi's* entire air group was gathered in the pilot ready room. The walls were lined with charts and blackboards, all of which had been conspicuously covered with cloth.

At precisely 1900 hours, the door opened, and several high-ranking officers entered, including the air group commander, Lieutenant Commander Itaya. Behind him were staff officers carrying folders and rolled maps. Every pilot recognized Vice

Admiral Nagumo among the group. His presence was significant, a clear indication that the briefing would be of the utmost importance.

Itaya stepped forward. "Thank you for your patience and discipline during these past weeks," he began. "You have demonstrated the utmost professionalism." He paused and nodded. "And now the time has come to discuss the purpose of our mission."

"The details of this mission have been carefully guarded for a reason," Itaya continued. "The operation we are about to undertake is one of unprecedented importance, not only for the Imperial Navy but for the Empire itself."

"We are going to attack the American Navy at Pearl Harbor."

A murmur rippled through the ranks before being swiftly silenced by Itaya's raised hand. The commander's expression remained calm as he continued. "This operation is critical to Japan's strategic objectives. It will determine the course of the war and the future of our Empire."

Itaya gestured to an aide, who stepped over and uncovered a large map on the wall. It was a chart of Oahu, with markers pointing out the locations of airfields, docks, and installations. One of the staff officers stepped forward, using a pointer to emphasize specific areas as Itaya outlined the plan.

"The attack will be divided into two waves," Itaya began. "The first wave will focus on crippling the American Pacific Fleet. Unfortunately, the American carriers are not in port, so our attack will focus specifically on the battleships as our primary targets. Their destruction will render the Americans incapable of challenging our operations in the Pacific for months."

Itaya continued, "Each squadron in the *Kido Butai* has been assigned specific roles to ensure maximum efficiency and effectiveness. The torpedo squadrons will spearhead the attack on Battleship Row, along with the high-level bombers."

The pointer shifted to the airfields marked on the map. "The dive bombers will concentrate on the enemy airfields at Hickam and Wheeler. Our goal is to destroy as many aircraft as possible on the ground to neutralize any potential counterattack from the Americans."

"Some of our fighters will remain behind to protect the fleet. The rest will provide cover for the bombers during the attack, and will engage any American aircraft that manage to take off."

Hideyoshi exchanged a glance with his wingmen. This would be their role.

Itaya paused, his gaze sweeping the room. Every eye was on him. "The first wave will consist of 183 aircraft, including torpedo planes, dive bombers, and fighters. The second wave will launch shortly after the first. It will include 170 aircraft, with a similar composition to the first. This group will focus on completing any primary objectives left unfinished by the first wave and on inflicting further damage to infrastructure and to any undamaged ships."

The pointer moved again, this time highlighting the attack routes to be taken by planes from each of the various carriers in the strike force. "Each carrier's air group has been meticulously organized to ensure a seamless execution of the plan. Timing and coordination will be crucial. The *Akagi* torpedo bombers will strike first, opening a path for the other groups. The *Akagi* fighters will provide cover for the bombers, engage any enemy resistance, and attack any aircraft that remain on the ground."

Itaya concluded the briefing with a solemn statement. "This mission is our chance to deliver a decisive blow to the Americans. The fate of the Empire rests on your shoulders. You are expected to do your duty to the utmost. Dismissed."

The pilots stood, saluting sharply before filing out of the ready room.

The next morning, *Akagi's* fighter pilots were gathered once again in the ready room, as they were briefed on their particular role in the mission. Hideyoshi's orders specifically assigned his *shotai* to escort the high-altitude Kate level bombers who had been tasked with attacking the American battleships. These Kates, unlike their torpedo-carrying counterparts, were fitted with armor-piercing bombs made from converted 18-inch shells originally intended for the immense guns of the *Yamato*-class battleships, designed to strike from the air and penetrate the heavily reinforced decks.

The decision to use level bombers reflected careful tactical considerations. The primary anti-ship weapon was the aerial torpedo, but because the ships at Pearl Harbor were parked side-by-side, these on the inside of Battleship Row would be blocked by those on the outside, and could not be hit by torpedoes. The solution, then, was to use high-altitude level bombers to reach them from above. The Kate attack bomber was capable of delivering either torpedoes or bombs, so a select number of them were being trained to drop their armor-piercing bombs in a group to bracket the target. Each bomber *shotai* was assigned a specific American ship as their target.

The Zeros escorting the high-altitude Kates had a dual mission. The first was to protect the bombers and neutralize any American fighters that might intercept them. "If the bombers fail to deliver their payloads effectively, the entire operation will fail," Itaya stated firmly "You must protect them at all costs."

"After the bombers complete their runs," the officer continued, "your secondary objective is to eliminate any enemy fighters still in the air and to strafe any ground targets of opportunity. Priority targets include parked aircraft and anti-aircraft emplacements."

Striking ground targets, Hideyoshi knew, meant descending into the thick of American anti-aircraft fire, where the risk of being shot down was much higher. The secondary mission, he thought to himself, was far more dangerous than the primary.

Igarashi leaned slightly toward Hideyoshi and murmured under his breath, "They're really asking us to do it all, aren't they?"

The briefing concluded with an exhortation. "The success of this operation, and the future of Japan, depends on every one of you."

Early on the morning of December 7, Hideyoshi stood near his Zero, watching as the ground crew swarmed around the aircraft. The sun had not yet risen, and bright stars still sparkled in the Pacific sky.

Aircraft were pushed to their designated positions by hand, with bombers, torpedo planes, and fighters carefully arranged for the fastest possible takeoff. The pilots, already suited in their flight gear, checked their aircraft for final adjustments, ensuring that weapons were loaded and engines were ready.

At the designated time, the *Akagi's* loudspeakers crackled. "Pilots, to your planes. All squadrons, prepare for takeoff." The pace of activity on the flight deck intensified.

Hideyoshi climbed into the cockpit of his Zero and automatically began the start-up procedure. With the engine running, he secured his flight helmet and strapped himself in. Glancing to his left, he saw Igarashi performing similar checks, and flashed a quick thumbs-up when their eyes met.

The Zeros were the first to take off, assigned to take high cover and watch over the slower bombers as they formed up. Hideyoshi's plane was tenth in line, with Igarashi and Yoshikawa positioned directly behind him. He watched as the first Zero, its engine roaring, surged forward, gaining speed as it raced down the deck, lifted smoothly into the air, and disappeared into the night sky. Each aircraft would be launched in timed intervals, their movements synchronized to get all of them into the air as quickly as possible.

When Hideyoshi's turn came, a bridge officer waved a flag as his signal to take off. He eased the throttle forward, feeling the Zero's engine respond beneath him. At the edge of the deck, he pulled back slowly on the stick and the aircraft lifted gracefully into the air. As he climbed, Igarashi and Yoshikawa quickly formed up on him.

Once all of the fighters were airborne, the bombers began their launches. The *Kaga, Soryu, Hiryu, Shokaku,* and *Zuikaku* were all mirroring the same operation, launching their own aircraft in staggered waves.

As the last *shotai* lifted off, the aircraft began to assemble in their designated formations. The sheer size of the strike force was breathtaking. The combined might of the carriers had put over 180 planes into the air.

Hideyoshi led his three-plane *shotai* in a tight vic, and the Kates they were assigned to escort appeared shortly after, their engines droning steadily as they climbed into position.

When the formation was complete, the signal for departure came: a flare arcing skyward from the *Akagi*. One by one, the aircraft turned southeast, setting a course for Hawaii.

The vast Pacific stretched endlessly in every direction, and for the pilots of the *Kido Butai* strike force, with no landmarks to guide them, navigation across such a featureless expanse posed a challenge. In the lead bomber formations, highly trained navigators, using detailed charts, compasses, and timepieces, calculated the course toward the Hawaiian Islands. The stars, faint but steady, provided the most reliable points of reference. By aligning their sextants to these celestial markers, navigators cross-checked their headings against their plotted routes. As the hours passed, the sky began to soften with the first light of dawn, and the navigators shifted their focus to the horizon and used the sun's position as their guide.

The sun was fully up by the time the strike force began its final approach to Pearl Harbor. As the island grew larger on the horizon, the mountains and valleys of Oahu became visible, and as the formation descended, the pilots could see the harbor in detail. The battleships were moored in a neat double row with smaller vessels clustered nearby. Oil tankers and auxiliary ships dotted the port, and a few small boats moved slowly across the water. It was a scene of apparent calm.

From his cockpit, Hideyoshi scanned the skies for any sign of activity. There were no American fighters in the air, the airfields — Hickam, Wheeler, and Ewa — were quiet, and the harbor below seemed blissfully unaware of the incoming strike. They had been entirely undetected and had achieved complete surprise.

The Kates in his group began to climb to their designated bombing altitude while the torpedo bombers descended down to the water. Hideyoshi and his wingmen maintained their escort positions with the Kates, tucking in slightly above and to the sides of the bombers. As they edged closer to their targets, Hideyoshi could make out tiny figures on the decks of the American ships, as sailors were beginning their morning routines and the naval base was coming to life with the mundane activities of an ordinary day.

The first wave descended upon Pearl Harbor. Leading the charge were the Val dive bombers, which had been ordered to make a simultaneous assault on all of the airfields across Oahu in order to cripple American air power. The planes peeled off from their formations and descended toward their assigned targets.

At Hickam Field, the lead bombers carefully aligned themselves with the long, straight rows of neatly parked P-40 Warhawks, and pushed forward sharply on their control sticks, angling their planes into steep dives. The pilots released their bombs, and a series of explosions rocked the airfield as they struck their targets, sending shrapnel through the parked planes and tearing apart hangars. The high-explosive bombs were particularly effective against the tightly packed targets. Fireballs erupted from fuel depots and ammunition stores.

Wheeler Field was the primary Army Air Corps fighter base on the island, housing several squadrons of P-40 Warhawks and P-36 Hawks, and it came under particularly heavy attack. The Vals targeted the parked aircraft as well as the airfield's maintenance hangars and command buildings. Their bombs detonated with devastating force, setting the airfield ablaze. Secondary explosions followed as munitions and fuel stores were ignited. Hangars crumbled under the concussive force of the blasts, and the fires that followed consumed whatever remained. Aircraft caught in the open were torn apart, their aluminum skins shredded by flying metal.

Sporadic anti-aircraft fire now began to rise from the ground, forcing some Vals to take evasive maneuvers. Despite this, the damage inflicted by the dive bombers was catastrophic. Smoke rose in thick columns, and the orderly rows of American aircraft were now twisted heaps of metal, blackened by fire and pierced with shrapnel holes.

Meanwhile, as the Val dive bombers were unleashing their devastation on the airfields, the Kate torpedo bombers were executing their own assigned mission: the assault on the American battleships. This was the centerpiece of the attack, aimed at neutralizing the Pacific Fleet's ability to project American power in the Pacific. The Kates, flying low and steady, carried specially modified torpedoes which had been fitted with wooden fins to run in the shallow waters of the harbor—an innovation which had been developed specifically for this operation.

As the torpedo bombers roared in, each pilot adjusted his approach to line up with his assigned target, skimming just above the water to release his torpedo at the right moment.

The first torpedoes hit their marks with deadly accuracy. The *Oklahoma* was among the first to be struck. Torpedoes slammed into her port side, and within minutes she began to capsize, trapping hundreds of sailors below decks. Nearby, the *West Virginia* took multiple hits, and fires quickly engulfed the ship.

The Kates, however, flying at slow speed and low altitude to ensure accurate torpedo drops, were particularly vulnerable to the defensive anti-aircraft fire which now began to be directed at them. Several planes were hit, and some went down in flames. The rest pressed on.

Other ships, including cruisers and destroyers, were also targeted. The *Helena*, moored at the Navy Yard, was struck by a torpedo that caused severe damage, while the *Utah*, an older battleship which had been converted into a target ship for aerial practice, capsized after being hit.

By the time the torpedo bombers completed their runs and began to regroup, the waters of Pearl Harbor were a scene of chaotic destruction. Nearly all of the US Navy's prized battleships lay crippled, their decks aflame and their crews desperately fighting to save what they could. Thick oily smoke billowed into the sky, mingling with the haze from the burning airfields and the continuous explosions rocking the harbor.

After the torpedo bombers completed their runs, the Kate level bombers moved into position. As they approached, they encountered the same rising storm of anti-aircraft fire that had greeted the torpedo bombers, and the sky above Pearl Harbor now sparkled with flak bursts and streaking tracers. Despite the bedlam around them, however, the bomber crews maintained strict discipline and focused on their targets.

One of the bombs released by the Kates scored a direct hit on the *Arizona*, penetrating her deck near the turrets and exploding in the forward ammunition magazine. The resulting detonation was devastating. A massive detonation tore the *Arizona* apart in a spectacular fireball, destroying the ship, sinking her almost immediately, and causing the loss of more than 1,100 sailors. The inferno would continue to burn for days.

The *Nevada*, despite being heavily damaged by earlier torpedo strikes, also drew the attention of the level bombers as she attempted to get underway to escape. Several bombs fell around her, with one striking her bow—forcing her captain to ground the battleship near the harbor entrance to prevent her from sinking in the channel and blocking the harbor entirely.

The *California* and *West Virginia*, both also already heavily-damaged from torpedo hits, now became targeted again by the Kates. Bombs struck them both, adding to the destruction. As the Kates completed their runs and began to withdraw, the harbor below was a scene of utter destruction.

While the battleships burned, the Zeros now peeled off to take on their secondary objective: neutralizing any remaining American aircraft on the ground or in the air.

Hideyoshi turned his *shotai* towards Hickam Field, where a number of Warhawks, Hawks, and a few B-17 Flying Fortresses remained undamaged, parked wingtip to wingtip in tight clusters on the apron. The Americans had aligned their planes in close rows to guard against sabotage, but this arrangement now made them ideal targets for strafing runs.

The three Zeros swooped low as they lined up their first pass. From his cockpit, Hideyoshi could see people on the ground scattering in confusion and scrambling for cover, with many diving into trenches or behind vehicles. He squeezed the trigger on his throttle control, and the Zero's cowl-mounted 7.7mm machine guns erupted, their tracer rounds slicing through the air. Bullets ripped into the fuselages and fuel tanks of the parked aircraft, sending plumes of fire and smoke into the sky as gasoline ignited and shattered debris flew in all directions.

Yoshikawa and Igarashi followed suit, strafing another row of parked planes. The American fighters were rendered useless in seconds.

Hideyoshi's next target was Wheeler Field. Here, rows of P-40s and P-36s were being systematically strafed by Zeros from another *shotai*. As Hideyoshi approached, he noticed one P-40 managing to get airborne, but it was quickly intercepted and shot down by one of the circling Zeros.

Another strafing run tore through a row of parked planes. One P-36 exploded in a fireball, its ammunition cooking off in a series of deafening pops. Hideyoshi caught sight of a fuel truck engulfed in flames, its thick black smoke adding to the growing clouds that now hung over the airfield. Even in his closed cockpit, he could detect the smell of burning fuel and charred metal.

Hideyoshi regrouped with Igarashi and Yoshikawa, their Zeros still pristine despite all the tracer rounds that raced towards them from the ground. They glanced down at the devastated airfields and knew that they had struck a decisive blow.

An instant later, a bright flash from Igarashi's wings caught Hideyoshi's attention as he fired a brief burst from his machine guns, one of the signals for "enemy planes". Looking in the indicated direction, Hideyoshi saw two specks in the distance, closing fast. Two American fighters, P-40s, painted in olive drab with gleaming white star roundels, had managed to get airborne and were now approaching. Their pilots were undoubtedly aware of the monumental odds stacked against them, and Hideyoshi could not suppress a feeling of admiration for his enemy's bravery.

Hideyoshi raised his left hand, signaling for an attack, pointed to the lead P-40, then tapped his chest to indicate he would take the first pass. Igarashi and Yoshikawa nodded in acknowledgment, falling back slightly to cover him as he pushed his Zero forward.

The distance between Hideyoshi and the lead P-40 shrank rapidly. The American pilot broke sharply to the left, evading the initial burst from Hideyoshi's machine guns. The other P-40 dove low, splitting their formation and complicating the Japanese pilots' pursuit. Hideyoshi signaled his own wingmen to follow the American, then turned after his own target with a steep turn.

The dogfight became a violent ballet of spirals, dives, and climbs. The P-40's engine roared as it struggled to gain altitude and outmaneuver the relentless pursuit, but Hideyoshi's combat experience proved decisive. He anticipated the American pilot's next maneuver and fired another burst, and the rounds struck the P-40's fuselage, sending up sparks as the plane began to trail a faint hint of smoke.

Below, Igarashi and Yoshikawa worked together against the second P-40. While one engaged directly, forcing the American fighter into evasive maneuvers, the other cut off its escape routes.

Hideyoshi stayed locked on his target, his focus narrowing as he maneuvered for a decisive shot. The P-40 pilot, now desperate, attempted a sharp turn to escape. It was a fatal mistake: the Zero could out-turn any airplane in the sky, and Hideyoshi followed easily. At the critical moment, he squeezed the trigger again, and his 20mm cannon rounds arced out, tearing into the P-40's engine and cockpit. Flames erupted from the stricken aircraft as it began a spiraling descent.

Hideyoshi pulled up, watching briefly as the P-40 crashed into the harbor, sending up a plume of water and debris. Once more a moment of respect crossed his mind for the enemy pilot's bravery, but he quickly refocused on the mission. There was no time for reflection.

Below him, the second P-40 was already limping away, trailing smoke but still airborne. Igarashi and Yoshikawa rejoined Hideyoshi, and the three Zeros slid back into formation.

As his Zero banked gently, Hideyoshi's eyes darted across the scene below. The American Pacific Fleet was now reduced to burning hulks. The *Arizona* was a fiery inferno, and the *Oklahoma* lay on her side, her upturned hull jutting out of the water like the belly of a beached whale. The *West Virginia* and *California* were also listing heavily, with thick flames engulfing their superstructures.

Looking further out, Hideyoshi could see the green mountains of the Hawaiian landscape, an unsettling contrast to the fiery carnage below. It was, he thought philosophically, a jarring reminder of the chasm between nature's indifference and humanity's destructive tendencies.

The second wave of the attack on Pearl Harbor arrived shortly after the first wave had completed its devastating assault. This wave consisted of 171 aircraft, including 54 high-altitude Kate bombers, 78 Val dive bombers, and 36 Zero fighters. Unlike the initial strike, which had prioritized surprise and focused on crippling the battleships, the second wave aimed to exploit the chaos and insure the complete neutralization of Pearl Harbor as a military base. The focus now expanded to include auxiliary ships, repair facilities, and fuel depots, as well as any surviving ships or planes that could pose a potential threat to the Japanese carrier fleet that was waiting just a few hundred miles offshore.

The dive bombers came in fast and swooped down low, and the hangars that still stood were now engulfed in flames, collapsing under repeated hits. The high-altitude Kates focused on any ships in the harbor that had been spared or only lightly damaged by the first assault, and the cruisers and destroyers anchored along the docks became primary targets, as did auxiliary vessels and tankers. Bombs rained down, striking with devastating force. Fuel depots and ammunition storage facilities were also hit and repair facilities and workshops were heavily bombed, insuring that any surviving ships could not be repaired without extensive delays.

As the second wave completed its mission, the aircraft began to regroup and head back toward the *Kido Butai*.

In just under two hours, the American fleet had suffered ruinous losses. Eight battleships were either sunk or severely damaged. Three cruisers, three destroyers, and several auxiliary ships sustained varying degrees of damage. Aircraft losses were equally devastating. The Japanese had destroyed over 300 aircraft on the ground, and only a handful of American aircraft had managed to take off during the attack. And the human toll was staggering. Over 2,400 Americans were killed, including military personnel and civilians, and more than 1,000 were wounded.

Strategically, the attack had temporarily paralyzed the Pacific Fleet. The destruction of so many battleships and aircraft left the US Navy severely weakened. However, key facilities at Pearl Harbor, including fuel depots, repair yards, and submarine pens, remained largely intact.

Additionally, the three American aircraft carriers—*Lexington*, *Enterprise*, and *Saratoga*—were not in the harbor during the attack. The Americans had taken a bloody nose and were put on their knees, but they had not been knocked out.

Hideyoshi was relieved by the sight of the *Akagi*. Like most of the combat pilots, he had expected that he would not survive.

Landing a Zero on a carrier required focus. As Hideyoshi lined up his approach, he adjusted for the slight crosswind and carefully managed his airspeed, his eyes fixed on the carrier deck as it swayed up and down with the waves. At the right instant, he guided his aircraft down and cut the power, feeling the jolt as the wheels touched the deck and the arrestor hook caught the wire. Deck crews rushed to secure the plane and tow it to its assigned position, clearing the way for the next arrival.

Hideyoshi climbed out of his cockpit, his muscles stiff from the tension of the mission. Mechanics immediately swarmed his Zero, inspecting the airframe for damage and preparing to refuel and re-arm it if the order came. His aircraft, like so many others, bore the scars of battle—several rows of bullet holes in the fuselage. Nevertheless, it had brought him back safely.

As Hideyoshi stood by his plane, a crew member approached him with somber news. Two planes from *Akagi's* complement had not returned. Among them was a Zero piloted by Lieutenant Inoue, a veteran aviator well-respected by his peers. The second loss was a Kate torpedo bomber and its three-man crew, led by Ensign Matsumori. Hideyoshi felt a pang of grief. They had lost good men.

After the planes had landed and the deck crews had cleared the aircraft, the pilots were directed to the ready room for a debriefing. Each man was asked to describe his actions and observations, providing details of the attack and noting any difficulties encountered. When it was Hideyoshi's turn, he saluted and reported succinctly, "We encountered two American P-40s. My wingmen and I successfully engaged them, downing one and driving the other off. Afterward, we continued to provide cover and strafed anti-aircraft positions before returning."

Lieutenant Mikatsu nodded as he jotted down notes. "Any mechanical issues or observations?" he asked.

Hideyoshi hesitated, then mentioned the strain of prolonged flight without radio communication. "Coordinating with wingmen in such an environment remains a challenge, especially during dogfights."

Mikatsu acknowledged the point with a sharp nod, noting it on his clipboard.

As the pilots dispersed, Hideyoshi lingered for a moment, reflecting on the day's events. The tactical success of the attack was undeniable—Pearl Harbor lay in ruins, the American fleet had suffered a terrible blow, and the Japanese had taken only minor losses. Yet, as the initial rush of victory began to subside, a deeper unease began gnawing at the edges of his thoughts.

He walked up to *Akagi's* flight deck, the cool night air brushing against his face. They had achieved the seemingly impossible, catching the Americans completely off guard and dealing them a punishing blow. And yet, it was impossible not to think about the enormity of what they had set into motion.

Hideyoshi leaned on the railing, staring out at the sea. From the ready room, he could hear the sounds of pilots celebrating their crushing victory.

"We've awakened a giant," he thought. The Americans were slow to act, perhaps, but their capacity for retaliation was overwhelming. Japan had struck first, but could it sustain such a war? The Empire's strategic gamble hinged on breaking the will of a nation far larger and wealthier than it, a nation that could command vast reserves of manpower and material that Japan could never hope to match.

He had no illusions about his role in this unfolding drama. As a pilot, his duty was clear: to fight with skill and courage for the Emperor. But as a man, he could not shake the sense that this war, begun with such triumph, would demand a terrible cost.

He glanced up at the horizon. Somewhere out there, the American carriers were still unaccounted for, their potential counter-strike an ominous question mark looming over Japan's grand strategy. The attack on Pearl Harbor had been a masterstroke, but it was only the opening move.

Turning away from the railing, Hideyoshi was lost in thought.

"We've won a battle," he said to himself, "but can we win the war?"

Chapter 10
Darwin (February 1942)

Japan's campaigns in early 1942 were textbook examples of rapid military expansion through combined naval, air, and land operations. By February, the Empire was systematically dismantling the defenses of Allied territories across the Pacific and Southeast Asia, leaving the world to marvel — and tremble.

The Philippines, an American colony and a key strategic location in the Pacific, became one of Japan's earliest targets, with Japanese forces launching their invasion only hours after the air raid on Hawaii. General Douglas MacArthur's forces were forced into a desperate defense, retreating to the Bataan Peninsula and an eventual American surrender in April. On the same day as the invasion of the Philippines, the Japanese launched a bold amphibious assault on the northeastern coast of Malaya, and British troops, including Indian and Australian contingents, suffered heavy losses in battles at Jitra and Slim River. Singapore, Britain's key stronghold in Asia, fell in February 1942.

In the Dutch East Indies, the campaign began in January, and the Imperial Navy quickly won an important victory in the Battle of the Java Sea in late February. By March, the Japanese had occupied Sumatra, Java, and Borneo, securing the vital oil supplies needed to sustain their war machine.

By early 1942, Japan's empire covered a vast stretch of the Pacific and Southeast Asia, reaching from the edge of the Aleutian Islands in the north to the Solomon Islands in the south, and from Burma in the west to the Gilbert Islands in the east. The militarists in Tokyo basked in the glow of their victories, confident now in the inevitability of their domination of Asia.

New Guinea had also become a focal point for new Japanese expansion, as its strategic location made it a convenient staging stepping stone for further operations in the South Pacific to protect their conquests in Southeast Asia. The campaign began with the invasion of Rabaul, a vital naval and air base, in January 1942. From Rabaul, the Japanese turned their attention to New Guinea itself, and landed troops at Lae and Salamaua on the Huon Gulf.

The Japanese advance into New Guinea was part of a broader effort to isolate and neutralize Australia as a potential threat, allowing Japan to control the air and sea lanes in the region and cut off Australia's ability to support American and British operations in the Pacific. It also put northern Australia itself within striking range.

Darwin, the largest city on the northern coast of Australia, quickly became a vital military base for the Australian and American allies. Its deep-water port was essential for the movement of troops, equipment, and supplies from Australia to the Allied forces fighting in the Dutch East Indies. The port's strategic location also allowed the rapid deployment of Allied warships to counter Japanese advances and to intercept potential air raids on Australia's major population centers like Sydney and Melbourne.

Despite its strategic value, however, Darwin's defenses were limited, hampered by the city's isolation and its relatively small population. While anti-aircraft emplacements and coastal defense batteries had been hastily constructed, they were nowhere near enough to drive off a serious invasion attempt.

For the Japanese, then, Darwin presented a tempting target. Its destruction would cripple Allied supply lines, disrupt communications, and weaken Australia's ability to contribute to the war effort in the entire Pacific.

For the crew of the *Akagi*, the voyage south was uneventful, almost boring. They had no idea where they were heading or how long it would take to get there, and while much of their time was taken up by drills and routines, everyone had their share of time off.

A day without flying was both a blessing and a curse for the men aboard the carriers. It gave pilots like Hideyoshi a reprieve from the intense pressure of flying missions, but it also sometimes left them grappling with the monotony of life at sea. The men sought ways to occupy themselves.

The wardroom, the heart of the pilot's off-duty life, was a frequent gathering place, and on their non-flying days, pilots and navigators would often meet here. Hideyoshi usually found himself drawn into a *hanafuda* card game — *Koi-Koi*, or *Hachi-Hachi* — with his fellow pilots. Gambling was something that was culturally frowned upon in Japan, so money rarely changed hands in these games; instead, they played for small tokens like cigarettes or promises of chores to be done.

Shogi, or Japanese chess, was also popular. Like Western chess the object was to capture the opponent's king, but *Shogi* differed in that it allowed captured pieces to be reintroduced on his own side by the player who had captured them.

Below decks, the enlisted service crew passed their time in equally creative ways. A volleyball net stretched across the floor of the hangar deck, and occasionally someone would produce a baseball bat.

Evenings often brought organized entertainment. The officers and crew sometimes gathered on the flight deck, where a small stage would be erected from spare parts. Performances ranged from comedic skits to traditional *Noh* plays, with sailors playing all the roles. One night, a pilot named Watanabe had donned a makeshift *kimono* and performed a hilariously exaggerated *kabuki* dance, earning roaring laughter and applause from the audience.

One enterprising sailor with a knack for handiwork began scavenging pieces of scrap wood from the carrier's maintenance shop, using a hand saw to shape them into a vaguely guitar-like instrument with a crude sound-hole cut into the center. Screws salvaged from a discarded engine part served as tuning pegs, and the strings came from scrounged lengths of thin wire — some stripped from old electrical cables, others begged from a mechanic who understood the universal need for music aboard. The sound was raw and uneven, but passably musical. It became an instant morale booster.

On one memorable occasion, a captured projector, scavenged from Dutch forces during the campaign in the East Indies, had been patched together by the technical crew. Alongside it was a collection of Dutch cinema reels, stored in battered cases bearing faded titles that none of the Japanese sailors could read.

Word spread quickly through the carrier that there would be a film screening that evening, and anticipation soared among the crew. After weeks of monotonous routines and relentless training drills, even the prospect of watching foreign films in an incomprehensible language was a welcome distraction. When the appointed hour arrived, the men filed in, settling onto benches or the bare floor, eager for the rare luxury.

The first film flickered to life on the improvised screen—a white sheet strung taut against a row of crates. After the incomprehensible opening credits, footage showed a cheerful Dutch village, complete with windmills and cobblestone streets. The characters on screen spoke animatedly, in dialogue that no one understood.

"What are they saying?" one pilot asked, mystified, drawing chuckles from the men around him. Another sailor quipped, "Probably complaining about the weather—just like us."

Despite the language barrier, the crew quickly found ways to enjoy the experience. Laughter erupted as the sailors provided their own dubbed-over commentary, turning mundane conversations into ridiculous exchanges. When an angry-looking man appeared on screen gesturing emphatically, someone in the back shouted, "He's telling them their rations are being cut!"

The second reel featured what appeared to be a melodrama. A woman wept by a canal while a man in a suit shouted and stormed off. "She just found out he's a pilot!" someone joked, prompting a round of laughter.

By the third film, a slapstick comedy, the language barrier no longer mattered. The physical humor—bumbling characters slipping on ice, a chase through a crowded market—translated universally. The hangar echoed with genuine laughter as the men momentarily forgot the tensions of their duty.

The evening drew to a close with applause and calls for another showing. For a few hours, the war seemed a little farther away

Though the men on *Akagi* were warriors, these pursuits revealed another side of them—resourceful and humorous. It was a reminder that, even in the heat of war, life continued in its own small ways.

Akagi's pilots quieted as the senior flight officer strode to the front, carrying a map of northern Australia.

"Tomorrow," he declared, "we strike a critical enemy base. Darwin is the key supply and logistics hub for the Americans in northern Australia, and its destruction will cripple their ability to interfere with our operations in the Dutch East Indies."

The officer's pointer tapped specific targets on the map: the airfields at RAAF Darwin, the town's harbor, and the shipping lanes leading into the port. "Your mission is to neutralize Darwin's air power, destroy its port facilities, and eliminate any shipping present. Surprise is on our side, but the Australians are not fools. They will fight back."

"You will be joined by aircraft from the *Kaga, Hiryu* and *Soryu*."

The officer continued, addressing the specific roles of each squadron. "The torpedo bombers will strike vessels in the harbor, targeting transport and warships alike. Dive bombers are assigned to eliminate the airfield infrastructure, fuel depots, and anti-aircraft positions. Fighters, your job is to eliminate any threats from the air. Once the dive bombers have completed their runs, you will continue by strafing targets on the ground and suppressing anti-aircraft emplacements."

The officer moved on, detailing the formation plans for the attack. "The first wave will depart at dawn. Maintain your formations and adhere to the strike timeline. Timing is everything. Fighters will take off ahead of the bombers and establish air superiority before they arrive. Dive bombers and torpedo planes will follow in staggered waves to minimize congestion and maximize effectiveness."

The briefing concluded with a final word from the senior officer. "This is a critical mission, one that will further Japan's rightful place in the Pacific. I expect every man to fulfill his duty with honor. Dismissed."

The process of "spotting" aircraft on a carrier deck was critical for ensuring the success of any mission. The arrangement was carefully planned by the flight operations team, which determined the order of launch based on the mission's objectives. Fighters like the Zeroes were arranged at the front to provide immediate air cover, while the larger bombers and torpedo planes followed. Using raw manpower, deck handlers maneuvered each aircraft into its designated position on the flight deck, aligning them in neat rows facing the bow. Space was at a premium, and every inch of the deck was utilized efficiently. Once the planes were in place, they were secured with chocks to prevent any movement from the rolling of the ship or the strong ocean winds.

As soon as the planes were spotted and ready, any unnecessary personnel and equipment were cleared away from the flight deck, and the pilots received the signal to start their engines. The air thundered with the roar of dozens of radial engines coming to life. One by one, the planes then taxied to their launch positions, waiting for the flagged signal to take off.

It was a coordinated and disciplined dance which insured that the maximum number of planes could be launched in the least amount of time. A good crew could launch its entire air group within fifteen minutes.

Hideyoshi glanced at his instruments, insuring that everything was in good order. He exchanged a silent nod with his wingman, Igarashi, who gave him a thumbs-up from his cockpit. Yoshikawa, to the right, adjusted his goggles and focused ahead.

As the Zeros lifted off the deck, they formed up into a tight V-shaped formation, leading the first wave of dive bombers and torpedo planes toward their target. Behind them, the rest of the Air Fleet followed in staggered waves, each group maintaining a carefully calculated distance to avoid midair collisions.

After a time, the coastline of northern Australia emerged on the horizon, a faint strip of land against the blue sea. Hideyoshi and the other flight leaders adjusted their altitudes slightly to maintain visual contact with the bombers below. The town's layout began to take shape beneath them: the airfields to the east, the port facilities sprawling along the shoreline, and the cluster of anchored ships.

He signaled to Igarashi and Yoshikawa, who nodded in silent acknowledgment.

As they neared the harbor, anti-aircraft fire erupted from the ground, sending bursts of black smoke into the sky. From his cockpit, Hideyoshi observed the lead bombers releasing their payloads over the town. Explosions erupted across the airfields, warehouses, and military barracks, and columns of smoke spiraled upward as buildings crumbled under the impact of the bombs. A split second later, a chain of explosions rippled through the harbor as bombs struck the ships moored there. Several vessels erupted in flames.

Hideyoshi watched as one of the bombs struck the *Neptuna*, an armed merchant vessel, setting off a massive explosion that rocked the harbor. Another bomb pierced the deck of the *Peary*, an American destroyer, igniting a blaze that quickly consumed the ship.

Meanwhile, the torpedo bombers moved in for their runs. Flying just above the water, the Kates unleashed their payloads toward the larger ships in the harbor, and torpedoes streaked through the waves, leaving white trails. One after another, they struck their targets with devastating force. Hideyoshi watched the *Zealandia*, a transport ship, list heavily to one side and belch fire and smoke before sinking beneath the surface.

Amid the confusion of tracer fire and the bursts of flak, Hideyoshi spotted a speck approaching rapidly from the northwest. It was a solitary Australian P-40 Tomahawk which had managed to take off and was now clawing for altitude towards them.

Hideyoshi dipped his wings and tapped the side of his cockpit, signaling Igarashi and Yoshikawa to stay with him. Igarashi acknowledged with a brief waggle of his wings, and the three Zeros turned sharply to intercept the Tomahawk.

The P-40 pilot charged head-on toward the formation, and as the distance rapidly closed Hideyoshi saw the P-40's machine guns begin to sparkle, sending a burst of tracers zipping above his canopy. He yanked the control stick and rolled his Zero into a sharp turn, the maneuver pulling him out of the Tomahawk's line of fire. Igarashi and Yoshikawa veered in opposite directions, splitting the attention of the Australian pilot. Hideyoshi glanced over his shoulder, watching as the P-40 reversed and turned after him. The Allied fighter lacked the maneuverability of the nimble Zero, but its speed and durability made it a dangerous opponent in the hands of an experienced pilot.

Hideyoshi pitched his Zero into a tight loop, the aircraft responding effortlessly. The P-40's nose briefly aligned with him, and a burst of bullets ripped through the air, several striking the edge of his left wing. The Zero shuddered but held steady. Hideyoshi gritted his teeth and continued the loop, aiming to come out behind his opponent.

As he completed the maneuver, the P-40 overshot its mark. It was now Hideyoshi's turn to attack. He pushed the nose of his Zero down and fired a short burst from his 20mm cannons. The shells streaked toward the Tomahawk, punching holes in its left wing and tail. The Australian pilot, realizing his precarious position, rolled his plane into a steep dive, trying to escape.

Hideyoshi followed. The heavier Tomahawk could dive much more rapidly than the lighter Zero, but now they were low and close to the water, and the P-40 pilot did not have enough room to dive away. He was forced to level out, allowing Hideyoshi to close the gap. The two aircraft hurtled across the harbor, the P-40 zigzagging in an attempt to evade him. Hideyoshi timed his shots carefully, and squeezed the trigger only when he was certain of a hit. Another burst of cannon fire found its mark, striking the P-40's fuselage. Smoke began to trail from the damaged aircraft, but the Tomahawk still continued on.

The panicked P-40 pilot made one final, desperate maneuver, pulling into a steep climb to gain altitude. It was a mistake. The Zero surged upward with ease, and within moments Hideyoshi was directly behind his opponent. He fired another burst, this one tearing through the P-40's engine, and the Tomahawk jolted, with smoke and flames pouring from its nose. The Australian pilot bailed out, his parachute opening moments later. His aircraft plummeted into the sea below.

Hideyoshi eased his Zero out of the climb, the adrenaline still surging through his veins. He glanced at the falling wreckage of the Tomahawk. It was his fifth air victory: he was now an ace. Igarashi and Yoshikawa rejoined him, their Zeros sliding into formation on either side, and Igarashi gave a quick salute, acknowledging the achievement.

The return flight to the carrier group took them out over the Timor Sea, where, despite the empty sky, the pilots remained vigilant, scanning the horizon for any sign of enemy aircraft. As they neared the rendezvous point, Hideyoshi spotted the faint silhouettes of the carriers and their escort ships ahead, their long wakes visible as they cut through the water. *Akagi* and *Kaga* were in front of them, and *Hiryu* and *Soryu* were out on the horizon. He checked his instruments again, and was satisfied that his plane would make it back, though he could feel the vibrations from the damage that the Australian P-40 had inflicted on his Zero.

When they arrived at the carrier group, the Zeros joined a growing cluster of returning planes circling above the *Akagi*. As a damaged aircraft, Hideyoshi was given priority to land. He throttled back and aligned his plane, and adjusted his glide path with small deliberate movements of the stick. The wheels touched down, and Hideyoshi exhaled a deep breath as the deck crew rushed forward to secure his aircraft, their shouts barely audible over the roar of the engines. Moments later, he was signaled to cut his power.

As he climbed out of the cockpit, the deck chief approached, gesturing toward the damage on his wing with a look of concern. Hideyoshi nodded in acknowledgment, grateful that the damage hadn't been worse.

Before he could remove his flight helmet, a ground crewman ran up to him with somber news.

"One of our Zeros is missing," the young sailor said, his voice subdued. "It's Sobachi. He hasn't return from the raid. Also, two of the Vals from our bomber squadron are confirmed lost. No word on the crew."

Hideyoshi's throat tightened. He had known Sobachi only briefly, but enough to feel the sting of his absence.

Even in victory, the cost of war was always present.

As Hideyoshi made his way toward the pilot ready room for debriefing, he glanced back at his damaged Zero being pushed across the deck.

The raid on Darwin was a tactical success for the Japanese. They had left the strategically vital port and airfields a wreck, crippling its military and logistical capabilities. Japanese bombers had sunk eight ships and damaged more. The two airfields were obliterated, destroying 23 Allied aircraft on the ground. Over 240 Allied personnel and civilians were killed in the attack, with hundreds more injured. And the psychological impact was penetrating, as Darwin's population realized the vulnerability of their city to direct enemy attack. They were now on the frontlines.

The raid on Darwin led both the Japanese and the Allies to make significant strategic adjustments as the Pacific War entered a new phase. For the Allies, the attack on Darwin was a shocking demonstration of their underestimation of Japanese capabilities. For Japan, the success of the attack reinforced their control of the region and confirmed their strategy of conducting rapid coordinated strikes against Allied positions. Following the raid, the Japanese Navy shifted its focus to maintaining control over key territories and securing the vital sea lanes from the Dutch East Indies and Malaya.

As Hideyoshi sat on the edge of his bunk aboard the *Akagi*, the faint hum of the carrier's engines reverberated through the steel walls. The adrenaline of the mission had long since faded, replaced by the introspection that always crept in during moments of solitude.

From a pilot's perspective, the mission had been flawless. Hideyoshi took a moment of pride in his contribution, particularly in his aerial combat with the P-40. It marked his fifth confirmed victory in air-to-air combat, a personal milestone that would have been celebrated in other nations. Yet, in Japan, individual achievements were not recognized or rewarded. Instead, the emphasis was on the collective success of the *shotai*, the squadron, and, ultimately, the Empire. Hideyoshi accepted this ethos without question.

But still he was troubled. "Victory fever," he muttered to himself. That was what some of the officers had whispered in the mess hall when they thought no one could hear them. Japan had won so much, so quickly. The Philippines had fallen, Malaya was conquered, and now the Dutch East Indies. Each triumph had fed the belief that Japan was invincible, that her Empire was destined to stretch unchallenged across the Pacific and perhaps beyond. But Hideyoshi had seen enough to know better.

The raid on Darwin, while impressive, had not delivered the hoped-for decisive blow. The Allies had been caught unprepared, certainly, but the damage inflicted had been more a disruptive jab than a crippling blow. Ports could be repaired, airfields rebuilt, and reinforcements sent. What the raid had truly accomplished, Hideyoshi realized, was to galvanize the enemy. Just as Pearl Harbor had awakened the Americans, Darwin would stiffen the resolve of the Australians. The brutality of the attack, the civilian casualties, the devastation—these would not demoralize the enemy. They would enrage him.

Later, Hideyoshi found himself granted a rare leave onshore at the naval base in Rabaul. The bustling port city offered a brief respite from the monotony of life aboard the *Akagi,* and he wandered through the narrow streets, past teahouses and shops, savoring the sense of freedom, however fleeting.

In the evening, he found himself at a small *izakaya* frequented by Navy men. The room buzzed with chatter, laughter, and the clinking of *sake* cups. Hideyoshi sat at a corner table, nursing his drink and enjoying the warmth of the space, when a man approached and gestured to the empty seat across from him.

"Mind if I join you?" the man asked.

"Not at all," Hideyoshi replied, motioning for him to sit.

The man introduced himself as Petty Officer Kamashima, a torpedo bomber pilot from the *Shokaku.* They exchanged pleasantries and spoke of their respective carriers, but it wasn't long before Kamashima steered the conversation toward recent events.

"I heard the *Akagi's* been running non-stop since Pearl Harbor," Kamashima said, taking a sip from his cup. "But you've missed some action lately."

"Oh?" Hideyoshi leaned forward.

"The Coral Sea," Kamashima said, lowering his voice. "A real fight down there. The *Shokaku* was in the thick of it. We tangled with the Americans near New Guinea.

Hideyoshi nodded. "We heard it was a great blow to the Americans."

But Kamashima slowly shook his head. "I don't know if I'd call it a victory. They were a lot tougher than we expected."

"Tougher how?"

Kamashima set his cup down and leaned back, his expression turning serious. "They're adapting. Their carriers *Lexington* and *Yorktown*—they launched a counter-strike before we could finish them off. We lost the *Shoho,* and they damaged the *Shokaku* badly. She's still in dry dock. And the *Zuikaku*? She's sitting out too. Lost too many planes to keep her operational."

Hideyoshi nodded thoughtfully. "But you held the Americans back?"

"For now," Kamashima said. "We sank the *Lexington,* and we think we got the *Yorktown.* Still, the Americans are learning fast. They're not just sitting still anymore. They'll be back. They're not giving up."

Hideyoshi swirled the remains of his tea, his mind racing. The Coral Sea was the first major naval engagement fought entirely by carrier air power—the kind of fight that *Akagi, Shokaku,* and their sisters were built for. Yet the cost Kamashima described was sobering.

"Do you think it's a turning point?"

Kamashima hesitated, looking off into the distance. "Hard to say. We've proven we can push them back, but they're not afraid to fight. And their industrial strength ..." He trailed off, shaking his head.

The conversation turned to lighter topics after that, but Hideyoshi knew the import of Kamashima's words. The Americans were already fighting back, and they had not yet even brought their massive economic strength to bear. As he returned to the *Akagi* the next morning, he wondered how long the Empire's momentum could last.

Japan had reached far and wide in its ambitions, but every new conquest stretched their supply lines thinner and strained their resources further. The planes they flew were marvels of engineering, but how long could they maintain such technological superiority when the factories of America were now starting to churn out new war machines at a stupifying pace? The enemy had time and industrial might on their side, advantages Japan could not hope to match. The military leadership in Tokyo, however, seemed to be blinded by its recent victories, apparently believing they could sustain this pace indefinitely. Japan was overreaching. Her early victories were breeding a smug complacency — and her enemies were already gathering strength.

Chapter 11
Ceylon (March 1942)

Ceylon, nestled in the heart of the Indian Ocean, was strategically vital to Britain. The island, known today as Sri Lanka, served as a critical naval and air base, guarding the sea lanes that linked Britain to its colonies in India and Southeast Asia and protecting the routes over which enough American Lend-Lease aid was flowing into China to keep over a million Japanese troops tied up there. The harbors of Trincomalee and Colombo provided the Royal Navy with key anchorages for their fleet, while several airfields across the island offered a base for RAF bombers and fighters.

For Japan, then, striking at Ceylon would achieve two goals: to disrupt British naval power in the region, and to sever the vital supply routes through which military aid was flowing to China. By striking quickly and suddenly, Japanese planners hoped to deal a blow so severe that it would cripple the British Eastern Fleet and force the Allies to divert resources away from the Pacific.

The British Eastern Fleet under Admiral Sir James Somerville expected a Japanese attack (Tokyo did not know that the Allies had broken the Imperial Navy's code system), but it was not prepared to face Japan's *Kido Butai* carrier force. The Royal Navy had lost its two most powerful ships in the Pacific, the battleships *Repulse* and *Prince of Wales*, in the fighting around Malaya, and the remaining fleet in the Indian Ocean was composed of five older battleships like the *Resolution* and *Warspite*. The carriers *Indomitable* and *Formidable* were quickly rushed to the scene, where they joined the light carrier *Hermes*. But the British air forces were a mix of outdated aircraft like the Fairey Swordfish, with just a handful of modern Hurricane fighters. Britain's topline military power, Tokyo knew, was desperately needed in Europe.

The British had just one potential advantage: their Fairy Albacore biplane torpedo bombers, while slow and vulnerable, were equipped with radar — something the Japanese did not have — which allowed for night attacks.

The Japanese plan for the Ceylon campaign, code-named "Operation C", therefore centered around a bold naval and aerial assault. The *Kido Butai,* the same carrier strike force that had attacked Pearl Harbor (minus the *Kaga,* who had been damaged after accidentally running aground on a shallow reef and was still undergoing repairs), was now redeployed for the mission, accompanied by another task force centered around the light carrier *Ryujo.* Their goal was to sweep into the Indian Ocean undetected, strike at Ceylon's key installations, and destroy any British naval forces in the area before withdrawing.

The fleet's approach was meticulously calculated to prevent detection and maximize surprise. Sailing south from the Japanese-controlled Dutch East Indies, the *Kido Butai* skirted the vast expanse of the Indian Ocean, avoiding all of the known British reconnaissance patrols. Mimicking the Pearl Harbor attack, the first raid was to be launched on Easter Sunday, when it was expected that the British would be least prepared.

One evening, though, as the Japanese fleet made its way, rumors swept through the *Akagi* that they may have been detected. The fleet's radio operators had intercepted British signals suggesting that the Eastern Fleet may have left port and was preparing for a battle. The thought of a major naval engagement electrified the men, and as they approached the waters south of the Andaman Islands, Admiral Nagumo issued orders for increased vigilance. Anti-aircraft crews were instructed to be at the ready around the clock, and the pilots were reminded of the importance of rapid response should the fleet encounter Allied reconnaissance planes. Each day, the Japanese cruisers launched their seaplanes to scout the area for any sign of enemy ships or aircraft, but none were found.

As the fleet drew closer to Ceylon, the final briefings were given. Hideyoshi took his place among the other Zero pilots, a folded map in hand. Around him, the other airmen chattered in low tones, sharing snippets of conjecture about the mission ahead.

At the front of the assembled group stood Lieutenant Commander Minoru Genda, the man who had planned the Pearl Harbor operation and who was now the chief planner of Operation

C. Every pilot knew him as a brilliant tactician, and his calm, authoritative demeanor commanded the room. Many considered him as almost a war god.

Behind him, a large map of Ceylon and the surrounding waters was pinned to a display board. Key locations, including the ports of Colombo and Trincomalee, were circled in red, with additional notations for coastal defenses and likely naval anchorages.

"The objective," Genda announced, "is to neutralize British forces on and around Ceylon. Our primary targets are the port facilities and airbases at Colombo and Trincomalee. Intelligence suggests that elements of the Royal Navy's Eastern Fleet are stationed in these locations, including capital ships and probably aircraft carriers. If successful, this operation will eliminate a key Allied stronghold and secure Japan's dominance in the Indian Ocean."

He pointed to Colombo on the map. "The fighters will concentrate on the airfields on the outskirts of the city, where Hurricanes and other British aircraft are believed to be based. Take out anything in the air, then hit anything that is left on the ground."

Hideyoshi leaned forward, studying the map. The pilot next to him whispered, "Hurricanes. I've heard they're tough." Hideyoshi nodded but kept his thoughts to himself. RAF pilots had a reputation for skill, and Hurricanes had already proven to be formidable opponents in the skies over England, where they had beaten back the German Luftwaffe.

Genda's shifted his pointer to Trincomalee. "This harbor will be the focus of follow-up strikes, but intelligence reports suggest that the primary concentration of ships is in Colombo."

Genda then outlined specific flight assignments, while officers distributed mission maps to each pilot. Hideyoshi received his with a nod, scanning the sheet for details. His *shotai* was tasked with escorting dive-bombers during the first wave.

"Maintain discipline and adhere to your formations—this is not the time for heroics. Dismissed."

As the *Akagi's* loudspeakers blared the order for launch, Hideyoshi and his wingmen climbed into their cockpits, and the Zeros roared into the air one by one, followed by the bombers.

As the harbor of Colombo came into view, a smattering of anti-aircraft fire from British naval ships greeted them. Hideyoshi signaled his *shotai* to stay above the bombers. Looking down, he was disappointed to see that the British had known they were coming, and their battleships and carriers had already left the harbor and headed out into the open sea. Only a small group of destroyers and auxiliary ships remained. The bombers nevertheless moved in for the attack.

Soon enough, the distinct shapes of Hawker Hurricanes began climbing up towards them from the airfield below. Hideyoshi signaled Igarashi and Yoshikawa to hold position and follow his lead.

The dogfight that followed was fast and chaotic. Hideyoshi's sharp eyes tracked a Hurricane that attempted to loop around and attack one of the bombers. A quick dip of his wings alerted Yoshikawa to cover him as he dived to intercept. Before the Hurricane could close the distance, Hideyoshi's approach forced the British pilot to break off the attack and circle away.

Meanwhile, Igarashi engaged another Hurricane that had attempted to climb directly into their formation. The Zero's agility proved decisive as Igarashi outmaneuvered his opponent, forcing the British fighter into a defensive turn.

The Zeros, despite their superior agility and firepower, adhered strictly to their orders to protect the bombers. Hideyoshi had drilled this priority into his wingmen during countless briefings. His hand signals directed Yoshikawa to fall back into formation after his unsuccessful pursuit: they did not want to stray too far from their Vals and leave them vulnerable.

As the bombers completed their runs and began to withdraw, the British fighters, unable to match the Zeros' climb and speed, also broke off their attacks and retreated to their airfield.

Returning to the *Akagi*, Hideyoshi barely had time to remove his flight cap when an officer approached him.

"You guys have missed out on the action," he said. "Our search planes found the cruisers *Cornwall* and *Dorsetshire* fleeing the harbor. Planes from *Hiryu* and *Soryu* are already on their way to intercept."

"What about *Akagi*? Are we launching?"

"The order was given for us to prepare for launch, but our aircraft weren't able to be refueled and rearmed in time after the Colombo raid. The *Hiryu* and *Soryu* were closer and they were ready to go. They've already launched their strike force."

For the next hour, the pilots waited for word, exchanging idle banter to pass the time. Then, the confirmation came. The *Cornwall* and *Dorsetshire* had been sunk by *Hiryu* and *Soryu's* Vals. The room erupted in a chorus of cheers. One pilot clapped Hideyoshi on the back and said with a grin, "Well, I guess *Akagi's* planes weren't needed after all."

That evening, Hideyoshi reflected on his encounter over Colombo. The British pilots had displayed courage and skill, but their aircraft were not as maneuverable as his, and their tactics were constrained by the limitations of their machines. Still, while not superior to the Zero, the Hurricane was no slouch, especially if it had a good pilot at the controls. They would have to be careful.

After the attack on Colombo, Nagumo's attention turned to Tricomalee.

As *Akagi's* air group approached the British harbor, Hideyoshi's *shotai* of three Zeros flew high above the bomber formation, scanning the airspace for incoming threats.

Hideyoshi caught movement in the distance, and he could see small dots moving swiftly in their direction. Hurricanes. With a quick hand signal, Hideyoshi alerted his wingmen and led them in an arc to gain altitude, his mind already working through the tactics. The British fighters, faster in a dive and well-armored, would try to climb above the Zeros and attack from superior positions.

The lead Hurricane broke away from its formation, angling toward Hideyoshi. Its pilot, an RAF veteran of the fighting in North Africa, seemed confident as he ascended. The rugged Hurricane had earned a reputation as a tough workhorse in the desert campaigns.

Hideyoshi moved to intercept.

The British pilot, seeing the Zero match his climb, adjusted course and attempted to dive for a deflection shot, but Hideyoshi anticipated this move, rolling smoothly into a split-S maneuver. The Zero responded with perfect precision, arcing beneath the Hurricane and leveling out behind it.

Hideyoshi closed the distance with deliberate care, the Hurricane's broad wings and distinctive silhouette growing larger in his gun sight. The British pilot weaved, banking hard to shake him, but the Zero's unmatched turning radius kept it locked onto the Hurricane's tail. The British pilot, likely expecting a slower turn, hesitated for a crucial second, giving Hideyoshi the advantage.

Hideyoshi squeezed the trigger, sending a burst of rounds streaking toward the enemy aircraft. Sparks flared as the bullets found their mark, peppering the Hurricane's fuselage. The British pilot, realizing the danger, banked hard to the left, but the Zero's nimbleness allowed Hideyoshi to stay with him. A second burst caught the Hurricane squarely in the engine cowling. Smoke poured from the stricken aircraft, and the pilot was now fighting to regain control. Hideyoshi maintained his position, watching as the Hurricane's propeller sputtered to a halt. Finally, the canopy slid back and the pilot ejected, his parachute opening a few seconds later. Hideyoshi eased off, watching the stricken aircraft spiral down into the sea below.

The trio of Zeros re-formed above the bombers, continuing their protective sweep. As Hideyoshi led his *shotai* in another circuit, he glanced back at the parachuting pilot. He imagined the man's confusion and frustration—probably expecting to face a plane akin to the Bf-109, only to be outmaneuvered by an agile aircraft that he had never encountered before.

Hideyoshi's eyes scanned the chaotic airspace, and as the Zeros looped back to cover the bombers, he spotted another Hurricane diving toward the formation, its guns blazing.

Signaling to his wingmen with a sharp wave of his hand, Hideyoshi peeled off to intercept. The British fighter seemed unaware of their approach, its pilot focused entirely on a damaged Kate limping away from the battle. The Hurricane closed in, tracers streaking across the sky and punching through the bomber's wing.

Hideyoshi felt a surge of anger at the attack on the already-wounded bomber. "He's already out of the fight!" he shouted out loud. "Let him get back!" He pushed the throttle forward, closing the distance rapidly.

The British pilot must have sensed the danger at the last moment, abruptly breaking off his attack and pulling into a steep climb. Hideyoshi followed, the Zero's superior climb rate enabling him to stay in position.

The Hurricane looped into a series of sharp turns, trying to shake its pursuer. It was a tactic that worked well against slower or less maneuverable aircraft like the German Bf-109, but against the Zero, it was futile. Hideyoshi expected such a move, and was able to stay just inside the Hurricane's turn radius while gradually closing the gap.

This pilot was far more skilled than the first, Hideyoshi said to himself.

The Hurricane suddenly changed tactics, diving sharply to gain speed and distance. Hideyoshi followed and quickly aligned his gunsights with the enemy fighter.

A burst of machine-gun fire erupted from the Zero, the bullets slashing across the Hurricane's tail. The British pilot jinked left, then right, trying to evade, but Hideyoshi adjusted with each move, firing short, controlled bursts. One volley struck the Hurricane's right wing, shredding the metal covering and sending fragments spinning into the air.

Smoke began trailing from the Hurricane's engine as Hideyoshi fired again, this time aiming for the wing roots. The bullets found their mark, and the enemy fighter shook from the impacts before losing altitude. The pilot made one last desperate maneuver, banking hard to escape, but his aircraft was now too damaged to maneuver.

The Hurricane rolled over, its propeller now windmilling as it nosed downward. Hideyoshi watched the stricken plane tumble toward the jungle below. He saw no parachute and felt a pang of regret—whether the pilot had been too injured to eject, Hideyoshi would never know. But the man had fought well.

Hideyoshi's thoughts were interrupted by the sudden sight of a Fairy Fulmar fighter diving out of the sun. Its pilot seemed to have spotted Hideyoshi, turning toward him with clear intent.

As Hideyoshi instinctively pulled back on the stick, sending his Zero into a steep climb, out of the corner of his eye, he saw a familiar silhouette—a Zero, streaking in from the side. One of his wingmen had spotted the danger and had come to his aid.

The British pilot, too focused on his prey, never saw it coming. The Zero closed in quickly, positioning itself perfectly on the Fulmar's tail. A burst of fire erupted from the Zero's 20mm cannons, the tracers slicing through the air and into the British fighter.

The Fulmar shuddered as the explosive rounds tore into its fuselage and wings. Smoke began pouring from its engine, and the aircraft wavered in the air before it began a slow, spiraling descent toward the jungle below. Hideyoshi caught a brief glimpse of the Fulmar's pilot struggling to maintain control before the plane disappeared into the treetops.

Relieved, Hideyoshi signaled his thanks with a quick wing waggle. His wingman, whom he now recognized as Yoshikawa, returned the gesture before falling back into formation. The bombers were returning towards the *Akagi*, and the remaining Hurricanes, outnumbered and outclassed, began to withdraw.

When Hideyoshi had landed back on *Akagi*, he learned to his chagrin that he had once again missed the real action. As he walked across the flight deck, he heard a voice call his name and, turning, he spotted Izuma jogging across the deck toward him with a wide grin.

"You missed it," Izuma said excitedly.

"Missed what?"

"The British carrier *Hermes*," Izuma replied. "We found her, and the reserve force took her out."

Hideyoshi turned to him. "What do you mean, 'we found her'? How?"

"One of the scout planes spotted her south of Trincomalee while you guys were out over the harbor. As soon as the report came in, the reserve force was ordered to launch."

"You were part of it?"

Izuma nodded, his grin widening. "Yes! We scrambled as soon as the order came down. Twenty-seven of us. The carrier didn't stand a chance. She had no aircraft ready to defend her, and just one destroyer. We sunk them both. It was over before we knew it."

Hideyoshi exhaled slowly. Like any other fighter pilot, he had the aggressive instinct that was so vital for success in the air, and the heart within him always wanted to be in the middle of the danger zone, to face the enemy directly and, like a *samurai* of old, to prove his superior skill in the test of one-on-one combat.

Izuma saw the flicker of disappointment in his eyes and clapped him on the shoulder. "Don't let it get to you, buddy. There will be other chances."

The Ceylon campaign had delivered a severe blow to the British forces in the Indian Ocean. The attacks had destroyed a number of ships, including cruisers and a carrier, and the Royal Air Force had suffered heavy losses, with over half of its Hurricanes, Fulmars, and other aircraft destroyed in the air and on the ground. For Japan, the losses were light, with 36 aircraft shot down by fighters and anti-aircraft fire.

As the *Kido Butai* sailed back to Japan, Hideyoshi found moments of solitude to process the whirlwind of events. The British pilots had been formidable, their combat experience evident in their tactics and tenacity. Yet, for all their experience, the British pilots were unprepared for the agility of the Zero.

The mess hall aboard the *Akagi* buzzed with the usual chatter of sailors and airmen swapping stories and speculations about the war. Hideyoshi, seated near the bulkhead with a bowl of rice, barely paid attention until he heard a familiar voice.

"Did you hear about it?" said Natsuo, a maintenance crewman who always seemed to know the latest rumors. He leaned over the table. "Something happened in Japan. Some kind of raid."

Hideyoshi looked up sharply, his chopsticks hovering in midair. "A raid? What are you talking about?"

Natsuo glanced around conspiratorially before sitting down across from Hideyoshi. "I heard it from a guy who works with the radio operators. They picked up something on a British civilian broadcast from Ceylon. American planes bombed Japan—Tokyo, Yokohama, Nagoya. Hit all over the place."

The table fell silent as others leaned in to listen. Hideyoshi's brow furrowed in disbelief. "American planes? That's impossible. Their carriers are too far away. How could they reach Japan?"

Natsuo shrugged. "That's the strange part. They say it wasn't carrier planes. These were bombers—big ones, twin engines. B-25s, I think. They couldn't have come from any carrier."

A wave of murmurs spread among the group.

"What else did you hear?" asked one of the younger pilots.

"Well, NHK back home is reporting that the Americans bombed a few cities, but the damage wasn't serious," Natsuo replied. "The government is saying most of the planes were shot down before they could get away."

Hideyoshi's mind raced. The notion of enemy planes striking Japan itself was deeply unsettling, even if the damage was minimal.

"Do you think it's true?" someone asked.

Natsuo spread his hands. "Who knows? They're keeping it quiet, so maybe it's worse than they're letting on. But it's got to mean something if the Americans could pull off a stunt like that."

"If it's true," Hideyoshi said quietly, "it means the Americans are more daring than we thought. And, that they won't give up so easily."

The table fell into a pensive silence.

It did not take long for the Japanese Navy to learn that the raiding American B-25s had taken off from aircraft carriers, and had been part of a deliberate retaliatory action.

The Doolittle Raid, carried out on April 18, 1942, was one of the most daring operations of the early Pacific War. Planned as a direct response to the attack on Pearl Harbor, the raid was intended to demonstrate that the United States could and would strike back at Japan's home islands, puncturing the prevailing notion of Japanese invulnerability.

The raid was the brainchild of Lieutenant Colonel James Doolittle, a pioneering aviator and aeronautical engineer. The plan called for sixteen B-25 Mitchell bombers to be launched from the aircraft carrier *Hornet* — a feat which had never before been attempted with land-based medium bombers. The B-25s were modified to reduce weight enough to allow them to take off from a carrier deck. The bombers, however, could not land back on the carrier; instead, the plan required them to land in China.

On the morning of the raid, the *Hornet*, escorted by the *Enterprise* and other ships, approached within 650 nautical miles of Japan's coast. The bombers launched earlier than planned after the task force was unexpectedly spotted by a Japanese patrol boat. They targeted military and industrial facilities in Tokyo, Yokohama, Nagoya, Kobe, and a few other cities.

The raid's immediate military impact was minor, but its psychological effects were profound as, for the first time in the war, Japanese military leaders experienced an attack on their own homeland. The operation shattered the illusion that Japan's islands were beyond the reach of enemy forces.

The raid had far-reaching consequences on both sides. In the United States, it was celebrated as a morale-boosting victory, demonstrating American ingenuity and resolve. Doolittle and his crews were hailed as heroes.

In Japan, the raid triggered outrage and a desire for retaliation, and spurred Japanese leaders to accelerate their plans to eliminate the American Navy's carrier fleet. To prepare for this new action, the *Kido Butai* was withdrawn from Ceylon.

Preparations for the new campaign began as soon as the task force had reached home waters. The success in the Indian Ocean had demonstrated the reach and power of Japan's carrier strike force. Now it would be put into action again.

Chapter 12
Midway (June 1942)

Midway Atoll, a small cluster of coral islands surrounded by the vast expanse of the Pacific, held strategic importance far out of proportion to its tiny size. For the Americans, it served as a forward operating base which protected the approaches to Hawaii. For the Japanese, possession of Midway would extend its defensive perimeter, keeping the American carriers out of range of the home islands and creating an extended buffer zone against any repeats of the Doolittle attack.

But the Imperial Navy had other reasons for planning a campaign against Midway. The US carriers had survived the Pearl Harbor strike untouched, and the Doolittle Raid had proven that they were still a serious threat. So, the attack on Midway was designed to provoke the Americans into action, forcing them to commit their carrier force in a desperate bid to defend the important outpost. Intelligence reports indicated that the Americans had only two carriers left in the Pacific. They were vulnerable, and the superior power of the Japanese forces, Admiral Yamamoto concluded, would be able to annihilate the entire American fleet by drawing it into a carefully prepared trap.

To execute this ambitious idea, Japan once again turned to the *Kido Butai* "Mobile Unit", with Vice Admiral Nagumo in command. He was, at the time, the most experienced carrier officer in the world, and he had four carriers — *Akagi*, *Kaga*, *Hiryu*, and *Soryu* — along with nearly 250 aircraft, at his command.

What the Japanese did not know, however, was that the Americans knew about the plan all along.

The US Navy's cryptographic team at Station Hypo, based in Pearl Harbor, had successfully penetrated the Japanese Navy's JN-25 code, which was used to transmit the fleet's operational orders. By mid-1942, the team had managed to partially decrypt enough Japanese communications to piece together the basic outline of the upcoming operation, which was targeting a location that the Japanese identified only by the code letters "AF".

The exact location of AF was not clear, but analysts suspected that it referred to Midway. To confirm their guess, a clever ruse was devised. The American base on Midway was instructed to send out an uncoded message reporting that its freshwater distillation plant had broken down. Shortly after, a series of Japanese communications were intercepted by Station Hypo reporting that "AF" was short of fresh water, thus confirming beyond doubt that Midway was the intended target.

The decrypted messages also provided the Americans with the makeup of the Japanese forces and the invasion schedule. Crucially, the intercepts also revealed that the Japanese were planning to make a diversionary attack on the Aleutian Islands, designed to draw the American ships out from Hawaii. The Japanese naval leadership seemed to have a penchant for inordinately complicated plans — and this one was very complicated.

Armed with this knowledge, though, the American admiral Nimitz was able to position his three available carriers — *Enterprise, Hornet,* and *Yorktown* (hurriedly repaired after the Coral Sea battle) — for an ambush.

As Hideyoshi and his comrades aboard the *Akagi* accompanied the *Kido Butai* towards Midway, they had no idea that their plans had been laid bare, and that the enemy was laying in wait for them.

Nagumo's first task was to neutralize the threat that Midway's small airfield posed to his fleet. The island's aircraft included B-17 Flying Fortress and B-26 Marauder bombers, a few PBY Catalina flying boats for reconnaissance, and a number of old F2A Buffalo and newer F4F Wildcat fighters for close-in air defense. The airfield was also protected by radar, still a relatively new technology at the time, which provided early warning of incoming Japanese aircraft and gave the defenders precious minutes to get their fighters into the air.

To destroy this threat, Naguma ordered an air strike with 108 aircraft.

Hideyoshi would not be going with them: he had instead been ordered to lead his *shotai* on combat air patrol, circling over the fleet to protect it from any enemy planes that might arrive. He tried to hide his disappointment: he was a fighter pilot, and the idea of circling the fleet and babysitting the carriers while the attack was going on felt like being banished to the sidelines. Still, duty came first, and he would carry out his assigned mission. He tucked his orders into his flight suit and strode purposefully toward his Zero.

His wingmen Igarashi and Yoshikawa were already at their aircraft.

"Combat air patrol," he informed them tersely as they gathered. "We're protecting the fleet while the strike force attacks."

Yoshikawa frowned. "I thought we'd be part of the main action."

"So did I," Hideyoshi admitted. "But this is where we're needed. Let's not let our guard down." The combat air patrol, he knew, was critical. Nobody knew when an attack might come, and the carriers, the heart of the fleet, had to be protected at all costs.

As they climbed to altitude, the three Zeros flew in unison in a vic formation. Below them were *Akagi, Kaga, Soryu*, and *Hiryu*, surrounded by their protective screen of cruisers and destroyers. The fleet stretched almost from horizon to horizon. It was an awesome display of force.

By midday, after several hours of flying, the patrol returned to the *Akagi* to refuel and prepare for another sortie. Hideyoshi wearily climbed out of his cockpit, his muscles stiff from sitting for several hours in the cramped space.

The Japanese strike force, meanwhile, was steadily droning across the sky towards the American island, and soon the bomber radios crackled with terse commands as they tightened up their formations, their targets now clearly in sight—runways, hangars, fuel depots, and anti-aircraft gun emplacements.

On the ground, the island erupted with activity as the Japanese planes drew near. Air-raid sirens wailed as men ran to their anti-aircraft guns. Pilots quickly scrambled into the cockpits of their Wildcat and Buffalo fighters and lifted off to intercept the attackers.

The Vals dove towards their targets and bombs came down on the airfield, tearing craters into the coral runways and sending up black clouds of smoke from the hangars. Secondary explosions erupted as fuel depots ignited. The anti-aircraft defenses roared to life, and the Japanese pilots weaved through the barrage.

The American fighters struggled against the nimble Zeros. The Buffalos were slower, less maneuverable, and poorly armed compared to their Japanese counterparts. Several of the stubby little planes were shot down in quick succession, their burning wreckage arcing into the Pacific or crashing onto the island below. The Wildcats proved to be more formidable, with better armor and heavier firepower. Several Japanese planes went down in flames.

As the strike force completed its attack, the flight commander was able to see significant damage to the island's structures, but also noted that the airstrip runway, though cratered, still remained operational. The message was sent back to Nagumo over the radio: "Damage insufficient to neutralize enemy air capabilities. Requesting follow-up strike." Midway's defenses had been pounded hard, but they had not been broken.

On the bridge of the *Akagi*, Nagumo read the radio report, and decided that a second strike on the island was necessary. Although the American carriers were not expected to arrive for several days yet, he had nevertheless withheld half of his aircraft, armed with torpedoes, as a reserve in case any US ships were found in the area. Now, he gave the order for the ground crews to remove those torpedoes and replace them with bombs for another attack on Midway.

Above them, Hideyoshi was once again circling the fleet on combat air patrol. For over an hour, he had scanned the horizon, alert for any sign of enemy aircraft.

Now, his eyes caught a glint of sunlight reflecting off metal far below him, almost on the water's surface. At first, it was barely noticeable, but as the formation drew closer, he could see them— American torpedo bombers, their stubby outlines unmistakable. Their intent was clear: they were making an attack on the carriers.

Hideyoshi gestured sharply with his wings to catch the attention of his wingmen, pointed the nose of his Zero toward the incoming bombers and dipped his wings again in the signal to attack. His *shotai* responded immediately, spreading out into a loose formation as they followed his lead.

The American planes were TBD Devastators, aging torpedo bombers that had served as the backbone of the American Navy's carrier force in the years leading up to the war but were now in the process of being replaced with newer TBF Avengers. Hideyoshi had never encountered them before, but their sluggish speed and lack of maneuverability were evident even from this distance.

He scanned the skies for their fighter escort, expecting to see a protective force of Wildcats, but, to his astonishment, there were none. His eyes narrowed. It was unthinkable that the Americans would send an attack force without fighter cover — but here they were, flying straight into the teeth of the *Kido Butai's* air defenses. Either their escort had become separated, he speculated, or the Americans were so desperate to strike the Japanese carriers that they had launched an unprotected mission.

The Devastators moved in a loose formation, their engines straining as they pushed toward the carriers. Hideyoshi could see the torpedoes slung beneath their bellies. Although they were his enemy, he felt a flicker of respect for the men piloting these aircraft. They were flying outdated bombers low and slow into a huge fleet that was heavily protected by anti-aircraft guns and fighters. They must have known the dire odds that they faced, yet they pressed on their attack with brave determination. He could not help but admire them. The thought crossed his mind that they must have *samurai* blood in them.

As the Zeros dove toward the torpedo bombers, the enemy formation began to react. The tail gunners swung their guns around and tracers began to streak through the air, but the Zeros were too fast and agile for them.

Hideyoshi rolled his plane into a sharp dive and put the crosshairs of his electric gunsight onto the nearest bomber. It all felt too easy. But he knew that this was not a sporting contest: his duty was to defend his carrier group, and the torpedo that this plane carried was a deadly danger.

He fired a short burst, and the TBD lurched, trailing a burst of smoke and flame before dropping into the sea. Around him, the rest of the squadron engaged the other Devastators. The tail gunners continued to fire back, and one Zero was struck, trailing smoke as it peeled away. Hideyoshi glanced briefly at the damaged plane, relieved to see the pilot managing to stay airborne. His focus returned to the bombers. The remaining Devastators were pressing forward, but their formation was unraveling under the relentless guns of the Zeros.

A bomber veered off, flames licking at its wings as it spun down into the water just below. Another dropped its torpedo prematurely, the weapon splashing harmlessly into the water too far from its intended target. Hideyoshi whipped over in a tight rolling turn, this time aiming at a bomber that was already trailing a thin white stream of fuel and was struggling to keep its position in the formation. His bullets found their mark, and the plane disintegrated in a fiery explosion.

Within minutes, the torpedo squadron was all but annihilated. A few stragglers managed to limp away, but most of the Devastators were now gone, and their crews along with them. Despite their reckless courage and sacrifice, they had not scored a single hit: most of them had not even been able to get close enough to drop their torpedoes.

Hideyoshi pulled his Zero back into a climb, scanning the area for any remaining threats. At first the sky appeared empty. Then he saw dark dots high in the sky, and his blood went cold. These were not the sluggish torpedo bombers from earlier. Their silhouettes revealed them as SBD Dauntless dive bombers. Two thoughts instantly flashed through Hideyoshi's mind: this many bombers meant there was at last one American carrier in the area, and these planes were already nosing down for their attack dive.

They were, in fact, from the *Enterprise,* and had been using the clouds to conceal their approach. The torpedo attacks earlier had drawn all of the Zeros down to sea level, leaving this higher altitude clear, and the SBDs were taking full advantage. It was a textbook tactic, and it was working.

The realization hit Hideyoshi with a cold jolt—there was not enough time for them to intercept the Dauntlesses before they could drop their bombs. The dive bombers were already positioning themselves directly above the carriers.

"Climb, climb!" Hideyoshi gestured frantically to his wingmen. Desperately, he slammed his throttle full forward, his Zero straining against gravity as he pulled the control stick back into his lap. The screaming engine vibrated through the fuselage as the fighter clawed for height. He watched the bombers closely, tracking their speed and calculating angles, but he already knew that the distance between the Americans and the *Akagi* was closing too quickly.

Hideyoshi silently urged his Zero higher and faster, and the airframe began shuddering with the stress. He cursed under his breath, knowing full well that he wouldn't reach them in time. Below, every anti-aircraft gunner in the fleet had opened fire, and black puffs now blossomed around the bombers, but the SBDs lowered their nose and dived. There was no way they could miss.

The first bombs hit with practiced accuracy. From his vantage point, Hideyoshi saw the lead bomber strike the *Kaga* squarely near the forward elevator. The bomb pierced the flight deck and detonated inside the hangar below, where the floor had been littered with loose bombs and torpedoes as the ground crews worked on re-arming the planes. A second hit followed moments later, smashing into the aft section. The resulting explosions sent fiery debris cascading into the sky as fuel tanks and aircraft ignited in chain reactions.

The ship's deck became an inferno and soon a sea of flames lapped at the sides of parked aircraft, each one loaded with fuel and bombs in preparation for the next strike. Crewmen scrambled amid the chaos, some desperately fighting the fires while others abandoned their posts, leaping overboard to escape the hellish scene. Columns of black smoke belched high into the air. *Kaga* was a mortally wounded giant.

The *Soryu* was next. Hideyoshi caught sight of three Dauntless bombers diving almost vertically. The first bomb struck near the midsection of the carrier, shattering the deck and ripping through to the hangar below. Explosions followed in rapid succession as more bombs found their marks. Flames erupted along the entire flight deck, and Hideyoshi could see tiny figures—crewmen—scattering like ants, fighting futilely against the growing inferno.

His heart sank when he turned his gaze to the *Akagi*. A lone bomb from an American dive bomber had plunged through the flight deck near the midsection, hitting a fuel storage tank in the ship's hangar. The explosion was immense, triggering fires that spread rapidly among the aircraft and weapons stored below. Another bomb landed forward, blowing apart the deck and sending flames roaring into the bridge. The *Akagi's* crew worked desperately to extinguish the fires, but they were hampered by the smoke and heat that rapidly engulfed the carrier.

Hideyoshi circled helplessly, watching the devastation. From above, the scene was surreal and horrifying. Flames and smoke poured from all three carriers. He caught glimpses of men on the *Akagi*, some clinging to the railings, others fighting fires. Their tiny figures seemed fragile. A number of aircraft were being pushed to the edge of the deck, just moments away from detonating and adding to the destruction. The waters around the three carriers were dotted with men struggling to swim clear of the burning wreckage.

Hideyoshi's tapped his fuel gauge. He had been flying for hours now, and it was getting disconcertingly low. He urgently scanned the sea for any sign of a remaining carrier. None appeared. The *Akagi, Kaga,* and *Soryu* were consumed by fire and smoke, and the *Hiryu,* the only surviving flattop, was nowhere to be seen. The sinking realization hit him: there was nowhere for him to land.

He looked around and spotted a Japanese destroyer cutting through the waves. Its deck was alive with sailors, some pointing toward the skies, clearly tracking the handful of Zeros still airborne. It was his only chance. Without a carrier deck to return to, Hideyoshi would have to ditch in the sea.

Banking toward the destroyer, he steadied his nerves. Ditching a Zero was risky; the aircraft was lightly-built and might not withstand the impact of a water landing, and even if it settled onto the surface in one piece it would sink quickly. He adjusted his throttle, set his flaps, and set a shallow glide angle.

The Zero hit the water hard and cracked a wing, but it held together, skimming a short distance and bouncing before slamming into the surface and coming to an abrupt stop. Water surged under the canopy and into the cockpit as the plane began to submerge. Hideyoshi wrestled with the harness and managed to free himself just as the cockpit filled with water. He scrambled out, the cold water shocking him as he kicked away from the sinking plane. It disappeared in seconds, leaving only a faint trail of bubbles.

"Over there!" voices shouted from the destroyer as crewmen pointed. A fast-moving ship's launch was already being lowered into the water, and the sailors aboard readied lines and rescue gear. Within minutes, they had reached him, and several pairs of hands gripped his arms, hauling him onboard. Hideyoshi collapsed into the bottom of the boat, breathing hard. The sailors wrapped him in a blanket and the launch quickly returned to the destroyer.

"You're lucky we were close," one sailor said, handing him a canteen.

Hideyoshi nodded, taking a quick drink.

A short while later, Hideyoshi, wrapped in a blanket, stood on the deck of the destroyer as he watched the *Akagi*, his home for so many months, being consumed by fire. The blackened hulk was listing slightly, flames flicking across her deck as explosions erupted intermittently from within.

A junior officer approached Hideyoshi with a grim expression. "They're trying to save her," he said. "Damage control teams are still onboard, but it doesn't look good."

Hideyoshi nodded but said nothing.

Around him, other survivors of the *Akagi* moved around the cramped deck in silence, many staring blankly at the burning ship.

A voice interrupted his thoughts. "Sugiyama, is that you?"

Hideyoshi turned to see a familiar face—Susei, a tail gunner from one of the Kates.

"Yes, it's me," Hideyoshi replied, managing a faint smile. "You made it out, too."

"Barely," Susei said, shaking his head.

For a moment, neither spoke. Finally, the gunner broke the silence.

"Did you see much of the battle?" he asked.

"Enough," Hideyoshi replied grimly. "And you?"

Susei sighed and rubbed his temples. "We made it to the target, dropped our torpedo, but we never saw if it hit. The flak was too thick, and we barely escaped. Then, on the way back ..." He paused. "We saw one of ours in the water. A pilot, clinging to some wreckage."

His expression darkened. "There were American fighters circling, strafing anything that moved. I saw one of them make a pass at him. The poor bastard didn't stand a chance."

"They were strafing a helpless pilot?"

He nodded slowly. "There was nothing we could do. It felt like abandoning a comrade."

After a moment, Hideyoshi murmured, "I wonder who he was."

Susei sighed. "Someone brave, no doubt. They all were."

The two men sat in silence, each lost in their own thoughts.

Now, other destroyers were circling the *Akagi*, sending launch-boats toward her in a desperate bid to rescue crew members. From his vantage point, Hideyoshi could see sailors clinging to wreckage in the water. Others were floating face-down on the oil-slicked surface.

An enormous detonation suddenly rocked the huge ship, sending a giant fireball into the air. The shockwave reached the destroyer moments later, making everyone on deck stagger. Hideyoshi's knuckles turned white as he gripped the railing tighter.

The destroyer's captain appeared on deck, speaking briefly with his officers before turning to several nearby sailors. "Prepare for more survivors," he ordered. "We're moving closer to assist."

The ship adjusted course toward the *Akagi*. The carrier's condition became even clearer at closer range. Her hull was scorched and buckled in places, and the flames were spreading. Part of the flight deck had collapsed into the inferno below. Another explosion rocked the carrier, this one smaller but enough to send more debris flying.

"Do you think they'll scuttle her?" a young sailor nearby asked quietly.

Hideyoshi didn't answer. He didn't know what to say.

Many of the rescued were injured, their uniforms blackened and torn from the blasts. Others stared blankly at the chaos, their faces frozen with shock. Hideyoshi recognized some of them. The scene felt surreal, like a nightmare.

As night fell, the destroyer *Arashi*, instructed to scuttle the carrier in order to prevent her from falling into enemy hands, launched several torpedoes into her starboard side. The massive hull began to tilt, her stern sinking first as seawater rushed into her breached compartments. The bow lifted momentarily before sliding beneath the waves, leaving behind a field of oil and debris. On the rescue ships, sailors stood silently, bowing their heads in respect. Many were openly weeping.

The attack had left the *Hiryu*, with Rear Admiral Yamaguchi in command, as the fleet's only remaining carrier. She managed to launch a counter-strike which had hit the American carrier *Yorktown*. It exacted a small amount of revenge. But shortly afterwards, *Hiryu* herself was hit by more dive bombers and, after burning all night, was scuttled. Yamaguchi stayed on the bridge of his ship and went down with her.

Defeat came hard for the Japanese.

Admiral Yamamoto, commanding the Combined Fleet from the bridge of the battleship *Yamato*, had initially intended to continue with the Midway operation, despite the ruinous carrier losses. His strategy relied on the hope that his remaining surface fleet of battleships and cruisers could still draw out and destroy the American carriers in a decisive night engagement. However, as reports continued to filter in, the true scale of the catastrophe became undeniable, and Yamamoto reluctantly gave the order to withdraw. The Japanese Navy's previously unbroken string of victories was at an end.

For the Japanese high command, consumed by "victory fever", the retreat from Midway was a bitter pill to swallow. It shifted the entire balance of power in the Pacific and forced them to turn from aggressive expansion to a hardened defensive strategy. They would never again regain the initiative in the war. From now on the Americans would be calling the shots.

Chapter 13
Reassignment (July 1942)

The journey back to Truk was a somber affair. The surviving crew of the *Akagi*, packed into a crowded transport vessel, spoke little as the ship lumbered through the vast Pacific. Many of the men, their faces hollow and pale, avoided each other's eyes. The once-proud pilots and sailors were now haunted by memories of fire and blood.

When they arrived at Truk, the survivors were quietly offloaded and shuffled into barracks that had been hastily repurposed for their arrival. Guards patrolled the perimeters, ostensibly to maintain order, but it was clear that their presence also served to confine the survivors. It soon became apparent why they had been gathered together in this isolated place. Conversations about certain topics, especially with civilians, were discouraged. No one spoke of Midway. Everyone had the silent understanding that to do so would invite trouble. For the men of the *Akagi*, it felt less like a rescue and more like a prison.

Hideyoshi sat on his cot one evening, staring at the ceiling. His thoughts were interrupted by the sound of boots approaching. An officer stepped into the room, carrying a clipboard. "Sugiyama," the man called out.

Hideyoshi rose, his uniform rumpled from days of wear. "Here, sir," he said, stepping forward.

"You're to report to the operations office immediately," the orderly said, then turned and left without waiting for a response.

At the operations office, Hideyoshi was handed a sealed envelope. "These are your transfer orders. You're to report to Kasanohara Air Base in Kagoshima Prefecture. Departure is scheduled for tomorrow."

Hideyoshi accepted the envelope, his mind racing. Kasanohara? It was situated far from the front lines, nestled in southern Kyushu. A quiet exile. "Understood, sir," he replied, saluting before stepping back into the corridor.

The barracks were quiet when he returned. A few men glanced up as he walked to his cot and began packing his belongings. "Transfer orders?" asked a mechanic named Sukoda.

Hideyoshi nodded. "Kasanohara."

Sukoda frowned, leaning back on his cot. "That's where they're sending all of us. To keep us out of sight."

"What do you mean?"

"They don't want the truth about Midway getting out," Sukoda explained. "Better to isolate us. Let the official story take hold."

The words lingered in Hideyoshi's mind as he finished packing. By the time the first light of dawn crept through the barracks windows, he was ready to leave. The transport plane that carried him and several others to Kyushu was cramped and noisy, the roar of the engines drowning out any attempts at conversation. Hideyoshi wasn't in the mood for talk anyway, and he stared silently out the small window, watching the endless ocean.

When they landed at Kasanohara, a Lieutenant greeted the new arrivals with a canned speech emphasizing the importance of discipline and discretion. "Your experiences are valuable," the officer droned. "But they are not for public discussion. You are here to recover and to prepare for the next stage of your service. That is all."

Hideyoshi felt bitter as he settled into his new quarters. The barracks were clean but spartan, and the men who occupied them carried the same air of muted resignation that he had seen at Truk. As he unpacked his belongings, he caught sight of a photo of his family tucked into his bag. He stared at it for a moment before placing it on the small table beside his cot.

It was at Kasanohara that Hideyoshi began to hear the steady drumbeat of propaganda filtering out through all of the radios and newspapers. Radio and newspapers all blared stories that had been carefully orchestrated to portray Midway as a monumental triumph for Japan. According to the official accounts, the Imperial Navy had sunk multiple American carriers and crushed the enemy fleet. Bold headlines screamed of victory, accompanied by exaggerated depictions of American ships sinking beneath an unrelenting fall of

Japanese bombs. Reports gave embellished tales of Japanese bravery, hailing it as a momentous step toward final victory in the war.

Hideyoshi felt a deep discomfort. He had seen the chaos of that day—the dive bombers, the flames that consumed *Akagi*, and the grim faces of the men as they abandoned ship. The truth of the matter was seared into his mind as vividly as the smoke and flames that had billowed into the skies above Midway. He knew that the fleet had been gutted—he had seen it. And yet, here was the press, turning their crushing defeat into a story of triumph.

Hideyoshi sat in the base's small mess hall, a bowl of rice untouched before him. Pilots and ground crew around him laughed and nodded as they listened to a radio broadcast detailing the supposed annihilation of American forces. An announcer's voice swelled with pride as he told the story, painting a picture of shattered American naval power and unchallenged Japanese supremacy.

"That's not what happened," Hideyoshi muttered under his breath, his chopsticks idly poking at the rice.

Across the table, Lieutenant Kunio, a pilot newly transferred from China, raised an eyebrow. "What was that, Sugiyama?"

Hideyoshi hesitated. The urge to voice his frustrations boiled within him, but he knew the consequences. They had all been ordered to remain silent, and varying from the official narrative could mark him as unpatriotic—or worse. The *Kempeitai* military police were everywhere.

"Nothing," he replied, with a forced half-smile.

Kunio shrugged and returned to his food, seemingly unbothered. But Hideyoshi couldn't shake the feeling that he was surrounded by men living in a fabricated reality.

Over the following weeks, the disillusionment deepened. Posters plastered across the base showed stylized images of Zeros flying in formation and bombs exploding over enemy ships. During mandatory morale meetings, *Kempeitai* officers regurgitated the same tired rhetoric about Japan's inevitable victory over the soft Americans who lacked warrior spirit and who didn't have the belly to make sacrifices in a hard fight.

Late one night, Hideyoshi sat on his cot staring at the photograph of his wife and son back in Sakurada. His thoughts wandered to his younger self, the idealistic boy who, inspired by his uncle's stories, had dreamed of defending Japan with honor and courage. Was this what he had signed up for? To serve under leaders who buried their failures beneath layers of lies?

He longed to confide in Aiko, to unburden his heart to the woman who had always been his steady rock. But he knew better.

The *Kempeitai's* watchful eyes scrutinized every letter, and even a careless phrase could be twisted into "disloyalty" or "defeatism". The risk to her and their families was unthinkable. With a heavy sigh, he dipped his brush into the ink and instead began writing a carefully crafted but innocuous letter.

"My dearest Aiko,

"I hope this letter finds you and Ichiro in good health and high spirits. I am well, and there is no need for you to worry about me. The weather here has been quite hot lately, but I am managing fine. The food is simple but adequate, and I am staying strong.

"Military necessity forbids me from telling you where I am, and we are somewhat remote and isolated here, but all the news we get about the progress of the war continues to be good.

"I think of you and Ichiro every day. I miss you both more than words can express, but knowing you are safe and together gives me comfort. Please give my regards to Mother and Father, as well as to anyone else who asks about me.

"I hope everything at home is going smoothly. Let Ichiro know his father is proud of him, and that I am looking forward to the day we can all be together again. Until then, please take care of yourself and stay safe.

"With all my love,

"Hideyoshi"

It was safe, harmless, and sounded unbearably hollow, but it was all he could do. Folding the paper with deliberate care (but leaving it unsealed for the military censor's inspection), Hideyoshi silently prayed that his unspoken thoughts would somehow reach her across the miles.

By mid-July 1942, however, Japan's need for experienced combat pilots had become urgent. The shattering losses at Midway had gutted the ranks of its elite aviators, and the Imperial Navy was scrambling to fill the gaps. Combat-experienced pilots who had survived Midway, like Hideyoshi, were now more valuable than ever, and commanders could no longer justify keeping them out of action.

Hideyoshi had just finished breakfast when the base adjutant, entered the mess hall with a stack of sealed orders. "Sugiyama!" he called. Hideyoshi set down his bowl of rice and stood.

Kuroda handed him a folded envelope. "Your transfer," he said simply.

Hideyoshi opened the orders. "You are re-assigned to the 5th Kokutai fighter group. You will report for duty at Kahili Airfield on Bougainville." The orders required his departure within forty-eight hours, allowing just enough time to pack and prepare.

Kahili was in the Solomon Islands, a region he had only heard of in passing. It had seen some action a few months ago, supporting the Japanese moves into New Guinea and the Dutch East Indies, but was relatively quiet now. According to the rumor mill, the Navy had plans to concentrate a striking force in the Solomons that would extend Japan's control of the sea lanes towards Australia and serve as a staging area for a thrust towards Fiji and Samoa, cutting the vital supply lines between the United States and Australia. A large airfield was already being constructed on one of the southern islands. The 5th Kokutai was headquartered at Rabaul, but most of its aircraft had been spread to a number of runways around Bougainville, where they could provide air cover until the new airfield was completed. Kahili was one of these dispersed runways.

Returning to his quarters, Hideyoshi began packing. His possessions were few: a spare uniform, a carefully folded *furoshiki* containing his personal items, and a collection of letters from Aiko and his parents.

Word of his reassignment spread quickly. In the barracks, the other pilots — some destined for similar orders — offered farewells. "Bougainville, eh?" one of them had said. "You might get to see Australia."

"I already have," Hideyoshi replied, recalling his combat over Darwin's harbor.

On the morning of his departure, Hideyoshi carried his bag to the airstrip, where a twin-engine K5Y transport aircraft waited. A handful of ground crew worked to load crates of supplies onto the plane, and he climbed aboard, finding a jump seat near the rear. The engines began turning, and the plane taxied down the runway. Looking out the small window, Hideyoshi watched Kasanohara recede into the distance. He was not sorry to see it go.

The transport plane banked low over the dense jungles of Bougainville, revealing a first glimpse of Kahili. The airstrip, carved out of the jungle and framed by towering coconut palms, looked rough but functional. Surrounding it were a handful of parked aircraft and clusters of hastily constructed huts, supply sheds, and maintenance bays. Kahili was clearly a frontier post, a far cry from the polished decks of the *Akagi*.

The K5Y jolted along the uneven runway before coming to a stop near a line of Zeros. Hideyoshi unbuckled his harness and gathered up his gear. The cabin doors opened, and the hot and humid jungle air rushed in.

An officer in a sweat-soaked khaki uniform approached the plane as Hideyoshi disembarked and gave a quick bow of greeting. "Ensign Sugiyama, welcome to Kahili. I'm Lieutenant Mori, adjutant to the squadron commander."

"Thank you," Hideyoshi replied, returning the bow.

Mori gestured toward a truck parked nearby. "We'll get you settled in. Major Kageyama is eager to meet you."

Hideyoshi climbed into the vehicle, balancing his gear on his lap, and Mori drove slowly down the dirt road leading away from the airstrip, carefully avoiding ruts and potholes. Along the way, they passed makeshift hangars and maintenance crews working in the shade of palm-thatched roofs. Mori provided a running commentary. "The conditions here are challenging. Supplies come in irregularly, and the humidity wreaks havoc on the planes. But the men are resourceful. You'll find that out soon enough."

The jungle loomed just beyond the perimeter of the base, its sounds an ever-present backdrop—chirping insects, distant bird calls, and the rustling of leaves in the warm breeze.

The truck came to a stop near a row of wooden barracks, and Mori pointed to one of them. "This will be your quarters. It's basic, but it's yours. The mess hall is just down the path, and the briefing room is in the central building. I'll leave you to get settled, but Major Kageyama will want to see you shortly."

Hideyoshi stepped out of the vehicle, his boots sinking slightly into the soft mud. The barracks were simple structures, elevated on wooden stilts with open sides to allow airflow in a failed attempt to beat the oppressive jungle heat. Inside, the accommodations were sparse—a cot, a small desk, and a wooden trunk for personal belongings. A mosquito net hung over the bed.

After a quick meal in the mess hall—rice and dried fish—Hideyoshi reported to the central building as instructed. The briefing room was a small, dimly lit space dominated by a large map pinned to the wall. Major Kageyama stood near the map, surrounded by a few junior officers. When Hideyoshi entered, he looked up. "Sugiyama, I presume."

"Yes, sir," Hideyoshi replied, bowing deeply. Kageyama stepped forward. "Welcome to Kahili. We're stretched thin here, but I expect you'll adapt quickly. Your experience will be invaluable."

"I will do my best, sir," Hideyoshi said.

The major nodded. "Good. We'll probably need it. The Americans have been becoming more aggressive, and this airfield is important to our operations in the Solomons. I'll have you flying patrols as soon as tomorrow."

Hideyoshi set out from his barracks to explore the base. It was obviously a temporary facility, and it had none of the polish or permanence of Japan's homeland airfields, let alone the orderliness of a carrier like the *Akagi*. It reminded him of the auxiliary airstrips he had seen in China.

The main runway stretched out in a wide, cleared area of packed coral and gravel. There were a few scattered Zeros, their green paint dulled by the tropical sun. Ground crews moved between the planes, hauling tools and spare parts. Hideyoshi watched as a group of mechanics struggled to patch a fuel line on a battered aircraft, their shirts soaked through with sweat.

Beyond the airstrip lay a series of makeshift hangars. These were little more than large canopies of palm thatch supported by wooden poles, offering some protection from the intense sun and torrential rains. Nearby, fuel drums were stacked in uneven rows, partially covered with tarps to shield them from the elements.

Farther out, a medical tent had been set up on a cleared patch of ground, and several men lay on stretchers or makeshift beds, their faces pale and drawn from malaria. The medical staff, visibly tired and obviously overworked, moved briskly between them.

Near the edge of the base, an armory and supply depot had been constructed, its contents protected by a couple of canvas tarps. Crates of ammunition and spare parts were stacked haphazardly, and a lone guard sat on an overturned box, fanning himself lazily with a piece of cardboard.

As Hideyoshi continued his walk, he passed a group of pilots gathered near the briefing area, smoking and chatting quietly. They nodded in acknowledgment as he walked by, a silent gesture of welcome. Hideyoshi knew that the old-timer pilots tended not to socialize with the new arrivals—after all, they probably would not be here after a few weeks anyway.

The morning after his arrival, Hideyoshi reported to the briefing tent to meet his new squadron members. The tent was crowded with pilots seated on mismatched chairs and crates. Out here in the frontline jungle, the atmosphere was far less formal than what he had grown accustomed to aboard the *Akagi*.

Standing at the front of the room was Captain Toyatomo, the detachment leader. As Hideyoshi entered, the Captain beckoned him forward. "You must be Sugiyama," he said. "I've heard about your experience. We can use someone with your skill here. Welcome to Kahili."

"Thank you, Captain," Hideyoshi replied, bowing. "I'm ready to serve wherever I'm needed."

Toyatomo nodded approvingly and gestured for Hideyoshi to introduce himself to the rest of the squadron. Hideyoshi turned to them and bowed. "I am Ensign Sugiyama. I flew off the *Akagi* until … well, until recently. I look forward to flying with you all."

The pilots responded with nods and greetings. Toyatomo then took over, introducing the pilots. Among them were Hideyoshi's assigned *shotai* wingmen. The first was Takumi Takeda, a rather plump man with a quick smile and a knack for storytelling, who immediately stood out as the group's unofficial morale booster. Next was Yukio Fukuhara, a quiet and methodical pilot whose calm demeanor belied his sharp instincts in the air. Takeda had just a handful of sorties to his name, while Fukuhara was a slightly more seasoned aviator, but they both lacked real combat experience.

"Stick with us, Sugiyama," Takeda said with a grin. "We'll show you the ropes of jungle warfare. It's not the same as carrier operations."

Hideyoshi gave a smile. "I'll do my best to keep up."

As the meeting broke up, Takeda clapped Hideyoshi on the shoulder. "Come on, let's grab some tea," he said. "You need to hear the real stories about this place."

Sitting on a bench under a canopy of palm leaves, Hideyoshi listened as Takeda and Mishima recounted their experiences. They spoke of shortages, sick calls, and the daily struggle to maintain their planes in the unforgiving jungle environment.

Mishima repeated a story that, he said, had been told to him in a bar by a rear gunner in a Val dive bomber, back during the operations to capture Rabaul.

"I'll tell you something, boys," the man had said, his voice low. "The war taught me plenty, but there's one lesson I'll never forget. Crocodiles are scarier than bullets."

The table fell silent, save for the occasional clink of cups. The young men, now captivated, leaned in closer.

"It was over the Solomon Islands not far from here," the rear gunner continued. "We were flying a mission in our trusty Val, my pilot Yukawa and me. Everything seemed normal until we ran into them—American Wildcats. They came at us fast, tearing through our formation like hawks diving on pigeons. Before we could react, tracers were everywhere."

He paused, staring into his cup. "Yamata-*san*, he was good, one of the best pilots I ever flew with. But skill doesn't mean much when you're outnumbered. A burst from one of those Wildcats caught us square in the engine. The Val shuddered, coughing smoke like an old man with a bad chest. I managed to return fire, but it was no use."

His hand shook slightly as he raised the cup to his lips and took a long sip, as if to steady himself.

"The engine went out, and we were going down. Yamata tried to hold her steady, but another burst came, and I felt the impact—it hit him. He slumped forward, and I knew it was over. I didn't have much time to think. The plane was spiraling, and all I could do was jump."

The young men listened, their drinks forgotten.

"I landed in a shallow bay, surrounded by mangroves. The water was warm, almost comforting, until I realized it was dragging me down. My parachute had tangled in the branches underwater, and I was struggling to free myself. That's when I saw them—a small wooden canoe, paddling toward me. Natives, four of them, shouting in a language I couldn't understand."

He chuckled dryly. "At first, I thought they might be headhunters. My training had warned me about hostile islanders, and here I was, completely helpless. But instead of attacking me, they grabbed me by the arms and hauled me into their boat, their voices frantic."

He paused, his expression darkening. "They stood me up, and one of them pointed to the water where I'd just been thrashing around. At first, I didn't understand what he was trying to show me. Then I saw it—a pair of glowing eyes just above the surface. Then another. And another. Crocodiles, big ones, circling where I'd been tangled. If I'd stayed in that water even a minute longer—"

He trailed off, shaking his head. "Those natives saved my life. They didn't owe me anything, didn't know a word of Japanese, but they risked their own necks to pull me out of there. They were probably used to pulling fishermen or their own out of those waters, but I was just a lost stranger to them."

The man drained his cup and set it down with a clink. "War teaches you a lot about humanity—sometimes the worst, but also the best. And let me tell you, boys, bullets are scary, but crocodiles? Those are nightmares you don't wake up from."

The next morning came another briefing, for a routine patrol over the construction site for the new airfield. Hideyoshi looked at the map, searching for the island. "That's the place," Takeda said, tapping the map with a finger. "Guadalcanal. Looks like a nightmare to me. A jungle airfield in the middle of nowhere. Hot, humid, crawling with insects—and that's before we even talk about the Americans."

Fukuhara leaned in, squinting at the map. "The commander said the runway's nearly ready. A coral strip, he called it. I've seen what coral can do to a plane's landing gear if it's not packed right."

"They're in a hurry," Hideyoshi replied. "It's all about getting a foothold. They want an airfield to control the area, as soon as possible."

Takeda shook his head slowly. "Must be hell for the construction crews. They're probably working day and night out there. I bet they're using whatever they can get their hands on—bamboo huts for housing, jungle trees cleared to make room for the runway."

"And us?" Fukuhara asked. "You think we'll be sent there as soon as it's operational?"

Hideyoshi sighed. "It sounds like it. This base at Kahili—it's temporary. Once that new airfield is ready, it'll be the focal point. We'll be expected to move in and operate there."

Takeda grimaced. "Great. Just what I wanted—living in a swamp, dodging mosquitoes the size of aircraft."

"That's the least of your worries," Hideyoshi said with smile. "We'll be flying constant sorties once we're there. The Americans won't leave us alone, not for a moment. Guadalcanal is probably going to be a hot spot, and we'll be right in the middle of it."

Fukuhara frowned, crossing his arms. "Do you think we'll have enough supplies? Fuel, ammunition, parts? I overheard some mechanics saying it'll be a nightmare to keep everything running out there."

"We'll manage," Hideyoshi said firmly, though he shared the same concerns. "We have no choice. This is the war we're fighting now."

The three men stood in silence for a moment. Finally, Takeda broke the quiet with a forced chuckle. "Well, at least we know what to expect. Heat, bugs, and Americans shooting at us. Sounds like a tropical paradise."

Hideyoshi smiled, appreciating the attempt at humor. "Get used to it, Takeda. That place will be home soon enough."

Chapter 14

Guadalcanal (August 1942-May 1943)

By mid-1942, Japanese forces had established a strong presence in the Solomon Islands, with key military bases on Bougainville, Guadalcanal, and Kolombangara. From its port at Rabaul on New Britain, the Imperial Navy had already begun reinforcing the seas around Guadalcanal, sending destroyers, cruisers, and light vessels to secure the area, and on Guadalcanal itself, construction laborers were working furiously to complete the new airfield.

After their crushing victory at Midway, however, the Americans, seeing that the balance of power in the Pacific had now shifted in their favor, were looking to go on the offensive, and they too turned their attention to the Solomon Islands. They realized that the Japanese airfield on Guadalcanal, if left unchecked, would serve as a springboard for further attacks on Australia and the South Pacific, while if the US had control of the Solomons they could serve as a jumping-off point to move up towards the Philippines, and eventually on to Japan.

And so the Americans began planning for a counteroffensive to seize control of Guadalcanal and its airfield from the Japanese. US ships began to arrive in the area, reinforcing the Australian ones that were already there, and reconnaissance flights over Rabaul and Bougainville became more frequent.

The Japanese, aware now that something was in the works, reinforced their own positions and braced for a possible attack on Guadalcanal.

It came on August 7, 1942.

At first light, a massive Allied task force, including three aircraft carriers, several battleships, and countless transport ships, had converged on the island. In the early hours, naval bombardments and carrier-based airstrikes pummeled Japanese positions near the airfield. The bombardment was relentless, and the construction crews quickly scattered, abandoning their half-finished project.

The first wave of American forces, drawn primarily from the 1st Marine Division, approached the beaches aboard amphibious landing craft. They quickly encountered resistance, but it was far less than they had expected. The Japanese garrison on Guadalcanal had been minimal, just some construction engineers, workers, and a few infantry units, most of whom were caught completely off guard.

The airfield, though incomplete, was seized with minimal losses by noon. The Americans named it "Henderson Field" and immediately brought in Seabee construction crews of their own to finish it. Unlike the Japanese workers, who had labored with shovels and buckets, the Americans had bulldozers and steel mats. Within a week the runway was ready for operations, and an entire functional airbase had been built within two months. Squadrons of Dauntless dive bombers and Wildcat fighters moved in. Since the invasion had been given the code name "Operation Cactus", the motley collection of American airplanes was quickly dubbed the "Cactus Air Force".

The Japanese commanders at Rabaul scrambled to assess the situation. The scale of the American operation and the speed with which they had moved had caught everyone by surprise, and for the first time, the Japanese forces seemed to be on their back foot. Messages were sent to nearby bases, including Kahili, demanding immediate action. Pilots were ordered to prepare for missions over Guadalcanal, while troop commanders devised plans for a counteroffensive. The Americans, meanwhile, dug in, bracing for the inevitable Japanese response.

The fighting on Guadalcanal quickly turned into a brutal and unforgiving struggle. After the initial American landings, Japanese forces were poured onto the island and launched a series of counterattacks, attempting to recapture Henderson Field.

One of the first major confrontations occurred along the Tenaru River. On August 21, Japanese forces, primarily from the Ichiki Detachment, launched an assault against the US Marine positions near the river. Under the command of Colonel Ichiki, the Japanese troops were confident in their ability to drive the Americans off the island, and they advanced under cover of darkness, hoping to take the enemy by surprise in a night attack.

The Marines, however, had prepared well. Machine gun nests and barbed wire defended their lines, and artillery was positioned to cover the approaches. As the Japanese troops charged, the Americans opened fire, and the Tenaru turned into a killing zone as wave after wave of Japanese soldiers screamed "*Banzai!*" and rushed at them. By dawn, Ichiki's entire force were either dead or retreating into the jungle. The Americans counted over 900 Japanese bodies, while their own losses were minimal.

The failure at the Tenaru did not deter the Japanese high command, which continued to send reinforcements to the island. In September, they mounted a larger offensive, centered on Edson's Ridge, a critical line of high ground overlooking Henderson Field. If the Japanese could seize it, they would have a perfect vantage point to put point-blank artillery fire onto the airfield.

Led by Major General Kawaguchi, the Japanese force of 3,000 men advanced through the jungle, once again intending to launch a surprise night attack. The Americans, however, were prepared once more. Colonel Edson and his Marines had fortified the entire ridge, creating a defensive network of interlocking foxholes and machine gun emplacements.

The Japanese assault began on the night of September 12 and quickly devolved into close-quarters combat, with Japanese soldiers using bayonets and grenades to try to overwhelm the American lines. The Marines, however, held firm, their machine guns relentlessly cutting down the attackers as, for two nights, they repeatedly charged up the hill. By September 14, the Japanese forces had been pushed back, leaving hundreds of dead behind. The Americans had suffered significant casualties, but they had successfully defended Henderson Field.

The Guadalcanal campaign was brutal. Diseases, particularly malaria, took a heavy toll on soldiers from both sides, sometimes claiming more lives than the fighting itself. The jungle terrain favored ambushes and close combat, and the tenacity of the Japanese troops ensured that every inch of ground gained came at a steep cost. The fight became a bloody war of attrition, with both sides pouring an ever-growing amount of resources and manpower onto the island.

It was as much a battle against the environment as it was against the enemy.

For the Japanese, the challenges began with the distance. Supplies had to be transported all the way from the home islands and pass through Rabaul before reaching the front lines. The sea lanes around Guadalcanal were patrolled by American ships and aircraft, which quickly gained superiority and forced the Japanese to rely on their famed "Tokyo Express", using fast destroyers and smaller vessels to deliver men and supplies under the cover of darkness, dashing in and unloading before quickly retreating to avoid the Americans.

While daring, the Tokyo Express was not able to deliver badly-needed food and ammunition in sufficient quantities. The Japanese troops on Guadalcanal soon found themselves rationing rice and resorting to hunting what little wildlife they could find in the jungle, and occasionally, whispered stories said, to cannibalism. Hunger became a constant companion, weakening their physical and mental strength. They bitterly referred to Guadalcanal as "Starvation Island".

For Hideyoshi and his fellow pilots at Kahili, the struggle in the air became crucial, since the side that had air superiority would be the ones who would then be able to safely bring in supplies and reinforcements.

Ever since the war had begun, the Zero had given the Japanese control of the skies. But, Hideyoshi knew, things were different now. The American pilots they were facing here were no longer the inexperienced adversaries of earlier campaigns. These men had learned hard lessons from the opening months of the war and had adapted their tactics accordingly. Their F4F Wildcats were slower and less maneuverable than the Japanese Zeros but they could absorb more damage, and their six .50-caliber machine guns could shred their opponent in seconds. The American pilots increasingly avoided one-on-one turning dogfights, at which the Zero excelled, and employed the "Thach Weave," a defensive maneuver designed to cover one another's tail. This tactic frustrated Hideyoshi and his fellow pilots, who found their usual attacks from behind being thwarted by the disciplined teamwork of the Americans.

The Japanese were also being hindered by the declining quality of their pilots. The disaster at Midway had cost the Imperial Navy a large portion of its best pilots and its most experienced ground crews, and in order to replace them as quickly as possible the Navy had begun to shorten its training regimen. While Hideyoshi and his fellow students had racked up over 300 hours of flying time before they were sent to China, he was now seeing new replacement pilots, fresh from advanced fighter training, with just a few dozen hours in the Zero. The Americans, by contrast, seemed to have an inexhaustible supply of planes and pilots, and the forces against him seemed to be growing every day. Hideyoshi often found himself outnumbered in the sky over Guadalcanal.

"Stay sharp and watch each other," he always reminded Takeda and Fukuhara before they took off. His leadership was calm and confident and he never showed any doubt or hesitation, even as the odds grew higher and higher against them with each passing week.

Yet the toll was undeniable. Nearly every day there were one or two pilots, often the new ones, who were absent from the evening mess hall. Some had never even had the chance to unpack their meager belongings before being sent on their first—and last—mission.

Hideyoshi's first combat mission over Guadalcanal began with a clear objective: establish air superiority and provide support to the Japanese ground forces struggling to hold their positions against the American advance. Flying from Kahili airfield at dawn, their mission that day was to escort Japanese bombers targeting the critical airbase, which had just been captured by the Americans.

As they neared the island, Hideyoshi spotted the distinct blunt-nosed stubby shapes of F4F Wildcats in the distance. He raised his arm, pointing toward the incoming enemy planes to alert his wingmen, and as the Wildcats closed in, Hideyoshi tilted his wings sharply, signaling his *shotai* to prepare for engagement.

The ensuing dogfight was furious. The American pilots moved in disciplined pairs, making it difficult for the Zeros to secure clean shots. Hideyoshi swung his Zero in a tight arc, leading Takeda and Fukuhara into position to intercept a pair of Wildcats chasing a damaged bomber. A quick burst from Hideyoshi's guns sent one of the attackers spiraling toward the jungle below.

The flight home was tense. Hideyoshi signaled a loose formation, keeping his inexperienced wingmen in sight as they made their way back. They all kept their necks on a constant swivel, knowing that an American fighter sweep could pop up at any time. Hideyoshi was relieved when they all touched down safely at Kahili.

Subsequent missions followed almost every day. Most times, they supported Japanese ground forces, strafing enemy positions along the Matanikau River or intercepting supply drops to American troops. These were alternated with bomber escort duty, protecting the single-engine Vals and the larger twin-engine Betty bombers as they hit American troop positions or bombed Henderson Field yet again. Occasionally, the Americans launched their own bomber raids against Kahili, and Hideyoshi and his *shotai*, often outnumbered, had to scramble into the air to drive off the B-25s and their escorts of P-40 Warhawks or the new (and more dangerous) P-38 Lightnings.

In one mission, the squadron was ordered to intercept an American naval convoy delivering supplies to the beach. Diving at a steep angle, Hideyoshi lined up his shots, strafing the decks of destroyers and cargo ships before pulling up to avoid the wall of tracer fire. They lost two pilots to the intense anti-aircraft defenses.

The next day, the mission briefing was straightforward: a fighter sweep over Guadalcanal to disrupt American air operations and draw out their fighters. The Zeros would go in fast and hard, hunting for any sign of American Wildcats and clearing them from the sky.

Hideyoshi led Takeda and Fukuhara in a tight V-formation, scanning the horizon. As they approached Guadalcanal, the dense jungle below appeared like a carpet of green, interrupted by the familiar outline of Henderson Field and its steel-mat runways.

Six Wildcats were already climbing toward them in pairs, and closed quickly. Hideyoshi banked hard to the right, narrowly avoiding the tracer rounds from an enemy plane that had locked onto him. He pulled his Zero into a sharp climb, taking him out of the Wildcat's firing arc.

As he leveled out, Hideyoshi spotted an opportunity. A lone Wildcat had unwisely broken from its formation, attempting to position itself behind Takeda. Without hesitation, Hideyoshi dived after it, pushing his throttle forward as he closed the distance.

The Wildcat's pilot, focused on his quarry, never even saw him. Hideyoshi calmly lined up his shot, the illuminated reticle of his electric gunsight falling on the enemy fighter's fuselage. He squeezed the trigger, and could see sparkles as the rounds struck home, ripping into the Wildcat's right wing and engine cowling. Thin smoke began to stream from the damaged aircraft, but the plane still held steady. The Wildcat, he knew, could absorb an unbelievable amount of punishment. Hideyoshi held his position for a moment longer, then fired another burst. The Wildcat veered down, now leaving a thick black trail behind. Hideyoshi pulled up sharply to avoid the debris as the stricken Wildcat plunged into the jungle below.

As he scanned for additional threats, he spotted Takeda in a precarious position, being pursued by two Wildcats, and rolled his Zero into a sharp turn to intercept. His sudden appearance startled the enemy pilots, forcing them to break away. Takeda took advantage of the distraction and executed a sharp climb to safety.

The remaining Wildcats turned for home, and Hideyoshi signaled his *shotai* to regroup. The Zeros climbed higher, putting some space between themselves and the Americans before circling back toward Kahili.

The ground crew greeted them with hurried efficiency, immediately checking the planes for damage and refueling them for the next mission. Hideyoshi climbed from the cockpit, his flight suit damp with sweat. Takeda and Fukuhara joined him.

"Good shooting today, *Taicho-san*," Takeda said. "Without it, that Wildcat would have had me."

Hideyoshi nodded, brushing off the praise. "We're a team. We survive by looking out for each other."

Later that evening, as the pilots were walking towards the mess hall, the air raid alarm blared across the airfield, sending them scurrying to their Zeros. The lookouts had spotted a formation of American planes heading toward the base.

As his Zero once again lifted into the sky, the bombers appeared as dark specks, flanked by a handful of smaller dots—American fighters providing escort. As they came ever closer, Hideyoshi identified the boxy silhouettes of Dauntless dive bombers.

Hideyoshi banked his Zero to the right, positioning himself to intercept the lead group of bombers. The Dauntlesses were already beginning their bombing runs. He pushed his Zero into a steep climb, angling to intercept one of the bombers as it lined up its attack. The dive bomber rear gunners around him opened fire, and a stream of tracers zipped past Hideyoshi's airplane, but he held his course, zigzagging slightly to throw off the their aim.

At the last moment, Hideyoshi rolled his Zero into an attacking angle, positioning himself just above the Dauntless. Cannon shells tore into the American plane's fuselage and wings. The pilot immediately jettisoned his bomb load to lose weight and gain speed, but it was already too late. Another burst, and the bomber spiraled down with flames trailing like a comet's tail.

Hideyoshi banked away sharply and looked around. A Wildcat streaked past him, its guns blazing at Fukuhara's Zero. Takeda swooped in from above, forcing the American fighter to disengage. With a quick hand signal, Hideyoshi directed his *shotai* to regroup and climb, pulling them out of the fray. Within minutes, all of the American planes had disappeared towards Guadalcanal.

Hideyoshi took a moment to examine the airfield. Several of the Dauntlesses had been downed, but a few had managed to drop their bombs before escaping. Below, plumes of smoke rose from Kahili's outskirts, but the runway itself appeared to be largely unscathed.

They brought their Zeros down on the pockmarked runway, the ground crew rushing to meet him. As Hideyoshi climbed down from the cockpit, Takeda was walking over, removing his helmet. "You got one of those SBDs good."

Hideyoshi nodded, his expression calm despite the adrenaline still coursing through him. "One less to bomb us tomorrow," he replied.

Fukuhara joined them, wiping sweat from his brow. "The damage isn't too bad this time. We held them off."

The craters in the runway were quickly filled in and patched, and Kahili remained operational, but Hideyoshi knew the Americans would be back.

The relentless pressure of the enemy raids was beginning to take its toll on pilots and planes alike, but the pace never let up.

A few days later, the *shotai* was part of a larger escort force assigned to protect another Japanese bombing raid. The sight of black flak bursts on the horizon told him the battle was already underway.

"Keep close," he signaled with a hand wave to Takeda and Fukuhara.

As they approached the engagement zone, Hideyoshi caught a flash of blue darting through the melee. A distinctive plane with an inverted-gull wing design—an F4U Corsair, one of the newest American fighters. He signaled his wingmen to drop back and cover him as he broke into a steep turn to engage. The Corsair had already seen him and was also turning into the fight.

The two aircraft spiraled around each other, each pilot testing the other's reactions. The Corsair opened fire first, its six .50-caliber machine guns spitting a stream of tracers. Hideyoshi rolled to evade. The American F4U was a match for the Zero in speed and climb, but the Japanese plane still had superior maneuverability.

The Corsair followed but didn't over-commit. It was a calculated pursuit, forcing Hideyoshi to adapt rather than simply react.

For several minutes, the two dueled through the sky. Hideyoshi pushed his Zero to its limits, diving, climbing, and rolling as each tried to get the other in his gunsight. But each time he gained an advantage, the Corsair's pilot countered, pulling into a defensive maneuver that left Hideyoshi chasing empty air. He quickly realized that this was not a novice—it was an experienced pilot who had likely flown dozens of missions.

On his fourth pass, Hideyoshi feinted a climb and then abruptly dove, forcing the Corsair to react. It was a split-second opportunity, but he seized it, pulling into a tight turn that placed him on the Corsair's tail. He lined up the shot, but the American twisted out of his sights with a barrel roll. Hideyoshi swore out loud.

The Corsair came around again, this time diving low to gain speed. Hideyoshi followed, their planes skimming treetops as they raced toward open water. The American pilot was trying to draw him away from the main battle.

"Clever," Hideyoshi said to himself.

Finally, the Corsair made a critical mistake. As the two planes briefly closed in on each other head-to-head, the American pilot pulled into a climb, exposing its vulnerable underside. Hideyoshi reacted instantly, pulling his nose up and firing a short burst from his machine guns.

The bullets ripped into the Corsair's engine. Smoke began pouring from the stricken plane, and its movements grew erratic.

Hideyoshi fired again, this time hitting the wing root. The Corsair nosed down and began to fall.

Rolling his plane inverted, the American pilot bailed out, and his silk parachute blossomed like a white flower. Hideyoshi slowed down and pulled closer, watching as the pilot drifted toward the jungle below, to be rescued by the American Marines who occupied nearly all of the island.

As he rejoined his wingmen, Takeda gave him a thumbs-up.

Hideyoshi nodded but said nothing. The skill of the Corsair's pilot lingered in his mind. Whoever that American was, he had been a master of his craft, and he had been defeated only because he had been the first to make a mistake. It could, he knew, just as easily have gone the other way.

Hideyoshi felt no triumph—only a sincere respect for an opponent who had fought well, with honor and courage.

The next afternoon, the air raid sirens at Kahili once again screamed. Troops ran to ready their anti-aircraft guns while pilots dashed to their Zeros. Hideyoshi climbed into his cockpit.

The raid was large and coordinated—B-25 Mitchell bombers escorted by American fighters. As he climbed for altitude, Hideyoshi could see the distinct forked tails of the bombers and the unmistakable silhouette of the P-38 Lightning escort fighters. The twin-engined P-38s were fast and heavily armed, making them formidable opponents.

"Pick your targets," Hideyoshi signaled. Takeda and Fukuhara acknowledged, their Zeros fanning out slightly but staying within easy reach.

The P-38s were quick to react. Two Lightnings peeled off to intercept Hideyoshi's group. Their guns blazed, forcing the Zeros to break formation. Hideyoshi looped back and caught one P-38 in his sights, firing a burst from his machine guns. The Lightning wasn't built for maneuverability, but it banked hard, narrowly avoiding the rounds.

Looking around, he saw Takeda lining up for an attack on one of the B-25s. But then, to his horror, a P-38 swooped in from above and came head-on at the Zero.

"Takeda, pull up!" Hideyoshi thought, but it was too late.

Both guns opened fire at the same time, with red and green tracers slashing across the sky at each other. The front of the P-38 sparked with several hits. But while the American plane was heavily armored and could withstand the damage, the Zero was not. Takeda's fighter shivered violently as .50-caliber rounds tore through its fuselage. Smoke began to trail from the crippled aircraft, then flames appeared.

Hideyoshi banked hard, trying to intercept the Lightning, but it was gone in an instant, diving away at full throttle.

Takeda's Zero spiraled downward, smoke and fire trailing from its smashed engine. Hideyoshi watched helplessly, hoping to see a parachute pop open. Seconds stretched into eternity as the crippled plane tumbled toward the jungle below.

"Takeda!"

The crash was obscured by dense jungle trees, but the plume of black smoke that followed was unmistakable. Takeda was gone.

Hideyoshi had no time to mourn. The Americans were still pressing their attack, bombs dropping down onto the airfield. He pushed his Zero into another climb, and managed to force one of the B-25s to jettison its bombs early. Another bomber was hit by flak and veered off course, trailing smoke. The raid ended as the Americans turned back toward their base.

As the remaining Zeros returned to Kahili, the mood was dark. Hideyoshi landed first, climbing out of his cockpit and waiting by the airstrip as Fukuhara's plane taxied in. The two men exchanged a glance but said nothing. No words were necessary.

Back in the barracks, Takeda's belongings sat untouched on his cot, a cold reminder of his absence.

"Another good man gone," Fukuhara finally whispered, breaking the silence.

Hideyoshi nodded, his voice low. "He fought well. He deserved better."

The order came a few days later: the Imperial Japanese Army was to withdraw from Guadalcanal. With supply lines severed, reinforcements impossible, and American forces growing stronger every day, the High Command had no choice. The "Tokyo Express" would now serve as the lifeline for the beleaguered troops, ferrying them away to safety under cover of darkness.

At Kahili, the mood among the pilots was grim as news of the evacuation spread. Hideyoshi sat in the pilots' ready room, reading the terse message pinned to the bulletin board. The announcement spoke of "repositioning to more advantageous positions" and "conserving strength for future operations." It did not mention "defeat".

Fukuhara stood nearby. "We've lost the island," he concluded.

Hideyoshi nodded. "They're doing what they have to. Better to save what's left of our men than throw them away in a hopeless fight."

On the first day of the withdrawal, Hideyoshi and Fukuhara were among the pilots assigned to fly protective patrols. Below, at dawn, Japanese destroyers were still creeping away from Guadalcanal's coast, their decks packed with soldiers.

The evacuation would continue for several nights to come, and by the time it was complete, over ten thousand Japanese soldiers had been rescued from Guadalcanal.

Just after the withdrawal had been completed, Hideyoshi, weary from another patrol, was summoned by Lieutenant Commander Hoshino. As he stepped into the dimly lit tent, he noticed the solemn expression on the officer's face.

"Lieutenant Junior Grade Sugiyama," Hoshino began, emphasizing the newly-awarded promotion in rank, "you've been assigned to a new posting." He was to report to Truk and join the fighter group of the carrier *Zuikaku*, one of the remaining fleet carriers. She had been covering the withdrawal from Guadalcanal, and was now due to leave for other assignments.

"You'll be leaving within the week," Hoshino added. "Congratulations on your promotion. This assignment reflects the Navy's confidence in your abilities."

"Thank you, sir." Hideyoshi saluted.

Back at his quarters, Hideyoshi found Fukuhara waiting.

"I've been reassigned," Hideyoshi said simply. "To the *Zuikaku*."

"The *Zuikaku*? That's a high-profile post."

For the next few days, Hideyoshi prepared for his departure. His Zero was checked and rechecked for the journey to Truk. The ground crews, many of whom he'd worked alongside for months, offered quiet farewells.

Fukuhara stayed close by, offering help where he could. On the evening before Hideyoshi's departure, the two men shared a quiet meal under the stars.

"You'll do well there, sir," Fukuhara said, raising a tin cup in a small toast. And we'll hold the line here. You can count on us."

"I know," Hideyoshi said. "Just make sure to stay alive. That's an order."

As Hideyoshi stepped into the hangar deck of *Zuikaku*, the carefully choreographed moves of the deck crew pushing around the parked aircraft brought a flood of memories rushing back— memories of the *Akagi*.

He took a moment to survey his surroundings. The *Zuikaku* was slightly smaller than his former ship but was much newer, having entered service just in time for the Pearl Harbor operation, but she bore the scars of battle—he could see patches of darker steel where repairs had been made.

The *Zuikaku*, along with her sister carrier *Shokaku*, had formed the backbone of Japan's fleet after the devastating losses at Midway. In actions around the Solomons, the two had damaged the American carrier *Enterprise* and had sunk the *Hornet*. During the withdrawal of the remaining Japanese forces from Guadalcanal, the *Zuikaku* had deployed its air group to conduct long-range reconnaissance and provide fighter cover for the operation.

"Lieutenant Sugiyama?" A voice broke his reverie.

"Yes." Hideyoshi saluted.

"Welcome aboard the *Zuikaku*. I'm Lieutenant Commander Okamura, the air group operations officer. I'll be overseeing your integration into the fighter squadron. Follow me."

"The *Zuikaku* is one of our finest carriers," Okamura said as they descended into the ship's interior. "You'll find we run a tight operation here."

The corridors were narrower than he remembered on the *Akagi*, but they were alive with activity. Sailors hurried past, carrying reports and supplies. Hideyoshi nodded politely to the crewmen who saluted as they passed.

They reached the air group's ready room, where a dozen pilots sat at long tables, studying maps and briefing documents. The room fell silent as Hideyoshi entered, and all eyes turned toward him. Okamura stepped forward, introducing him.

"This is Lieutenant Sugiyama, newly assigned to our fighter squadron. He comes to us with extensive combat experience. I expect you to learn from him and work together as a cohesive team."

The pilots rose, offering polite bows. Hideyoshi returned the gesture. Most of the men were younger, likely recent graduates from flight training schools.

After the introductions, Okamura led him to his quarters. Hideyoshi set his gear down. "Your first briefing is at 1800 hours," Okamura said. "Until then, I suggest familiarizing yourself with the flight deck layout and the squadron roster."

In late 1943, the Japanese Navy made an adjustment in its aircraft organization which reflected a new approach to tactical air combat.

The "vic" formation, which had been the staple of Japanese and other air forces at the war's start, consisted of three planes arranged in a tight V-shape. While this arrangement guaranteed that the leader could maintain close visual control over the wingmen who were there to protect his tail, it suffered from several flaws. The planes in the vic were closely spaced, and wingmen, especially the less-experienced, often had to focus most of their attention on staying in formation, which limited their situational awareness and left them more vulnerable to surprise attacks.

By contrast, the "finger four", named for its resemblance to the tips of four fingers on an outstretched hand, was a looser and more adaptable configuration. Made up of two pairs of aircraft, each with a leader and a wingman, the formation provided better visibility and flexibility with each of the two pairs able to operate independently when necessary.

Hideyoshi saw how this new arrangement allowed for greater freedom of movement, enabling pilots to react more fluidly to enemy actions, covering each other while still remaining able to switch smoothly between defense and attack. When attacked, the formation could quickly break into pairs or even single planes, making it harder for enemy pilots to track and engage. At the same time, the pair-based structure ensured that no pilot was left without a supporting partner, reducing the chances of being picked off in isolation — a vulnerability often exploited by the American fighters.

The German Luftwaffe, the British Royal Air Force, and the United States Army and Navy squadrons had already adopted the finger four early in the war. Japanese commanders, steeped in tradition, were initially hesitant to abandon the vic, but they had now been forced by reality to recognize that this tactical shortcoming had contributed to their mounting losses, and they were now keen to modernize their tactics.

The pilots spent the next several weeks practicing the new formation during flight drills. Hideyoshi quickly realized that while the finger four required better communication and coordination (and that was difficult since the Zeros were still mostly flying without radios), its potential for both offense and defense outweighed its complexity. He simulated these tactics during practice dogfights and noted the effectiveness of flanking maneuvers that would have been impossible with the vic.

By the end of the month, the pilots aboard the *Zuikaku* were comfortable with the new formation. The switch to the finger four had come too late to prevent some of the losses suffered at Midway and Guadalcanal, but it represented an effort to match the evolving strategies of their adversaries. In the coming battles, Hideyoshi knew, their survival and success would depend on how well they could wield this new tool in the skies.

Hideyoshi, however, had witnessed firsthand the increasing skill and aggressive spirit of the American forces. Japanese pilots were still flying the same Zero fighters that had fought three years ago in China, while the Americans were beginning to introduce superlative new fighters like the Corsair, Hellcat and Mustang. Japan no longer had control of the skies, and as a pilot Hideyoshi knew that wars could not be won without air superiority.

The meat-grinder on "Starvation Island" had, however, also revealed the limits of human endurance. The tropical conditions, malnutrition, and disease had taken a toll on everyone involved. Hideyoshi often thought of the ground soldiers who had fought and died in the stifling jungle, their sacrifices largely unacknowledged, as the Japanese government was reluctant to admit such losses. He wondered whether their leaders in Tokyo truly understood the cost of their decisions.

Chapter 15
Philippine Sea (June 1944)

The period following the Guadalcanal campaign marked a turning point in the Pacific War. The Americans set their sights on the nearby islands of New Georgia and Bougainville, and the New Georgia campaign saw especially fierce fighting. Further north, the Battle of Bougainville began in late 1943, and American forces invaded Tarawa in November. By mid-1944, the Americans had advanced through the Marshall and Gilbert Islands.

The *Zuikaku*, meanwhile, had joined the Japanese fleet near New Guinea, and Hideyoshi found himself flying escort missions for bombers attacking American airfields and supply depots along the northern coast. During one mission, his flight encountered a squadron of P-38 Lightnings and he managed to down one of them after a protracted dogfight—but also lost one of his wingmen. During the American assault on Truk in February 1944, he flew defensive patrols as part of *Zuikaku's* air group. By June 1944, Hideyoshi had scored over 25 confirmed aerial victories.

By this time, the Marianas had become the next target for the Americans. The islands were of critical importance because their location would put the new Boeing B-29 Superfortress, a long-range heavy bomber, within range of Japan itself, and establishing airbases on Saipan and Tinian would allow the US to begin a massive sustained bombing campaign against Japan's major industrial cities, reducing them to rubble and eliminating their ability to continue the war.

The Imperial Navy, recognizing that the Marianas had become a crucial location, now prepared "Operation A-Go", an aggressive plan involving Japan's carrier strike force, land-based aircraft, and surface fleet, to destroy the American carrier fleet in one single decisive battle. The carrier strike force was commanded by Vice Admiral Ozawa. His fleet, larger than the *Kido Butai* which had attacked Pearl Harbor, included three light carriers and six fleet carriers, among them the veterans *Zuikaku* and *Shokaku* and Japan's newest carrier, *Taiho*. Together, they carried over 400 aircraft. The Japanese strategy also relied on the support of land-based aircraft from airfields on Saipan, Guam, and Tinian. These planes were expected to supplement the carrier force by striking at the advancing American fleet. Finally, the Navy's battleships, cruisers, and destroyers were assigned to protect the carriers and to exploit any opportunities which might allow them to engage the American ships directly.

The plan called for a complex series of maneuvers to lure the American carriers into range. Ozawa intended to use his surface fleet to bait the Americans into committing their forces prematurely, and his carriers and land-based aircraft would then strike at them with overwhelming force.

The A-Go plan was rooted in Japan's traditional "*kantai kessen*" naval doctrine which emphasized an effort to destroy the enemy fleet with one fatal blow. This strategy had brought success at the Battle of Tsushima during the Russo-Japanese War, and the admirals hoped that it would now bring success again.

As the *Zuikaku* steamed towards the Marianas in June 1944, her crew worked to insure that the ship was prepared for battle. In the hangar deck, maintenance crews made sure that every plane was combat-ready. The carrier's complement included Zero fighters, newer Nakajima B6N "Jill" torpedo bombers (which had replaced the aging Kates), and Yokosuka D4Y "Judy" dive bombers (replacing the Vals).

Hideyoshi inspected his assigned Zero with the keen eye of an experienced pilot. He double-checked the tension of control cables, inspected the ammunition belts, and made sure everything was functioning properly. Like many veteran pilots, he trusted his ground crew, but he also wanted to perform his own personal inspection.

In the carrier's ready room, the pilots were shown charts of the Marianas, highlighting the expected American fleet positions and all of the potential attack vectors. The air operations officer told them,

"Our mission is to destroy the enemy carriers. Without their carriers, the Americans are crippled."

Among the younger pilots, however, there was a noticeable level of nervousness. They had all been hastily trained and quickly pushed into combat, and most of them had only limited flight experience. This would be their first major battle. Hideyoshi took it upon himself to reassure the young men in his squadron, speaking quietly to a few of them. "Focus on your training," he advised one nervous young pilot. "Stick to your formation, and don't try to be a hero. We succeed as a team."

The first skirmish of what would become the Battle of the Philippine Sea began on the morning of June 19 after the American carrier planes had bombed targets in the Marianas and landed Marines on Saipan. Hideyoshi and his wingman, Hiroshi Takahashi, had been assigned to escort a strike by Jills and Judys against the American fleet.

Hideyoshi and Takahashi formed up in their familiar finger-four *kutai* battle formation, side by side. "Stay alert," he signaled with a quick hand gesture. Takahashi gave a sharp nod.

Soon, the silhouettes of American aircraft appeared on the horizon, and a pair of F6F Hellcats, the US Navy's new replacement for the Wildcat, was rapidly closing in on their position. Hideyoshi quickly assessed the situation: the Americans outnumbered them, but he had the advantage of height. It was time to act.

Hideyoshi turned towards the nearest Hellcat. The American came at him with guns firing, but Hideyoshi was already moving, his Zero twisting in a sharp rolling turn. The Hellcat pilot had opened up too soon, and his rounds fell harmlessly beneath the Zero. Hideyoshi snapped his airplane back into position, now resuming the offensive.

The Hellcat tried to turn away, and Hideyoshi seized the advantage, pulling inside of the F6F's turn and cutting the distance between them. His hands pulled the control stick back just enough to maneuver into position. As the Hellcat tried to snap-roll in the opposite direction, Hideyoshi's sights aligned perfectly. His gunfire tore through the American fighter's tail, sending pieces of it spiraling away. The stricken plane plunged down into the ocean below.

For the rest of the day, Ozawa launched wave after wave of bombers against the American fleet, hoping to break through their defenses by sheer brute force. Each time, Hideyoshi and Takahashi were with them.

It was brutal.

Zuikaku's aircraft were back in the air as fast as they could be refueled, and once again the Zeros were escorting another wave of bombers towards the American fleet. When the Hellcats appeared again, Hideyoshi quickly directed the *kutai* into a defensive posture. They spread out a bit to cover each other and prepared for the clash.

As the Americans closed in, Hideyoshi focused on protecting the vulnerable bombers. Spotting a pair of Hellcats breaking toward the formation, he pulled back on his stick, climbing to intercept. Takahashi followed closely, protecting his tail.

One Hellcat peeled off to meet Hideyoshi head-on. The American pilot held steady, his guns blazing. Hideyoshi jerked the stick to the right, rolling out of the line of fire, and then banked sharply to cut across the Hellcat's path and turn behind it. The Zero's machine guns chattered as he fired. Tracers streaked through the air, and rounds punched through the Hellcat's wing and fuselage. Flames poured from the damaged plane as it rolled over and fell toward the ocean. Hideyoshi watched for a moment to confirm the crash, then scanned for his next target.

Takahashi was locked in a fierce fight with another Hellcat, his Zero darting left and right as he closed in on the American. Hideyoshi moved to assist but paused when another Zero streaked between them at high speed. Its pilot was expertly tailing another F6F with a series of deft moves. The trailing Zero fired a short controlled burst, and the Hellcat immediately erupted in flames, spiraling down to the water.

As the victorious Zero leveled out and drew alongside him for a moment, Hideyoshi recognized the markings on the tail and the cool demeanor of the pilot—Hiroyoshi Nishizawa, one of Japan's highest-scoring aces.

Nishizawa's Zero tilted slightly in acknowledgment before he accelerated to rejoin the fight. Hideyoshi nodded in return, though he wasn't sure if the ace had seen him. There was no time for greetings. Another wave of Hellcats was already diving toward the strike group.

With quick hand signals, Hideyoshi directed Takahashi and the rest of the *kutai* to engage the new attackers. Hideyoshi took position near the lead bombers, shielding them from the brunt of the assault. His machine guns drove one Hellcat away from the bombers while Takahashi forced another to disengage with a sharp dive.

The Japanese bombers began their attack runs as the Hellcats regrouped for another push. The American fleet came into view below, and the dive bombers peeled off one by one, descending toward their objectives. Despite heavy anti-aircraft fire, the bombers released their payloads and began their retreat.

Towering splashes appeared around the ships, which turned into expanding white rings. But Hideyoshi noted with disappointment that the inexperienced bomber pilots had all missed their targets.

Back aboard the *Zuikaku*, Hideyoshi stepped down from his cockpit, his gloves and flight suit drenched with sweat. He didn't say much as the maintenance crew swarmed the Zero, inspecting for battle damage and preparing it for another mission.

The final attack wave launched in the late afternoon. Hideyoshi's *kutai* had been whittled down to three planes after the earlier engagement, as one of the Zeros had been too badly shot up to fly. They again took up their position as escorts, as all of the *Zuikaku's* remaining bombers once again pressed an attack against the American fleet. The mood among the pilots was tense, and exhaustion was apparent on everyone's face after hours of relentless combat. Hideyoshi's adjusted his goggles and fought to keep his mind focused on the mission ahead.

As they approached the target area, it didn't take long for the American fighters to arrive. The engagement began abruptly, with tracer fire and cannon rounds ripping through the sky. A group of Hellcats dove straight toward the bombers, intent on breaking up their formation. Hideyoshi climbed to intercept, and his Zero, though pocked with scattered bullet holes, responded sharply to his control inputs. He focused on a Hellcat that was leading the charge.

The American pilot reacted quickly, veering to the left and pulling into a steep climb. Hideyoshi followed, keeping his aim steady. The Zero's maneuverability gave him the edge, and after a short burst of fire, 20mm rounds struck the Hellcat's wing roots. Smoke poured from the stricken plane as it wavered and then lost a wing, sending the American cartwheeling into the ocean. Hideyoshi banked sharply to rejoin the formation.

Nearby, Takahashi was engaged in a tight duel with another Hellcat. The two planes twisted and turned around each other, their engines straining as each pilot tried to outmaneuver the other. Takahashi managed to slip behind his opponent and, at the right moment, he opened fire, his bullets striking the American plane's engine. The Hellcat turned away, trailing smoke, before a parachute appeared, and the now-empty plane tumbled into the water to disappear in a spray of white foam. Takahashi wagged his wings briefly in acknowledgment as he rejoined Hideyoshi.

A sudden flash of fire and black smoke to their left drew Hideyoshi's attention. A Zero from another *kutai*, a replacement pilot, was hit by Hellcat gunfire. The Japanese fighter's left wing crumpled under the barrage, and the plane spun wildly before erupting in flames. Hideyoshi watched in grim silence as the burning wreckage fell into the ocean. The pilot never bailed out.

There was no time to dwell on the loss. Together, the two dived toward more Hellcats, forcing them to break their formation and keeping the enemy fighters at bay while the Judys made their attack runs.

Below them, the bombers dropped their payloads. Plumes of water and foam erupted around the American ships. The attack caused significant chaos within the fleet, but Hideyoshi could see only two hits, and one of the cruisers was belching a steady plume of smoke. As the bombers turned away, Hideyoshi and Takahashi provided cover, driving off a final pair of Hellcats before beginning their own withdrawal.

The flight back to *Zuikaku* was subdued. Hideyoshi glanced over at Takahashi's plane, relieved to see no visible damage.

After debriefing, Hideyoshi stood on the flight deck, staring at the horizon. Takahashi joined him, silent at first before finally speaking. "We did what we could, Lieutenant," he said quietly.

Throughout the day, sortie after sortie had been launched to meet the American fleet. The results were disastrous.

Hideyoshi's four-plane *kutai* had lost one Zero. Other units had been wiped out completely. *Zuikaku*'s air group had started the battle with a powerful contingent of Zeros and bombers: now less than a dozen remained intact.

In the ready room, entire rows of empty seats indicated those who wouldn't be returning. They included friends who had fought alongside Hideyoshi for months. Among them were Lieutenant Commander Nakamitsu, who had been shot down while diving his Judy against an American carrier, and Lieutenant Fujiwari, whose torpedo plane had exploded in midair after taking a direct hit from anti-aircraft fire.

The sheer numerical superiority of the Americans was proving to be overwhelming. Their Hellcats were faster, more heavily armed, and were being flown by experienced pilots. While the Japanese pilots had fought with courage, the younger recruits had struggled. Many of the hastily trained pilots had never even seen combat before this battle. For them, it was a trial by fire which they were not prepared for.

On the deck, mechanics worked tirelessly to salvage what they could. Damaged Zeros were stripped for parts, their engines and cockpits cannibalized to keep a handful of other aircraft operational. Torpedo bombers with bullet-riddled fuselages were pushed overboard. The *Zuikaku's* air officer paced the hangar deck, yelling out orders, his face sagging with exhaustion and frustration. "We need every plane we can get airborne!" he shouted to the crew. "We'll fight with whatever we have left!"

Hideyoshi and Takahashi lingered near their planes as they watched the frantic activity around them, until Takahashi finally spoke. "It's madness, Lieutenant. They're throwing us into the air just to get shot down."

Hideyoshi didn't respond immediately. He looked around at the chaos. "We don't have a choice," he said finally. "If we don't fly, the ship goes down. And if the ship goes down, so do we."

But the Americans had another heavy blow to strike.

On the *Shokaku,* crews had scrambled to launch yet another sortie. But unseen beneath the waves, the American submarine *Cavalla* lay in wait, its crew carefully tracking the carrier's movements. Positioned at the edge of Ozawa's fleet, the sub had spent hours shadowing the carrier group, avoiding the Japanese destroyers who had passed overhead on routine anti-submarine patrols. Finally, Captain Kossler gave the order: "Flood tubes one through six. Prepare to fire."

Three torpedoes struck *Shokaku's* port side, tearing through her hull and igniting the aviation fuel stored below decks. Flames reached up to engulf the hangar bays, where fully armed aircraft sat prepared for launch. The carrier listed sharply, her engines grinding to a halt.

On the bridge, Captain Matsubara ordered the crew to fight the fires, but the inferno proved to be uncontrollable as explosions from stored munitions tore the ship apart, sealing her fate. *Shokaku* rolled over and sank, taking 1,200 of her crew with her.

But the destruction was not finished: there was another American sub that was also prowling. Lt Commander Blanchard, on the submarine *Albacore,* had been watching the *Taiho,* Japan's newest fleet carrier, and ordered a torpedo attack.

A single torpedo struck *Taiho's* starboard side near the aviation fuel tanks. The damage seemed minor at first; the carrier maintained its speed and carried on with operations. However, a critical error was made by the inexperienced damage control crews: while trying to vent explosive vapors from the fuel tanks, they inadvertently spread the fumes throughout the ship, and an accidental spark set off a massive explosion. Fire consumed the ship, and *Taiho* went to the bottom.

The loss of the two carriers left the remaining fleet, including *Zuikaku,* dangerously exposed, and Ozawa gave the order to retreat. Their hopes for a decisive victory had been shattered by the overwhelming power of the American forces.

In *Zuikaku's* hangar deck, Hideyoshi and Takahashi sat with their battered Zeros.

"Do you think the Americans will follow us?" Takahashi asked.

"I think they will," Hideyoshi replied bluntly. "They know we're finished. They'll press their advantage."

The younger pilot looked down, his expression grim. Hideyoshi placed a hand on Takahashi's shoulder. "Survive the next fight, Takahashi. That's all we can do now."

But there was no pursuit. The Americans, satisfied with the damage they had already done, also withdrew.

"I saw Zaito's plane go down," Takahashi said quietly. "He was trying to cover the bombers."

Hideyoshi nodded but said nothing. There was nothing to say. For Hideyoshi, the "Great Marianas Turkey Shoot", as the Americans mockingly dubbed it, was more than just a defeat; it was a blunt confirmation of Japan's waning power.

Yet, as news of the battle began to filter back to the Japanese public, the story that emerged was starkly different from the grim reality.

Once again, the Japanese propaganda machine moved into overdrive, just as it had after the disaster at Midway. Radio broadcasts and newspapers triumphantly declared the operation a resounding success, claiming that the Imperial Navy had inflicted heavy losses on the Americans and had turned back their advance. The reports spoke of dozens of enemy ships sunk, hundreds of American planes downed, and bold Japanese pilots defending the homeland with unparalleled bravery.

Hideyoshi read one such report in a hastily printed news bulletin delivered to the ship. "Imperial Navy Victorious Over American Fleet in the Marianas," the headline announced. The article went on to list fabricated statistics of American losses, claiming the destruction of at least five carriers, two battleships, and an uncountable number of enemy planes. There was no mention of Japan's own crippling losses, no acknowledgment of the hundreds of half-trained pilots who had been lost, and certainly no admission of the crippled fleet's hasty retreat.

Takahashi, standing beside him, shook his head. "They can't possibly expect any of us to believe this."

Hideyoshi set the bulletin down, and his thoughts briefly flashed back to Midway. "It's not meant for us," he said quietly. "It's for the people back home. They need something to believe in."

The air aboard *Zuikaku* was heavy with resignation.

In Tokyo, however, the narrative of victory served a vital purpose. The government and military high command understood that the morale of the Japanese people was already beginning to falter, as what they had been told would be a quick war now approached its fourth grinding year. Announcing a crushing defeat would only further erode public confidence in Japan's ability to win the war for which they were making so many sacrifices.

But the truth could not be hidden from those directly involved. Ozawa's official report, classified as secret and circulated only among the highest echelons of command, painted a brutally different picture. He detailed the destruction of nearly 400 aircraft and the deaths of hundreds of pilots. The loss of *Shokaku* and *Taiho* had crippled the fleet's ability to project air power, leaving Japan's carrier force a mere shell. While Japan still had a number of remaining carriers, they did not have enough aircraft and pilots between them to equip a full air group, and Japan no longer had the means to replace them.

Sitting on the edge of the flight deck, Hideyoshi stared out at the clouds. He thought of the civilians in Japan, of his wife Aiko and their young son Ichiro, whom he hadn't seen in years. What would happen to them if Japan lost the war?

The war was still far from over, he knew, but it seemed clear that Japan was no longer fighting for victory — at best, it was fighting for survival.

Chapter 16
Leyte Gulf (October 1944)

After the disastrous losses in the Marianas, the *Zuikaku* underwent emergency repairs and resupply at Kure Naval Base, and was hastily prepared to face a new American push. Intelligence reports indicated that the US was already targeting the Philippines as their next major objective.

For the United States, the island of Leyte held strategic value, since control of its waters would intercept Japan's critical supply lines to the rich resources of Southeast Asia. The loss of the Philippines would render Japan's entire remaining Navy ineffective, as its ships and aircraft were completely dependent upon the oil flowing from Borneo and Sumatra.

But the Philippines also had an important geopolitical value. It was an American possession, and it had been a tremendous embarrassment to the US (and to General MacArthur) when the Japanese conquered it. Taking back the islands would vindicate MacArthur's morale-raising pledge "I shall return".

Planning for the invasion began months beforehand. The operation called for a massive amphibious assault on the beaches near Tacloban and Dulag, on Leyte's eastern coast. Over 200,000 troops from the Sixth Army, under the command of General Krueger, were slated to participate in the initial assault, with reinforcements ready to follow once a beachhead had been established. Over 700 ships from Admiral Halsey and Admiral Thomas, including carriers, battleships, cruisers, destroyers, and troop transports, were assembled for the campaign. It would be the largest naval operation in history.

The Japanese high command, in turn, prepared Operation Sho Go ("Victory Operation"), yet another bold plan to counter the invasion and destroy the American landing force. Virtually all of Japan's surviving naval ships would be divided into four groups, each assigned a particular role.

Commanded by Vice Admiral Ozawa, the Northern Force was built around the remaining carriers, including *Zuikaku*. Although the Japanese force of four carriers looked impressive on paper, the harsh reality was that nearly all of Japan's naval aircraft and pilots had been lost in the Marianas, and the remnants were far out-classed by the eighteen American carriers that were available. The Japanese carrier force, then, was slated to be nothing more than diversionary bait. Ozawa's force was to head north, luring Halsey's Third Fleet away from the invasion beaches.

Once Halsey had taken the bait, Vice Admiral Kurita's Central Force, containing most of Japan's remaining battleships and cruisers, including the super-battleships *Yamato* and *Musashi*, would move in and destroy the now-unprotected American landing ships.

This attack would be joined by two smaller groups under Vice Admirals Nishimura and Shima. The Southern Force was built around the battleships *Yamashiro* and *Fuso*. Sho Go depended on a synchronized, three-pronged attack in which the Central and Southern Forces would catch the American invasion fleet in a vice.

The American landings began on October 20. By that afternoon, the beach had already been secured, and MacArthur, always a master of publicity, waded ashore with his staff in front of American reporters and photographers and dramatically declared, "I have returned".

Ozawa, meanwhile, established his command center on board the *Zuikaku* and put his forces into motion. "We are the spearhead," he told his officers, "and it is our duty to ensure that the sword strikes true."

As the Japanese forces converged, however, American submarines found the Center Force, and sank the heavy cruisers *Atago* and *Maya*. By mid-morning, Halsey's forces were moving toward the northern edge of the Philippine Sea. The Japanese knew that the overarching priority for US commanders was to destroy the Japanese carriers, and Halsey had, as they had expected, taken the bait. His task force, containing the fleet carriers *Enterprise, Intrepid, Lexington,* and their escorts, surged ahead.

Aboard the *Zuikaku*, lookouts soon reported incoming American aircraft — dozens of them — as Halsey launched his strikes.

"Enemy bombers are inbound!" *Zuikaku's* loudspeakers called out. "Prepare for launch!"

Hideyoshi scanned the sky as the other three Zeros of his *kutai* joined him in a tight formation, Takahashi on his right flank. They climbed steadily to meet the Americans and turned toward the incoming wave.

The first shots were fired as the formations closed the distance and the Hellcats split into smaller groups to engage the Zeros. Hideyoshi climbed for more altitude, positioning himself to dive into the fray at an advantageous angle, then rolled his plane and swooped in from above.

Below him, Takahashi engaged one of the Hellcats in a tight dogfight. It was a deadly mistake on the part of the American: though the F6F out-classed the Zero, the A6M still had superior maneuverability, and every American pilot was taught to not get into a turning dogfight. Hideyoshi nosed over to assist, but a quick burst from Takahashi's guns had already caught the Hellcat, and it fell away, trailing flames.

More Hellcats swarmed into the fight, their sheer numbers threatening to overwhelm the Japanese defenders. A quick glance around revealed dozens of aircraft racing through the sky, as well as a number of smoke trails that arced towards the ground. Hideyoshi dodged a burst of machine-gun fire, rolling his Zero and climbing away to avoid a pursuing fighter.

After a time the Americans, growing short on fuel and ammunition, turned away to head for home, and Hideyoshi signaled for his group to return to the *Zuikaku*. As his Zero touched down on the deck, he noted the number of shot-up and damaged planes being pushed over the side to make room for them.

Within the hour, just as his plane had been refueled and re-armed, another incoming raid was spotted, and the Zeros once again scrambled to intercept. It wasn't long before the enemy appeared, a flight of Hellcats climbing towards them. As they closed in, Hideyoshi and Takahashi split from the defensive formation and dove.

Hideyoshi selected one of the lead planes and turned in behind it. The Hellcat jinked to the left, trying to shake him off, but he pressed the attack and fired a burst of rounds, aiming for the engine.

The American twisted away and tried to break off, but Hideyoshi tightened his turn, following the enemy pilot's next action and matching the Hellcat's every move.

The Hellcat went for a sharp left-hand turn and tried to outmaneuver the Zero by diving into a split-S. It was a classic move —break hard, gain some speed, and then reverse the situation. But

Hideyoshi was ready. As the Hellcat dove, he did not follow. Instead, he pulled up sharply into a high-speed loop.

As the Hellcat came out of its dive, the Zero was already waiting at the top of the loop, having gained enough altitude to position himself above and behind — the classic hunter's position. Hideyoshi rolled over the top of the loop and dove down onto the F6F.

The Hellcat was now in a wide, shallow climb, but the Zero's superior maneuverability allowed Hideyoshi to close the distance in an instant. The American pilot, realizing his mistake, tried to push his fighter into a dive, desperately trying to escape, but it was too late. Hideyoshi's finger was already tightening on the trigger.

The first burst struck the Hellcat's wing, spitting a cloud of debris into the air. The Hellcat struggled to stay level, and Hideyoshi fired again, this time targeting the engine. Tracers ripped through the fighter's cowling, and fire burst from the nose. As Hideyoshi watched, the pilot pulled his canopy open, stood up on his seat, and bailed out.

Hideyoshi dropped into a shallow dive, approaching another of the Hellcats that had split off from the formation. But as he prepared to fire once more, a flash of light below him caught his attention out of the corner of his eye. As he looked down, Hideyoshi's stomach dropped. A bomb had just struck the *Zuikaku's* flight deck, the explosion tearing through the wooden slats and sending a plume of black smoke into the air.

The American fighters were beginning to disperse, now, heading back to their own fleet.

As Hideyoshi flew toward his own carrier, he could see the damage more clearly now. There was a blackened hole in the flight deck, but he could also see firefighting crews working to control the flames. The carrier was still operational, and he was not waved away as he made his landing approach. The crew had cleared as much space as they could for incoming aircraft, and the elevators looked functional.

As he climbed out of his cockpit, he looked around at the damage. Firefighting teams were still spraying water on the remaining flames, and the air was thick with the smell of smoke and burning oil. But the *Zuikaku* was still alive.

Hideyoshi got no rest, however, as yet another wave of American bombers soon came pouring in. The Americans seemed to have an endless number of planes to send into the fight. Meanwhile, the *Zuikaku's* crew barely had enough time to load Hideyoshi's pockmarked Zero with fuel and ammunition before he was back in the sky again.

As the American bombers descended, Hideyoshi calculated the closing distance between him and the enemy, looking for the most advantageous angle of attack. He dove toward the approaching SBU Helldivers with Takahashi at his side, aiming for the rearmost bombers in the formation.

Hellcats peeled off to intercept them, but Hideyoshi positioned himself behind one of the bombers. Just as he squeezed the trigger, however, a burst of gunfire erupted from a Hellcat below him, striking his tail. The Zero jolted momentarily, then settled down as he climbed away. It was not a bad hit, but Hideyoshi silently cursed his rookie mistake: dulled by the stress and fatigue of flying all day, he had allowed himself to become fixated on his target and had not been paying enough attention to what was going on around him. It was a mistake that should have killed him.

As he broke off from the combat, he glanced down at the *Zuikaku* once more—and was horrified. The carrier had obviously been hit again, and was now a smoking wreck, with flames billowing out from her hangar deck. It was clear that he would not be able to land there, even if the ship managed to survive the day.

He turned his Zero westward, heading toward the nearest land base in the Philippines. His fuel would be stretched, so he throttled back and leaned out the mixture as much as he dared. It was now a race against time—he wasn't sure if he would make it all the way to the airstrip, but he knew there was no other choice.

His controls were sluggish now, and the row of holes in his tail reminded him that he wasn't out of danger yet. He glided low and hugged the wave tops.

Finally, after what felt like an eternity, the outline of the airstrip came into view. Hideyoshi could feel the jolt of the landing gear hitting the dirt as he touched down and the Zero rolled to a stop before it reached the end of the runway. He had made it.

By the afternoon of October 25, the Japanese carriers *Zuiho* and *Chitose* had also been sunk or severely damaged, marking the effective end of Japan's once-unchallenged carrier fleet. But as other battle reports poured in from the south, Halsey's decision was looking more and more like a mistake. The Japanese northern force was not the main body. He had pursued a decoy.

In the southern portion of the battle area, Vice Admiral Kurita's fleet had lost the heavy cruisers *Mogami* and *Chikuma* before retreating. He had never even come close to the American landing operations. By the end of the day Ozawa's Central Force had also been effectively wiped out. The Americans, by contrast, had suffered relatively light losses, with only a handful of aircraft lost and minimal damage to their fleet. The Japanese had suffered another crushing defeat.

At the Philippine airstrip, Hideyoshi climbed out of his cockpit and looked around. One of the mechanics, his face smudged with grease, handed him a dented canteen of water and he gulped it down, the warm liquid soothing his throat. Another crewman, an older man with weary eyes, offered him a small bundle of rice wrapped in a banana leaf. Hideyoshi nodded his thanks, his voice too hoarse to speak.

"Lieutenant, your aircraft is in bad shape," the older man said, gesturing toward the Zero. "We'll patch it up as best we can, but ..." He shrugged helplessly.

Hideyoshi took a deep breath and surveyed the rough runway. It was a small auxiliary airstrip, hacked roughly out of the jungle. The air was thick with unspoken tension, though: reports of advancing American forces had everyone on edge.

As Hideyoshi sat on a crate eating his makeshift meal, he heard the distant drone of engines above the fighter airfield. The sound was unmistakable—a twin-engine plane, but its hum was uneven and labored. His first thought was of an approaching enemy bomber, but as the dark silhouette emerged through a patch of low clouds, he saw the shape of a G4M Betty bomber. Smoke trailed from one engine, and the other sputtered unevenly. The plane wobbled in its approach, its flaps lowered, clearly struggling to stay aloft.

"Clear the runway!" someone yelled to the mechanics and ground crews, who scattered to make way for the incoming bomber. Everyone turned to look, watching as the aircraft lurched closer, its landing gear extended. The Betty hit the ground hard, skidding and bouncing a few times before it finally came to a stop near the edge of the strip. One of the tires had blown on impact, and the plane now tilted awkwardly to one side.

Hideyoshi grabbed his flight helmet and ran toward the aircraft as the engines sputtered to a halt. Smoke and steam hissed from the bullet-riddled fuselage, and the battered crew began climbing out. The pilot, a slender man barely older than Hideyoshi, stumbled onto the wing and jumped to the ground. He waved off the approaching medic and his gaze darted around nervously. The bomber's crew— five in all—gathered round their pilot, each man looking shaken but intact. One of them, a gunner with a bandaged arm, leaned heavily against the fuselage.

"We made it," the pilot exclaimed to them, with both relief and exhaustion in his voice. "Barely."

Hideyoshi stepped closer, noting the jagged holes riddling the fuselage and the black scorch marks streaking the wings behind the engines. "What happened?"

"American fighters," the pilot replied grimly. "They ambushed us on the way back from a mission near Leyte. We were lucky to get away."

One of the crewmen added, "We lost two planes from our group. They didn't stand a chance."

Hideyoshi nodded. "You were over Leyte? How bad is it there?"

The pilot hesitated, his eyes meeting Hideyoshi's. "Bad. The Americans are everywhere. Their fighters ... We barely saw them before they were on us. If I hadn't dropped altitude and hugged the waves, we'd be at the bottom of the ocean."

As they spoke, ground crewmen approached, offering water and cigarettes to the shaken men. The Betty's pilot accepted a cigarette and lit it with shaking hands. He took a long drag before looking back at Hideyoshi.

"How about you — looks like you've seen some action too."

In answer, Hideyoshi pointed silently at his shot-up fighter.

"I wanted to fly fighters," the bomber pilot said suddenly, with a wistful sigh. "When I enlisted, that was my dream. To fly hot fast machines like yours. I figured the pretty girls all loved fighter pilots. But —" He smiled and shrugged. "The Army said they needed bomber pilots more. So I trained for bombers, and here I am, driving a flying coffin."

"Bombers are just as important," Hideyoshi offered. "Without them, the fighters would have nothing to defend. You've done your duty."

The pilot smiled faintly, but his eyes betrayed his frustration. "Maybe. But when I see you fighter jocks zooming around through the skies, I can't help but wonder what it would've been like."

The conversation paused as a mechanic called over to Hideyoshi. "Sir, they're towing your plane to the far edge of the field. It's too damaged to repair here."

"Understood," Hideyoshi replied, before turning back to the bomber crew. "I'm trying to get to Manila." He glanced over at their shattered Betty, now sitting in a field with the other wrecks. "Looks like you won't be going anywhere for a while."

The pilot nodded. "We'll find a truck to get back. We all want to get back into the fight and give them some payback."

There was nothing more to say. "Well", Hideyoshi gave a slight bow. "Good luck out there".

"And to you", the pilot replied. "We're all fighting the same war, after all."

After finishing his rice, Hideyoshi walked back to his aircraft. Several mechanics were already assessing the damage, their tools clanging as they worked. The Zero's fuselage bore rows of fresh bullet holes, and one of the control wires was frayed.

"We've got orders to get you to Manila, sir," one of the crewmen said, looking up from his work. "They need every pilot there to prepare for the defense."

Hideyoshi nodded. "How long until the Zero is airworthy?"

The crewman hesitated. "Two hours, maybe three. Enough to get you to Manila anyway, but probably not much further than that."

Hideyoshi watched as they patched the bullet holes with sheet metal, replaced the rudder wire, and stripped some parts from other wrecked planes to replace damaged pieces. By the time they finished, the Zero looked battered but serviceable.

Hideyoshi's flight to Manila was anxious but uneventful. The Zero gave him no trouble, and though he stayed alert and kept vigil for roving American fighters, he saw none.

Hideyoshi's boots scuffed against the cracked tarmac as he walked across the Manila airbase. A number of battered aircraft were scattered across the field, most of them in various states of disassembly — missing wings, stripped engines, and bullet-riddled fuselages with missing panels.

Inside the command tent, an officer sat behind a desk cluttered with maps and radio equipment. He looked up as Hideyoshi entered.

Hideyoshi saluted. "Reporting from … from the *Zuikaku*, sir. I was ordered here after my aircraft sustained damage. I'm ready for assignment."

The officer leaned back in his chair, rubbing his forehead wearily. "Lieutenant, I appreciate your enthusiasm, but we have no Zeros for you to fly."

"None? Surely there must be one that can be made operational."

The officer sighed and gestured toward the airfield beyond the tent's flaps. "Look for yourself, Lieutenant. All of our Zeros are either destroyed or have already been cannibalized for parts."

Hideyoshi addressed the officer again. "Sir, if there's nothing for me to do here, what are your orders?"

"Formosa," the officer replied without hesitation. "We're evacuating as many of our pilots as we can to regroup there."

"When does the transport leave?"

"Within the hour," the officer said, shuffling through a stack of papers. "Head to the north end of the field. A transport plane is waiting for personnel heading to Formosa."

Hideyoshi nodded curtly and turned to leave, but the officer called out to him. "Lieutenant," he said, his tone softening, "I know how you must feel. But we're all doing what we can with what little we have. You'll do more good on Formosa than you can here."

Without replying, Hideyoshi made his way across the airbase. He passed by a group of mechanics working on a grounded Judy, and one of them glanced up and gave him a half-hearted salute.

"No planes to fly, Lieutenant?" the mechanic asked with a faint smile.

"Not here," Hideyoshi replied.

The mechanic nodded knowingly and turned back to his work.

As he walked away toward the transport plane, Hideyoshi glanced back and saw ground crew members already swarming over his Zero. They were dismantling it, removing the machine guns and ammunition. Every resource was being salvaged for the ground defense.

One of the crew, noticing Hideyoshi's gaze, gave a resigned shrug. "We'll use the guns in the trenches, Lieutenant. It's all we can do."

Hideyoshi said nothing. He merely nodded and continued walking. The sight of his dismantled Zero was a painful reminder of how far Japan's air power had fallen.

Climbing aboard the transport plane, Hideyoshi found a seat near the window. As the engines chattered into action, he watched the airstrip recede into the distance. His battered Zero remained where he had left it, now little more than a collection of parts for the men staying behind.

As he made his way back to Japan, Hideyoshi wondered what the future held for Japan—and for him. Would he survive the war? Would he ever return to Sakurada, to his family, to the life he had known before the war had consumed everything?

He didn't know.

Chapter 17
Divine Wind (November 1944-February 1945)

Hideyoshi's arrival at Taichu Airfield in central Formosa came with little ceremony. The transport plane touched down on the dusty runway and taxied to a stop near a row of the Army's Ki-43 Hayabusa fighters. Hideyoshi stepped off the plane, and was greeted by a junior officer who saluted smartly despite his tired appearance.

"Lieutenant Sugiyama," the officer said, "you're to board another transport for Japan. Orders from the 2nd Air Fleet."

Hideyoshi nodded wearily, still lagging from the fatigue and stress that had settled into his bones over the past few days. He followed the officer toward a small operations shack, where a makeshift desk was piled with papers and flight manifests. A ground crewman handed him a wrapped rice ball.

"Eat while you can, Lieutenant," the crewman said with a grin. "It's not much, but it's fresh."

Grateful, Hideyoshi sat on a wooden crate near the shack, unwrapping the rice ball and taking measured bites. Around him, mechanics swarmed over battered planes, patching holes and replacing shot-out parts. Pilots in oil-streaked uniforms moved between briefing tents and aircraft. A mechanic paused to nod at him, then returned to removing the engine cowling. After a short while he was directed toward an olive-drab twin-engine L2D transport plane.

Inside, a handful of other men—pilots, officers, and technicians—were already seated, their belongings tucked beneath the bench seats. Hideyoshi found a spot near a small window and stowed his bag before settling in.

The flight northward was uneventful but long. Hideyoshi stared out the window as the coastline of Formosa disappeared, replaced by the open waters of the East China Sea. The details of his reassignment were still unclear, and he wasn't entirely sure just where he was going.

The transport finally descended toward an airfield in southern Kyushu. From the window, Hideyoshi caught glimpses of a sprawling complex of runways and hangars nestled amid rolling hills. This was Kanoya Airfield, the base of the 2nd Air Fleet and one of Japan's most important air installations. As he disembarked, Hideyoshi was directed toward the operations center, a sturdy wooden structure at the heart of the base.

Inside, he was greeted by a senior officer with a clipboard in his hand. The man's eyes swept over him as he extended a curt nod. "Lieutenant Sugiyama," the officer said. "Welcome to Kanoya. You'll be briefed on your duties shortly."

Hideyoshi took his place at the long table with several other men, who appeared to be veteran pilots like himself. At the head of the room stood Captain Morita, who held a stack of documents that he laid on the table with deliberate care. After a quick glance to ensure everyone was present, he began.

"All of you are combat pilots, so you know that the Americans have introduced many new and advanced aircraft which can outperform ours. And as the Americans approach closer to our home islands, we must produce new aircraft capable of defeating them."

"Our focus here," Morita continued, "is to test advanced fighter designs that, when they enter combat, will turn the tide in our favor. These include the Mitsubishi J2M Raiden, the Kawanishi N1K Shiden, and the Nakajima C6N Reppu."

"The Raiden," Morita explained, gesturing to a technical drawing pinned to the wall, "is a high-altitude interceptor designed to engage the American B-29s. Its speed and climb rate are exceptional, but it has handling quirks you'll need to master."

As Morita spoke, Hideyoshi studied the diagram. The Raiden was sleek, with a slim fuselage and narrow nose. Planes, Hideyoshi knew, generally fly in a way similar to how they look. The Raiden looked aggressive, built for speed and power.

Next, Morita moved to a schematic of the Shiden. "The N1K, nicknamed 'George' by the enemy, is a strong dogfighter. It's heavily armed and can match the performance of any American aircraft."

Finally, he turned to the Reppu. "The C6N Reppu is still in development. It promises exceptional range and speed, making it a vital asset for our carrier forces."

"These prototypes represent our latest efforts to counter the enemy's technological and numerical gains. Each of you will be assigned specific models to test."

"Your aim," he concluded, "is not just to evaluate their performance but to push these machines to their limits, identify their strengths and weaknesses, and provide feedback to the designers and engineers. Lives will depend on the results of the work you do here."

The next morning, Hideyoshi was led to the flight line, where several test aircraft had been parked under tarpaulins. A mechanic standing beside a Shiden greeted him with a sharp salute. Like all test models, it had been painted bright orange for visibility.

"She's all ready, Lieutenant," the man said, patting the aircraft's cowling.

Hideyoshi approached it with a blend of curiosity and professional scrutiny, his eyes tracing its contours. The first thing he noticed was its size. The Shiden was larger than the Zero, its fuselage broader and more robust. Where the Zero embodied a certain delicate elegance with its slender frame, the Shiden appeared more rugged. Its wings were mid-mounted, sweeping outward with a slight dihedral angle that lent it stability in flight.

The engine was also different. The Homare 21 was more powerful than the Zero's Sakae, boasting 2,000 horsepower compared to the Zero's 1,130, but the larger engine came at a cost: the aircraft was heavier and less nimble than the Zero.

The armament was another marked improvement. The Shiden bristled with four 20mm cannons, two mounted in each wing. These weapons were far more destructive than the Zero's mix of light machine guns and cannons, and were capable of shredding even a huge B-29 with a well-placed burst.

The Shiden's cockpit was roomier and was armored, offering improved protection for the pilot. The bubble canopy provided excellent visibility in all directions, a critical advantage in combat. And there was a reliable radio.

An hour later, Hideyoshi was taxiing the Shiden to the airstrip, with its radial engine rumbling with a guttural roar. As he pushed the throttle forward, the Shiden rolled down the runway.

Hideyoshi climbed steadily, testing the Shiden's responsiveness as he gained altitude. The controls felt heavier than the Zero's and required more force to maneuver, but the plane responded with stability and accuracy. Banking into a wide turn, he noted how the aircraft handled smoothly despite its bulk, a testament to Kawanishi's engineering.

He leveled off at 5,000 meters and pushed the throttle to full power, testing the Shiden's top speed, and the wind howled past the canopy as the needle on the airspeed indicator climbed rapidly. But Hideyoshi was disappointed as the needle topped out at 485 kph. Not enough to match the Americans. He decided that the engine was underpowered for the airplane's weight.

Next, Hideyoshi tested the aircraft's climb rate. He pulled back on the stick, feeling the vibration as the Shiden climbed steeply. At 6,500 meters, he leveled off again, the plane steady and responsive even at high altitudes.

With the basics tested, it was time to explore the Shiden's maneuverability. He rolled the plane sharply, diving into a series of tight turns. Here, the differences from the Zero were most apparent. The Shiden couldn't match the Zero's effortless agility; it was heavier, slower to react, and could not execute such tight maneuvers. However, it compensated with remarkable stability, especially at higher speeds.

After an hour in the air, he began his descent. The approach was smooth, but as the wheels touched the runway, he felt a slight wobble. It was, he realized, the landing gear. The mid-body wing mount and the long propeller blades had necessitated unusually long landing gear struts. These, Hideyoshi sensed immediately, were a weakness during landing, and they probably would not stand up to repeated rough landings on an aircraft carrier. Still, the aircraft came to a stop without incident, and Hideyoshi taxied it back to the hangar. He mentally compiled a list of the adjustments that would be required to improve the plane, which he would report to the engineers.

Climbing out of the cockpit, Hideyoshi removed his flight helmet and looked back at the Shiden. It had its flaws, he decided, but it could be, if tweaked, a formidable machine.

Over the following weeks, Hideyoshi spent a considerable amount of time in the cockpit of the Shiden, each flight offering him new insights into the aircraft's capabilities and limitations as he grew more accustomed to its handling characteristics. He had quickly adapted to the plane's strengths, learning to use its firepower and stability to his advantage. However, the aircraft's bulk, particularly in sharp turns and rapid climbs, was a constant reminder of how different it was from the nimble Zero. One test flight took him up to an altitude of 8,000 meters. The air thinned as he leveled off, and Hideyoshi could feel the Shiden's engine working harder, but it held steady.

On another flight, Hideyoshi spent time at lower altitudes, simulating an engagement with enemy aircraft. He practiced tight turns and evasive maneuvers, testing the Shiden's ability to defend itself against a faster, more nimble fighter. The results were predictable: the Shiden couldn't match the Zero's agility, but it could absorb far more punishment and still bring the pilot home.

Hideyoshi's flight testing reached its climax with a series of mock dogfights, set up to put the Shiden to the ultimate test against some of its strongest adversaries.

The first mock engagement was against a Zero, the venerable aircraft that had once dominated the skies over the Pacific. In the first run, Hideyoshi quickly found that the Shiden could outrun the Zero in a straight line. Hideyoshi snapped the plane into a hard bank, forcing the Zero to overshoot, and then dove under it to gain a winning position.

The Shiden's heavy build, however, made it difficult to match the Zero's agility in close-quarters combat. Its superiority in firepower could be decisive in a real combat scenario—but only if the battle remained at range. In a close quarters turning fight, the Zero would still have the upper hand.

The next series of engagements was more complex—Hideyoshi faced off against captured American Hellcats and P-51 Mustangs, aircraft far faster, more maneuverable, and packed with superior firepower.

The Shiden could not outpace the Hellcat in a straight-line chase, and when it came to sharp turns, the American fighter had the advantage. Hideyoshi found that he couldn't match the Hellcat's quick rolls and turns.

Hideyoshi then shifted to engage the P-51 Mustang, a more challenging adversary. The American fighter came at him in a series of coordinated high-speed dives, trying to force Hideyoshi into a defensive position. The Shiden was slower to climb, and the Mustang closed in on him quickly, but Hideyoshi used the Shiden's excellent dive capabilities to extend the gap. He dove toward the sea and then pulled up sharply into a vertical climb. The Mustang, following the Shiden, misjudged the climb and overshot, giving Hideyoshi an opening to loop behind it.

As he descended toward the airfield, he reflected on how much better the Shiden was than the Zero in certain respects, but it was also too late—far too late.

Hideyoshi was also given the opportunity to test-fly the Reppu. This plane was light and agile, designed to be a true match for the American fighters. It was smaller than the Shiden, its wings shorter and the fuselage more compact. Hideyoshi examined the aircraft closely, noting its clean lines and the powerful engine that seemed to promise exceptional speed. It reminded him in many ways of the Zero.

As Hideyoshi climbed into the cockpit, he adjusted the controls and checked his instruments. The Reppu's layout was different from the Zero's, but the arrangement felt intuitive enough. The seat was lower, and the cockpit cramped, but the visibility was excellent. Hideyoshi took a deep breath, his gloved hand resting on the throttle as he prepared to taxi.

As he took off and climbed into the sky, the aircraft felt solid and stable, and accelerated crisply as it climbed.

When he reached cruising altitude, Hideyoshi began to put the Reppu through its paces. He engaged in several rolls and sharp turns, testing the limits of the plane's maneuverability. The aircraft was more stable than the Zero in most high-speed maneuvers, and it didn't require as much effort to maintain control at high speeds. The Reppu was certainly an improvement, but it lacked the flexibility and low-speed agility of the Zero.

Hideyoshi's next opportunity came when he was allowed to fly the Raiden, a sleek sharp-nosed fighter with a shark-like body that was intended specifically as a high-altitude interceptor to counter the B-29 Superfortress. Its primary armament consisted of four 20mm cannons. Just a few hits with its exploding shells would be enough to bring down even the huge American bomber.

The aircraft had a strong, reinforced fuselage. The nose was slightly more elongated, housing the powerful engine designed to propel the Raiden to altitudes where the B-29s would fly. The control stick felt heavier than those of the Shiden or Reppu, which suggested that, as an interceptor, the Raiden was not built for nimbleness. Unlike the agile Zero, which had struggled with high-altitude performance due to its older engine, the Raiden was capable of reaching the altitudes where American bombers operated and maintaining a solid performance there.

As Hideyoshi continued his test flights in the new fighter designs, though, a growing sense of frustration began to take root. While the Reppu, Shiden, and Raiden were impressive in their own right, they were ultimately bound by the grim realities of Japan's manufacturing limitations and lack of resources. Hideyoshi had seen for himself the constant shortages in spare parts and replacement planes on the frontlines, and he knew that despite their advanced design and impressive performance, these aircraft were the products of a nation that had already been severely hampered by years of war and a rapidly declining industrial base.

Even if these aircraft could be produced in sufficient numbers, the second major challenge facing Japan was the severe lack of trained pilots to fly them. These new aircraft, designed to exploit specific tactical advantages, demanded a high level of skill and experience to be used effectively in combat. But, Hideyoshi knew, most of Japan's experienced pilots had been lost in the devastating battles in the Solomon Islands, at Midway, and the Marianas.

Training new pilots was a challenge in itself. With the need for new pilots increasing at the same time that resources were growing thin, the instruction courses at Japanese training facilities were cut short and rushed. Pilots were often taught only the basics and were given minimal flight time before being sent directly into combat, which had led to disastrous results.

Hideyoshi, who had survived the brutal attrition of the war, knew this all too well. The young men now entering the fight were not the experienced and battle-hardened pilots who had fought in the early days of the war—now, they were green, unprepared, and had been thrust into the fight too soon.

Hideyoshi could appreciate the technological innovations behind the Shiden, Reppu, and Raiden, and he could see how they might change the course of the war if given time and resources. But Japan's industrial constraints and the shortage of trained pilots meant, he concluded, that these fighters would never reach their full potential.

After several months spent testing and evaluating new aircraft, Hideyoshi found himself reassigned to a new, far more somber duty.

His new orders promoted him to the rank of full Lieutenant and directed him to Matsuyama Airfield, located in Ehime Prefecture on the island of Shikoku. He had been ordered to train the next wave of pilots—young students, newly graduated from flight school—who had volunteered for suicide missions. These were the *kamikaze* pilots, who would fly their aircraft directly into American ships, destroying themselves along with the enemy.

When Hideyoshi arrived at the airfield, he found that the change in atmosphere was immediate. These were the faces of eager young men, most still in their late teens—nearly all of them raw recruits with only a few dozen hours of flying experience. "These are chicks barely hatched out of their shell," he thought.

The formation of *kamikaze* units was a response to Japan's increasingly hopeless situation as the war dragged on. By late 1944, Japan had suffered a series of crippling defeats, and the B-29 bombing campaigns were severely weakening the Japanese war effort. The military were suffering from critical shortages in aircraft, fuel, and experienced pilots, while the American forces continued to grow stronger, both in numbers and in technological advantage. The Marianas and Leyte had demonstrated the overwhelming strength of American air and naval power, and the Japanese knew that they could not match it through conventional means. And every pilot knew that his odds of coming back alive from any mission were not good.

In those conditions, the concept of the *kamikaze* — literally "divine wind" — was born. It had, in the eyes of many, become the only viable tactic left for a nation that was facing the inevitability of humiliating defeat. The young men were motivated by a sense of duty and patriotism, encouraged by propaganda that framed their actions as a noble sacrifice for the Emperor and their country.

In addition to the younger, less-experienced student pilots, the Japanese military also sought out experienced front-line pilots to volunteer for "special attacks", and many did — driven by a sense of duty, honor, and a belief that it was their last chance to defend their country.

The pressure to volunteer came not only from military leadership but from the very culture that defined Japan's wartime ethos, and even though the *kamikaze* pilots were all technically volunteers, the reality was that there was little room for refusal. The choice was portrayed as an honor, one that would ensure their legacy and show their unwavering devotion to the cause.

As a result, while many of the pilots did indeed volunteer willingly, believing they were giving their lives for a greater cause, others felt trapped by their circumstances. The pressure from their peers, their commanders, and their society was overwhelming, and for some, it was a matter of "volunteering" to avoid the shame of not doing so.

The new students, mostly young men barely out of adolescence, watched Hideyoshi as he inspected their training planes. His role was clear — he was there to impart the skills necessary for their final flights.

The lessons, however, were far from simple. Hideyoshi showed them how to navigate their planes in the most efficient way possible, how to pick the most significant targets, and how to ensure that their sacrifice would be effective. But despite his instruction, Hideyoshi felt a growing sense of disconnect between himself and the young pilots. They did not yet understand the true nature of what they were being asked to do, and were, for the most part, eager to prove themselves, to show their willingness to sacrifice for their country. Hideyoshi could see it in their eyes — the idealism that would soon be extinguished when they were sent out on their final missions. Most of them had never seen combat, let alone understood the true nature of the war. They were, Hideyoshi knew, in a fight that, in his mind, was already lost, and their deaths could not possibly change that. It was a hard truth that he himself was struggling to come to terms with.

Days turned into weeks as Hideyoshi ran drills, sharpening each student's ability to fly, dive, and aim with precision. Each session felt like it drained something from him—his heart heavy with the knowledge that these young men, who reminded him so much of his own earlier days in the air, were being groomed for certain death. There was no other outcome for them.

One afternoon, as Hideyoshi stood by a row of Zeros, one of them, a young man no older than twenty, approached him with a hesitant expression. His name was Takahiro, a quiet, earnest-looking student who had volunteered for the "special attack" missions, eager to give everything for Japan. He had been one of the first to enter the program, driven by a deep sense of loyalty to the Emperor and the nation.

Takahiro's question caught Hideyoshi off guard. "Sir," the young man began, his voice laced with uncertainty, "I have been wondering … why is it that you, an experienced fighter pilot, have not volunteered for a special attack flight? We all know how skilled you are, and you could do much to strike back at the Americans. So, why haven't you offered yourself for the same mission we are preparing for?"

The question hung in the air between them, and for a moment, Hideyoshi was silent, considering how best to respond. His first instinct was to avoid such a delicate conversation, but the sincerity in Takahiro's eyes gave him pause. Takahiro's question was not meant as a challenge, but as a genuine inquiry—one that reflected the reverence that young men like him held for the older generation of pilots, those who had fought in battles that now seemed a lifetime ago.

Finally, Hideyoshi spoke, his voice steady but with a hint of quiet sorrow. "Takahiro," he began, "I am the only son of my family. Navy policy prevents sole male heirs, like myself, from being accepted into the *kamikaze* missions. It's considered important that we continue the family line. My duty, in the eyes of the Emperor, is to carry on my father's legacy." He paused for a moment, his gaze distant, thinking of his mother and father, of Aiko and Ichiro.

Takahiro had a puzzled look. He had expected a different answer—perhaps something more akin to the stoic patriotism of his peers, but instead, he saw a man who had lived through the horrors of war and carried a burden far greater than any he had imagined. Hideyoshi's voice softened as he continued. "You must know that I honor you for choosing this path. You are acting out of duty and love for your country, and that is something I can never question."

Takahiro remained silent, absorbing Hideyoshi's words. The silence between them stretched, but there was a mutual understanding now—a recognition of the different paths that life had forced them to take. Hideyoshi's role, it seemed, was not to die for his country, but to guide those who would.

That night, in the dim light of the barracks, Hideyoshi sat at a small wooden desk under the flickering light of a single candle. He could not shake the need to write to Aiko. She had always been the one constant in his life amid the chaos of war. Writing to her felt like a fragile thread connecting him to a life outside of the war, a life he feared might slip beyond his reach.

He dipped his brush in ink.

"My dearest Aiko,

"I trust this letter finds you well. I think of you often, and I hope the days are gentle to you and Ichiro, though I know it is difficult for both of you in these times. Please give him a warm embrace for me. I long for the moment when I can return to you.

"I write to you now from a place that is far removed from the skies I once dreamed of. I have been assigned to instruct young pilots who have volunteered for special missions. They are not much different from the boys I once flew with, each eager to serve, to protect their homes. I see their faces, and I know their devotion. They are ready to give everything.

"As for myself, Aiko, I am torn. I am the only son of my family, and I am bound by a different duty. This has become both my burden and my responsibility—to continue the family name, to protect what is left of our legacy. There are days, however, when I wonder if it is enough—if this role, this duty, truly holds any meaning in the face of the great challenges that we are all enduring.

"I am unsure what the future holds. I can only hope that we are able to protect what we can for as long as possible.

"I will leave you with these thoughts, though I fear I am not the best at expressing them. I hold on to the thought of you, and Ichiro, and the life we had before this war. It is the only thing that sustains me as I carry out the tasks set before me.

"Please take care of yourself, and know that I am with you in spirit, even as I remain here in this place.

"With all my love,

"Hideyoshi"

He placed the pen down slowly, rereading the letter several times. The words felt inadequate, and he knew he could not truly capture his feelings in mere ink and paper. Yet it was all he had to offer. He folded the letter carefully, wondering how much of it would be censored before it ever reached her. Still, he hoped that she would sense the depth of his feelings through his words, even if they were filtered by the strict eyes of the military censors.

Hideyoshi sighed, leaning back in his cot. For now, all he could do was hold on to the faint hope that he might one day be with Aiko again

----

Hideyoshi stood at the edge of the airfield, the sharp winds of Formosa whipping past him. He had been reassigned again—no longer would he be working with trainees or testing the newest aircraft designs. Now, he was to take to the skies again, this time once again as a combat pilot.

The orders to send him to Taichu Field, in the central part of the island of Formosa, had come quickly and unexpectedly. Hideyoshi suspected that his letter to Aiko had something to do with it.

But now the Japanese Empire's focus had shifted almost entirely to the defense of the home islands. The relentless B-29 raids had necessitated a more immediate response, and Hideyoshi's new assignment would involve flying operational sorties to intercept the American bombers. And for these missions, he would be flying the Shiden Kai—an improved version of the Shiden fighter that he had previously tested.

He had heard about the improvements, of course. The aircraft had incorporated some of the design changes which he had recommended himself during his earlier test flights, particularly with the landing gear. The new Shiden Kai featured a low-mounted wing that enabled a shorter and stronger undercarriage that was designed to handle the stress of hard landings, something that had been a concern during his earlier test flights. But the most important change—one he had been hoping for—was the new improved engine, which gave the aircraft a boost in speed and climb rate, vital for intercepting incoming American bombers.

For Hideyoshi, his return to combat was bittersweet. He had fought through the entire war, had seen his comrades fall, and had witnessed the gradual crumbling of Japan's strength. Now, he was back in the cockpit, but the war was no longer the same. The skies had become a graveyard, and the number of experienced pilots like him was constantly shrinking. And, he knew, they were fighting a war which they could no longer win.

A few days later, as the plane lifted off for an interception mission, Hideyoshi's gaze was fixed on the horizon where the American bombers were expected to appear. He had heard reports of how tough the B-29s were—and he knew the rumor that most of the Superfortresses had removed all of their guns (except the tail gun) to save weight, counting upon their speed and altitude to keep interceptors away. But there was always the chance that he would encounter fighter escorts, which would be a far more difficult challenge. He'd seen the American Hellcats and Mustangs before, and he knew their capabilities.

The sighting came quickly. The huge B-29s, with their four engines and massive wingspans, were unmistakable. There was no fighter escort.

Hideyoshi signaled to his *kutai* with a waggle of his wings, and the four planes broke into pairs.

Hideyoshi and his wingman Tondabayashi swooped toward the left flank of the formation. As they closed in, tracer rounds streaked toward them like fiery needles. Hideyoshi banked hard to the left, narrowly avoiding a burst that could have shredded his plane. Tondabayashi followed suit, keeping pace. Their approach was methodical, darting in quickly to avoid prolonged exposure to the overlapping fields of fire.

On the other side of the formation, Hasegawa drew attention from the right flank, forcing the gunners to divide their fire. Araki remained slightly behind, prepared to pounce on any bomber that strayed from the protective formation.

Hideyoshi's chance came as one of the B-29s banked slightly to avoid a near-collision within the tightly packed group. The maneuver exposed its belly, and he seized the opportunity, diving beneath the formation and pulling up sharply into the bomber's blind spot. Lining up his sights, he unleashed a burst from his four 20mm cannons. The rounds tore into the B-29's underbelly, sending debris and flames cascading downward.

The bomber tail gunners around him fired wildly in response, but Tondabayashi darted in from above, adding his own burst to the attack. The combined firepower proved too much. Smoke poured from one of the bomber's engines and it fell behind. Its mates were unable to assist without breaking formation, and that would leave them exposed to the fighters.

Moments later, the wounded B-29 pitched forward, flames engulfing its left wing as it spiraled downward.

The mighty B-29 was not unbeatable after all.

The new intelligence reports came in about a week later: now, the B-29s were being accompanied by fighter escorts. The Americans had clearly learned from their losses and were now deploying Mustangs, formidable adversaries with excellent speed and firepower.

On their next mission, the familiar sight of the massive B-29s came into view. But just below and to the side of the bombers, they spotted the smaller shapes of the Mustangs.

At Hideyoshi's signal, the *kutai* split into attack formation. Hideyoshi and Tondabayashi would go for the escorts while Hasegawa and Araki focused on the bombers.

The Mustangs immediately moved to engage as the Japanese fighters closed in. The first, banking sharply to intercept, made a shallow dive to gain speed. Hideyoshi rolled left, cutting across its path to force an overshoot. The American pilot reacted quickly, climbing into an Immelmann to reverse direction and regain the advantage. But Hideyoshi executed a tight spiral that put him on the Mustang's tail as it crested the loop.

Lining up his sights, Hideyoshi squeezed the trigger and the American fighter wobbled, trailing smoke from its engine. The Mustang attempted a dive to escape, but Hideyoshi pursued, firing a second burst that shattered its right wing. The enemy plane spiraled out of control, vanishing into the clouds below.

His moment of victory was cut short as tracers zipped past his canopy. Another Mustang had closed in on him. Hideyoshi pulled into a sharp climb, his Shiden Kai groaning under the strain as the American pilot stuck close. The Mustang was gaining. Hideyoshi's mind raced. A prolonged climb, he knew, would end in his destruction.

Thinking quickly, he rolled inverted and pushed into a dive, a risky maneuver that momentarily stalled his pursuer's attempt to follow. Then Hideyoshi suddenly yanked the stick back, pulling into a high-G turn. The Shiden Kai shuddered but held steady. As the pursuing Mustang overshot, unable to match the Shiden Kai's tighter turn, Hideyoshi reversed his dive, placing himself on the enemy's tail.

The American pilot, recognizing the danger, dove for speed, but Hideyoshi stayed with him. He aimed and fired, and the Mustang jerked as the explosive rounds tore into its right wing and fuel tank. Flames erupted, and the enemy fighter tumbled toward the earth.

Breathing hard, Hideyoshi scanned the sky for his comrades. Tondabayashi was engaged with another Mustang, but the remaining P-51s were breaking off to rejoin the bombers. Hideyoshi, now low on ammo, regrouped with his wingman and signaled the *kutai* to disengage. The damage to the bombers had been limited, but two Mustangs were down, and Hideyoshi's squadron had managed to hold their own against the American fighters.

As they returned to Taichu Field, Hideyoshi reflected on the encounter. The P-51s were formidable and their speed and firepower were dangerous, but the Shiden Kai had proven itself.

Then the Americans changed their tactics again.

The first sign came as intelligence reported an unusual absence of B-29 raids during daylight hours for a few days. At first, Hideyoshi and his comrades at Taichu Field were cautiously optimistic, interpreting the lull as a temporary reprieve. However, this hope was short-lived. One night, the distant rumble of engines broke the stillness, and a fiery glow lit up the horizon — evidence of a low-altitude incendiary bombing run.

The B-29s had adapted. Realizing that the Japanese interceptors, even advanced fighters like the Shiden Kai, lacked the radar capability needed to operate effectively at night, the Americans shifted their strategy. Rather than risking high-altitude daytime bombing raids where their unescorted bombers could be attacked, they began flying at low altitudes under the cover of darkness. At night, they could drop incendiary payloads designed to create massive fires in urban and industrial areas, devastating Japan's infrastructure.

At the morning briefing, the mood was dark. The base commander slammed his fist on the map spread out before him. "They are exploiting our greatest weakness," he pointed out. "We have no radar-equipped night fighters, no way to intercept them effectively. This is a deliberate strategy to demoralize and destroy us from within."

The frustration was visible among the pilots. Tondabayashi, always the optimist, tried to rally the group. "They can't fly at night forever," he said. "Their maintenance crews will be pushed to their limits. Their pilots will tire."

Hasegawa, ever pragmatic, countered, "Even if they do, it's enough. Look at what they've done already. We're chasing shadows."

Hideyoshi remained silent. As a test pilot, he had evaluated many aircraft, some with the potential for night operations, but Japan's limited resources meant those designs had never materialized. He knew all too well that even the Shiden Kai, for all its power and maneuverability, was almost useless in the dark. The lack of radar and proper training for night operations had left them blind and defenseless.

In the days that followed, the Japanese air crews worked tirelessly to try to adapt. Maintenance teams experimented with modifications. Someone even managed to scrounge up an aerial radar set, but it was intended to be used in flying boats for reconnaissance missions, and the Shiden Kai could not carry it. (And in any case none of the pilots knew how to use it.)

Hideyoshi, desperate for some way to counter the threat, volunteered for a trial night mission and taxied his Shiden Kai onto the dimly lit runway that night. It was a failure. He spent hours chasing phantom targets, unable to find the dark shapes of the bombers above him.

During one morning briefing, the base commander spoke frankly to the pilots. "Our options are limited. The Americans have taken the upper hand with these nocturnal raids. Until we can develop a night fighter—or find a way to bring them back to daylight operations—we must endure."

The mess hall at Taichu Field buzzed with muted conversations as pilots and ground crew gathered for their evening meal. Hideyoshi sat near the back, his tray untouched before him.

A junior officer entered, carrying a stack of papers. "News from Iwo Jima," he announced.

The words silenced the room almost instantly, and the pilots turned their attention to the officer, who cleared his throat and began to read. "Fierce air combat continues over Iwo Jima. Special Attack units have struck multiple blows on the American fleet supporting the landings. Several enemy ships have been sunk, including one escort carrier, and another reported as heavily damaged." The suicide pilots were described as "examples of devotion to the Emperor", their attacks praised as acts of "unparalleled heroism".

Hideyoshi froze at the mention of the *kamikaze*. He had trained some of the pilots who were throwing their lives into these desperate missions. Now the faces of these young men—some barely out of their teens—flashed through his mind.

"Do we know which units were involved?" someone asked.

The officer nodded. "The 201st Air Group contributed to the attacks."

Hideyoshi felt a pang in his chest. The 201st was the unit to which many of his students had been reassigned. He could almost hear their voices, their questions during training, their hesitant laughter during rare moments of levity. For a fleeting moment, he wondered which of them had made it through and had died in a fiery plunge into an enemy ship.

Tondabayashi, sitting across the table, broke the silence. "They're brave, those boys. To go out knowing there's no return." He stared into his bowl, the unspoken words hanging in the air.

"Bravery, yes," Hasegawa responded. "But the Americans have the numbers, the equipment, and the training. What else can we do?"

Silence fell over the table again, the unvarnished truth of Hasegawa's words sinking in. Hideyoshi remained quiet. He had seen the flaws in the *kamikaze* strategy from the start—an unsustainable sacrifice of young lives, draining what little strength Japan had left.

But he couldn't voice these thoughts. Not here. Not now.

Another pilot, sitting nearby, spoke with subdued admiration. "Still, they've hit something. Even if it's just one ship, it's something. Better than sitting here while our cities burn."

Hideyoshi thought of the student who had asked him, weeks ago, why he hadn't volunteered for a *kamikaze* mission himself. He remembered explaining his exemption as an only son, but even then, he hadn't admitted the deeper truth: that he didn't believe in the strategy, that he saw it as the final act of a nation on the verge of defeat.

The room remained quiet for a long moment. Finally, one of the younger pilots said what they were all thinking: "I wonder how much longer we can hold out."

No one answered. Hideyoshi stared down at his tray, the rice growing cold.

The *kamikaze* attacks during the battle for Iwo Jima marked a grim evolution in Japan's desperate attempts to counter the overwhelming strength of American forces. As waves of young pilots, many barely trained, threw themselves into US warships, the psychological and tactical impacts rippled through both sides of the conflict.

From the Japanese perspective, the "special attacks" were heralded as acts of selfless bravery and sacrifice, with propagandists emphasizing their devotion to the Emperor and the homeland. News of successful strikes was broadcast widely, bolstering the morale of a populace increasingly battered by deadly air raids at home. For the soldiers and sailors entrenched on Iwo Jima or elsewhere, the *kamikaze* represented a defiant symbol of resistance, demonstrating that even in the face of certain death, Japan could still strike fear into the enemy and exact a toll.

The toll on American forces was indeed significant, but not crippling. During the Iwo Jima campaign, *kamikaze* pilots managed to sink several ships supporting the invasion, most notably the escort carrier *Bismarck Sea*. Other ships suffered varying degrees of damage. The fleet carrier *Saratoga* was heavily damaged when her flight deck and hangar sustained several hits, forcing her to withdraw for extensive repairs.

For American servicemen, the *kamikaze* attacks were both infuriating and terrifying. The suicidal nature of the *kamikaze* was something utterly alien to Americans, presenting the picture of an enemy who seemed to disregard self-preservation entirely. Watching a plane dive inexorably toward their ship, knowing that it would either hit them or die trying, left an indelible mark on those who survived these attacks.

Fleet commanders, however, adapted their tactics to deal with the threat, stationing destroyer radar-pickets further out from the main fleet to give advance warning of incoming *kamikaze* strikes. Fighter coverage over the fleet was also expanded. In the end, most suicide attacks were shot down long before they could hit anything. They achieved limited tactical successes and inflicted significant casualties, but they did nothing to alter the course of the war.

Hideyoshi sat cross-legged on his cot, once again staring at the blank sheet of paper in front of him. He had intended to write another letter to Aiko, but the words refused to come.

The news from Iwo Jima laid heavily on his mind. These were men he had personally trained—young eager faces that he had shared meals with, and now they were gone, reduced to names on a casualty list and perhaps a fleeting mention in an official report.

He thought of Yoshimada, the quiet but determined farmer's son who had shown a knack for navigation, and Takemori, whose boisterous laugh had once filled the training hangar. Both had volunteered for "special attacks" without hesitation, their faces confident, their spirits unshakable. Did they truly believe in the glory and honor that had been preached to them, or had they simply succumbed to the overwhelming pressure to serve as sacrificial weapons in a war that had spiraled beyond reason?

He had trained them to fly and, ultimately, to die. He had taught them the maneuvers they might need to evade enemy fire long enough to reach their targets. And now, he was left to wonder if he had done the right thing by preparing them for a mission he himself could not bring himself to accept. They had looked up to him, respected him, even idolized him. They had trusted him to guide them, to make them ready. Had he betrayed that trust by sending them to their deaths?

The military's policy exempting him from *kamikaze* duty as an only son had become both a shield and a burden. He had been spared the ultimate sacrifice, but the knowledge that others—many of whom had families just as dependent on them—had not been given that choice gnawed at him. How could he reconcile his role as a trainer with the deaths of those men who had followed his instruction?

Staring out the window at the moonless sky, Hideyoshi's thoughts turned to the Americans. Did they see these attacks for what they were—a sign of Japan's desperation? Did they hate the *kamikaze* pilots, or did they pity them? He wondered if the B-29 pilots on the other side felt the same struggle to justify their actions in the face of so much destruction of civilian cities. Did they see themselves as warriors, or were they simply men, like him, trying to do his duty and survive in a war that was consuming everything?

A sharp pang of regret pierced his heart. He felt the urge to scream, to demand answers from the heavens, from his commanders, from himself. Instead, he let out a deep, shuddering breath and closed his eyes.

That night, Hideyoshi wrote nothing. The blank page remained on the table as he finally lay down to rest, his thoughts still a storm of conflicting emotions. He did not cry, though he wanted to. He did not pray, though he felt he should. Instead, he stared at the ceiling, his mind racing with questions that had no answers.

Chapter 18
Okinawa (March-April 1945)

Okinawa, the largest island in the Ryukyu chain, held strategic importance in the Pacific theater during the closing months of World War II. Its location, just 340 miles south of Kyushu, Japan's southernmost main island, made it a vital objective for the Allied forces. Its airfields could support a variety of aircraft for missions over Japan, while its harbors were capable of anchoring parts of the vast fleets necessary for the final stages of the war.

For the Japanese, Okinawa's defense represented a last-ditch effort to delay or repel the Allied advance; they understood that the Allied invasion of the island was inevitable, and they were unable to prevent it. The strategy they devised, then, had the goal not of beating back the Americans, but of making them pay such a high cost, both in lives and in resources, that it would force them to forego an invasion of Japan and negotiate a settlement instead. "Operation Ten-Go," the Japanese plan for the defense of Okinawa, had the sole purpose of holding out for as long as they could and inflicting as much damage as possible on the Americans.

The defense of Okinawa fell to the Japanese 32nd Army, commanded by Lieutenant General Ushijima. His force consisted of 100,000 regular army men, naval troops, and local conscripts. Instead of confronting the Allies directly on the landing beaches, Ushijima adopted a defense-in-depth strategy and concentrated his forces in the rugged southern portion of the island. Here, the natural hills, ridges, and limestone caves were transformed into a series of bunkers, pillboxes, and artillery emplacements, and they hoped to delay the Americans as long as they could to buy time for Japan to prepare its final defenses on the home islands.

The American assault on Okinawa began on April 1, 1945, with 180,000 troops under the command of Lt General Buckner. The primary landing zones were on the central west coast of Okinawa, near the airfields at Kadena and Yontan.

Immediately after the invasion began, Hideyoshi was re-assigned to the 343rd Kokutai at Omura Air Base, near Nagasaki, with orders to fly support missions over Okinawa. The 343rd Kokutai was an elite handpicked squadron led by Captain Genda, who had planned the Pearl Harbor attack. Hideyoshi had served under Genda before, at the beginning of the war. Most of the other pilots were also seasoned veterans, survivors of earlier campaigns in the Pacific who had accumulated a wealth of combat experience. Unlike the fresh-faced students that Hideyoshi had recently trained, these men carried themselves with the confidence of those who had stared death in the face numerous times and lived to tell the tale.

That evening, Hideyoshi sat near the middle of the mess hall, his tray half-empty, his thoughts far away as he absently stirred his rice. Sitting across from him was Lieutenant Yamazaki, a heavy man with sharp eyes and an ever-present smirk. Next to him sat Ensign Nakahara, the youngest pilot in the group, and to Hideyoshi's right was Lieutenant Tanabe, a seasoned veteran. They were his *kutai* mates. Between them they had over 100 air victories.

The other pilots around them were talking among themselves.

"I hear Genda's still angry about the Americans pulling back their P-38s," Katsuo was saying. "He wanted to test the Shiden Kai against them. Can't say I blame him. It would've been a hell of a good fight."

"Good for the Shiden Kai, maybe," Takeshi chimed in, grinning. "Not so good for the P-38s."

The group chuckled, and even Hideyoshi managed a faint smile.

"What about you, Sugiyama?" Noboru asked, turning toward him. "You flew this plane back when it was being tested. Think it's as good as they say?"

"It's the best we have," he said simply. "It can out-fight a Hellcat, and it's good enough to take down a Mustang. But—" He paused, setting his chopsticks down. "It won't matter how good the Shiden Kai is if we're always outnumbered."

Noboru nodded gravely. "That's the truth of it. But it's all we've got. Better to fight with it than without it."

Takeshi leaned forward, his expression more serious now. "Do you think we can hold Okinawa? With what's happening down there, it feels like ..." He trailed off, unsure how to finish the thought.

Hideyoshi glanced at him, considering his words. "Okinawa is critical," he said finally. "But it's about timing. The longer we can hold them off, the more time we give our forces to prepare."

"And if there's no time left?" Katsuo asked quietly.

The table fell silent for a moment. Hideyoshi's gaze dropped to his bowl.

"We do what we've always done," Noboru said at last, his voice firm. "We fight. Until there's nothing left."

The conversation shifted after that, turning to lighter topics. Stories about the maintenance chief, and speculation about what meal would be served tomorrow. No one said what they were really thinking.

A few weeks later, during one American raid on the airfield, Hideyoshi was caught on the ground out in the open and had to dive into a nearby ditch. As he peeked out, he saw smoke trailing from a stricken B-25 bomber, its engines coughing as it descended in a slow, spiraling dive toward the dense jungle just beyond the airfield. He watched until the aircraft disappeared into the treetops, a dull thud moments later marking its crash. When the bombs stopped, he grabbed his sidearm and set off toward the site.

As he approached the edge of the clearing, a group of Japanese Army soldiers stood in a loose circle, their rifles slung across their shoulders. They had seen the crash too.

In the center of the group were four Americans, the surviving crew of the downed plane. They had their hands tied behind their backs, their shoulders slumped. One of them, a young man with soot-smeared cheeks, glanced up as Hideyoshi appeared, his wide eyes full of desperation.

"What's going on here?" Hideyoshi demanded, stepping closer. The Army sergeant in charge, a stocky man with a scar running down his cheek, turned toward him.

"These men are bombers," the sergeant snapped. "They've killed our people, destroyed our towns. They don't deserve mercy."

"They're prisoners," Hideyoshi shot back. "Isn't there a protocol for handling captives? Command would want to interrogate them and—"

The sergeant cut him off. "Command has given clear orders. No time, no resources for prisoners. You've seen what their bombs have done. Do you think they'd spare us if the situation were reversed?"

Hideyoshi stomach tightened as he looked back at the Americans. They didn't seem like killers now—just scared and battered boys.

The sergeant shouted an order, and two soldiers stepped forward, dragging one of the Americans—a tall man with a bloodied forehead—toward a large tree. They shoved him against the trunk, and he stumbled, nearly falling to his knees before they forced him upright.

The young man cried out, his voice breaking into words Hideyoshi didn't understand, though the meaning was unmistakable.

The sergeant raised his hand, and a soldier leveled his rifle. Hideyoshi's watched helplessly as the crack of the shot echoed through the clearing. The man crumpled to the ground.

One by one, the remaining Americans were led to the tree. One cursed loudly, his defiance cutting through the air until another rifle shot silenced him. Another wept openly, his sobs cut off abruptly as he too fell.

The last man barely stood as they dragged him forward. He stared straight ahead, trembling, his lips moving silently. Hideyoshi turned away just before the final shot rang out.

When it was over, the soldiers covered the bodies with loose dirt and foliage. The sergeant wiped his hands and, as they left, he turned briefly to Hideyoshi.

"This is war," he said coldly, as if that was all the explanation that was needed.

The next morning, Hideyoshi and his new *kutai* mates—Takagi, Shimada, and Okabe—were patrolling near Okinawa when the Shiden Kai's radio crackled with a message from the forward observers. "Enemy formation at 10,000 meters." Hideyoshi signaled the others, and his *kutai* fell into position, their fighters sliding into a finger-four combat formation. The American aircraft were B-29s accompanied by P-51 Mustangs.

As the Shidens dove toward the Mustangs, the American pilots reacted quickly, breaking formation and scattering. One Mustang peeled off and began to climb for altitude, and Hideyoshi pursued. The Mustang twisted into a tight corkscrew maneuver, but Hideyoshi followed and, aiming carefully and leading his target for a deflection shot, squeezed the trigger. The Mustang shivered as rounds tore through its fuselage.

Hideyoshi followed it down for a moment, watching as the pilot bailed out and the parachute opened. Hideyoshi knew that the downed pilot would likely be rescued by one of the American submarines stationed near Okinawa for just such an emergency. It was a luxury afforded to the Americans that the Japanese could not match. With no ships or resources to recover them if they were shot down, many Japanese pilots chose not to hook up their parachutes, not wanting to face the humiliating shame of capture or to test the stories they had been told of Americans torturing and killing captives. Hideyoshi had made the same decision long ago, a silent acknowledgment of the grim reality that they faced.

The air battle raged on as Hideyoshi and his *kutai* engaged the remaining Mustangs. Okabe managed to cripple another American fighter, its pilot also bailing out just before it spiraled into the ocean.

When their fuel began to run low, Hideyoshi regrouped with his *kutai*. Their aircraft bore the scars of the engagement — bullet holes in the wings and fuselages — but all four planes remained airborne.

As they descended toward Omura, Hideyoshi thought once again of the Mustang pilot's parachute drifting down to safety. It was a stark reminder of the harsh contrast between their situations. The Americans treated their pilots as a valued asset and made every effort to rescue them. The Japanese treated their pilots as expendable equipment.

For the next several days, Hideyoshi and his *kutai* continued to patrol the skies over the island, but the enemy's presence was becoming greater. A British carrier force had joined the American invasion fleet, assigned to providing air cover and anti-aircraft support for the operations. The Royal Navy's Fleet Air Arm had sent some of its best aircraft to aid in the assault — Sea Spitfires, navalized versions of the iconic Battle of Britain Spitfire. They had earned a reputation for being formidable opponents in dogfights, and their appearance in the skies over Okinawa brought a new challenge for the Japanese defenders, who were already stretched thin.

It was during one of these patrols that Hideyoshi found himself face-to-face with one of the British aircraft. His *kutai* was on patrol when the call came in: a group of Sea Spitfires was heading toward the island in a fighter sweep.

Immediately upon sighting them, the Sea Spitfires broke from the formation and made a sharp turn to engage, with one of them speeding straight towards Hideyoshi. The British pilot clearly intended to get the first strike in, his aircraft banking with impressive agility. But Hideyoshi had flown against such tactics before, and he was ready. He pushed his Shiden Kai into a diving turn, forcing the British pilot to overcompensate. With a quick split-S maneuver, Hideyoshi was on his tail and closed the gap. A burst of fire roared from the Shiden Kai's wings, and the British fighter veered sharply to the left, smoke trailing behind it, and plummeted into the Pacific below. The encounter was over in seconds.

The air battles over Okinawa intensified as the American ground forces pressed inland. Hideyoshi's days became a numbing cycle of sorties. One evening, after a particularly harrowing fight with another wave of American bombers and another fighter escort, Hideyoshi sat in the mess hall, quietly sipping his tea. The faces around him were silent, lost in their thoughts.

"We've been flying non-stop for days," Noda finally muttered. "I can't remember the last time I had a full night's rest."

Hideyoshi could only nod. The weariness had begun to seep into every corner of their lives. And yet, the pressure never let up. The Americans were relentless, sending wave after wave of bombers and fighters. The Japanese defenders, meanwhile, had nothing left to give but their lives.

Suganami spoke up. "How long do you think we can keep this up?" he asked, looking up from his bowl. "Every time we climb into those planes, it's like stepping into the abyss."

Hideyoshi knew the answer, though he couldn't bring himself to speak it aloud. They were outnumbered, outgunned, and out of options. The few planes they had remaining were steadily being worn down, and those pilots who were lost could not be replaced. Hideyoshi had heard of entire units being wiped out in single engagements.

As Hideyoshi glanced around the room, he saw the same exhaustion mirrored in the faces of those still with him—pilots who had once been full of confidence and pride, now drained and hollow-eyed.

And then came the worst blow of all: the loss of Shigeru Noda. He had been one of the most skilled pilots in the squadron, a high-scoring ace who had weathered many campaigns. But during a dogfight with American P-51 Mustangs, Noda's plane was hit. Hideyoshi watched in helpless silence as his aircraft went down, trailing smoke.

As the days bled into each other, Hideyoshi knew that they were all running out of time.

Not all of the deaths came from combat, though.

One morning as Hideyoshi stood near his fighter with the ground crew, a Yokosuka Judy dive bomber taxied for takeoff. The Judy's pilot and navigator gave a smile and a "thumbs up" as they passed by.

The plane rolled forward, its engine straining as it gained speed down the runway and the nose lifting slightly as the wheels left the ground. But then, something went terribly wrong. A sharp metallic clunk echoed across the field, followed by a jolt through the plane's fuselage. The Judy wobbled unnaturally.

"Something's wrong with that one," a mechanic stammered, shading his eyes to watch. Before anyone could react, the left wing struck the ground and the plane cartwheeled into the dirt with a deafening explosion. A fireball erupted as fuel ignited, sending debris hurtling across the field.

Shouts of alarm filled the air as men rushed toward the wreckage, some with extinguishers. Hideyoshi was among them, sprinting toward the burning remains of the Judy. The wreckage was a chaotic mess. One of the crew had been thrown clear by the impact, and now his body lay motionless on the grass. The other was still pinned inside the crumpled cockpit, with flames consuming what was left.

"Get back!" a crew chief shouted, waving the others away as ammunition in the bomber's machine guns began to cook off with sharp pops. The men retreated, unable to do more. The airmen were beyond any help now.

The fire burned itself out, leaving behind a smoldering wreck. The ground crew worked silently to recover what they could. In the mess hall later, the crash was the topic of some conversation, but quickly faded into memory. Crashes like this happened every week, and killed more air crews than combat did. Pilots and crew alike understood the risks.

It was a harsh impersonal end to two lives.

On Okinawa, meanwhile, the Americans were steadily gaining ground, and despite the stubborn resistance of the Japanese defenders, they were unable to stop the overwhelming advance. But it wasn't just the air superiority of the Americans that the Japanese had to contend with—it was the sheer number of ships that were being used to support the invasion. The Japanese military understood that if they could cripple or destroy these ships, they might be able to slow the American forces, to inflict heavy casualties, and to shift the momentum in their favor. And so they turned once again to "special attacks".

In late March 1945, the first large-scale *kamikaze* attack on the American fleet at Okinawa occurred, launching whatever aircraft they could scrounge up—Zeros, Judys, even seaplanes—that had been loaded with bombs and fuel to cause as much damage as possible. The fight for Okinawa was not about defending the island — it was about fighting to the last man, to the last plane.

The *kamikaze* attacks had some successes. The carrier *Bunker Hill* was struck by two planes in quick succession on May 11, killing over 300 men and causing massive fires. The battleship *West Virginia* was also hit, though it was able to continue fighting.

The *kamikaze* attacks became a regular feature of the battle, with Japanese pilots diving toward the American fleet nearly every day. Most did not make it past the patrolling Hellcats and the fleet's anti-aircraft fire, but each attack, whether successful or not, cost the Japanese forces more of their dwindling resources and manpower.

When Hideyoshi was ordered to fly as an escort for one of the "special attacks", he turned cold inside. He had trained *kamikaze* pilots, perhaps even some of the very ones he would be flying with, and he viewed the entire effort as a waste of lives and resources.

But he was a military man, and orders are orders, so he dutifully taxied his Shiden Kai down the tarmac and took to the air. His orders were simple: clear the skies of any American interceptors that might get in the way of the *kamikazes*.

He glanced over at Ensign Yukashi, one of the "special attack" pilots, who was flying just to his left, a 500-kilogram bomb secured to the belly of his Judy dive bomber. The young man's face revealed nothing of the fear that Hideyoshi knew must have been flooding his brain. None of them wanted to show weakness, not even in the face of approaching death.

Looking away, Hideyoshi scanned the skies again. He knew the Americans would be looking for them, ready to swat these planes from the sky like flies. Then it came: a flicker of movement in the distance. A formation of American Hellcats. Hideyoshi gave a quick signal to Nakahara and Yamazaki. They broke formation and dove toward the incoming Hellcats, guns ready. The fight had begun.

The dogfight was chaotic. Hideyoshi's first pass was a blur of tracers, and one of the Hellcats peeled away, smoke trailing from its engine but still steady in the air. Hideyoshi turned hard, latching onto another. This time, the Hellcat was ready, and they traded shots with each evading the other. Hideyoshi made a snap turn and pulled up sharply, and the Hellcat that had been behind him now passed into view. With a quick squeeze of the trigger, he forced it to break away. He could not pursue it: he had a different job to do. He glanced back at the *kamikaze* pilots beneath him, their planes still heading for the American fleet.

Puffs of flak began to pepper the sky around them as the *kamikazes* approached their targets. Hideyoshi watched from his position high above: he had been ordered to make a report detailing the attack's successes. The attackers split into two groups, with one climbing rapidly to height, from which they could dive down onto their target, and the other sweeping in low, just above the water. It was the tactic he had taught his students, to make it as difficult as possible for the anti-aircraft gunners to hit them.

The anti-aircraft fire became more intense. He could see hits, with one plane after another spinning crazily or arcing down into the sea trailing fire and smoke.

Only three of the attackers made it through. One of them flew too high, roared over the deck of an American carrier, and crashed into the water on the other side. Hideyoshi wondered if the pilot had involuntarily flinched at the very last instant.

Another had dived at too steep an angle and had lost control, plunging into the sea about 80 yards behind his target.

But the third came in fast and steady bearing directly down on a heavy cruiser. Hideyoshi could see the crewmen ducking for cover as the Zero smashed into the five-inch gun turrets amidships, sparking off a bright explosion and sending a thick column of smoke into the sky. The cruiser slowed noticeably and turned towards the center of the formation for protection.

Hideyoshi and his fellow pilots returned to base and made their reports.

The *kamikaze* aircraft were not the only "special attacks" that were put into use by the Japanese. A number of different weapons were being designed and produced. It was intended that they be held in reserve, stockpiled for the day when the Americans appeared off the shores of the Japanese homeland, but some of them were being tested at Okinawa. These included the *Kaiten* (a manned torpedo), the *Shinyo* (an explosives-packed speedboat), and the *Okha* (a rocket-powered bomb with a pilot inside).

Hideyoshi's squadron had been assigned a difficult mission: to escort a group of G4M Betty bombers carrying *Okha* rocket bombs against a British carrier task force. The rocket-powered *Okhas* flew too fast for a fighter to intercept, and once launched they could not be stopped. But the Betty bombers which carried them were slow and vulnerable, and Hideyoshi knew the British would have fighters on patrol to counter the attack. They would make every effort to shoot down the bombers before they could release their piloted bombs. It would be a hard fight.

As the group closed in on the British fleet, the Sea Spitfires were quick to engage, and Hideyoshi and his squadron immediately moved to intercept. But they were outnumbered, and although they managed to take out several of the British fighters, the rest got past them and reached the bombers. One by one, the Bettys fell from the sky. Hideyoshi saw one bomber spiral out of control, its wings shredded by enemy fire. Another exploded in mid-air. Soon only one bomber remained, though it too had been damaged. But as Hideyoshi watched, a pair of Spitfires streaked in head-on and fired directly at the Betty's cockpit.

The bomber pilot, likely overwhelmed by the attack, panicked and, in a desperate attempt to avoid the fighters, he dropped the *Okha*. It was too soon—the *Okha's* rockets only burned for 60 seconds of powered flight, and they were too far away from the target. Hideyoshi swore out loud as the rocket burned out and the *Okha* dropped harmlessly into the sea short of its target, exploding on impact. A waste. The Navy had lost nine Betty bombers and their crews as well as nine *Okhas* and their pilots—and had accomplished nothing.

By this time, the Americans had already captured the southern part of Okinawa, and now they were advancing onto the northern end. The Japanese had been forced to withdraw into the hills and caves, where they made their last stand. The fighting was fierce, but the Americans, despite the resistance, were closing in on their objectives. The battle for Okinawa was nearing its end.

As the battle for Okinawa reached its inevitable conclusion, Hideyoshi found himself battling more than just the Americans in the skies. The emotional toll of the war was beginning to wear on him. He had fought in many battles, each with its own losses, but the battles over Okinawa were different. The brutality of the fighting, the sheer destruction, and the overwhelming might of the American forces made it feel as if Japan's fate had already been sealed.

Hideyoshi thought of Aiko, his wife, and Ichiro, his son. What would come next? What would happen if the Americans made it to the Japanese homeland?

The thought was terrifying.

Chapter 19
Defending the Mainland (May-July 1945)

With the struggle for Okinawa clearly lost, the entire 343rd Air Corps was relocated to Matsuyama Air Base on Shikoku Island, part of a broader new strategy to reinforce Japan's air defenses against air raids and to prepare for the American invasion that everyone knew would now come. Alongside Hideyoshi's orders was another notice — his promotion to Lieutenant Commander.

Perched on the shore of the Seto Inland Sea, the airfield was strategically located for intercepting B-29 raids or carrier task forces that were approaching Osaka, Kobe, Nagoya, Yokohama or Tokyo. It was larger and better-equipped than the primitive airstrips in Bougainville or Formosa, but not, Hideyoshi thought, as comfortable as a carrier.

Genda met with his senior officers in the squadron's operations building shortly after their arrival. His sharp gaze swept the room as he laid out their mission. "Matsuyama is critical to the defense of Japan. From here, we will intercept the enemy's bombers and carrier strikes before they can reach our cities."

After the briefing, Hideyoshi joined his *kutai* mates to inspect their Shiden Kais. Yamazaki patted the wing of his brand-new plane and smirked. "Finally, a proper machine to give those Yankees something to worry about." Tanabe chuckled and turned to Hideyoshi. "Just remember to leave some for the rest of us, *Taicho*."

Hideyoshi allowed himself a smile. "There will be enough to go around," he said.

That night in the mess hall, Yamazaki told exaggerated accounts of his daring encounters with American Hellcats, while Nakahara spoke of his family in Kyushu.

Tanabe lightened the mood with tales of misadventures from earlier in the war. "Well, you see—" he leaned in and began "—I was on a little trip to Rabaul. A little rest and relaxation, you know?"

The other pilots exchanged looks. Rabaul was known for its less-than-ideal conditions, but it was still a welcome break from the daily grind.

"Rabaul? You went on leave?" Araki asked, raising an eyebrow. "I didn't know they let you off the base."

Tanabe's eyes twinkled. "Oh, I had the perfect opportunity. It wasn't all relaxation, though. I had a little adventure there."

"Of course you did," Hideyoshi said, already sensing that the story would get stranger from here. "What happened?"

"Well," Tanabe began, settling in with a dramatic pause, "I found a pig."

"A pig?" Hideyoshi said, blinking in disbelief. "You went all the way to Rabaul for a *pig*?"

"Not just *any* pig," Tanabe shot back with a grin. "This was a *big* one. Fat, healthy, and just waiting to be cooked."

The other pilots chuckled at the absurdity of it all, but Tanabe continued, clearly pleased with the attention. "So I thought, why not bring it back? The locals there didn't mind, and I thought it would be a great addition to the mess hall. A little surprise for everyone."

"Wait," Araki interjected, his eyes narrowing. "You didn't bring the pig *back* with you, did you?"

Tanabe's grin only widened. "I sure did. I didn't exactly have it on the plane with me, though. I found a local who was willing to sell it to me, and after some bartering, I arranged for it to be slaughtered."

There were guffaws of disbelief around the table. "You're telling us you smuggled a pig back to the base from Rabaul?" Hideyoshi asked with mock incredulity.

Tanabe nodded, completely unfazed. "I didn't just smuggle it—I got the whole thing wrapped up. Had to keep it hidden in the back of the truck, of course, so nobody saw it before the big reveal. But when we got back, I made a plan."

"And what was your plan?" Araki asked.

Tanabe grinned. "I'm glad you asked. I managed to get a few of the cooks in on it, and we had a big feast planned for the evening. The pig was roasted whole, right in the middle of the camp. The smell was so good, you could've sworn it was heaven itself."

Hideyoshi laughed at the surreal image. "Wait, you cooked the whole pig? Right there?"

"Oh yes," Tanabe said, grinning even wider. "We roasted it slowly over an open fire. It was so tender, so juicy, that even the officers who were supposed to be monitoring us couldn't resist sneaking a taste."

The other pilots laughed, imagining the scene. "I can just see it now," Hideyoshi said, shaking his head. "A whole roasted pig, surrounded by you and the cooks trying to keep everyone away."

Tanabe chuckled. "You know how it is. The moment the officers caught wind of it, they tried to claim their portion, but by the time they got there, the pig was almost gone. I'm telling you, it was every man for himself."

"And how did you end up with the biggest portion?" Araki asked.

"Simple," Tanabe said with a wink. "I made sure I had a piece before anyone else. You have to be quick in these situations. And besides, I had already put in the hard work—getting the pig, setting it all up. I earned it."

The pilots roared with laughter, imagining Tanabe slyly securing his share of the roast while the rest of the men fought over the remaining scraps.

"But it wasn't all smooth sailing," Tanabe added. "We didn't realize it at the time, but we had roasted the pig too long. It came out a little too crispy, and some of the boys could barely chew it."

"Of course you did," Hideyoshi said, shaking his head. "Leave it to you to turn a simple feast into a disaster."

Tanabe grinned sheepishly. "What can I say? I may have gotten a little carried away with the roasting process. But even if it was tough, it was still a great time. A lot of laughs, a lot of *sake*—and most importantly, we got to enjoy a bit of normalcy before going back into the fight."

"And I'm sure the rest of the pig made its way to the officers' table too," Hideyoshi said, smirking.

"Of course," Tanabe said with a wink. "They weren't going to let a whole roast go to waste, even if they were too late to the party."

The table erupted into more laughter, the stress of the war momentarily forgotten as the pilots enjoyed Tanabe's ridiculous story. In a time where food was scarce and the pressures of combat weighed heavily on everyone, a simple tale like this—a pig smuggled from Rabaul and roasted in the barracks—was exactly the kind of absurdity they needed to lighten the mood.

As the laughter died down, Hideyoshi leaned back in his seat, still chuckling. "Only you, Tanabe. Only you."

And in that moment, amid the harsh realities of war, the camaraderie among the pilots of the 343rd felt just a little bit stronger.

On his first patrol out of Matsuyama, Hideyoshi took his Shiden Kai out over the Inland Sea. The fighter handled beautifully, its engine roaring as he climbed to altitude. As he banked over the waters, he spotted the familiar sight of fishing boats below.

When he landed, Genda was waiting on the tarmac. "How does she feel, Commander?" he asked.

"Like she was built for this," Hideyoshi replied.

By May 1945, the air raids on Japan had intensified, and American B-29s and carrier-based aircraft were unleashing destruction by day and night. The raids targeted industrial centers, airfields, and transportation hubs, all aimed at crippling Japan's ability to oppose an invasion.

The relentless firebombs devastated Japan's civilian infrastructure, leaving cities in ruins and countless families without shelter, clean water, or access to food. Cholera, dysentery, and typhoid fever spread rapidly through the weakened population, claiming lives even as the bombings continued.

One afternoon, Hideyoshi and Kato paid a visit to one of their fellow pilots who was in the base hospital. Sakamoto lay on a cot, his face pale and gaunt. A nurse knelt beside him, adjusting the rubber tube on his IV bottle.

"Sakamoto!" Hideyoshi called out, forcing a cheerful tone as they approached. The lieutenant opened his eyes, glassy and sunken, and managed a faint smile.

"Sugiyama," Sakamoto rasped, his voice barely audible. "Didn't expect to see you here. Thought I'd be buried before anyone came to visit."

"Don't joke like that," Hideyoshi replied, crouching beside the cot. "You'll be back in the cockpit before you know it."

Kato held up a small bundle of rice balls wrapped in cloth. "We brought these for you, Tadashi. Not much, but better than what they're feeding you in here, I bet."

Sakamoto's eyes flicked to the bundle, but he shook his head weakly. "Thank you, but … I can't eat. Not yet. They say I have to keep the fluids down first."

"What happened?" Hideyoshi asked. "You were fine a week ago."

"I was stupid," Sakamoto admitted. "Drank some water from a well in town. I didn't think." He closed his eyes briefly. "The raids have destroyed so much. It was probably contaminated. Next thing I knew, I couldn't stop vomiting. Then the diarrhea started. I thought I was going to die that first night."

Kato glanced at the other patients in the ward. "The civilians must be suffering even worse."

Sakamoto nodded weakly. "They are. I saw some of them brought in when I first got here. Children, old men. They're barely hanging on. It's not just the bombings anymore—it's everything that comes after."

Hideyoshi placed a hand on his shoulder. "You just focus on recovering. We'll keep things in the air until you're back with us."

"Don't get shot down without me," Sakamoto murmured as they left. "I still owe you a round at the mess hall."

On one bright, cloudless morning, radar stations on Shikoku picked up a large formation of incoming planes—carrier-based fighters and dive bombers sweeping inland from the coast. The alarms sounded, and the base erupted into action.

Dozens of Hellcats and Corsairs screamed through the skies, escorting Helldiver dive bombers. Hideyoshi radioed his *kutai* to follow as he dove into the swirl of airplanes. His first target was a Helldiver breaking from its formation. He fired a burst that shredded the bomber's rudder. But the escorting fighters protected their bombers ferociously, and Hideyoshi found himself constantly on the defensive. Two of the squadron's Shiden Kais did not return.

As days turned into weeks, the raids only grew more intense. Though most of the B-29 missions were still carried out under cover of darkness, the Americans were increasingly risking daytime strikes, emboldened by the dwindling Japanese defenses. On one such day, the roar of B-29 engines filled the air as they made their way towards Nagoya. Climbing to meet the enemy formation, Hideyoshi targeted the lead bomber, darting through streams of tracers. He fired a long burst, the 20mm cannon rounds smashing into the B-29's engine. Flames erupted from the bomber as it broke apart, its crew bailing out one by one. Still, the other bombers pressed forward until the Shidens were forced to break contact and turn back to their base.

In the mess hall that evening, the pilots discussed the raids. Tanabe, usually jovial, shook his head. "It's like they're determined to leave nothing standing. Towns, factories, even the fields—they're burning it all."

The sun was dipping low when the distant roar of an approaching aircraft reached those still on the ground. Mechanics paused their work, squinting at the horizon. A single Shiden Kai appeared, limping toward the airfield and trailing smoke.

Hideyoshi and several other pilots stood near the mess hall, their conversation cutting off as they turned their heads in unison. Tanabe announced, "Looks like Nagura's bird."

The plane wobbled precariously, its engine sputtering. The Shiden Kai hit the runway hard, sparks flying from a mangled wing as the left landing gear collapsed on contact. The plane skidded to a stop, and ground crews ran forward with extinguishers, surrounding the battered fighter.

The cockpit popped open and Nagura climbed out shakily, waving off assistance. A group of pilots quickly gathered around him as he trudged over to the mess hall. "What in the world happened up there?" someone asked.

"Ambushed," he said, exhaling heavily. "We ran into a patrol of Corsairs. Must've been a dozen of them, circling like vultures."

The group went silent as Nagura continued. "They came at us from above and behind. I barely saw the first one before it started throwing lead. I thought it was over right there. The plane shook so hard, I could feel the bolts rattling loose under my boots."

"What happened to the others in your flight?" Tanabe asked.

"I don't know. They scattered when the attack started. I couldn't keep track of anyone."

He reached up, gesturing with his hands. "One Corsair got right on my tail, close enough I could see the pilot's face behind the canopy. He must've emptied everything he had into me. Holes in the wings, the fuselage, the tail ... even the engine was coughing oil."

"I dove low, hugging the water, trying to break free," Nagura continued. "The Corsair stayed with me, though, closing in. Then, I don't know, luck, maybe? He peeled off. Maybe out of ammo. Whatever it was, I was glad to see him go."

A mechanic poked his head into the mess hall, shaking his head in disbelief. "Nagura, your bird looks like it's been through hell. How it stayed in one piece is beyond me."

Nagura chuckled weakly. "That's the Shiden Kai for you. If I'd been in a Zero, the gulls would be picking pieces of me out of the ocean right now."

"You're lucky to be alive," said Yamazaki.

"Lucky?" Nagura replied, his grin fading. "That Corsair could've finished me if he'd had a few more seconds — or a few more rounds."

Hideyoshi placed a hand on Nagura's shoulder, a gesture of quiet solidarity. "Rest up. You'll need it. There'll be more of them tomorrow."

Genda drilled the pilots relentlessly, instilling in them a doctrine of teamwork over individual heroics. His oft-repeated mantra was: "Protect each other and survive the fight."

The Shiden Kai, with its powerful engine and sturdy frame, was well-suited to Genda's tactics. Unlike the fragile Zeros of earlier years, the Shiden Kai could take significant punishment and still stay in the fight. Genda advised his pilots to take advantage of the fighter's strengths. Rather than engaging in turning dogfights like the Zero, they were to strike quickly, using diving attacks to deliver devastating blows before pulling away to regroup. This hit-and-run approach allowed them to avoid getting overwhelmed by the sheer number of Allied planes.

One of the most innovative tactics the group developed was the use of the "rolling ambush." When a formation of B-29 bombers was detected, a flight of Genda's pilots would first attack the escort fighters. The P-51s, drawn into combat, would leave the bombers vulnerable. A second wave of Shiden Kais would then attack the bombers directly.

Under Genda's command, the 343rd made every sortie count. Their Shiden Kais inflicted a heavy toll on the Americans.

Genda's leadership extended beyond strategy. He brought a sense of camaraderie and purpose to his pilots. He was often seen walking the flight line, speaking to mechanics and pilots alike, offering encouragement and advice. Hideyoshi admired Genda's approach, finding in him a leader who understood both the technical and human elements of aerial combat.

For the second time in a day, Hideyoshi ran to his Shiden Kai. American carrier-based aircraft had been detected heading toward the southern coast of Shikoku, their likely targets being one of the naval facilities. Beside him, his three *kutai* mates—Yamazaki, Nakahara, and Tanabe—prepared their own aircraft. These men had become more than comrades; they were a tightly knit team whose lives depended on mutual trust and coordination.

Minutes later, the four Shiden Kais roared down the runway, climbing rapidly toward the reported altitude of the incoming raid.

"There they are," Yamazaki called out. Hideyoshi adjusted his goggles and squinted. In the distance, dark specks—Helldivers flanked by Hellcat escorts.

"Yamazaki, you and Nakahara engage the escorts," Hideyoshi ordered. "Tanabe, you're with me. Let's go after the bombers." The Helldivers were always the first priority. Yamazaki and Nakahara broke left, drawing the escorts away in a series of sharp maneuvers.

Hideyoshi and Tanabe continued on toward the bombers, through bursts of defensive fire from the tail gunners.

Hideyoshi slid into position behind a Helldiver and the Shiden Kai's guns roared as he pressed the trigger. He could see sparks as his rounds tore into the bomber's right wing, and there was a fiery burst as the plane hit the water.

At the same time, Tanabe's cannons shredded the tail of another Helldiver, and its crew bailed out as smoke poured from the cockpit. "That's two down!" Tanabe called.

The remaining bombers pressed forward. Hideyoshi banked sharply to avoid a Hellcat that had turned to engage him, then set his sights on another Helldiver. He fired in short bursts, aiming for the engine, and the plane began to lose altitude. Only one of the crew bailed out.

Above him, Yamazaki and Nakahara were locked in dogfights with the Hellcats. Yamazaki managed to land a hit on one of the escorts, a thin white plume of fuel trailing from its engine as it broke off. He would probably not make it back to his carrier.

Then, simultaneously, the remaining Helldivers nosed over into a steep dive. The Shiden Kais could not follow. A series of explosions rippled across the port, and flames poured from the docks.

Hideyoshi signaled to regroup, his *kutai* forming up as the remaining Helldivers and Hellcats left for home.

But once again, the American bombers had reached their targets.

Back at the airbase, the pilots gathered in somber silence. Yamazaki's plane bore fresh bullet holes, and Nakahara's required extensive repairs.

"It's like throwing pebbles at a stone wall," Tanabe said, shaking his head.

The Americans had perfected their methods, and each successive strike brought more devastation than the last. The skies over Japan were now constantly filled with the sound of B-29s, heavy with firebombs and with their sights set not only on military targets but on civilian infrastructure. Their payloads were designed to incinerate entire cities.

In one particularly harrowing raid on the nearby city of Kochi, Hideyoshi had watched from the skies as massive plumes of smoke and flame rose into the air, reddening the horizon. The city's wooden buildings had fueled fires that raged unchecked for days.

Hideyoshi's *kutai* had been ordered to intercept B-29s on many occasions, but the raids were still relentless. Even when they were successful in shooting down a few bombers, the effect on the raid was imperceptible. Soon, Japan's entire fighter force had been reduced to such a level that orders came from Tokyo to no longer launch interception missions against the raiders except for the direst emergencies. Instead, all of the remaining fighters were to be carefully husbanded and protected so they would be ready for the inevitable invasion of Japan, which was now just a matter of time. The American bombers and fighters, flying from new airbases on Okinawa, had free reign.

Hideyoshi could hear the conversations in the mess hall. "They say the firebombing raids on Osaka are the worst yet," one of the pilots had said. "The city's been reduced to rubble. Half the population's homeless, and there's barely any food left."

Another pilot nodded grimly. "I heard that over one hundred thousand people were killed in just one night in Tokyo. The fires just wouldn't stop burning. The city center is nothing but cinders now."

Hideyoshi didn't respond. He knew that this was the reality of war — the relentless, unstoppable force of destruction that seemed to consume everything it touched. The war was no longer confined to the front lines, and Japan itself was under siege. The American raids were not just about destroying Japan's military capacity — they were systematically breaking the nation's spirit, leaving nothing behind but devastation.

The brutal efficiency of the American air campaign left Hideyoshi with a growing sense of frustration and futility. Night after night, the B-29s appeared. For every bomber they shot down, two more seemed to take its place. For every city they defended, another would burn.

Japan was being systematically destroyed, one city at a time.

Chapter 20
Hiroshima and Nagasaki (August 1945)

August 6 began as an ordinary day. Hideyoshi stepped out of the barracks, adjusting his cap and squinting against the glare of the sun. His morning had been uneventful: a breakfast of stale rice, followed by a cursory briefing with the other pilots. He was scheduled for a routine patrol that afternoon, and his Shiden Kai already sat waiting for him near the end of the runway. The maintenance crew moved around it, methodically performing their final checks.

Hideyoshi passed by a few ground crewmen lounging in the shade of a hangar, their cigarettes glowing faintly as they swapped quiet jokes. Other pilots gathered near a table where someone had scrounged up a set of *hanafuda* cards. He glanced at the sky, where thin, high-altitude clouds drifted lazily.

At around 9 a.m., though, whispers began to spread among the personnel. Something unusual had happened in Hiroshima.

At first, the rumors were vague, almost nonsensical. Some spoke of an accident—perhaps a massive explosion at a munitions depot or a catastrophic fire. Others speculated about an American air raid, though no one had seen or heard any B-29s flying in that direction.

The tension grew when the Matsuyama radio operators reported that they couldn't establish contact with any Navy facilities in Hiroshima. Repeated attempts were met with static or silence. The operators looked visibly shaken as they relayed their findings up the chain of command. "It's like the entire city vanished," one of them said under his breath.

Then word came from a destroyer patrolling offshore: one of its officers had reported seeing a bright flash in the direction of Hiroshima at roughly 8:15 a.m. The description was chilling—like a second sun had risen, blindingly intense even from miles away. It was no ordinary explosion, they said, but something entirely different.

The only thing everyone knew for certain was that they had not detected any B-29 formations moving in the direction of Hiroshima, though some outposts had reported sighting a single bomber flying over the city, apparently a weather reconnaissance.

The development of the atomic bomb was born out of a race against time, driven by the fear that Nazi Germany might create a super-weapon first.

By the late 1930s, physicists had made significant strides in understanding nuclear fission—the process by which splitting an atom's nucleus releases a tremendous amount of energy. In 1939, scientists Leo Szilard and Albert Einstein, both refugees from Europe, co-authored a letter to President Roosevelt, warning that Germany might be working on nuclear weapons and urged the United States to begin its own research into the military potential of uranium. In 1942, the US Army launched the Manhattan Project— which quickly grew into one of the largest and most expensive wartime efforts in history, employing over 125,000 people and costing nearly $2 billion.

By mid-1945, the Manhattan Project had succeeded in creating two bomb designs. The first, code-named "Little Boy," used uranium-235. The second, "Fat Man," was more complex and used plutonium-239.

The weapons were ready by July 1945, and although Germany had surrendered in May, Japan showed no signs of giving up, and the US was already planning for the invasion of Japan.

President Truman, who had assumed office after Roosevelt's death in April 1945, faced a decision. Military planners estimated that an invasion of Japan could result in hundreds of thousands of Allied casualties and millions of Japanese deaths. The atomic bomb, it was argued, might compel Japan to surrender quickly, avoiding those huge losses.

On July 16, 1945, the first successful test of an atomic bomb, code-named "Trinity," was conducted in the New Mexico desert, and the Americans moved quickly to ready it for use it in combat. Hiroshima, a major military and industrial hub, was chosen as the first target. Nagasaki was designated as a secondary target.

On August 6, 1945, the B-29 bomber "Enola Gay" dropped the "Little Boy" bomb over Hiroshima. The weapon detonated with the force of approximately 15 kilotons of TNT, obliterating the entire city and instantly killing tens of thousands of people.

By mid-morning, the rumors were no longer idle speculation. Genda had summoned all of the senior command to a hurried briefing, and soon an unusual number of staff officers were moving briskly to and from the command center. Their faces all bore grim expressions.

A short time later, Genda ordered the pilots and ground crews to assemble.

"I have received reports from Naval Command," he announced. "Hiroshima has suffered a major attack. Details are limited, but we know the damage is catastrophic."

Murmurs rippled through the group, some asking questions, others simply shaking their heads in disbelief.

"An air raid?" someone asked.

"No," Genda replied. "It appears to have been a single, powerful strike. We have no specifics on the weapon used, but communications with all naval installations in Hiroshima have been lost. That is all we know."

"What could cause such destruction?" one pilot finally asked.

"That," Genda said gravely, "is the question Command is trying to answer. For now, focus on your duties. There may be more information to come."

As the pilots dispersed, Hideyoshi knew that something was very wrong, and none of them, not even the top brass, had the faintest idea what it was.

That evening, the officers once again gathered in the command center, and Genda called another assembly. He cleared his throat before addressing them.

"We've just received new intelligence reports," he said. "The Americans have made a public statement. Truman has announced that the United States has used what they are calling an 'atomic bomb' on Hiroshima."

"An atomic bomb?" one officer exclaimed. "What does that even mean?"

Genda raised his hand for silence. "It's some kind of new super-weapon. They claim it has unprecedented destructive power, equal to twenty thousand tons of explosives, and Hiroshima was just their first target. More will come."

Several officers exchanged incredulous glances. Hideyoshi leaned against the wall, arms crossed, trying to process the words.

Genda continued, "NHK has begun broadcasting the news. They're reporting that an entirely new type of weapon was used, capable of destroying an entire city in a single strike. This aligns with the reports we've received about Hiroshima's condition. Communications with the city still remain nonexistent."

"We don't yet know the full extent of the damage or the specifics of this weapon," Genda finished. "But one thing is clear: we must be prepared for whatever comes next."

In the hours that followed the announcement, the base was flooded with speculation about what exactly an "atomic bomb" could be. Not even the base ordnance officers had ever heard of such a thing.

"I heard it creates a fire so hot it melts everything," one mechanic said.

A young ensign interjected, his face pale. "What if it's a weapon that can summon an earthquake? Hiroshima's destruction sounds like an entire city collapsed. Only an earthquake can do that."

Another pilot leaned forward, his voice low. "I heard the Americans have been working on splitting atoms to create a weapon. Maybe this is what they mean—something that uses the power of the sun."

"The power of the sun?" Tondabayashi snorted, shaking his head. "Don't be ridiculous. How would they control something like that? If they were experimenting with such a thing, they'd blow themselves up before they could drop it on us."

Araki, who was usually quiet, now spoke. "Whatever it is, the Americans seem to think it's the weapon to end the war."

Hideyoshi shook his head. "All this talk about sun power and earthquakes—no one knows what this thing really is. All we have are rumors and guesses. Until we know more, we're just scaring ourselves with fantasies."

Then one of the older lieutenants, Nishida, rubbed his chin thoughtfully. "You know," he said, "years ago—maybe twenty-five years ago—I read an English novel by H G Wells. It talked about 'atomic bombs.' If I remember right, they weren't like normal bombs. These things kept exploding, for days, maybe even weeks, burning and destroying everything around them. At the time, it seemed ridiculous, like something out of a madman's dream." He shook his head slowly. "But now, hearing about this 'atomic bomb' in Hiroshima, it makes me wonder. Could the Americans have actually built something like that?"

The room fell silent. No one wanted to admit it, but the idea didn't seem as absurd as it might have a day ago.

The next day, a transport plane landed at Matsuyama, and from the rear emerged a handful of figures. Among them was a Navy nurse. The scuttlebutt spread quickly—she had come from Hiroshima, and she had seen what happened there. She was immediately escorted to Genda's office

In a low voice, trembling slightly, the nurse recounted her story.

"It was an ordinary morning. The air-raid sirens had gone off earlier, but they stopped right away, and we assumed it was another false alarm. I was outside hanging linens to dry when I saw the flash." She paused, staring at the wall as if she were reliving that moment. "It wasn't like anything I'd ever seen before—blinding, white, and it seemed to fill the entire sky. For a second, it felt like the sun itself had fallen to the earth."

"The shockwave came next. It knocked me off my feet and shattered every window in the building. When I got up, I could see a huge column of fire and smoke rising from the direction of the city. It looked like a monstrous mushroom growing out of the ground, twisting and boiling. It climbed into the sky. We didn't know what it was."

The nurse's hands clenched into fists. "Within an hour, the injured began to arrive. They came by foot, by cart, carried on makeshift stretchers. Many of them were burned—horribly burned. Skin hung from their bodies like rags. Some of them didn't even look human anymore, their faces were so swollen and blackened."

"The smell—" She shuddered involuntarily. "The smell was unbearable—burned flesh, charred wood, and something else, something I can't even describe. Metallic. It clung to everything, no matter how far you moved from the injured. And then there were the ones who looked fine, at first. They walked in on their own, asking for water, but within hours, they collapsed. Their hair was falling out in clumps, and their skin turned an ashen gray. Some started bleeding from their gums or ears. We didn't understand it— none of us did."

Genda shifted uncomfortably in his seat and asked, "How many injured did you see?"

The nurse shook her head slowly. "I couldn't begin to count. Hundreds, maybe thousands, but most of them—they didn't make it. We ran out of supplies almost immediately. No bandages, no clean water, no medicine."

"In the city, the fires kept burning, even when it began raining. But the rain was strange. Thick, and black. Almost like oil." She shuddered again. "Every time I close my eyes, I can see the city. It wasn't a city anymore — it was a wasteland. Buildings were flattened, rubble piled up as far as you could see. And the people, they were wandering through the ruins, calling out for family members."

Her voice broke, and she pressed a trembling hand to her mouth. "I've seen injuries before. I've seen death before. But this — whatever this was, it was like nothing I've ever seen. It wasn't war — it was annihilation."

Genda finally broke the silence. "Thank you, Nurse. You've done your duty in bringing us this report. We'll do what we can to get the wounded from Hiroshima all the help they need."

The nurse nodded numbly.

Genda turned to one of the junior officers standing nearby. "Gather every available medical supply we have on base — bandages, morphine, anything we have. Pack them up and have them sent to Hiroshima on the next transport plane, immediately."

That night, Hideyoshi lay awake, thinking of his wife and son, back in Sakurada. Were they safe? If this weapon could destroy an entire city, no place seemed safe anymore.

The morning of August 9 was overcast but warm as Hideyoshi and his *kutai* took off for a patrol over the city of Kokura. Hideyoshi was concerned: the cloud cover would limit their visibility and make it hard to detect enemy planes. He knew that the Americans didn't like bombing through cloud cover, but he also knew that their radar systems were good enough to allow them to do so if they really wanted to.

Hideyoshi adjusted his position and glanced at the other pilots. Yamazaki gave a quick thumbs-up, Nakahara followed, and Tanabe brought up the rear. "Stay alert," he called into the radio. "If they're up there, we won't see them in this weather."

"Do you think they'll come today?" Yamazaki's voice broke the silence.

"They might," Hideyoshi replied firmly. "Let's stay focused."

The conversation ended, and the patrol continued. Below, farmers worked in the fields, and villagers occasionally glanced up at the sound of the planes. Everything seemed calm.

A crackle came over the radio. "Looks like another quiet day," Nakahara said, trying to lighten the mood. "Maybe the Americans decided to take the day off."

"Let's hope they did," Hideyoshi replied, though he wasn't convinced.

By the time the patrol reached its final leg, the fuel gauges on their planes were nearing the point at which they would just have enough to get back home. Hideyoshi glanced at his clock, calculating how much time they had left before they would need to head back to Matsuyama.

"Time to wrap it up," he radioed to his formation. "We'll turn back in five minutes. Lean out your mixture so we have some gas if we run into trouble on the way."

Just as Hideyoshi reached over to adjust his fuel mix, a brilliant flash lit up the horizon to the south. He instinctively shielded his eyes.

"What was that?" Yamazaki's startled voice came over the radio.

Hideyoshi didn't answer immediately. His mind raced, trying to make sense of what he had just seen.

"Something's happened," Hideyoshi finally replied. "South of us. It might be Nagasaki."

Moments later, a towering column of smoke and debris began to steadily rise on the horizon, twisting as it expanded outward in a massive mushroom-like shape. Even at this distance, some 50 miles away, they could see the cloud's interior boiling with brilliant reds, oranges, pinks and purples.

Nakahara broke the silence. "What *is* that?"

"It's ... enormous," Yamazaki said.

For a moment, no one spoke, then Hideyoshi grabbed his radio transmitter. "Matsuyama base, this is Commander Sugiyama. Be advised, we've just witnessed an event south of Kokura—an enormous explosion near Nagasaki. There's a massive cloud, over 30,000 feet high. It resembles what was reported over Hiroshima."

A brief silence followed before the radio crackled back to life, and a tinny voice answered, "Commander Sugiyama, say again? A large explosion near Nagasaki?"

"That's correct," Hideyoshi confirmed. "A mushroom-shaped cloud rising far into the atmosphere. No sign of enemy aircraft in the area."

The controller was silent again for a few minutes, likely relaying the message up the chain. Then, a new voice came over the radio. "Sugiyama, this is Matsuyama command. Proceed to Nagasaki for reconnaissance. Report on damage and conditions." Hideyoshi responded, "Matsuyama, we are already low on fuel. Request alternate orders." A brief pause, then the reply came. "Make your observations over Nagasaki, then divert to Kokura for landing." There was no room for argument.

Hideyoshi acknowledged the order, then switched to his formation's channel. "Okay, boys, we've been instructed to divert over Nagasaki and then land at Kokura. Follow me in tight formation. And keep your eyes open."

As Hideyoshi descended toward Nagasaki, a thick haze of smoke and dust obscured nearly everything below. Through gaps here and there, he was able to see only fleeting glimpses of the devastation—enough to see that a vast, scorched field of rubble now stretched out where a city had once stood. Buildings lay flattened in jagged heaps, and fires were smoldering everywhere. Along the river, bridges had collapsed into the water. Hideyoshi banked his Shiden Kai, searching for any sign of movement below—but there was nothing.

On the ground, Hideyoshi made his way quickly to the office of the airfield commander at Kokura, saluted sharply, and stepped forward.

"Commander Sugiyama reporting, sir. My *kutai* observed a large explosion south of Kokura. A bright flash, followed by an unusual mushroom-shaped cloud—"

"No time for that, Commander," the Major snapped, cutting him off in mid-sentence. "We've just received orders. A major attack has hit Nagasaki. The situation is disastrous."

The commander abruptly rose from his chair. "A truck is leaving for Nagasaki in five minutes to assist with supplies and to evacuate the wounded. I need every man I can get—so that means you're going too."

Hideyoshi opened his mouth to protest ... why him, a fighter pilot? What was he supposed to do in such a situation? But this was not a debate. "Get moving," the Major ordered.

Hideyoshi saluted again and turned on his heel. Outside, a group of soldiers and pilots were gathered around a truck parked near the edge of the tarmac. Its cargo bed had been hastily piled with crates and bundles. Somebody yelled to him, "Get in back, we're leaving right now," and, still uncertain of what was happening, Hideyoshi climbed into the truck, settling awkwardly among the crates.

The truck rumbled forward.

Ninety minutes later, they were still half an hour away from Nagasaki, but the first signs of destruction had already appeared as they crested a hill overlooking the city's outskirts. A small village lay below them, and they could see rooftops sagging in and burn marks on the wooden walls.

"Is this from a bomb?" one of the soldiers wondered, his voice barely audible over the engine noise.

Nobody answered.

As they got closer to Nagasaki, the damage became more severe. Entire neighborhoods had been flattened into charred rubble and smoldering ashes. Here and there, the remains of cement-brick buildings leaned at awkward angles. Fires still burned in some places. The road grew more difficult to navigate, blocked by fallen trees, overturned carts, and burned pieces of masonry.

"Look at that," one of the men whispered, pointing toward a twisted railway track that arched grotesquely into the air before disappearing into an unrecognizable pile of wreckage.

The truck slowed as they reached what had once been a busy thoroughfare leading into the city. Bodies lay scattered along the roadside, most charred beyond recognition, a few unnervingly intact.

"Gods above," someone said.

They passed a group of survivors huddled beneath the remnants of a collapsed bridge. Their faces were gaunt and ash-streaked, their clothes tattered and burned. Some cradled small children; others simply stared blankly into the distance. One man, his face half-obscured by bandages, stumbled into the road, waving weakly at the truck. The driver hesitated but kept moving, his expression grim. They could not stop.

After another hour of maneuvering through and over rubble, the truck lurched to a stop in front of what had once been one of Nagasaki's hospitals. The building was still standing, but barely. Large sections of the roof had caved in, and jagged shards of glass were all that was left of the windows.

A nurse in a blood-streaked uniform hurried toward the truck. "You've brought supplies?" she asked curtly.

"Yes, we have medical supplies and food," the petty officer replied, waving to the men to begin unloading.

"Good. We're running out of everything."

Standing outside the hospital, Hideyoshi looked back toward the city center. It looked like the entire world had been swallowed by a firestorm. What had once been the heart of Nagasaki was now a barren ruin.

Fires still raged everywhere, illuminating everything with an orange glow. The thick smoke blotted out the sun, making it hard to see more than a few hundred meters. In the dim light, Hideyoshi could make out the faint silhouettes of half-standing buildings in the distance.

Hideyoshi turned to see a group of soldiers unloading boxes of supplies from the truck, carrying them into the hospital. He stepped aside to let them pass, and his eyes were drawn to a small group of patients huddled near the entrance.

One man, his back burned and blistered, stumbled forward, a child clinging to his legs. A woman sat cradling a baby who was silent and motionless, her tears streaking trails through the soot on her face. Another man, his skin charred black and peeling in places, stared vacantly ahead. Next to him, a young boy clung to his mother's hand, his face smeared with ash. Bodies littered the streets around them, some of them so charred he could not tell their fronts from their backs.

The nurse interrupted him. "This way," she said, motioning for Hideyoshi to follow her inside.

As they entered the building, the stench hit him immediately — a sickening combination of burned flesh and disinfectant. The moans of the injured filled the air, sometimes broken by an occasional wail of pain or a muffled cry for help. In one corner, a nurse tried to calm a woman whose face was swollen and disfigured, her eyes barely visible beneath layers of bandages. "Get that saline over here!" someone shouted. The doctors, their faces haggard and pale with fatigue, worked with what they had, applying bandages, setting broken limbs, injecting what little medicines they could into the injured.

The nurse reappeared, her arms laden with rolls of bandages. "We've been overwhelmed since this morning," she said. "There are only three doctors left who can still work, and half of our nurses are injured themselves."

He followed her back outside to an open area that had been transformed into a kind of admissions center. Everywhere he looked, there were injured and burned people. They were lying on the ground or propped against whatever rubble they could find for support. Their skin, burned and blistered, hung in tatters, with blackened and roasted flesh exposed beneath layers of charred clothing. Some of them had no skin left at all; it had slipped off in large wet flakes, leaving behind raw flesh. Many were nearly naked, with most of their clothing burned away by the blast. Some of the women appeared to have had the flowered patterns of their *kimono* burned into their skin. Many of the wounded were too weak to even lift their heads. Some of them lay still. The most desperate cry that filled the air, however, was for water. "Water, please!" they called. "Water! Water!"

The nurse turned to him. "The people on the stretchers with red tags, stay. Those patients who can walk and any stretchers who have a green tag go inside. If you run out of green tags, start with the yellow ones."

In that moment, Hideyoshi understood the triage calculation being made by the doctors and the nurses, and his role in it. Those few who could still be saved had to be given priority. The others, those whose burns were too extensive or whose injuries were too severe, would be allowed to die. There was no way to save everyone. The hospital staff, themselves worn down by wounds and weariness, had to make the brutal choice to save as many lives as they could with the meager resources that they had left. They couldn't waste any effort on those who would not survive.

Hideyoshi's hands trembled as he reached for his first stretcher, his eyes catching those of a woman, crouched next to it, who had been left aside. She was barely conscious, her face covered in blackened burns, her lips puffed and bleeding. She stared at him with an expression that was equal parts pleading and resignation, and her eyes seemed to ask him the question that no one dared to speak aloud: am I going to survive? It was a question without an answer that Hideyoshi could provide, no matter how many times he tried to tell himself that it wasn't his decision.

This wasn't a place of healing—it was a place of sorting. It was a harsh and necessary process, but one that could never erase the toll it took on his soul.

And still the city burned.

The hours stretched on, merging into a long, exhausting blur. Hideyoshi hardly noticed the passage of time as he moved back and forth, stretcher after stretcher, his arms growing heavier with each trip. The cries for water, for help, for life. Hideyoshi's hands were stained with blood.

The most unbearable part of the night was carrying away the dead. When he wasn't carrying a stretcher with someone still breathing, he was carrying someone who was already dead. It was of course an inevitability, one that he had already seen too many times during the course of the war. The corpses—their face sometimes frozen in pain, sometimes peaceful in death—were stacked in the back of the hospital like so much rubble waiting to be taken away.

By the time the sun began to rise, Hideyoshi's body was worn out, his movements sluggish from fatigue. His hands were raw, his legs aching from the constant lifting and carrying. But it wasn't the physical exhaustion that weighed on him the most. It was the psychological toll—the endless parade of suffering, the cries for help that he couldn't answer. As a pilot, he had seen people die, watched men burn in their cockpit, traced their impact into the ground. But like every other pilot he had salved his conscience with the thought that it was the machine he was shooting at, an aircraft, not the man inside it.

But now, in the heart of Nagasaki, he was seeing the true cost of war. This was something new, something terrifyingly inhuman. What could they do against an enemy that had such a weapon, a weapon that could erase a city in an instant? Nothing—nothing—could stop this. Japan was fighting something so powerful that no amount of courage or self-sacrifice could counter it. A single bomb had done this, and there were more. There would be more.

And in that moment, as he looked out over the ruined city, the truth became undeniable. Japan could not win this war. Perhaps, Japan could not even survive it.

Tokyo received word of the second atomic bomb on the afternoon of August 9, 1945. The message came from the Japanese consulate in Switzerland, where neutral channels had been used to transmit news from the United States. The confirmation that another atomic bomb had been dropped, this time on Nagasaki, hit Japan like a hammer blow and altered the landscape entirely.

At the Imperial Palace, officials rushed to convene an emergency meeting between the Emperor's advisors and the military leadership. The Chief of Staff, General Umezu, along with the other senior commanders, were shocked by the reports coming in from Nagasaki. The first bomb had been terrifying enough, but now there was the horrifying prospect of another. And another. And another.

The conversation quickly turned to the state of the war. Japan had already been dealing with devastating losses from the relentless air raids, the sinking of its fleet, and the ongoing pressure from American island assaults, and had also been rocked that very morning by the sudden entrance of the Soviet Union into the war. As they debated what to do, reports from China indicated that the Soviet Red Army had brushed aside the Japanese forces in Manchukuo and were now racing towards Korea. They seemed to be unstoppable.

The possibility of continuing the war, even with the hope that Japan could negotiate more favorable surrender terms, seemed more and more impossible. The United States had issued the Potsdam Declaration several weeks earlier, calling for Japan's unconditional surrender. The Tokyo government had rejected it, hoping for a negotiated peace that would preserve the Emperor's position and protect Japan's sovereignty. But the atomic bombs had changed everything.

"Should we not hold out in order to seek terms?" General Umezu asked. "If the Americans demand unconditional surrender, it will mean the end of the Empire as we know it."

"We cannot stand against these bombs," said a voice from across the room, one of the Emperor's advisors. "The military's will to fight can only carry us so far, and now, the civilians are paying the price. We can no longer allow our people to suffer this way."

Prime Minister Suzuki, long reluctant to embrace the idea of unconditional surrender, finally gave in to the pressure. "There is no more fighting left to be done," he said, his voice quiet but firm. "We must accept the surrender, for the sake of the people. It is the wish of the Emperor."

Japan would accept the terms of the Potsdam Declaration and surrender.

The morning of August 15, 1945, dawned grey at Matsuyama Air Base. The crews were doing routine maintenance to prepare aircraft for patrols that never seemed to end, while pilots stood ready to scramble in an instant to intercept any incoming Helldivers.

Around mid-morning, though, word began to spread that an "important announcement" was coming that afternoon. The radio operators, who had been receiving transmissions throughout the morning, could only pass along the cryptic orders to have all of the base personnel gather together by the loudspeakers outside the command building.

Genda stood by his office, scanning the horizon, his face as unreadable as ever.

The pilots, now gathered together in loose formations, exchanged nervous glances. "What's this about?" one of them asked. Nobody knew. Hideyoshi silently assumed that it would be just another pointless exhortation to keep fighting and win the war.

Finally a message came through the speakers. "The Imperial Headquarters has ordered an assembly of all personnel. Please report to the designated area for an important announcement."

Genda turned to his officers. "Get everyone in formation." Within minutes, the pilots and ground crew were lined up, forming neat rows in the open field. The entire base was quiet.

For a few moments, there was only the faint hum of the loudspeakers as the radio operator prepared to broadcast. Then, the voice of a news reader in Tokyo came through. "All personnel, please remain silent and stand by for the Imperial Government's announcement." As one, every man saluted and bowed deeply: the divine voice of the Emperor was to be given the same deference as if he were standing in front of them himself.

As a voice began to speak, no one moved. For a few moments, there was confusion. Some pilots exchanged puzzled looks, unsure if they had heard correctly. Was this really the Emperor speaking? His voice had always been reserved solely for the very highest ranks of government and military officials. It was the voice of a symbol—an Emperor who reigned but never directly governed.

The words were slow and deliberate, as if the Emperor were carefully choosing them, weighing the significance of each one for his people.

"To our good and loyal subjects," the speech began.

"After pondering deeply the general trends of the world and the actual conditions obtaining in our empire today, we have decided to effect a settlement of the present situation by resorting to an extraordinary measure.

"We have ordered our government to communicate to the governments of the United States, Great Britain, China and the Soviet Union that our Empire accepts the provisions of their joint declaration.

"To strive for the common prosperity and happiness of all nations as well as the security and well-being of our subjects is the solemn obligation which has been handed down by our imperial ancestors and which lies close to our heart.

"Indeed, we declared war on America and Britain out of our sincere desire to ensure Japan's self-preservation and the stabilization of East Asia, it being far from our thought either to infringe upon the sovereignty of other nations or to embark upon territorial aggrandizement.

"But now the war has lasted for nearly four years. Despite the best that has been done by everyone—the gallant fighting of the military and naval forces, the diligence and assiduity of our servants of the state, and the devoted service of our one hundred million people—the war situation has developed not necessarily to Japan's advantage, while the general trends of the world have all turned against her interest.

"Moreover, the enemy has begun to employ a new and most cruel bomb, the power of which to do damage is, indeed, incalculable, taking the toll of many innocent lives. Should we continue to fight, not only would it result in an ultimate collapse and obliteration of the Japanese nation, but also it would lead to the total extinction of human civilization.

"Such being the case, how are we to save the millions of our subjects, or to atone ourselves before the hallowed spirits of our imperial ancestors? This is the reason why we have ordered the acceptance of the provisions of the joint declaration of the powers.

"We cannot but express the deepest sense of regret to our allied nations of East Asia, who have consistently cooperated with the Empire towards the emancipation of East Asia.

"The thought of those officers and men as well as others who have fallen in the fields of battle, those who died at their posts of duty, or those who met with untimely death and all their bereaved families, pains our heart night and day.

"The welfare of the wounded and the war-sufferers, and of those who have lost their homes and livelihood, are the objects of our profound solicitude.

"The hardships and sufferings to which our nation is to be subjected hereafter will be certainly great. We are keenly aware of the inmost feelings of all of you, our subjects. However, it is according to the dictates of time and fate that we have resolved to pave the way for a grand peace for all the generations to come by enduring the unendurable and suffering what is insufferable.

"Having been able to safeguard and maintain the National Spirit of Japan, we are always with you, our good and loyal subjects, relying upon your sincerity and integrity.

"Beware most strictly of any outbursts of emotion which may engender needless complications, or any fraternal contention and strife which may create confusion, lead you astray and cause you to lose the confidence of the world.

"Let the entire nation continue as one family from generation to generation, ever firm in its faith in the imperishability of its sacred land, and mindful of its heavy burden of responsibility, and of the long road before it.

"Unite your total strength, to be devoted to construction for the future. Cultivate the ways of rectitude, foster nobility of spirit, and work with resolution – so that you may enhance the innate glory of the Imperial State and keep pace with the progress of the world."

The war was over.

Silence followed the Emperor's speech. For a few seconds, Hideyoshi stood motionless, the impact of the words still hanging in the air. Around him, the others remained just as still, their faces blank as they tried to absorb what had just been said. No one knew how to respond.

Some, like him, remained quiet, their thoughts locked inside. But there were others who could no longer hold back their feelings. Hideyoshi noticed one of the pilots beside him, Lieutenant Akito, struggling to hold back tears. His face, usually stoic, was now wracked with grief and his shoulders shook with barely contained sobs.

Beside him, Ensign Takeshi wiped his eyes quickly. He had hardly been old enough to drink before he enlisted, but now the war's end seemed to crush him. This was the only adult life he had ever known, the world that he had built his whole life around ever since his first flight, his first air victory.

"It's over," he whispered under his breath, though Hideyoshi was close enough to hear it.

Genda stood nearby. He didn't cry, didn't flinch, but there was a deep sadness in his eyes that no amount of discipline could mask. For a moment, it looked like he might speak, but he held his tongue. There was nothing left to say. He was a man of action, a leader who had given everything for the war effort. The weight of his own failure hung over him like a cloud. The mission, the dream, the honor—it was all gone now.

Some of the ground crew were already moving away from the assembly, their eyes glazed over. They whispered to each other, their voices low, their reactions subdued. Some of them seemed to be almost in a daze, as if they couldn't quite comprehend what had happened. Some were muttering curses under their breath, shaking their heads in anger.

One of the Lieutenants had his back to the group, and when he finally turned around, his face was tight with rage. "They've surrendered," he growled to no one in particular, clenching his fists at his sides. "We were so close. We were so close to victory."

Some of the pilots, gripped by an overwhelming sense of dishonor and unable to accept the reality of defeat, would make their way back to their barracks, lock themselves in their quarters, and use their short swords or service pistols. For these men, death was preferable to living with the shame of Japan's surrender.

And yet, not all were so consumed by despair. Some, like Hideyoshi, stood at the edge of the precipice but chose to look directly down into the abyss. The war was over, but there was still a future to be faced.

Chapter 21

Post-War (Sept-Dec 1945)

The Navy's formalities ended with little fanfare. Hideyoshi stood in the corner of the office as an officer read a prepared statement officially discharging him from service. When they handed him the certificate marking the end of his military career, he could only nod. The paper was thin and impersonal, much like the ceremony itself.

Stepping out of the small administrative building, Hideyoshi made his way directly to the main gate, past the now-quiet hangars. Hoisting a duffle bag over his shoulder, he walked away without looking back.

At a small fishing village not far from the airfield, he spotted a man working on a motorboat moored at the dock. The gray-haired fisherman was bent over the engine, grumbling curses under his breath. When Hideyoshi approached, the man straightened, wiping his hands.

"I need a ride across to Tsu," Hideyoshi said, then reached into his pocket and retrieved the envelope that Genda had handed him before he left the airfield. It contained a portion of the money which the commander had set aside during the war for emergencies, which he had now divided up among the pilots. It was more than a month's pay. "I can pay you," Hideyoshi added, holding up a few folded bills.

The fisherman eyed the money, then Hideyoshi, before muttering, "All right. But if that motor gives out, you're the one paddling."

A smile tugged at Hideyoshi's lips. "Fair enough."

As the fisherman prepared the boat, Hideyoshi stepped aboard, instinctively checking the hull's condition and the engine mount. His father's fishing boat had been similar in size, though powered only by sails and oars.

"Sturdy build," he said, running a hand along the gunwale.

The fisherman gave him a sideways glance. "You know boats?"

"My father's a fisherman," Hideyoshi explained. "I grew up helping him on the water."

The man's demeanor softened slightly. "Then you'll understand if she sputters a bit. She's seen better days, like the rest of us."

Hideyoshi settled near the bow as the boat moved through the water.

After a while had passed, the man asked, "You said you're heading home?"

Hideyoshi nodded. "It's been years. I don't know what to expect."

The fisherman grunted in understanding. "War doesn't leave much behind. But you've got family waiting?"

"A wife and son in Tsu. My parents are still in Sakurada."

"Well, good luck to you. Not everyone has that kind of fortune."

The journey across the bay took most of the afternoon. When the boat finally bumped against the dock, Hideyoshi handed over the agreed amount, along with an extra note.

"For the repairs," he said.

After stepping off the fishing boat, Hideyoshi paused for a moment, taking in the sights of Tsu. The dock was quieter than he remembered, though there was still some movement—a few people walking briskly, fishermen carrying nets and crates, and children playing by the water's edge.

Hideyoshi adjusted the pack on his back. As he walked, his gaze wandered from street to street. There were the markets where he and Aiko used to shop for vegetables, the alleyways where they had once mingled with neighbors exchanging pleasantries. The small bridge over the stream where Hideyoshi had once stopped to fish with his father. The parks where he and Aiko had stolen quiet moments. All of that was still here, but it seemed faded. The vibrancy he had remembered was gone.

A handful of people greeted him as he passed, but none of them seemed to recognize him. Time, after all, had done its work.

Finally, Hideyoshi could see his destination in the distance—the house he had shared with Aiko. He reached the small wooden gate that separated the front yard from the street, hesitated for a moment, and then pushed it open. The house was still there—unmistakably the same, though it seemed to have aged in his absence. The garden, once meticulously cared for by Aiko, was overgrown now in patches.

For a moment, he wasn't sure whether to knock or simply walk in. But the thought of making a grand entrance felt foolish, so he quietly stepped forward and slid the door open.

And then, there she was.

Aiko stood in the dim light of the entryway, her hands clasped tightly in front of her. She was thinner than he remembered. Her black hair, which had once framed her face in soft waves, was now pulled back into a simple bun. Yet, in that moment, Hideyoshi saw her as she had always been — the woman who had been the center of his world, the one he had promised to return to.

For several seconds, neither of them moved, as if the world had paused around them. Aiko's eyes widened in disbelief. Her lips parted, but no words came at first.

"Aiko," he said, his voice thick with the emotions he had kept bottled up for so long.

She took a step forward. For a heartbeat, it seemed as though neither of them could quite believe it was happening. Then, without warning, Aiko threw her arms around him, pulling him into an embrace so fierce it almost knocked the breath from him. Her small frame trembled as she clung to him, burying her face in the crook of his neck.

"I was afraid you would be …" her voice broke, and her grip tightened.

Hideyoshi held her just as tightly, his hand pressed to the back of her head. For a moment, he let himself forget the war, forget the years that had passed. It was just Aiko, his Aiko, in his arms again.

"I'm here," he whispered. "I'm home."

Finally, she pulled back, her eyes scanning his face as though she feared he might disappear again if she looked away for even a second.

"I'm sorry," he whispered. "I never wanted to stay away so long. I thought — "

Aiko placed a finger on his lips. "You're home now. That's all that matters."

Then Hideyoshi's eyes drifted to the *shoji* sliding door, where a small figure stood, watching them in silence.

Ichiro.

The boy was taller, his eyes deeper, but there was no mistaking the resemblance. Ichiro was almost seven now, no longer the toddler he had last seen in 1941.

Hideyoshi froze, his heart stuttering.

The boy stood there for a moment, his expression indecipherable, before his face softened into a tentative smile. "Papa?"

Hideyoshi didn't say a word. He took a step toward his son, then knelt down, his heart racing. Ichiro hesitated for a moment, then ran into his arms, burying his face in Hideyoshi's chest. He could feel the boy's small shoulders shaking.

"I'm here," he whispered again. "I'm sorry I wasn't here for you."

Ichiro didn't answer, but just clung to him. Hideyoshi held him tightly, feeling the weight of all the lost years, all the moments they had missed.

Aiko stepped forward, placing a hand on Hideyoshi's shoulder. "He's grown so much," she said softly.

Hideyoshi nodded, blinking back tears. "I can see that." He held Ichiro a moment longer before lifting him into his arms, holding the boy as though he were still the toddler he had left behind.

"Papa, can I show you something?" Ichiro asked, his voice a little shy but eager. Hideyoshi nodded, smiling warmly, and he scrambled to his feet, running to the corner of the room where a small wooden box sat. He opened it carefully, revealing a collection of small, hand-carved airplanes.

Hideyoshi chuckled softly. "You like planes?" he asked, his voice filled with both surprise and affection.

Ichiro's face lit up as he nodded. "I like them a lot, Papa! Mama says you were a pilot. Are these the kind of planes you flew?"

The boy held up one of the models, an approximation of a biplane, and made buzzing sounds as he wove it through the air.

"Yes," Hideyoshi said, his voice heavy with memories. "I flew planes just like these. They were very fast, and they could do incredible things in the sky. Twists and turns."

He smiled at the sight of his son's enthusiasm. "You'll have to tell me everything you know about planes, Ichiro. Maybe you'll be a pilot someday, too."

Ichiro's eyes grew wide, and his chest puffed out with pride at the thought. "I want to be a pilot just like you, Papa!"

He was surprised at how little time it took for him to feel at ease with his son again, even after so many years apart.

Aiko watched quietly, a soft smile on her face as she observed the exchange. Hideyoshi turned to her.

"You told him all about me, didn't you?" he asked, his voice teasing.

Aiko nodded. "But he needs to know you as you are now, not as the man I've talked about."

"I see," Hideyoshi whispered.

Ichiro, still absorbed in his play, looked up at his mother with a bright grin.

Aiko smiled, but there was a trace of sadness in her eyes.

"I'm glad you've come back to us, Hideyoshi. But ... What happens now?"

He met her gaze and took a deep breath, setting the toy plane down on the mat beside Ichiro.

"I don't know, Aiko. I can't say. The world has changed, and we have to find our way through it. We've all survived a war that nearly destroyed everything, but that doesn't mean we can just pick up where we left off."

Her face softened with understanding, but the concern in her eyes didn't fade. "We've all changed, Hideyoshi. You ... you've changed too. The man who went away and the man who came back are not the same."

Hideyoshi felt a pang of guilt in his chest. She was right, of course. He had come back, but he had changed in ways even he didn't really understand. The war had taken so much from him.

"I know," he replied. "But I'm here now, and that's all I can promise. We'll have to take it one step at a time."

Aiko nodded. "I've been raising Ichiro alone for so long. I never thought this day would come, Hideyoshi. I thought I would have to face whatever came next without you. I wasn't sure how much I could hold on to. But now you're here, and I don't know if I'm ready to start again."

"We'll start together," he said, his voice steady. "We'll rebuild, not just the house, but everything. What's been broken can still be fixed."

Aiko was quiet for a moment, and then she gave him a smile. "I've missed you, Hideyoshi. I missed this — this life. I didn't want to give it up."

He reached out, taking her hand in his, squeezing it gently. "I missed you too, Aiko. More than you know. Let's rebuild it, together."

Their quiet conversation was interrupted by Ichiro, who suddenly stood up and began running around the room, pretending his plane was zooming through the sky.

Aiko laughed, and the tension in her shoulders eased just a little. For a moment, the weight of the past seemed to lift, and Hideyoshi felt, for the first time in a long while, that perhaps the future didn't have to be so uncertain.

Then Aiko's face clouded for a moment as she looked down, her fingers absentmindedly smoothing the folds of her *kimono*. Hideyoshi, sensing the change in her mood, grew quiet. She finally spoke, her voice soft but now filled with sorrow.

"Hideyoshi," she began, her eyes still on the floor, "there is something else I need to tell you. Something you won't like to hear."

He frowned slightly as he turned to her. "What is it, Aiko? You can tell me anything."

Her gaze lifted briefly, meeting his with an expression of grief. "My father, Hiroshi ... he was killed during one of the firebombing raids in Kobe. He was there on business when it happened, and ... and he never made it out."

Hideyoshi's heart sank at the words. "I'm so sorry," he said quietly. "I didn't know. I can't imagine what that must have been like for you, Aiko."

"It was a terrible shock. We had hoped he would be safe, but the raids were so devastating, especially in the cities along the coast."

"It wasn't just his death, though," she continued, her voice faltering. "It's everything. Mother is still grieving. She ... she couldn't stay in the house alone after that. So, she's living with Michiko now, my sister."

"I didn't realize," Hideyoshi said softly. He had been so focused on the hardships of his own life, the things he'd seen and endured in the war, that he hadn't thought about the suffering of others back home. "I'm sorry, Aiko. I should've been here for you, for your family."

She looked up at him. "There was nothing you could have done, Hideyoshi. I know that. But things have changed. We're all trying to find a way to move forward in a world that's been torn apart."

Hideyoshi took a deep breath and reached out to take her hand. "I will do whatever I can, Aiko. For you. For your mother and Michiko. I'll make sure they're taken care of."

Her eyes searched his face. "You've always been the strong one, Hideyoshi. Even when I thought I had lost you, I hoped you would come back. And now that you're here, maybe . . . maybe we can begin to heal."

"I promise you, Aiko," he said firmly, "I'll make sure we have what we need. We'll rebuild. We're a family, and I'll make sure no one goes without."

Her lips quivered, and for a moment, she looked as though she might say something more, but then she swallowed hard and held him.

Hideyoshi gave her a reassuring smile, the same one he had worn back when they were young, before he had left for the war. "We'll get through this. Together. All of us."

Aiko nodded. Whatever they had lost, they still had each other.

The day was just beginning as Hideyoshi, Aiko, and Ichiro made their way towards Sakurada, the village where Hideyoshi had grown up. Aiko walked beside him, her hand tucked into his, while Ichiro skipped ahead, his small figure a blur of energy. The closer they got to Sakurada, the more Hideyoshi could feel his heart beat faster. He had not seen his parents in a long time.

As they approached the edge of the village, Hideyoshi began to see the familiar sights of his youth—the row of small homes with thatched roofs, the narrow roads lined with bamboo, the rice paddies stretching out into the distance. It was all so unchanged, so familiar, and yet so foreign to him after everything he had been through.

Finally, they arrived at his parent's house. Aiko gave his hand a reassuring squeeze, and Ichiro, sensing the significance of the moment, quieted down, his eyes wide with curiosity.

Before Hideyoshi could announce himself, the door slid open, and there stood his mother, Haruko. Her hair was now touched with gray, but her smile was still as warm as ever. For a moment, neither of them spoke.

"Hideyoshi . . . " Haruko's voice trembled as she stepped forward, her hands reaching out for him. "My son. You're home. You're really home."

Tears welled up in his eyes as he embraced her, holding her tightly. The years of war, of uncertainty—all of it seemed to melt away in this single moment.

"I'm here, Mother. I'm here," he whispered.

She pulled back slightly, holding him at arm's length and studying his face as if she were trying to make sure it was really him. "You've changed, my son ... but you look so much like your father now."

Hideyoshi smiled. "I've seen things, Mother. I've been through a lot, but I'm here now. And I'm not going anywhere."

Aiko stepped forward, bowing slightly. "Haruko-*san*, it's good to see you again."

Haruko nodded, then her eyes fell to Ichiro. She crouched down, reaching out to him with a delighted chuckle.

"And my grandson!" she exclaimed.

Ichiro smiled. "Hello, *oba-san*".

Haruko stood up and guided them all into the house. "Come in. We have tea waiting, and you must be hungry after your journey."

As he entered the familiar space, Hideyoshi couldn't help but notice how little had changed. The room still smelled of *tatami* and wood smoke from the *hibachi*, and the low wooden table where they had all sat for meals was still there, surrounded by the same worn cushions.

Just as they were about to settle in, a familiar voice interrupted the moment. "Is that you, Hideyoshi?"

From the next room came his father, Hideyuki. His frame was stooped with age, and his face had softened with the passing years, but his gaze was as sharp and steady as ever.

"Father," Hideyoshi said, his voice catching again as he stood up to greet him. "It's good to see you."

Hideyuki stepped forward, his strong arms enveloping him in a warm embrace. "You've come back to us, son. I never stopped hoping, never stopped praying that you'd come home."

"I'm here, Father. I'm here," he replied.

The family gathered around the low table, and the conversation shifted to quiet topics—the village, the fishing boat, the weather, the simple things that had carried them through the war. Haruko and Hideyuki told him of the years, how Aiko and Ichiro had made the journey back and forth between Tsu and Sakurada when circumstances allowed, and how they had always been welcomed with open arms. They spoke of Ichiro's growth and how proud they were of him, even as the boy had showed his longing for the father he barely remembered.

Hideyoshi looked over at his parents. "I can't thank you enough for looking after Aiko and Ichiro during these times," he said. "I know it hasn't been easy, and I don't know what we would have done without you."

Haruko placed a gentle hand on his arm, smiling softly. "Your family is our family, Hideyoshi. We are always here for you, and we're just happy that you're home."

The war was over, and though there was much uncertainty ahead, he was home at last.

In the aftermath of World War II, Japan was a nation in ruins. Years of intense firebombing had left the country devastated, and the major cities, once thriving centers of industry, commerce, and culture, were now unrecognizable. The economic heart of Japan had been obliterated, and the infrastructure that had supported its rapid industrialization lay in tatters. Kobe, Nagoya, Osaka, Tokyo—all were bombed-out shells.

The countryside was no better off. Although the rural areas had not been targeted by airstrikes, the long-term effects of the war were still felt there. The food supply had been severely affected. Fields once cultivated with rice, wheat, and vegetables had been trampled by the forces of war. The labor force had been decimated, and those who remained in rural areas faced the daunting task of replanting and rebuilding with limited means. Transportation across the country had broken down, and cities could no longer be supplied with the essential goods they needed. Much of the urban population found themselves facing starvation and sickness.

People who had already endured years of hardship during the war now found themselves in the midst of an even greater struggle. Those who had lost family members, homes, and livelihoods were left to pick up the pieces of a shattered world. Many had lost hope, resigned to the belief that their country had been destroyed beyond repair. The emotional toll of the war was no less damaging than the physical destruction, and in many ways, the two were intertwined.

And then the Americans came.

With Japan's surrender, the American occupation forces swiftly arrived. Under the command of General MacArthur, the Supreme Commander for the Allied Powers, American troops took control of the country, as they worked to enforce the terms of the capitulation and begin the process of rebuilding Japan under a new political and social order.

At first, there was fear that the Japanese nation would be split in two. The Soviet Union had only entered the war just as it was ending, but they had occupied a huge portion of Manchukuo, and there was genuine fear that they would demand the right to occupy the northern parts of Japan itself—which would very likely have then become a Communist puppet state. But in the end the Russians satisfied themselves with their buffer states in Eastern Europe, and it was only the Americans who entered Japan.

In the early days of the occupation, the sight of uniformed American soldiers patrolling the streets was a harsh reminder of Japan's defeat, and it was met with a measure of resentment. The cultural gap between the Japanese people and the American forces was wide, with language barriers and differences in customs leading to frequent misunderstandings.

For the most part, though, the presence of the occupation forces brought a sense of calm to an otherwise fractured society. The American military worked closely with Japanese police forces, who had been restructured under the occupation's guidelines, to ensure that order was restored.

As part of the occupation's mission to reshape Japan, the American forces also worked to demilitarize the nation. They dismantled the Imperial Japanese Army and Navy, disbanded military factories, and prohibited the production of weapons. American soldiers conducted raids to confiscate firearms and other weapons from civilians, and military personnel were often involved in monitoring and dismantling Japan's industrial capabilities. At the same time, the American military sought to foster economic recovery by overseeing the distribution of aid, food, and resources. This included providing emergency food rations to help alleviate the widespread famine that affected much of the population.

The introduction of new political, social, and economic systems set the stage for Japan's recovery and its eventual rise as a global economic power.

Meanwhile, as Japan struggled to recover from the devastation of the war, millions of young men who had been serving in the Japanese Army and Navy were returning home to a country in ruins. These veterans were now faced with the challenge of reintegrating into a society which had been reshaped by the American occupation and was in the throes of rebuilding itself from a militaristic empire into a Western-style democracy.

Japan struggled with how to accommodate these returning soldiers and how to offer them a meaningful place in a post-war society. Veterans often returned to find their homes destroyed, their families altered, and their once-revered social status diminished, while the lingering memories of the war continued to haunt them.

For Hideyoshi, the experience of returning home was filled with both relief and stress. Like other veterans, he had spent years in a brutal world of "kill or be killed". Yet now, the war was over, and he had returned to a Japan that was no longer the place he had known before. He had to learn how to become a part of that post-war world.

Yet as he sat in the quiet of his home, the war seemed to linger in the spaces around him, never truly leaving. He found himself constantly revisiting the horrors of combat, the faces of the lost young men who had once been his comrades, and the cruel reality that, in the end, war destroyed everything and everyone, no matter which side they were on.

The futility of it all pressed heavily on his heart. He had fought for a country, for an empire, and now that same empire was shattered and broken. What had all the bloodshed accomplished? Only more pain, more suffering, more loss. The more he thought about it, the clearer it became: war was not a path to glory — it was a path to destruction. None of it was worth the price.

And yet, despite everything, Hideyoshi felt a lingering hope. Perhaps the future could still be something different. Perhaps, in the rebuilding of Japan, there could be a chance for peace — a chance for men like him, scarred by the past, to create something better.

In the years that followed the end of the war, Hideyoshi found a new sense of purpose. He began to think about the future, not just for himself, but for the generation that would come after him. They needed to understand the consequences of conflict and the importance of peace, not just for the sake of their own lives, but for the survival of their country and the world.

He began to seek out opportunities to speak with young people. In schools, he spoke to groups of students eager to hear the stories of the past. In his soft, steady voice, he would recount the days of the war — how he had joined the Navy as a young man, how the sky had been filled with fire and destruction, and how, in the end, it had all been for nothing.

He did not glorify his past. There were no tales of heroism or triumph in his stories — only the harsh reality of loss. His talks were not about medals or victories but about the human cost of war. He spoke of the men he had flown with, of their youth, and the shattered futures they had left behind.

But Hideyoshi didn't just focus on the past — he wanted to show them a better future. After every lesson about the war, he would ask them to think about what they could do to ensure peace in the future. He would ask them to take responsibility for the world they would inherit, to reject the ideologies that had led to the destruction of his generation, and to work together to create something new, something better.

In time, he came to understand that his own healing was tied to the healing of his country. The wounds of war would never be fully healed, he knew, but they could be faced, understood, and used as a foundation for a better future. His efforts to educate the young people of Japan were his way of atoning for the years of destruction.

And perhaps, in teaching peace to the next generation, Hideyoshi could begin to find some peace for himself as well.